RAVEN QUEEN, ASCEND

AN EPIC FANTASY SAPPHIC SEDUCTION FULL OF MAGIC & REVENGE

TEMPLE OF VENGEANCE
BOOK TWO

DAVE REED

Edited by
SUSAN BISCHOFF

© 2025 Dave Reed

Raven Queen, Ascend

An Epic Fantasy Sapphic Seduction Full of Magic & Revenge (Temple of Vengeance Volume 2)

First edition, October 2025

Book Shaman

Georgetown, Texas

davereed.me

Editing: Susan Bischoff, bischplease.com

Cover Designer: Katrina Curry, crimsonphoenixcreations.com

Interior Formatting: Dave Reed

ISBN: 978-1-958316-04-7 (e-book)

ISBN: 978-1-958316-05-4 (paperback)

ISBN: 978-1-958316-06-1 (hardcover)

For my lovely and gracious warrior-queen Samia,
to commemorate every glorious battle
in all our lives together, forever and always.

A thousand years before mortals forsook their faith in the divine, I was there at the second breaking of the world.
This is the litany of my errors, the story of my arrogance, the tale of my loves, and a reckoning of all my needful darkness.

CONTENTS

PREVIOUSLY IN THE TEMPLE OF VENGEANCE

This book stands alone. However, because you have waited impatiently for a long time (or haven't read *Death Descends* or *Raven Queen, Arise* or *Righteous Disobedience*), there is a summary of important characters and spoilers from the previous books to refresh your memory (and mine) at the end of this story.

Perhaps being as unreasonable as Illyria can be at times, I assume that we all remember what went before. This saves us both a lot of didactic prose and allows us to dive directly into the next, fresh story with Illyria, her lovers, and her haters, new and old.

If you haven't read or don't remember, perhaps give it a read first.

AS THE STORY RESUMES...

At the end of *Raven Queen, Arise*, Illyria had just begun to settle into her tender, new relationship with her pair of lovers, Z'nnek and Tourak, knowing full well that she has been summoned to Conclave with the high gods and the old in four days' time.

Illyria has no intention to comply with the tyrant Twin Gods' summons.

CHAPTER 1

*A*n eyeblink ago, I was not at risk of having statues made in my image. Now, it seemed, on the eve of my wedding, both of my future husbands felt obligated to further immortalize me in some embarrassing manner. As a newborn goddess, they would have *me* forever. What need would they have for a mere statue? I refused, repeatedly, on principle and on my own authority as the proposed subject of the statues. Such arrogance was the cause of many wars and much destruction. I'd done my best to slice away the part of me that still burned to complete my vengeance upon Saevera, last living among the Chosen of Tyrr.

Harmony for all was my new, self-appointed goal. Since I was a goddess, I reasoned, I got to decide how I applied my will and to what end. I told myself that all I yearned for was peace to enjoy my lovers and my marriage for the rest of eternity. In fact, I wasn't quite sure why we needed a wedding at all!

At last, I agreed, if only for the distraction from my dread of the high gods' summons to Conclave. Nothing good could come of acquiescence. Nothing good could come of defiance. I was damned either way if I were to ever visit the sun-kissed lands again. For my wedding day, at least, I would pretend there was nothing beyond the bounds of my underworld home.

It turns out that when there is no higher authority in your realm, you can just declare yourself to be married. You may do as you please if there is neither ruler nor overseer to impose will or whim of their own. What are laws and rules and customs but arbitrary impositions an individual first devised to inflict upon others? Traditions always begin in some form or fashion, for some inconvenient reason or another. Such as when a goddess gets an urge to make a proclamation. For when a deity decides, I'm given to believe that her priests and priestesses simply must obey. After all, what care the divine for the opinions of mortals?

Of course, my lofty position in the afterlife did not accrue to me without anxiety.

Or without being harangued into wearing an uncomfortable gown on my wedding day.

"My guests and friends," Z'nnek said in a voice that suffused the entire underworld, "thank you for joining us today in welcoming Illyria home." He spread his arms high and wide as if embracing the entirety of our under-world realm. "Today, she shall wed all of Nethe as your new queen!"

In point of fact, I had agreed to no such thing. Not explicitly, anyway. I was only here to marry my lovers because it made them happy to have a silly ceremony: nothing more, nothing less. They'd nagged me sufficiently to squeeze into a gown of midnight velvet and scarlet lace. In my opinion, I looked more like a ridiculous confection than a bride. But I would suffer—a little—to bring happiness to my marriage and to my men.

Tingling worry, similar to what had always accompanied the approach of the seasonal festa orgies, filled me. Unlike the rest of my highland kith and kin, I was not favorably inclined to group sex. Only Tourak's dutiful presence at my side kept me from bolting down the steps of the gilded ziggurat to lose myself in the vineyard jungle of my new home. As far as I was concerned, we were already married enough.

Z'nnek stood to my left. I tried to look demure as I gazed at him through my lashes. Though he did not often flaunt his crown, he wore it now. The thin circlet of black gold, its entire circumference studded with purple diamonds, nestled amongst his tight, nappy curls. It was an elegant, under-stated piece, like my lover. He wore a charcoal velvet ensemble with flared sleeves over a maroon blouse that was open from throat to halfway to his navel. I approved not only of the exposed skin, but the attractive pair of bone amulets he wore. I knew them to be the mantles of his angelic hosts—the symbols of his leadership and emblems of his power. One bore the effigy of a roosting vulture. The other featured a swooping buzzard. I'd never thought to wear my own raven totem as jewelry. Perhaps I would wear it to bed tonight.

"...her joyous coronation..." he continued to drone.

It would not be much of a coronation without a crown, I mused, but didn't interrupt. It was just like Z'nnek to use words in slightly the wrong way or make obtuse the mundane.

In his mild, effeminate voice, Z'nnek carried on at length, though the words weren't meant for me and passed beyond my awareness. I considered him—dark of skin, tight curls shorn close to his scalp, wine-colored eyes, full kissable lips—and wondered how he had captured my heart. He was faithful and devoted and gentle and kind. Yet so far from the type I had enjoyed in my time under the sun. At least the ubiquitous quakes of the underworld had given me the marriage gift of their absence today.

I sighed and glanced to my right.

His oldest friend, Tourak, with one scarred eye, ruddy skin, and long flowing tresses, was no less strange compared to lovers I'd known as a mortal woman. Yet I had chosen them in eternity. And they had chosen me. The least I could do was humor them for a day.

Tourak stood, impassive and patient as always, his dark raven wings folded quiescent at his back. I wondered if my more laconic lover would speak at all during the ceremony. He had been silent but accepting of all of Z'nnek's many wedding preparations. He met my gaze with a slight, long-suffering but loving smile. My heart lightened with the knowledge that I did not suffer alone. Without words, we agreed to let Z'nnek enjoy his moment at our expense.

"...as all they shall," Z'nnek declared, waving both of his thin, elegant hands at the flights of our winged angelic hosts soaring overhead. Raven wings. Vulture wings. Buzzard wings. Crow wings. So many different feathers of birds associated with our shared domain: all of the unclaimed dead. Ten thousand angels honored us in well-coordinated formations.

They shall what? I wondered.

Suppressing my orgiastic anxieties, I chose trust and patience. My soon-to-be-husbands knew my heart and mind on the subject. Though, I really should have paid attention to what Z'nnek was committing me to. But I didn't much care—I'd do whatever my love required, within reason, despite how little patience I might have for it. I distracted myself by taking in the statue-less splendor and spectacle. Which is probably what he had intended.

With one arm, Tourak hugged me between himself and Z'nnek. Placing a hand on his ancient friend's shoulder behind my back, probably in hope of hurrying this along. But my red-skinned lover's mild smirk warned me that he knew his efforts would be of no avail.

My king of the sunless realm had insisted on an enormous ceremony with unstated expectations. I should have pressed for more specifics in the past two days of delirious lovemaking. It cost him nothing but unimaginable quantities of magic to lavishly feed and entertain millions. He had done so every day for the past ten thousand years, so it was only a mild difference in degree. At his invitation, an ocean of immortal shades had flowed toward our wedding ceremony from all corners of our realm, leaving their other eternal occupations to celebrate with us. As far as I could see were shades of every race and culture enjoying themselves with endless abandon. All who had been deemed unworthy to claim by the high gods.

This ceremony, Z'nnek's long-winded speech, and the plenty which surrounded me were alien to my frugal highland upbringing. In Alamar, people came together as they wished and parted as they saw fit. A few might seek counsel from their warlord or advice from the love-men and love-women of the village, but no one needed permission or ceremony to live together any more than they needed such dispensation to fuck. Among my kith and kin, couples or groups were wed when they declared themselves to be and unwed when they chose. There were celebrations and feasts aplenty during the seasonal festas and the rites of the high gods of the Litanies. But electing to set up a household together was hardly an event uncommon enough to warrant so lavish an expense as a wedding.

As one of many nuptial surprises, my lord of the unclaimed dead had erected a vast new underworld temple for us. The broad, flat terraces of the massive stone ziggurat seemed to stretch halfway up to the stone sky of Nethe. Overhead, the multicolored stars danced their erratic rhythm. I wondered what they were, and why they were, as much as I wondered why

Z'nnek felt I needed a temple. He'd accommodated my only stipulation: no statues.

I hadn't really wanted a temple, either, because I wasn't yet comfortable then with being worshipped. So, he constructed it much like the rooftop garden of our palace—where we'd spent some part of our recent lusty nights —but much grander than I could have imagined. Our countless guests filled the tree-lined terraces and spilled out into the orchards and vineyards surrounding the ziggurat. They helped themselves to the fruit of the always ripe trees and vines and tables of fresh breads and cheeses and roast meats. Minstrels played. Jugglers tossed and caught. Acrobats tumbled alone and together. Singers crooned and swooned and swayed. In all of Z'nnek's reign, no shade of his dark realm ever suffered hunger or boredom or scarcity of choice. He allowed all of our guests to choose their eternal occupations.

My dead kinfolk filled the highest terraces of the pyramid in our new temple garden closest to the expansive flat apex. Those who'd been unclaimed at the end of their mortal lives. And those whose souls had not been extinguished by death eternal. I refused to be maudlin on my wedding day, but I'd not dishonor the memory of Padra or Nerren or our kin sacrificed upon the wheel of woe by sweeping them out of mind. I'd give anything to share this day with them. Padra had been an honorable warlord and devoted father—I would honor him every day in my heart. Nerren, in some way, lived on in the memories he'd gifted to me when I'd consumed his accidentally stolen soul to recover from my second defeat at the hands of Provax.

Madra, who was quite reasonably still mightily pissed with me, set aside her several, valid grievances to stand with the wedding party behind us in a place of honor atop the central plateau. Among all the gods my loves had invited, only Mawzi, my bloodsworn sister, Goerranu, my erstwhile frenemy, and Urth of the old gods attended.

All of this was more than I ever dreamed. I'd lived with the expectation to die unmarried. And I supposed I had, after all. In life, I had wished only to serve the high god of justice, Torr, as a Temple Judge. My disappointment at awakening to eternity in the underworld a month past was fading. I had been unclaimed by any of the high gods. Perhaps unchosen was a more generous characterization—not for lack of service or worship of the high gods, but because this strange small god of the underworld had claimed me. Z'nnek had claimed my soul in flagrant violation of the Accord with the high gods. Not because I had distinguished myself in any way to him in life. But because Tourak had asked him to.

Warmth of that young memory filled my heart. I had unintentionally sacrificed my own childhood remembrance of it in my recent quest for vengeance. Tourak had restored it to me by sharing his own recollection.

My reverie was shattered when Z'nnek turned to me and removed his crown.

Uncertain, I took the circlet of dark metal he offered me. Immense power and vast knowledge rested in my palms. I could feel the weight of it against my skin. I wanted to retreat, to refuse the responsibility which surely came with any crown. A warm presence at my back, Tourak rested his hands on my hips, a comforting restraint. Questions for Z'nnek I couldn't form with my lips crowded my expression.

"It is but a token," Z'nnek said with a wistful grin up at me.

His hands beneath mine lifted the crown and placed it upon my unready brow.

A vast sense of the underworld welcomed me. It was eerie and banal at once to feel as if I might know each rock or tree or vine or the name of each shade should I simply wish it so. Then he kissed me. Through his lips, love and devotion and support washed away my awe and trepidation. In that moment, I believed I would never have to bear the weight of the crown alone. So, I did not refuse him.

"Thank you," I whispered.

More words from Z'nnek filled the now blurry eternal night until Tourak gently pulled me around to face him. In one hand, he held a raven feather, dyed crimson along its edges. Behind me, I felt Z'nnek tense unexpectedly and place his hands upon my shoulders.

Tourak inclined his head more solemnly than a bow. His one dark eye sparkled with love. In his rough, gentle voice, he said, "I have no crown to give, only myself." He lifted my hands together to wrap my fingers around the long decorative flight feather.

A deep sense of peace exuded from the token. I felt the joys of home and love and family. Closing my eyes, I inhaled the male scents of him. Oiled leather. Cookfire smoke. Lemongrass. Though strange, I felt a stronger connection with him through the feather than I already held deep in my heart.

Electric realization shot through me. "I— I did not think to bring—" I stammered.

Z'nnek smoothly maneuvered my stunned self into a triangle with Tourak. "I have a gift for you as well," he said, "husband of my bride."

The confused look on my archangel's face morphed to horror as Z'nnek unclasped his buzzard amulet. My husband held out half of his divine power to my other husband. It was a most generous gift—matched only by the one Z'nnek had given me a month past when he had allowed me to choose the raven mantle in exchange for the right to court me himself.

Horror replaced confusion. "No!" Tourak stepped back.

I blinked in surprise, looking back and forth between my husbands.

The long-time lord of the underworld seemed nonplussed rather than angry, as I might have been. But I didn't understand the offer or its refusal. My husbands had known each other ten millennia longer than I'd been in existence. Tourak had faithfully served Z'nnek for all that time. I blinked and thought furiously, trying to determine the problem.

"You tempt me with equality now?" Tourak demanded. "When taking up that mantle will separate me from her?"

"We're to be married, Tourak," I said. "Nothing will ever separate us."

A grim expression on his face, Tourak turned to me. "I've no desire to rule a host. I belong only to you. I *want* to belong only to *you*."

His nonplussed expression burned away as a simmering anger suffused Z'nnek's features.

Hells' frozen fuck demons. I'd never witnessed Z'nnek to be more than mildly annoyed. Well, not with anyone but me. I couldn't imagine whether my further intervention would improve the situation or exacerbate it.

The lord of the underworld still held forth the leadership of an entire angelic horde. "I do not seek to separate you, *old friend*," he said in a low, firm voice. "I seek to empower you to her best protection." Z'nnek sighed. "Need I remind you of the Conclave two days hence?"

Of course, Z'nnek would remind me of my date with the gods of war and justice, which I had done my best to forget. He assumed that I would attend, despite my oft-stated intentions to the contrary. Even with the much-vaunted mercy of Amuun, mother of the gods, presiding over the Conclave, I feared its outcome. To my mind, 'twas best not to go at all. But I understood his purpose behind the gift now, and it was well-meant. The sharing of power broadened our options to respond politically and militarily to whatever opposition we faced together.

Though I had no doubt Tourak understood as well or better than I, intellectually, I felt his reaction was much deeper. Whether it was through our shared membership in my unkindness of ravens or through the feather token he had gifted to me, I felt his soul-deep refusal. My archangel would walk away from our marriage before he relinquished his position as first among my flock.

I needed to do something to prevent this moment from spilling over into the rest of my eternity. But the only thing I could think to do was the last thing I wanted to do in public.

Yet I would be damned before I ever let anyone of accuse me of inaction in the face of fear.

With a sway, I twirled between my men. "Are we taking our clothes off already?"

My best idea was to mimic the dance I'd seen clan love-women perform to showcase their talents prior to festa orgies. Truth be told, I often left the festa early every season when those dances began. A war dance held the only steps I was comfortable performing. But in the name of marital harmony, I began to shed pieces of the overly ornate gown of midnight I'd forgotten they'd dolled me up in. Good riddance to impractical clothing.

Erotic magic rose up around me, flowing from my new crown and out through the crowd, all down the ziggurat. As awkward as I felt, pretending to know what I was doing, my own arousal rose. And I witnessed the same effect on Tourak and Z'nnek beneath their clothing.

At least their eyes were on me now, not each other.

As subtly as I was able, I refastened Z'nnek's amulet about his neck under the guise of removing his coat and shirt. I struggled to find a rhythm that enabled me to touch them both at once and disrobe all three of us. The musicians and singers began a new song, joining their rhythm and harmony in time with my awkward prancing. As my foreplay continued, the crowd increased in their amorous attentions. The more aroused they got, the more aroused I became.

Through the necromancy of the crown, I felt Nethe itself begin to change. The strange orchards with their pulsating fruit and eerie, endless vineyards *shifted*. That's the only way I could describe the sensation. The sensibility of Nethe *settled*, and I felt as much as saw its flora and construction become more like the sun-kissed lands of my birth, less surreal and odd and more like *me*.

Soon, I was drunk with anticipation. I forgot my inhibitions as sexual energy flowed into me from all directions. Overhead, our hosts of angels coupled in the sky. Ten thousand angels fucking must have been a sight to see, but I had neither time nor inclination to pause in my own amorous endeavors: my eternal marriage was at stake. Throughout my underworld realm, my people worshipped me in one vast lovemaking. I felt as if I were one with them all.

My lovers forgot their quarrel, at least for the moment, and paid me the marital homage I was due on my wedding day.

It was good to be the Queen.

CHAPTER 2

I'd just had the most amazing orgasm of my brief eternal life. My world had shaken, but not from one of the usual quakes that had been quiescent since before the wedding earlier in the day. Lying between my sweaty lovers upon purple silken sheets, I panted to recover myself. The earthy, sanguine scent of the blood candles which lit the room lingered in my nose and on my tongue. Languidly, I opened my eyes. Z'nnek's effeminate features were relaxed, eyes closed. Pillowed against the bronze of my breasts, his deep black cheek was beautiful. On my other side, Tourak's long black hair was unbound and scattered across wine-colored silk pillows. His one eye was closed, but I always had a sense the other, the eye-scar, was watching me.

As a living woman, I'd tired of lovers quickly, in days or weeks. In the mere month since I'd met them both, my fascination had only grown. If I'd gods to pray to, I'd beg them for this feeling to continue to intensify forever. But I had yet to discover who we gods pray to for favors. Perhaps Amuun, the mother of the gods, would grant me that small mercy in eternity. I would give much for that kind of peace.

I surveyed the half dozen others of our current orgy who shared the enormous bed canopied with iridescent shadows. Some hours ago, we'd fought—sparring, of course, but with true weapons—in what Z'nnek had come to call my version of "foreplay." These six angels had proved a worthy challenge, in battle and in bed.

Still, I had thousands more to choose from and an eternity to relish them and to be worshipped by them. That thought shivered through me with anticipation.

Somewhere in the echoing halls of my palace in the depths of the underworld, someone in chainmail and hobnailed boots stalked the halls. I smiled. If I'd not been so thoroughly satisfied, I might have taken the sound as an invitation to more foreplay. In my state of bliss, I didn't even care to use my newfound awareness of my domain to reach out through the crown and seek their identity. To each their own was my new philosophy.

As I stared at the bed hangings in my languor, ripples of midnight pulsed through the spidersilk canopy in time with my heart. I wondered if its magic was in tune with mine or vice versa. Since Z'nnek gifted me with the black gold crown, more and more of Nethe became in sync with me. Or...I became more and more in sync with Nethe. Unlike my magical weapons and armor that rested comfortably in the depths of my soul until I had need of them, I proudly wore the nameless crown now. In truth, it was the only thing I wore at the moment. The thin circlet of dark metal, studded with purple diamonds, would need a name. In due time.

Lolling my head, I gazed lazily about. Each of my immortals lay in a state of disarray and satisfaction similar to my own. In my nineteen mortal years, I'd eschewed public or group sex. I had even fought the entire Elysian Foreign Legion rather than be forced into an orgy. Right before I'd been murdered, as it happened.

I'd hated the very idea. Until I'd wed not only Z'nnek and Tourak, but all of the vast and terrible underworld. As part of my ritual coronation earlier in the day, I learned what I'd been missing. At least I had eternity to make up for that mortal lack now.

Or did I? Urth had delivered the high gods' summons to Conclave to me two days past. While I hadn't exactly agreed to attend, I wasn't sure I could simply avoid it forever. But I was going to damn well try. *I am a sovereign of the underworld. Who can make me do any fucking thing I don't choose?* I'd demanded four days of mourning my beloved dead—including those I'd killed myself. If I wished, I would ignore any summons for as long as I liked. I hoped.

The haunting, metallic stride and rattle of armor jangled closer. Lazily, I wondered who it was. Our host of angels and the horde of shades inhabited the palace. Plus Goerranu and Mawzi, but neither were the noisy sort, and neither had been interested in our invitation to join our newly consecrated wedding rituals. I was too sated, too lazy to sort through so many familiar souls. I closed my eyes and smiled.

On this third day of my self-imposed mourning period, the angels who had joined this tryst were all from among my raven-winged unkindness, none from among Z'nnek's flocks of crows, buzzards, and vultures. Four of my males from various darker skinned realms in the sun-kissed lands, though none as dark as Z'nnek himself. And a lovely pair of enthusiastic, flame-haired, befreckled Azzarrean twins.

The latter reminded me more than a little of my first and only priestess, Conseca, who ministered to my few faithful under the sun. I suppressed a twinge of guilt for my incomplete vow of vengeance—sworn to her for herself and for my highland kith and kin. Instead ruminating upon the dead, I lazily inspected the sleepy fair-skinned nudes. I suspected, given their amorous attentions to Z'nnek earlier in our collective bedplay, that they'd been trying to share his bed for millennia. I wondered why he'd never indulged them. Given my current level of satisfaction with their participation, I should have squelched the jealous impulse immediately.

Of course, my mother chose that very moment to invade my opulent boudoir.

I'd hoped to avoid that inevitability…for all eternity.

Dressed in her customary breastplate and chainmail, she rattled as she walked, hobnailed boots striking sparks from the marble tile. Her highland spatha hung at her hip, because I'd not made time to teach her how to create one by magic on demand. Nor had I made time to elevate her station above the common, unclaimed shades. I squelched my neglectful daughter shame and sighed. Though wrinkled like well-worn leather, her skin was as healthy a bronze as my own. Her steel gray hair, though naturally free-spirited with curls like mine, was tamed in severe braids. The pinned style resembled a helmet. She looked much the same as the day I'd killed her.

Madra wore disapproval like a veil. "How much of eternity are you going to fuck away, *Goddess?*" Her tone was far less the respectful tone of a worshipper and much more the disdain of a disappointed matriarch.

She wasn't livid about the debauchery. I'd witnessed my mother's ardent participation in many a festa orgy more often than I cared to recall. I hadn't noticed if she'd joined my wedding festivities or not. But being taken to task for irresponsible sex by my mother's shade would be preferable to the real reason for her ire. Of course, if I'd already done as my lovers advised and anointed her into my unkindness of raven-winged angels, perhaps her allegiance would be less...hostile? I would never lord my position or title over anyone, especially my mother. Still, I snorted to cover a giggle at the thought of Madra being obsequious.

Her eyes narrowed. "Have I said aught to humor you?"

Sitting up, I resisted the temptation to sigh as Z'nnek's nappy hair tickled my nipples. "Nay, mother mine."

With help from Tourak's strong, red-skinned hand, I slid off the end of the bed and stood. Creating a carmine silk robe from the magic of my underworld realm, I draped it over my nakedness. I gave no thought to why I felt I needed clothing to face my mother.

I didn't want to, but I offered the highland custom, "Say your piece."

Madra reared her head back and looked down her nose at me.

Before she responded to my insolence, I spied my erstwhile allies lurking in the doorway from the sitting room. *Damn them. And damn me for inviting them into my realm.* No good could come of them skulking about my palace. Not more than they already had. Perhaps accepting their company on my long walk to Nethe after my interment in the family tomb had been a mistake born of loneliness and grief. But that wine had already been spilt.

I did sigh at that, even as I waved them in. Mawzi wore her male face, which I'd come to associate with her more aggressive, hostile intentions. Her skin was blacker than Z'nnek's and blacker than her knife-encrusted leather armor. Goerranu preened like a tiny bird, which looked odd in her simple homespun brown robes. Her hair, her skin, her clothes were all nondescript shades which were so unmemorable as to be forgotten when you looked away. Behind me, my lovers and my angels reclined, content to watch my family tableau without involving themselves directly. Of course. For them, it was fresh entertainment in a long and boring eternity.

Madra strode across the room to stand in front of me. "Have you a plan for demanding redress of the high gods?" She crossed her arms over her chest with a metallic clank. "Or will you simply declare war?"

There it was. To her, everything was black or white. All or nothing. She didn't see the glimmer of hope for peace that Z'nnek and Tourak assured me was possible. They'd kept eight thousand years of détente since the Accord. Despite having attempted to sacrifice herself to death eternal to stop my mortal war with Elysia and the Chosen of Tyrr, Madra stood before me all but demanding I start a second godwar. As much as I might want to complete my vengeance, could I afford to?

"After all, you do have to attend the Conclave two days hence, my love," Z'nnek drawled from his silken repose behind me. "That would be a perfect time to ask for reparations."

I knew what he and Tourak wanted—more of the same conciliation from the past eight millennia. Appear and apologize. Maintain the status quo. Go along with the high gods' whims in the name of peace. Luxuriate in underworld debauchery. One option, perhaps, but I wasn't convinced it was my path. I might be disinclined to further bloodshed and destruction in my name, but neither was I disposed to bend over at anyone else's demand. I ignored him and focused on my mother.

Her desperation had not been self-sacrifice, but depression and suicide. I understood her reasons, but I felt differently. Now, her despair was buried beneath anger at me for thwarting her and exacerbated by my allies' goading us all toward godwar, for reasons I couldn't yet fathom. The guilty parties, Goerranu and Mawzi, took station two or three strides behind Madra. None of them saw that too much blood had been shed already. In my name.

I resisted the urge to embrace my mother, to comfort the agonizing loss boiling beneath her skin. Her stoic nature would not welcome the intimacy. Instead, I collected the black-skinned Book of the Forbidden from the polished mahogany nightstand. And assumed the pose of polite waiting, with the large Book resting upon one hip. "Very well, Warlord," I said, using the title she'd earned in the sun-kissed lands. "Counsel me. What would you have me do?"

Madra eyed the Book with suspicion. Goerranu eyed it greedily. Mawzi ignored it and watched me instead. The other eyes in the room, I could feel moving with lazy interest between me and Madra. I knew what each of them wanted. But I didn't know what I wanted. Except that I'd prefer to climb back into bed with attentive, luscious lovers with the stamina of the divine.

Meeting my gaze, Madra said, "Slay the high gods for me." She scoffed. "Tyrr and Torr, at the least. But the rest deserve it for sitting idly by while injustice is done in their names."

I suppressed a wince for all the violence already done by my faithful in my name. And by my own hand. I'd slain angels and demigods and mortals alike. To my mother, perhaps, the murder of a god or two did not seem beyond my reach. Perhaps it wasn't, if I wished.

Not long ago, Conseca had demanded a similar vengeance from me. In pursuit of that vengeance for her as my priestess, I'd inflicted terrible casualties upon friends and foe alike. I had brought the entire world to the brink of a second godwar. I'd even killed my mother to save her from a worse fate, an act of intended mercy that had brought us inevitably to this moment.

Tilting my head as if considering her request, I felt and heard Z'nnek shift restlessly upon the silken sheets behind me. I debated asking him to explain to my mother why he had chosen precisely to *not* do as she demanded. Eight thousand years past, long before we'd been born, Z'nnek had nearly won the godwar—the first godwar. But on the eve of his conquest, for reasons known only to him, he surrendered to the high gods and the old. He'd refused to tell me why. But I ached to know. And to know why he'd agreed to the double-damned Accord.

Madra and I regarded one another for many long heartbeats.

Perhaps he'd tell her?

Madra neither moved nor twitched. Mawzi perhaps was making odds about who would break first. Goerranu hadn't taken her covetous eyes from the Book. The goddess of secrets and lies had been given her promised turn with the Book, but it had refused to open for her.

15

"What then, Warlord?" I asked. "Let's pretend I have the fire to rain death eternal down upon *your* foes."

She flinched at my emphasis upon *your*.

I began to pace the wide, lush ermine carpet between my bed and a scattering of unoccupied gilded chaise lounges. I reined my mind back from remembering all that I'd enjoyed upon those recumbent chairs. *Always focus on the moment,* I heard Madra's voice from my childhood remonstrate.

Madra glared at me without speaking. I felt Goerranu's gaze leave the Book and settle upon me for the first time since I'd picked up Araeda'h's prison.

I continued into the gaping silence. "Let's pretend Z'nnek will give me leave to raise the hordes of the damned—"

My lover, king, and god of the unclaimed dead sat up on the bed, but remained silent.

"—and lead them from Nethe up into the sun-kissed lands to wreak devastation and havoc there. To lay siege to the gates of paradise once more. What of the mortals and shades who would suffer and die eternal in that conquest?"

My mother's face was stony and impassive.

I stopped pacing and crushed my own desire for retribution. "Let's pretend I lay siege to the Twin Paradises. Let's pretend I overthrow the gods of the Litanies and the Tales. What then? What do I demand of Amuun and the high gods?" I ignored the triumph that surged in my heart at the proposal. I threw up my free hand in mock exasperation.

Madra wasn't the sort to roll her eyes, but she scowled at my faux histrionics and waited patiently for me to continue.

"Would that make me more righteous than Tyrr, who incited his bastard Chosen to sacrifice our people upon the wheel? Or Torr and Amuun, who stood by and allowed them to resume forbidden human sacrifice?" I asked. "How would that bloodshed make anything better?" But my heart sang: *It would be right!*

Either my mother's heart had become so hardened that she didn't care about the consequences for innocents who would be ravaged, or she'd not thought beyond the satisfaction of her bloodlust over the loss of her husband and her son and her kin to death eternal. And her daughters. Well, at least Kausae was out of reach in service to Torr as an angel of justice. I was here. But perhaps I was not enough for her to savor in her afterlife. My heart twinged.

Madra was no stranger to gore or war. She herself had taught me most of what I knew of violence and death and vengeance. *Did she simply want it more than I?*

Deep inside, beneath the blood-soaked guilt, my rage still simmered. I'd not completed my vow to Conseca. I not slain Saevera, perhaps the worst and most conniving of the self-styled Chosen of Tyrr. No, that wasn't entirely true. Tired of bloodshed and death, I'd allowed her to escape. That fact grated upon my sense of justice. *Was justice enough reason to risk the slaughter of countless mortals? Was spite?*

We stood staring into one another's eyes, as we had many times in my nineteen years.

At last, I lost the contest of patience. Again. "Leave me to think," I said.

Madra scoffed at the inviting, exposed flesh of my interrupted orgy. "Is that what you call it, daughter?"

Irked, but refusing to let her see my pique, I replied in a cool tone, "As is tradition, I will give you my answer upon the morrow."

CHAPTER 3

I slumped upon the plump cushions of a gilded chaise, still clutching the Book. Madra clanked from the room. With a puzzled but hopeful expression, Mawzi slunk away behind her. Goerranu looked toward me, but her eyes were faraway and unfocused. Without ever meeting my gaze, she meandered out, too deep in thought to engage with me further. The remaining nudes lounged about collecting their second or subsequent wind, so to speak, polite enough to wait until I was ready. My libido felt far away.

While I could allow myself to become righteously angry, it wouldn't solve my dilemma. Pouting around the palace might feel cathartic, but that wouldn't give me insight. I locked eyes with Z'nnek for countless heartbeats and then with Tourak for just as long. Both smiled, but neither took pity upon me. They'd already given me their advice. I could pour out a measure of the memories of stolen souls I'd bottled up in the wine rack of my mind, though I doubted any of those had knowledge that would be of use in this dilemma.

Even the soul of Provax, fallen mortal son and Chosen of Tyrr, would know nothing of use to me. I didn't know what I was going to do with him, other than burn his essence to power my magic, perhaps. Though not before I'd learned the secret of Tyrr's invulnerable skin from him. First, I'd need a much greater mastery of magic than I yet possessed. Z'nnek was a patient, thorough teacher—and glacially slow in his process.

Returning myself to the matter at hand, I decided aloud, "I am going to speak with Araeda'h." *Again,* I thought to myself. I waved a hand dismissively and added, "Feel free to get started without me." Though I secretly hoped they wouldn't.

I wondered, for just a moment, why Z'nnek refused to commune with Araeda'h. In recent days, I'd offered him many opportunities to join me in my visits with the imprisoned goddess of magic. Each time I'd paused to open the Book, I'd asked if he would join my much more aggressive magic lessons and bizarre conversations with her. In fact, he'd had most of a day alone with the Book of the Forbidden while my kin, allies, and I fought Provax and the Legion. But he'd said he chose not to open it. I chose to believe him. My secret jealousy was grateful that he abstained. Someday, perhaps, he would be prepared to tell me who the ancient, mad goddess was to him. I schooled my mind not to imagine trouble for myself.

Peeling back the black leather covers, I stepped into the now-familiar tropical garden. Though it was empty of Araeda'h's lovely naked servants, the same ruby and topaz game board dominated the central clearing atop its marble table. A glance told me that the pieces were in the same arrangement as before: the ruby Queen threatened by the topaz Archer, Dragon, and Sorceress. The beleaguered sovereign huddled between and behind three ruby pawns.

Games with rigid, restrictive rules bored me. Why should a Queen restrict herself to such limited modes of movement? Moving in only straight lines or diagonals was naïve and predictable. Waiting for an enemy to consider his next move would get any warrior killed in her first battle. Sillier still, half of a real army wouldn't vanish from the field just because the King or Queen were slain. The rules of the game were stupid.

Like the occult rule she'd drilled into me over the past few days: Magic attains efficiency in time, not in effort. I hated that doing something with magic would take just as much energy as it would be to do it the hard way— just maybe doing it faster. What was the point of arcane knowledge if it couldn't accomplish something with no effort? That would be like winning a game at the cost of all your pieces. I admired that level of commitment but hoped to avoid ever needing to be that ruthless myself.

Still, I wondered what moron had chosen such a flawed strategy for the ruby army. Why advance only pawns and no powerful pieces? I decided, again, that I didn't care enough to ask after it. Clearly, Araeda'h was playing against herself and found the situation an interesting enough stalemate to ponder it for days. Or it was intended to trap me into inquiring. I would not.

The mad goddess of magic herself slumped lazily in one of the uncomfortable chairs attending the game table. Her costume was an uproar of radiant colors. Loose pantaloons and a flowing chemise rippled across her dark skin in a breeze I couldn't feel. Whorls and curls of obsidian hair with a life of their own rioted atop her head. Hypnotic eyes with metallic motes in the deep black irises focused on me. She indicated the empty chair. "Will you play, Preema?"

I pulled the carmine robe tighter and cinched the velvet belt. I resisted the urge to fidget with my own unruly curls. Was *Preema* what she called the game? Herself? She was old enough to have many names. Had she simply forgotten me again and confused me with someone else? Engaging with her delusions was never a winning move.

Putting on as patient an expression as I could, I said, "I'd prefer to speak of the Conclave. If I go, what should I expect? How can I win?" It would be well to find out what consequences I was bringing upon myself by not attending—and if I must go, how to beat my enemies.

She startled then, as if seeing me for the first time. "Did you tire of the orgy so quickly?" Her lascivious smile reminded me that, though she could not seem to affect the world, she certainly could perceive it—at least her immediate environs. She batted her eyelashes at me, which was just annoying.

I thought to remark that her own naked playthings were missing from the garden, but thought better of it. I hadn't come to provoke her. The game might be preferable to our first combative encounter. When we first met, Araeda'h had thought me a tool of the Hierarch and attacked with ferocity. Today, though, I was in no mood to be her toy.

"Swordplay, then?" I asked hopefully. "Or perhaps another magic lesson while we speak of the high gods?" I asked, less hopefully. Though my skill and knowledge had progressed quickly under her tutelage, it was neither entertaining nor comfortable. Learning to bend the world to my will required learning to bend my own mind. Perhaps she'd broken herself and that was why she frequently forgot what we were doing or who I was. Or maybe pretended to, when she tired of my company?

Araeda'h had taught me more of the primordial tongue of language that was every mortal's birthright. She couldn't tell me—or wouldn't tell me— why the Litanies had banned the use of all magic after the Accord. Z'nnek and Tourak seemed to retain the ability, and Goerranu managed to keep some limited capacity for spells. I'd never observed from anyone else the ability to perform more than simple, idiosyncratic magic: fly with their wings, light a sword on fire, and so on. Mawzi could not describe how she walked in shadow or manipulated her body to change her shape and size— she simply could. Tyrr's Chosen and war angels had performed only the most limited miracles in my presence, nothing like what Z'nnek and Tourak and I could do.

The self-proclaimed goddess of magic shrugged and shook her head. "When will Amuun arrive?" she asked.

Narrowing my eyes at her, I wondered if she'd acquiesced to my discussion of the Conclave or was having a mad conversation orthogonal to mine. "I presume it's customary for Amuun to attend a Conclave... But I don't know in what order the delegations arrive."

"You should arrive first, of course," Araeda'h said obtusely. "It's always better to be waiting than to have someone waiting for you."

We squinted at each other for a long moment. Like me, she thought the Conclave would be an ambush.

At last, I resumed, "I don't intend to go."

Araeda'h gifted me with her crooked grin. She raised her eyebrows at me quizzically and then studied the game board and its poorly arranged pieces. Stroking her temples, she seemed deep in concentration. "But how else will you fulfill your promise?"

Shocked, I demanded, "What promise?"

The mad goddess narrowed her eyes at me shrewdly. "The promise your priestess made in your name." The metallic flecks in her magical eyes sparkled. "The promise that bought you converts and worshippers among your kin and clansfolk."

She swept the topaz Archer to a new position that threatened the ruby Queen.

I didn't know what had transpired in the four days during which I'd lain like the dead. After falling to Provax a second time on the bridge, I woke to find my clan already steeped in my worship. Not sure I wanted to know, I'd avoided direct inquiries of Conseca and everyone else involved. If I knew, it might obligate me. Clearly, Araeda'h thought I should be obligated. I closed my eyes and sighed.

"What promise?" I asked again in a small voice.

She looked to the side and frowned. Either she couldn't recall or was trying to work out how much I knew and how much she could stretch the truth. I wished that I'd had the foresight and fortitude to gather more information from Conseca and my kin. Such was my life.

Just as I'd decided that I would get nothing further from her in the moment, she turned her face up toward me. Her eyes were lit with fervor. "Take me to Conseca. Tell her to follow my direction and I will consider our promise fulfilled."

"Why should I lend you my only priestess?"

The mad old woman gave me a sly smile. "Because I don't have one of my own?"

I snorted and pretended to examine the pieces on the board. My likely strategy of pushing out the ruby corner Dragons early would have resulted in the topaz Archer taking one or both. Perhaps there was something to a more defensive strategy than I was naturally inclined.

"You denied me a reprieve from my prison once already," Araeda'h said in an aggrieved tone. "Your ginger priestess did the same, but promised your aid in my eventual escape in exchange for my help and my tutelage."

With a sigh, I agreed, "You have been a wise tutor to us both, and I am grateful. What could I possibly do that you have not already tried?"

"We must find the Pillars of Creation," she said with a mystical flair.

"Do you even know where to look?"

She scowled at me. "Just tell—"

"I heard you," I interrupted. "I will consider your request. Everyone seems to want me to attend this godsdamned Conclave." I grunted in annoy-ance. Did *I* want to go? Did I actually have a choice? My inclination was to spite the high gods and their infernal demand.

Araeda'h grinned. "Tell Conseca to choose her next move carefully!"

Realization tickled through me. Conseca had been playing this silly game against Araeda'h. And she'd stymied the mad old goddess. With pawns. New appreciation for my self-appointed priestess filled my heart.

"She might benefit from Z'nnek's mentorship," Araeda'h mused in a tone that sounded like calculated nonchalance.

The suggestion made me irrationally jealous. I refused to consider why and held my tongue. Something about that man stirred up feelings I'd never felt before about anyone.

Araeda'h muttered to herself, "Most gemstones can be trusted, but garnets cannot!"

She waved her hands frantically at me. "Soon!"

I'd be getting nothing further from her today but nonsense.

With a deep sigh, I closed the Book.

CHAPTER 4

$\mathcal{U}$nsettled and no longer in the mood for orgy, I wandered aimless through the mutable, inconstant halls of the underworld palace I called home. It never occurred to me in those days to wonder why Nethe was ever changing. The question of what to tell my mother on the morrow was locked in a dungeon cell in my mind. Trapped inside my own preoccupation, I sought an answer to the question of what I wanted in eternity instead. Z'nnek was a magnanimous co-ruler, a gracious partner, and a generous lover—he shared me without complaint and no small measure of joy. Though, the more he and Tourak overcame their ancient monogamous jealousies, the more mine secretly increased.

When I first arrived, nigh a month past, I'd found this place foreboding. The idiosyncrasies that had seemed so eerie then were a comfort now. The neglected armories no longer disappointed. They signaled a long, lasting peace. Weapons and armor unneeded since the Accord—eight thousand years before I was born. Implements of war Madra would see put to use once more. I sighed as I strode past them.

The musty libraries drew me now rather than repelling—I had come to reckon knowledge was power in its own right. Between orgies, I'd found refreshment in books in a way I'd never had as a living woman. I'd been exposed to fresh alternatives and perspectives, including that of the mad goddess trapped in the Book of the Forbidden. My lovers' worldview had edged its way toward becoming my own. The jumbled architectures and concepts that had once seemed incongruous were now my home. And Nethe had begun to change since I donned the crown. Some of the dust and rust and disuse had begun to fade, perhaps to heal, in the vibrant stillness of the underworld.

Something disturbed that quiescence. Far above, someone not of my own fell through a hole in the stone sky of Nethe. I did not recognize the presence as one of the gods I knew, nor their angels. A winged being with the power of flight. An angel then. But the sense of the servitor was unfamiliar. I'd not met enough of my new divine counterparts to recognize them all, let alone the angels of their hosts. Not yet.

Disinclined to visitors, I left the new problem to Z'nnek. *Let him deal with it*, I thought. *He left me with enough to ponder on my own.*

Beyond the tall windows of the greeting hall, our angels appeared at intervals, one at a time, carrying unclaimed souls down from the sun-kissed lands. Not so many as the Elysian betrayal had dropped on Spring Festa, but a consistent trickle. One in three of those angels were mine—and one in three of the slumbering souls they carried. I wondered how many of those newborn shades would be capable of ascendance to join my flock. By my standard, of course. The high gods had not claimed them for their own. Therefore, to the world above, they were already prejudged unworthy, damned for eternity.

Still, they were mine to care for and perhaps to lead. Z'nnek and I disagreed upon the latter. He tended the unclaimed dead like the gentle vintner he was: caring, feeding, shaping, nurturing. I felt they should be given meaning, purpose...something. I just didn't know what. Not yet. What I knew with certainty was that I did not want that purpose to be war.

The unknown flyer circled above, out of sight, but not out of mind. Why wasn't Z'nnek greeting the emissary of the high gods? It wasn't like him to suffer interlopers. I'd no taste for meeting someone sent as a reminder of the looming Conclave.

My meandering feet led me up a familiar, narrow, winding staircase. This time, instead of the spurs and boots I'd worn a month ago, I wore silken slippers of my own creation. Instead of plate and chain armor, I was clad in my now customary burial wrap—a sinuous black and crimson affair. This style, a copy of a duplicitous gift from Goerranu, had apparently been the custom for dead priestesses of some long-lost tribe or clan or cult. A people burned to ash by Amuun and the high gods for disobedience ten millennia or more past. Their traditional clothing was comfortable and pretty. I should ask the goddess of secrets and lies about them—when I stopped avoiding her. Perhaps I might even believe the tale she told me.

Stepping out of the musty, twisting stairway, I took in the rooftop where I'd unwittingly accepted my goddesshood only a month gone.

The benighted garden was the same...and different. The fruit on the trees no longer pulsed ominously. Now, they produced lush fruit just like their sun-kissed cousins. The ornamental trees were healthy and green beneath the multicolored lights that flitted far overhead. Whether Z'nnek's recent visit to the world above or my own fresh influence had changed things, I was glad of the difference. Nethe itself was adapting for the better. Though I hadn't acquainted myself with all of my new realm, I at least felt more at ease here than I had when I first arrived.

The unsettling presence rippled through my awareness, lower now, skimming the treetops, unescorted and unchallenged. The palace was visible from anywhere in Nethe, which meant the intruder chose not to come straight here. Such a trespass must be answered, regardless. If Z'nnek would not, then I must.

Steeling myself to suffer the summons to Conclave again, my eyes searched the dark sky for the place that felt...*wrong*. One flyer, low in the sky, stood out among those that I knew by sense. They soared above an orchard a few leagues away, far below the stone ceiling of my underworld realm. A sense distinct from those who called Nethe home. My angels and Z'nnek's were purposeful, attentive. They knew their business and they went about it with efficiency and aplomb. We'd no need to guide them in every detail. They cared for and loved our charges—the unclaimed shades— as much as we, in their own way.

The newcomer circled as if confused or searching for something. I'd trusted that Z'nnek would greet our unexpected "guest" and he had not. Many of my nearby unkindness were attentive but would not intervene unless I bid them. Though we'd nothing to hide, I'd not suffer a stranger to traipse about in my realm unannounced. No, that would not do at all. I sighed.

As Z'nnek had taught me, I drew upon Nethe's magic rather than exhaust my own. With the slightest of intent, my raven-feathered wings emerged from my shoulders, pushing aside the strips of the burial wrap. I launched myself high and away from the interloper to gain altitude and advantage.

Circling broadly, I angled back toward my prey from many furlongs' height. I loved to fly, but I pushed the joy of it away to focus on my hunt. The stranger was descending toward an odd grouping of three sepulchers I'd not noticed before. The three round-domed tombs marked three points around a large, circular pool of dark water with some sort of winged statue at its heart. So many strange ruins dotted Nethe that I'd ceased to notice them.

A feminine form alighted beside the pool in a dainty way. High above her, I watched as she furled her hawk-feathered wings without hurry but did not release them—as if she did not intend to tarry at the edge of the black pool. She seemed to be entranced by the slow, black ripples that oozed on its surface. Such unwelcome curiosity and trespass should be punished.

While her back was to me, I had the perfect opportunity to strike. I took it.

Curling my body and wings, I fell into a stoop so fast I couldn't breathe the air. I'd no intention to give her any warning. My aim was perfect as I fell straight toward her, not even slowing to pull out of the dive.

I crashed into the rough, charcoal tiles, shattering them with the energy of my attack. The force of my impact was so great that I nearly bounced into the pool.

Pain radiated through every part of me, but I ignored it and absentmindedly drew magic from Nethe to heal. I levered myself up, knowing that, some-fucking-how, I'd missed. Furling my wings tight against my back, I chose not to release them in case I should need to retake to the air again with a quickness.

My prey was gone.

Only a haunting, feminine laugh remained.

Expecting a rapid counter, I shook off the embarrassment of my failed attack. I drew Grievance from the depths of my soul. The black steel blade rasped across my heart like a whetstone. The silvery razor edge gleamed in what passed for starlight in my realm. Whirling in my war dance guard, I sought the invader.

She stood impassively, her mocking laugh still twisting her carmine lips, just out of lunging distance. A strong-featured woman, with dark skin and verdant eyes that turned up at the corners, watched me with curiosity. A child of mixed parentage, she had the look of both the lovely, olive-skinned islanders from the east and the handsome, black-skinned Swalli of the south. Pretty, in a wild sort of way. She seemed unperturbed, neither by my armed, aggressive stance nor my failed assault. Her level of danger increased in my estimation.

She wore light armor of emerald steel chased with rose-gold filigree. The decorations were of predators and prey: hawks and doves, hounds and stags. I could guess whom she served: the goddess of hunters and the hunted. Perhaps some of her goddess's wild magic had saved her from my ambush. Elsewise, I couldn't've missed. An ornate longbow hung across her back betwixt her wings. A pair of scimitars rode at her hips.

She nodded to me, which bobbed her short, intensely curly black hair. "Illyria, mistress of Nethe?" Every bit of her aspect radiated boredom and displeasure. She did not want to be here.

Not sure who else she thinks I'd be. "I am Illyria," I said, hiding my indignance. "Queen of Nethe." Because she was being nominally polite and still unarmed, I sheathed Grievance in my heart, who groaned silently with reluctance at being put away unblooded.

"Just so," the hawk-winged angel said, without sounding the least bit impressed. "The crown gave you away." She crossed her arms behind her back and struck a formal pose, one foot presented at a cant. Athletic but not overmuscled, she had the small breasts and lithe build of a Swalli dancer. Her stance reminded me of the legendary duel-fighters of the monks from her east islands origin. Her voice took on a rehearsed tone. "The Lady of the Dread Hunt inquires as to your intentions."

Taken aback, I managed to not sputter stupidly. "My intentions?" *What did the goddess of hunters and the hunted want with me?* To give myself time to think, I took a long breath and blew it out. *Why would Huund send an emissary? She had no dog in this hunt beyond kinship to the Twins.*

"Urth's report of your period of mourning to the Lady's brothers was—"

I laughed, which seemed to disconcert her. I wondered how old she was. One of the many problems with divine beings is that no one seemed to look their age.

She waited, covering her irritation at being interrupted, reminding me of my mother. Where was Madra? More urgently, where was Z'nnek? He should've arrived by now to greet this emissary of the high gods. *Where is my royal lover to answer this intrusion? And why had they chosen an angel of their elder sister's host to play messenger? Urth themselves had delivered the original summons to Conclave with the high gods.*

"I can imagine how the Twins received the news of my delay to their summons to Conclave." I gave her a wicked grin. "Was there yelling? I do hope there was yelling. Possibly screaming. That would be nice." I heaved a faux sigh. "It's been such a fraught morning, what with the wedding and all! I could use some cheering up with news like that."

The angel of the Dread Hunt sniffed. "I would not know, my—uh..." She seemed to flail about for a title of address.

She couldn't very well call me queen, now could she? No one but Z'nnek and Tourak and my angels seemed to believe I'd earned that title nor properly been given it. Well, my lovers and my priestess, Conseca. For sure, the high gods would not acknowledge my sovereignty.

Without mercy, I said, "You may call me Queen or Your Highness or Your Imminence or..." I smiled with feigned politeness to cover my discomfort with pomposity. "Illyria."

"Illyria then."

Before she could speak further, I asked, "What is your name?"

She forced the word out past her surprise, as if no one ever asked the name of messengers. "Siti."

I smiled. "Well met, Siti." It sounded like an eastern islander's name. I was curious about her background, her mortal life, who she was. I wondered what her name meant in her culture, but I didn't want to prolong this encounter. I wanted her to leave. "Peace and hospitality for you in my realm for your brief visit."

With an odd head tilt, she narrowed one eye at me. "Will you attend?"

Single-minded, this one, I thought. What to tell her? I'd been wandering aimlessly through this conversation, trying to avoid that particular question. It might be fun to tell her that I planned to blow off the entire affair. How would she react? But what would that mean for my fledgling religion? My fresh new faithful? Conseca? My highland kinfolk? They might be punished by the high gods and the old for my fit of pique. No, I was certain Alamar would be punished.

My mother wanted me to use the opportunity of the Conclave to declare war. Or perhaps just slaughter the high gods in return as their followers had slain us. That would disappoint both of my lovers, not to mention set the world aflame with godwar. Again. Though such an outcome would please Goerranu and Mawzi more than a little, I found that I alone stood between vengeance denied and an ocean of blood. I did not enjoy the position.

Huund's herald became more still the longer I gazed at her. Her bearing was much like her Mistress, the Lady of the Hunt portrayed in the Litanies. My mind swirled. Her hawklike posture was a predator ready to swoop and pounce. This angel stalked my reaction with her predator eyes, waiting for the answer as to my attendance.

I opened my mouth to speak, then thought better of it, since I'd no idea what I would say.

There had to be some middle path between capitulation and oblivion.

But I couldn't see it. Yet.

I stalled for time. "What are your Lady's expectations?"

Siti blinked and stifled a yawn. "The Lady of the Dread Hunt expects you to attend the Conclave, as promised."

Whenever I couldn't see a path through the darkness, all I could do was hold the torch high and walk forward until I could see further.

"Very well," I said. "Inform your Lady and"—I forced a laugh—"her brothers to expect me at dawn in two days." I thought for a moment. *Should I ask where? Not my fault if they didn't tell me where to meet. Neither had I said precisely that I would attend.*

Nodding, Siti replied, "As you say."

I waved at the multicolored lights that fluttered against the stone sky of my world, seeking their final exit back into the sun-kissed world they desperately craved. "I trust you can find your way out?"

Siti stretched her wings and launched herself high. Flapping effortlessly, she spun in a lazy circle overhead, spiraling higher and higher. Annoying as her presence was, her hawk-winged beauty was a joy to behold.

"The Conclave will be held in the circle of standing stones," the distant voice of the lovely angel called like a ghost on the wind, "where you last celebrated Spring Festa, at the first light of Amuun rising."

Though the huntress angel was nearly out of sight, I fought with my face to keep the conflicted flurry of emotions hidden.

Of course, they would choose to Conclave upon the ground where I'd been killed.

Fuck me.

CHAPTER 5

Though the huntress angel was long out of my sight, I stood sentinel until her presence had left Nethe. Through the crown I became aware of being watched. One of my nearby shades was curious, yet hesitant to approach. Well, they would or they wouldn't, as they willed. I was disinclined to rush the business of others in their own eternity. My mind was preoccupied.

Still standing in the small crater I'd left in the charcoal-colored slate tiles, I scanned all around me. The black pool was large enough for fifty or more friendly people to play in, with room to spare. Its surface rippled with slow, complex, overlapping patterns. The liquid stank of a foul vintage that I knew too well. Many, if not most, of Nethe's shades imbibed it willingly and with relish, but I loathed that particular liquor and what it represented.

At its heart, a winged statue posed high upon an ornate pedestal in the midst of the vast pool. Her immaculate image, done in painted ivory, evoked auburn curls, hazel eyes, and pale skin. Midnight-feathered raven wings, spread in a sheltering pose, marked her as one of mine, but I'd never seen her face before. Something in her stance or expression gave the impression of fragility, but she was beautiful. Her raised hands held a crude flagon to her lips as if she were about to drink. The statue was lovingly crafted and well-kept. Her name was inscribed upon its base: Kragh.

I was not too proud to admit to myself the twinge in my heart. I'd no love for those who wanted statues made of them. Yet my Z'nnek had clearly loved this delicate beauty enough to memorialize her as he'd wanted to do for me in our new temple ziggurat. She was not his first wife, Ru'mael, lost to him as a mortal man. He'd told me of her ebony skin and strong vintner's frame. The fragile Kragh was undoubtedly another who'd possessed his heart since Z'nnek had ascended to the throne of Nethe. Yet he'd never mentioned her.

Three sepulchers crouched atop crepidomas spaced equidistant around the black pool. From each, a spillway dumped dark fluid in a curtain-like fall. Waves rippled away from the falls, flowing toward the statue, meeting in a complex triumviral pattern around her base. Three channels flowed out of the pool, one betwixt each sepulcher. Curiosity engrossed me in trying to determine the purpose of these ruins.

"I am tired," a woman's voice whispered behind me, "and I am ready."

Startled and unnerved that I'd lowered my guard so far, I turned to find a shade of a tan-skinned race I couldn't place. Standing within easy reach, she regarded me with a vacant expression. She was frail and faded, as if she'd lived aeons in Nethe, drinking Z'nnek's wine of oblivion. Her aura was midnight, marking her not as one of Z'nnek's, but one of mine. Her style of clothing was unfamiliar—the once-fine fabrics were worn at the seams. Above the hollows of her cheeks, her dark eyes were sunken and devoid of liveliness. My already sensitized heart ached for her emptiness.

The grinding of heavy stone upon stone crushed the air. The great double doors to the sepulcher in my direct view opened in ponderous fashion. Glances over both shoulders warned me that all three tombs had yawned together. Hooded figures emerged and walked silently down the steps toward us as if summoned by the shade's whisper. They did not glide with the effortless grace I'd observed many of our shades to adopt. These cowled figures of many races moved heavily, as if with great age. Horrific, mutilated faces lurked in the shadows of their hoods. Their eyes and nostrils and mouths were sewn shut with heavy, imperfect stitches. My skin prickled at the sight of them.

They converged upon us.

I resisted the urge to draw Grievance again. Knowledge stayed my hand.

Knowledge that Z'nnek would suffer nothing truly dangerous to inhabit our lands or threaten our shades. Resolving to epitomize my new philosophy of patience and long-suffering, I held my ground unarmed, but interposed myself between the faded woman and the newcomers—at least as many as I could. I counted thirteen approaching from three directions at once, circling the pool.

"What do you intend?" I demanded. My words felt odd, as if I were echoing Siti's recent query to me.

The oncoming shades did not slow. They emanated emotion so cold it struck me with its power. Several blinks passed before I identified the icy feeling: wrath. Though it was not directed at me, this much wrath from thirteen mutilated shades was nigh overpowering. I could not fathom its origin nor its target. They did not *feel* wrath. They had *become* wrath.

I'd danced with wrath myself only once: in my third and final fight with Provax two long days ago upon the now-destroyed bridge to Alamar. Once the need for vengeance cooled so deeply, it became irresistible. In truth, I was more comfortable with warm anger or hot rage or boiling fury—my own or others'. Those emotions were weapons I could wield or counter. Wrath was an uncontrollable armament I'd no wish to ever employ nor suffer.

I didn't understand what was happening. Still, my instinct was to protect this innocent woman from whatever these terrors of the grave intended. She was mine to defend.

I defied the mob. "You may not have her!"

Before I could choose to draw my sword or even call for aid from my unkindness of angels, the faded woman stepped past me. Her feather-light touch upon my arm held me in place.

"I called them," she mumbled. "They've come for me." Her short, shuffling steps took her close to the stocky woman who led the terrors.

"No!" I shouted, pulling the woman back behind me. I whirled us away, to interpose myself between her and the oncoming thirteen.

All of them wore the wine-colored aura of Z'nnek's shades. I did not wish to raise arms against them. My mind scrambled, seeking a way to save my helpless charge.

The mutilated dead moved in silence to array themselves in a circle around us.

Then they advanced.

Instead of Grievance, I reached up to the unnamed crown Z'nnek had gifted to me only yesterday. The black gold circlet encrusted with purple Azzarrean diamonds rested upon my head. I shoved my intention to command into it. All around me, the muted colors of Nethe came alive with vibrance. My awareness of the underworld—its magic and its presence—filled me. Nearby sources of power and unexplored novelty called to me. Controlling my attention to remain focused on the immediate threats became difficult.

"As your queen, I command you to halt!"

The thirteen halted. Stopping in midstride, they put their feet down in unison. They didn't precisely come to attention, but it was clear that they watched me and waited for my direction. Through their frigid wrath, I also sensed curiosity bubble up, fresh and new—as if they'd not felt such an emotion in a long time.

"No!" the shade behind me screamed. Her feeble fists beat upon my back. "You tyrant!"

Shocked, I released my hold on her and turned about face. "What? I am no tyrant!"

The translucent woman was distraught beyond words. Many sounds emerged from her throat, but none were intelligible to me.

Mastering my own surprise, I said, "I do not force anything upon you. Not upon any of my people!" I could not fathom her accusation.

At least she spat, "You would deny me what is mine by right?"

"I deny you nothing," I declared, confused. "I only seek to protect you from those who intend you harm."

"I called them," she said again, as if that explained everything.

I looked over my shoulder at the impassive, stitched-scarred wraiths. "Called them to what end?"

"To my end," the shade whispered. "I am ready to be done."

Two unexamined things in my core clashed together. The pain of that collision jarred me with agony that even being nailed to the wheel of woe had not. Afraid of her answer, I had to ask, nonetheless.

"Tell me what you need," I pleaded, reaching to cup her sallow cheeks in my palms in the most maternal way I knew. "If I—or Z'nnek before me— were not generous enough…" I spread my arms wide as if offering her all of Nethe. "What do you want that you do not have here?"

She pursed her lips and shook her head.

It was not lost upon me that Z'nnek had made me the same offer a month gone. And I, too, had refused.

"I haven't even gotten to know you or your name!" How many millions of my shades languished in Nethe unknown and uncounted?

Her face, though full of its own despair, erupted with pity—for me. "It doesn't matter. I don't want it anymore."

There lay my dilemma: protect her from herself or accept her sovereignty over herself.

I had always fought to preserve lives, and when I failed to do so, to avenge them and thus preserve others in the future. But also, I believed no one owns anyone but herself. Three days past, I'd confronted this same choice—and I'd killed my mother to preserve her immortal life against her will. Had I been right? She didn't think so. And she might hate me for it.

"Will you let me go?" asked the shade who looked nothing like my mother.

Embarrassed now to wear the crown, I tore it from my head. And stepped aside.

The nameless woman glided past me toward the waiting wraiths. I followed on her heels.

All thirteen encircled her at the edge of the oozing black pool. They didn't touch me, but somehow edged me out until I was standing isolated. The pitiful shade stood in the center of them. I was taller than many of the terrors and had no trouble watching as twelve efficiently stripped the shade of her clothes.

The stocky leader strode across the water toward Kragh.

Her feet did not ripple the water. The hem of her cloak did not drag through the deep bath of the wine of oblivion. It was as if she were immune to it and her very existence repelled the toxic brew. Perhaps her wrath overpowered the entropy of the wine. I hated that vintage and what it represented. I realized then that the three channels leaving the pool were not intended to keep the pool from overflowing.

Those channels were the font of the three powerful rivers that flowed throughout Nethe, carrying the forgetfulness so many shades seemed to crave. This place was the origin of the wine of oblivion, the draught that eventually caused every shade to wither to nothing and seek the stone sky in a vain effort to escape back into the sun-kissed lands.

The leader of the terrors returned, bearing the flagon taken from the statue at the heart of the black pool. Even before she bent to scoop wine from the pool of oblivion, I knew what they intended for the nameless woman I should be protecting. Only her willful consent stayed my hand from stopping this awful rite. Who was I to bar someone from the fate she chose?

The naked shade took the flagon and drank greedily. Before she finished the draught, she collapsed and spasmed upon the broken tiles where I'd missed my prey. Wine of oblivion splattered upon the damaged stone. The flagon clinked and rolled to a stop at my feet. No sound emerged from her wracked lips, which seemed to scream in agony.

The cloaked terrors carried her into the pool then.

And began to drown her.

Surely, this can't be what she wanted?

My heart clenched, and I squeezed my fists so tightly they ached.

The bubbles and thrashing quickly ceased. The thirteen who stood in the pool, yet seemingly unaffected by it, stepped back, maintaining their circle around the shade they had sunk. They raised their hands to the sky in benediction.

An amorphous, glittering, sand-colored blob flitted up from beneath the black waves, shedding drops of oblivion as it rose. Inside the misshapen bubble, I could see a frozen moment in time, like a memory. A younger version of the faded woman, vibrant and alive, caring for an elderly woman who could be her mother. A tender moment I would never have with Madra.

Then what was left of the woman wobbled toward the sky to join the other aimless, multicolored stars in my eternal night sky.

CHAPTER 6

Soundless but for their ponderous, shuffling gait, the hooded terrors filed back toward their respective sepulchers in groups of four. Without thinking further, I followed the stout leader who made the fifth of the group who followed her. They tramped up the massive stone steps. I trailed behind, carrying the crown in my hand, uncertain what to do with it now. A foulness weighted the air as I approached the heavy stone portal. The stench was as much a crawling sensation upon my skin as an olfactory assault. It was a reek akin to the pool, only thicker and more rank.

"Illyria!" Z'nnek's voice called to me from far overhead. "Don't!"

I glanced up at where he circled overhead, vulture wings spread wide in the windless underworld night. My annoyance with him flared into disappointment and anger. I didn't speed up my stride, but neither did I slow. *He knows better than to command me!*

The stout figure at the top of the steps turned. As the other four filed past her, she stood braced in the midst of the yawning doorway. I thought she meant to bar my path. A grim smile split my face.

Her posture and twisted expression were meant to convey something. I could not be sure what, though. Perhaps her skin had been too long confined by the rough stitches to pull into any position but a wrathful scowl. As I approached, she made no move to block my progress, though I could sense that she did not sanction my passage into the darkened interior.

Behind me, I heard Z'nnek alight on the stone, his lambskin boots scuffing softly.

"Illyria, please!" he begged.

Three strides away, I placed the crown back upon my head as I faced the stocky woman in my path. I made no effort to decipher her wordless attempts to dissuade me.

In those days, I was too arrogant to heed warnings.

The hooded horror stepped aside and preceded me.

The dark mouth of the sepulcher swallowed me.

The stone entry was three strides deep. The huge doors as thick. While I should not have been surprised that underworld denizens with eyes stitched shut would not need light, I was. The crown gave me knowledge of any part of my domain I chose to concentrate upon, so I didn't precisely need to see —but I was still accustomed back then to seeing with my own eyes. The source of the foulness demanded exploration with my own senses.

I wanted light. Therefore, I created it.

With a word and an intention, I converted the darkness of Nethe within the stone tomb into daylight. Four hooded creatures stood at the four corners of a blood-guttered altar. Their hands clutched flensing knives and other implements of butchery. The fifth stood apart, just slightly to my left, watching me with anticipation through stitched-shut eyes.

Chained upon the altar before them was an enormous vulture-headed demon, expertly stripped of his skin. Even the feathers had been plucked from his head and taloned feet. Every muscle was excruciatingly revealed. I thought him—for it was a well-endowed man's body beneath the neck— skinned and dead. The massive corpse had to be eight feet tall, from skinless talons to featherless crest.

Then I noticed the slightest pulsation of his exposed arteries, barely perceptible.

Each weak throb pumped tiny squirts of purpling, near-black blood onto the altar which drained through the gutters into runnels in the floor of the raised platform. Fascinated and horrified, my eyes traced its flow. Beyond the edge of the raised area, the runnels emptied into what looked like wine aging casks. The barrels were full to the brim with something that was less blood and more the consistency of wine. The thick proto-wine oozed out into tracks that fed the spillway. I'd found the origin of the pool's source and it was more awful than I'd imagined.

No stranger to battlefield gore or hunting offal or animal slaughter, I'd not been truly shocked until I saw that he lived. I'd never seen any beast live through such an ordeal.

As I watched, a tiny sliver of skin began to regrow upon one of his shoulders. The nearest hooded figure deftly sliced it away with a flensing knife. The tormentor flung the bloody gobbet into one of the runnels in the floor. The little hunk of flesh flowed on the tiny current toward the row of wine casks where it plopped and began to dissolve.

The ravaged monstrosity lifted his beaked head. Chains rattled as he contracted his limbs. Black vulture eyes met mine.

"FREE ME!" he screamed in a voice that was more concussion than speech.

The sepulcher shook with agony. The very foundation rocked. Of a sudden, I knew the epicenter of every quake that rattled Nethe—for just a moment. Before the sheer force of it blew all thought from my mind.

The power of his compulsion drove me to my knees. My ears rang. My head spun. Demonic will crushed down upon mine. The crown slipped from my bowed head. The black gold circlet rang upon the stone floor in the breathless silence that followed the terrible shout. Or perhaps it was the phantom ringing deafness after the aural assault.

My will broke. The light in the tomb flashed back to its natural darkness.

Every regrettable mistake. Every moment of weakness. Every weighty self-doubt. Every low point in my short nineteen years poured out of my unconscious to attack me like demons of the Hells.

My unintended slaughter of my brother.

My mindless escalation of the war with the Chosen of Tyrr.

My desperate battle that destroyed the ancient bridge.

My reckless disregard of my mother's will and her murder.

"You were never worthy of my crown," the demon purred.

Unreasoning despair clutched my heart and squeezed. I wanted to defy him. No air would fill my lungs. I'd lost the power of speech. The fingers of my left hand scraped at the nub where my right middle finger had been lost in ignominious defeat.

"Free me," he purred, "and I will give your pitiful life meaning."

Giving in would be so simple, so easy. Who was I to pretend to be a goddess? I'd done nothing but fly from one disaster to the next all my life. Even my mother thought so, I was sure. The allure of obedience beckoned. Never in my life had I complied without a struggle. Putting down all the burdens I'd picked up, though, would be a relief. Someone with true power could put all the things I'd broken to rights.

"I will give you power to be the envy of all," he tempted, "if you release my shackles."

In my heart, I'd never sought to be a goddess. I'd only thought to serve justice—in life and in the afterlife. Even in my innermost dreams, I'd failed, despite lifelong encouragement by my parents, my family, and my clan. Especially my father. Padra had told me, *Don't seek power for its own sake. Possess it only to do good.* I couldn't tell if that were my memory or Nerren's. The recollections he'd sacrificed to me along with his immortal soul had merged with my own, so perhaps it didn't matter which were whose. Submitting to anyone, least of all a demon, would not solve my pain.

"You—"

"No," I whispered, cutting him off as if I'd shouted.

Recovering my crown from the dark-hidden floor, I hoisted myself to my feet. Pushing up against the weight of existence bearing down on my shoulders was harder than rising from the wheel of woe I'd been nailed to less than four days past. But I rose.

"Light," I commanded with a snap of the fingers on my damaged hand.

Illumination blew through the room, clearing some of the putrescence from the space that had seemed huge when I entered. Even the demon that dominated the altar seemed smaller. Beady eyes that had their lids carved away glared at me.

I met his bloody gaze as I put my crown on my head in triumph. *No*, I thought, *that is its name: Triumph.* The circlet nestled its slight weight into my curls, feeling more a part of me now than it had before.

Without a word, four hooded horrors turned to me, wielding their bloody implements. Their leader, the fifth, bowed deeply to me and held her pose until the others joined her. I felt, in that moment, that I had earned something intangible from them. I wasn't sure I wanted it.

"You may rise," I said to the demon's keepers, "and return to your task."

As one, they straightened and wordlessly resumed their stations around the bloody bier.

How much time had passed in our contest of wills, I know not. But before I could speak further, Z'nnek rushed in behind me. I turned toward him as I felt him, and his fear, approach through the gaping maw of the sepulcher.

"Illyria, don't let Baal—"

"FREE ME!" the demon thundered.

I ignored the gale of the demon's impotent rage upon my back, watching Z'nnek. My lover scarcely flinched, his eyes only for me. His gaze searched mine, hopefully and fearfully. I smiled to reassure him.

The demon cackled, low and ragged. "All these uncounted millennia after you took what was mine by right! I waited for you to visit me, you treacherous bastard," he said, "and I wasted my pent up wrath upon *her*." He made a rude clucking sound. "Now, I can't even make the cowardly vintner grovel. End me and be done."

My lover and co-ruler and I stared at one another in surprise for a long moment. Baal's self-deprecating plea washed over us unnoticed.

"You aren't—" he started.

"You didn't—" I began.

We both took a breath to stop interrupting each other.

"You deserve to have died in your last assault upon Heaven," the demon snarled. "Still, your arrogance will be your downfall, Preema! You have been gone for too long. Far too much has changed. Beware, lest the sun and the hawk steal your prize."

That was the second time today I'd heard that name. Had Araeda'h confused me with Preema, whoever they were? I wasn't about to ask nor trust Baal in any way. I ignored the demon. Z'nnek would tell me later or I'd find out in my own way in my own time.

"Kill me," Baal said, but his voice carried no command, only pitiful resignation. "Do not leave me to the untender ministrations of your Unspeaking…"

42

"Never, Baal," Z'nnek said, glaring at the demon with eternal rage. "You've only begun to suffer for what you—"

I glanced at my husband in surprise. He was not the vengeful sort. Yet he had either created or empowered these Unspeaking tormentors of Baal, and presumably Raam and Sett.

My lover bowed his head in shame.

Whatever he believed his sins to be, this was not the place to deal with them. Nor my place to judge him. When Z'nnek looked up again, I waved toward the yawning mouth of the sepulcher for him to precede me.

The stout, bestitched leader of the Unspeaking nodded to me as she took my place in the tomb at the foot of the sacrificial altar.

CHAPTER 7

I flew higher into the stone-ceilinged sky and deeper into thought, at war with myself as much as with disappointment and surprise. I needed to regain my perspective. *Did these new facts change my need to disregard the Conclave?* The gentle god of the unclaimed dead who defied the tyranny of the high gods and the old in open war wanted me to not do the same. What mystery had I not yet solved which would explain the contradiction?

The fact that Z'nnek had secrets shouldn't—didn't—surprise me. The reality of them did. New truths about the world had surfaced which abrogated what I thought I knew. The Litanies told few stories of Z'nnek, but his overthrow of the demon lords of Nethe was one every child learned.

My mind churned with the many other Litanies, given the lie as I'd witnessed with my own eyes. The mortal man who had braved the netherworld on a hopeless quest to reclaim his wife and unborn child from death. The humble vintner who had deceived and conquered and destroyed the three demon lords who ruled Nethe. Including Baal. Not destroyed. Still alive and in torment. In my realm. Perhaps at the behest of, but certainly with the full knowledge of my mild and gentle Z'nnek.

Baal's wrathful torment didn't shock or dismay me. If Z'nnek felt obliged, it was surely due and deserved. What irked me was that Z'nnek had left me to handle Huund's messenger alone. And he hadn't ever warned me about Baal. What other unpleasant surprises, hidden for eight thousand years, lay in ambush for me in my new realm? I supposed the other two sepulchers contained the other demon lords: Raam and Sett. The eternal torture of all three must be the source of the quakes that frequently rocked Nethe. But not so much as all the other secrets I'd uncovered shook me.

Who was Kragh? Who was Preema? They appeared neither in the Litanies nor the Tales.

More importantly, who were they to Z'nnek? What were they to Z'nnek?

Do I confront him about them?

Did he love them more than me?

Am I so petty and jealous as that?

The recalcitrant king of the underworld had followed me into the sky, eventually. Should I care what caused his hesitation? Whether I should mattered not—I cared. I could feel him in the distance, below and behind. While not intent on outpacing him, I was not about to slow down and wait for Z'nnek. He would have to work to catch up.

Dancing lights overhead caught my eye. I feared those contained hard truths and painful secrets, too. Every one. I angled higher and flapped harder.

The inconstant stars above Nethe were doubtless not angels, as they were in the sun-kissed lands. But I'd never flown so close before. After witnessing the drowning of one of my shades, I feared what I would find in those many-colored lights in my sky. *Trust everyone, but count the coins,* Madra always said. Still, I rose higher with broad strokes of my wings, struggling to lift the heaviness in my heart with my love of flight.

Would my every joy in the afterlife become bittersweet?

Misshapen balls of varicolored light danced along the rough rock ceiling of Nethe. They were not like the gold and silver stars above my childhood highland home. According to the Litanies, those brilliant guardian angels patrolled the veil of night against the incursion of the Hells' demonic hordes. Was that even true? I shook away the pointless questioning.

These shapeless, incoherent clouds of memory beat aimlessly against the roof of the underworld, hopelessly trying to regain the life they'd lost. Not ordered sequences of memories—as every soul I'd ever stolen were—but single, poignant moments. Each little bubble a singular recollection. One tiny but most significant moment.

Z'nnek caught up sooner than I'd expected. He'd assumed his vulture form to fly faster. Perhaps in time, he would cease to please me, but for now, I'd embrace his sweet-and-sour novelty. In my anger, I hoped he wouldn't try to converse, so I could brood in silence.

My hopes were dashed by his querulous screech. "Illyria, allow me to explain!" he gronked in avian speech.

I'd not forgive him so easily. I pulled on my own raven and flew higher faster, still drawn to the shining lights. I felt the bigger, slower vulture struggle to give chase. What I craved was distraction from the shaken beliefs at my core.

Even the feeblest shade possessed enough strength to keep their secrets, if they wished, unless taken by force. As I soared below the stars of the underworld, my immortal sight allowed me to peer into each slice of remembered time from some unclaimed soul's mortal life. Like the woman I'd watched drown in oblivion, none of them had a defense against my invasion of their privacy. These remnants were bereft of anything but one clear obsession, a singular nostalgia. The surface of each fragile soul capsule rippled like clear mountain pools as my gaze touched each in turn.

A pale greenish blob was a father's fond memory of a girl-child's birth.

The gleaming orb that caught my eye next was an indistinct wedding ceremony. In a culture I'd never known beneath the sun, three new wives exchanged silver circlets with one another. The remembrance belonged to the person officiating.

An irregular crimson teardrop enclosed an agonizing death scene, the final fatal sword stroke eternally rising and falling, piercing down between clavicle and neck. *Why would the memory of that moment be the eternal core of a person?*

No stranger to death scenes myself, that one stung. They all did, in some way, but not equally. Not for me. *Why would anyone seek to return to death and pain?* Like this nameless warrior, I knew the answer of my heart.

Z'nnek had asked me once when we first met: *Take you back to what, Illyria? To pain? To suffering? To death?*

I'd told him I'd suffer it a thousand times over to save my family. *Was I wrong then? Am I so different now from a month ago? Are those who suffered and died in my name any less worthy than my mother? Do I owe them enough to burn the world in godwar?*

In my reverie, I'd slowed, perhaps intentionally, to allow Z'nnek to catch up. He waited patiently now instead of trying to gain my attention. We flew over our domain for many wingbeats in blessed quietude.

A memory of Araeda'h's voice echoed in my mind. The mad, book-bound goddess of magic had said to me: *We are all only what we remember.* I had thought she quoted the Tales. Perhaps she did. I wondered idly who promulgated the blasphemous Tales. Were they truer than the false Litanies? Did truth even matter when all that was remembered were lies?

The wine of remembrance came unbidden to mind. Those moments I'd shared with Z'nnek, and later with Tourak, were the truest I knew—the opposite of oblivion. I wondered why so many shades preferred to forget. Asking Z'nnek now would invite conversation, if he truly even knew the minds of our guests anymore. Still, I grappled with this unpalatable verity. I felt it was connected to the Conclave somehow, but the link eluded me. My eyes were drawn back to the tiny, weak bubbles of souls.

These fluttering, unclaimed mortal spirits had withered down to the most powerful event of their lives. With so little left of their shades to weigh them down, these poor souls sought the sky. Countless eons later, they still clung to a single defining moment. And—just like I had done not so long ago—they struggled blindly to return to the world above and recapture what they'd lost. Perhaps we mortal spirits are nothing but the essence of our memories. When those fade or are stolen or consumed to power magical spells, we die eternal. Like my vanquished enemies. Like Padra. Like Nerren. *What happened to the latent power of all the other memories they shed? Was it just washed downriver to feed the orchards and vineyards of Nethe? Was that the sad point of it all? Why would someone create such a place?*

The lovely rainbow of underworld stars were the last remnants of souls after they'd whiled away some long portion of eternity in Nethe. Perhaps their lack of will to continue was the end for all those shades who'd drunk too much of Z'nnek's wine and forgotten all but their most essential selves. At the last, they'd sought final oblivion in the pool. *Perhaps soon, they would*

fade away entirely into the ambient magic and be no more? Was nothing the ulti-
mate end for us all in death eternal? If not, where were they trying to go?

I hadn't flown up here to seek this truth. But I was saddened and glad-
dened both together. It was a reminder that I no longer belonged to the sun-
kissed realm above. Nethe was my home now. Perhaps that was reason
enough to eschew the Conclave and keep the fragile détente with the high
gods. I circled lower in a lazy spiral.

"Illyria," Z'nnek called in the manner of birds, "will you hear me now?"
His vulture call was deeper than his voice as a man. His meaning was
carried not only through sound, but through his posture, the movements of
his wings, and infinitesimal twitches of his talons. All the minutiae of his
mannerisms contributed to the totality of his avian speech.

With a raven's eye, I could take in all his nuance. I was again struck by
how expressive avian speech could be with such economy. My introspective
silence was broken. Though his intrusion irked me, I knew I could use
Z'nnek's experience in the Little War to formulate a plan for the inevitable
consequence of ignoring the summons to Conclave. To remain here, I must
defend Nethe.

Angling toward one of the openings in the stone sky that lead through
twisting tunnels into Urth's realm, I soared high again. Z'nnek dutifully
followed.

"We must make this defensible," I complained. "Did you seal them all
during the Little War?" *It had taken no effort for Huund's emissary to invade my
domain.*

Surprise jolted his frame, and he beat his wings hard twice to maintain
his altitude. "No." His avian reply carried shock and confusion in its under-
text. "What does that—"

I swooped past his beak, cutting him off literally and figuratively. "Our
realm should not be so open to outsiders." I soared in a half circle to his
other side. "We should lock our bedroom doors, no?" *We might not have been
interrupted this morning,* I thought, *and I might not be here now, knowing what I
know.*

He tried to respond. "Who would—"

With a rude squawk, I interrupted again. "All those shades," I said in the
manner of birds, "roaming about unguarded. There are no angels in sight!" I

fell into a steep dive toward one of the many haphazardly tended vineyards that littered Nethe.

Z'nnek followed me down with a grumpy buzz. In the near distance, I could feel Tourak winging toward us. *I'm not in the fucking mood for both of them.* One downside of being a raven is the apparent inability to sigh. I braced myself to be pressed again, by both of them, with the importance of attending the Conclave and bending over for the high gods and the old. I refused.

My archangel wasn't rushing, but neither was he sedately soaring. His approach was intentional. My feathers rankled to remember that he'd kept Z'nnek's secrets just as he'd told me he would—just as I hoped he kept my own. I wondered abstractly when hypocrisy had become normal for me. I'd no doubt of his loyalty or devotion to me, even when he believed he best served me by siding with Z'nnek.

As we got closer to the ground, I pondered the terrain above and below. Protecting all of Nethe would require more airborne power than we could muster. My host of angels and Z'nnek's combined totaled less than fourteen thousand strong. Nowhere near enough to hold the vastness of Nethe against the might of the high gods and the old, should they pour through the sieve of my stone sky. If the Litanies were to be believed.

"During your rebellion," I inquired with a squawk and a flutter, "how many battles were fought in Nethe?"

Z'nnek's responded with a raucous snort. "None! Though, it was hardly a rebellion," he retorted. "Wouldn't you say, Tourak?" he asked the other raven who sailed down to join us on my other wing. To box me in.

How was that possible? "The Litanies say—"

Tourak buzzed a mocking call that passed for sardonic laughter. "Would be rude to respectable rebellions to call it such. More like a temper tantrum, my old friend, I hate to say."

The jocular amusement between friends who'd shared millennia grated on me today.

A gacking sound that I knew to be a polite chuckle was Z'nnek's reply.

Incredulous and annoyed that they were both laughing at me, I sputtered, "You're telling me that you laid waste to the cities of men among sun-kissed lands and threatened the very gates of the Twin Paradises… And that was just a 'tantrum' to you?"

Turning his head away, Z'nnek didn't answer. Tourak opened his beak and clacked it shut without making any other sound. We three soared in silence.

"All three paradises," Z'nnek chirped softly at last. His plumage ruffled like a shudder.

"But—" I protested, suddenly feeling ignorant and inexplicably ashamed. "The Litanies only name two!"

Sailing closer, Tourak rasped, "They changed the Litanies…after."

My mind whirled with the new revelation. *Z'nnek had destroyed a paradise? One now struck from the Litanies as if it never was? How? Why? The everlasting Litanies had been changed?* All my questions tangled up and I couldn't get any of them out.

We sailed through the eternal night sky together in silence for a long time, boosted on an updraft that rose from a cliff face below. I was lost in thought about how Z'nnek had accomplished so much with so few in his host of angels. The Litanies called them the hordes of the damned. I'd thought they'd meant hosts of angels, merely given a deprecating term. But I hadn't put the puzzle pieces together until now.

"You led the shades to war," I accused. My gaze encompassed all the lazy, indolent shades that lolled without apparent purpose about the underworld below us. My underworld. *How had he urged them to fight?* "Is that why you pamper them so? In your guilt?"

"There are things you don't understand about the world yet," Z'nnek said after a painful pause. "The destruction… The waste…"

Tourak picked up where Z'nnek trailed off. "The high gods and the old could do nothing to resist our advance." He made a mournful chirrup. "Only after we'd laid waste to scores of cities and temples…"

"That doesn't make any sense," I said when he paused long enough for me to think he'd stopped explaining.

Tourak quorked sadly. "Up until the end, our angels fought their angels. In those days, only Amuun and Huund had hosts. Huund's Dread Hunt fought most ferociously." He gacked in respect which I found irritating, based on my one encounter with the huntress's minions.

"Huund must take after her father," I mused, "since Amuun is so merciful."

With a laughing caw, Z'nnek interjected, "Amuun is not so merciful as her priests' propaganda might have you believe." He waggled his wings in amusement. "Don't presume she stopped wanting to burn the cities and temples of her enemies to ash simply because she hasn't since my—" The vulture god clacked his beak. "Since the Accord."

I tried to let that sink in, but it didn't align with my learned image of Amuun, the merciful mother of the gods. The Litanies were clear that only the demon-worshippers and practitioners of the forbidden had been punished. Practitioners, like Z'nnek. And like me.

Tourak resumed his reminiscence. "It might have been different, if Amuun had given mantles to Tyrr and Torr sooner."

Z'nnek gave an ambivalent buzz.

The Litanies said that the birth of the Holy Twins, Tyrr and Torr, and their golden and silver hosts had turned the tide. *Another lie?* "Given mantles?" I asked. I recalled Tourak's reaction to Z'nnek's offer of the wedding gift. "Where do they come from?"

"Mantles are just part of the world," Z'nnek said noncommittally. "Like the crowns of the paradises. And your crown. Wearing a mantle confers the form and the dominion of a flock."

"And the ability to claim souls?" I asked.

Z'nnek whistled an affirmative. We soared long in silence while my lovers let me think upon that. I loved them more for knowing my need to ruminate and granting me time to do it.

Eventually, Tourak continued, "Our mortals fought their mortals. The damned outnumbered the living by a hundred times or more. They'd never truly had a chance."

My raven lover's avian posture was proud, the opposite of Z'nnek, who was ashamed.

Tourak said, "Once we figured out how to lift our horde to the Paradises..."

Z'nnek fluttered his wings as he shook his entire body as if waking up. "Only after we'd laid siege did we realize the divine should never fight the mortal."

51

Tourak watched his old friend for a moment before he spoke. "We had broken the sacred balance." He tilted his head against the wind to look at me. "Do you understand now why we must keep the status quo?"

"The divine must never again make war upon the mortal," Z'nnek repeated emphatically, just as the Litanies described the Accord.

I blinked, trying to process what that meant. How these revelations meshed with what I'd observed myself. And whether any of it changed my intentions. The events of the prior month had lain dormant in my mind, a tangled mess that was easier to ignore than explore. The fingers of my mind twitched at all the loose ends.

We soared aimlessly, or so I'd thought, until we came within view of our palace.

"But I fought mortals," I said at last, focusing on the one thing I understood. I tried, in vain, to alight upon my rooftop garden with grace. I stumbled, of course, with no one to fight and nothing to occupy my mind and keep me from overthinking every movement.

I righted myself and released my raven form with care to avoid self-inflicted pain. I resumed the more familiar mortal shape with a last slight stumble. "I killed demigods and mortals alike. Am I not divine?"

My lovers landed beside me, taking their own human forms more gracefully than I could yet manage. "You are truly divine, love," they sang in unison, love and humor both in their voices. They shared another chuckle at my expense.

That wasn't what I'd meant, and they knew it.

"Spending the eternal lives of the unclaimed was too high a price to pay," Z'nnek said with an earnest frown when they were done laughing at me.

"But—"

Z'nnek interrupted to answer my real question. "Just because you can do a thing, love, doesn't mean you should, yes?" He gave me his endearing, lopsided smile.

Unlike the high gods and the old, Z'nnek had forgiven me my sins.

We strolled without speaking for many heartbeats. My strategic brain whirled into so many patterns. The high gods and the old were vulnerable. I had weapons they could not defend against. *Was I willing to use them? Could I wield people like weapons? Should I?*

"You were something else," Z'nnek said at last, when my continued seriousness pulled at him. "Something new and unexpected. The realm of flesh and spirit merged." He reached between us to tap the heart-shaped scar between my breasts—the magical scar he'd given me to bind my soul to my corpse. "I hadn't meant to upset the careful détente we must keep." He smiled. "But you left your corpse on a burial shelf and now must assume the responsibilities of the divine."

When he said it like that, there was no fucking way I was going to the Conclave.

I stopped walking to think. So did my lovers.

Why did the scar follow me into the afterlife? Instead of asking the obvious, I asked, "Did you know that would happen?"

"No," Z'nnek continued is his abashed voice, "Araeda'h didn't explain everything, before—" He took a deep, controlled breath. "But none among the high gods have matched the mastery of magic she taught me." He smiled wanly. "Little good it did me at the end."

"You did as I asked," I said with an appreciative smile tempered with my more recent irritation with him. I didn't want his confession to dry up, so I asked, "Was it a mistake?"

"I won't say I made a mistake," he said with chagrin, "since you've come to understand, at least in part, why I...surrendered."

I blinked at him. I'd meant him helping me rescue my kith and kin, but he was still talking about the Little War. And his inexplicable surrender.

"No, I don't understand," I said. "You had your enemy at your mercy!"

"Everyone has a part to play." Z'nnek sighed. "Mine is not to rule the world."

"But why agree to the Accord?" I demanded. "Why accept banishment to the underworld when they could not hold you here against your will even if they wished?" I was missing some crucial detail.

"What do I need among the sun-kissed lands?" he asked, turning in a circle, arms wide as if to embrace all of Nethe. "I can do the most good for the most souls here."

I looked again, truly looked at the surreal excuse for the world above. In a month, it had changed somewhat. The flora was more like their sun-kissed counterparts. Songs of the night insects that marked the distinction between days were less eerie. Many of shades I'd chanced to meet walked and worked with renewed vibrancy. I fancied that I'd played a small part in those improvements. But Nethe was still a far cry from the vibrant, living world of my youth.

"You truly can't see it, can you?" I boggled at him. "It's been so long since you lived beneath the sun that you've forgotten what it's like to be alive."

Turning on my heel, I marched toward the stairs. "You allowed the Accord to trap you here, embracing but a shadow of life."

I left him there in the benighted garden, where two fortnights past he'd doomed me to eternity in the dark.

CHAPTER 8

Z'nnek and Tourak were idling in a moldering library when I found them. I'd needed time alone to absorb and digest all that my lovers had revealed. Now I was ready to hold my own. I would not bend on my refusal to attend the Conclave.

Z'nnek was drinking wine, of course. Tourak sipped something from a dainty porcelain cup. Tea, I presumed, from the scent of cinnamon and cardamom on the air. A forgotten game board lay close to hand, both sides decimated. Z'nnek's pieces were roughly chiseled from Azzarrean purple diamonds. Tourak's looked to be melted from black opal from some western wasteland. They could create anything they wished, and yet they fell into the familiar.

They'd been mid-conversation, talking excitedly past one another as only old friends could. The Book of the Forbidden lay between them, with Z'nnek's free hand lazing upon its cover. I brushed my reflexive jealousy aside. For later. After all, I had asked him to keep her safe in my absence.

They ceased to speak when I crossed the threshold and turned as one to face me.

"Tell me not to go to Conclave," I demanded.

Z'nnek grinned. Tourak frowned. They both shook their heads.

I refused to let my resolve deflate. "It's a waste of time!"

Instead of stamping my foot like a child, I strolled to the small table where they sat. The heavy woolen carpet underfoot was a style I didn't recognize, probably from an age long before I was born. A fire crackled merrily in the hearth behind my lovers. Rather than disturb the comfortable mood, I decided to take a different tack. I would shatter it.

Reaching into my soul, I drew Grievance from my own essences of shadow and spirit. Her edges rasped upon the whetstone of every slight and wrong and injustice I carried in my heart. The black steel of the big two-handed blade rang in the heavy air.

I grinned.

Tourak smiled and flowed up from his chair, drawing his own pair of short blades in the same way. It occurred to me that I would have to ask him their names.

"New rule!" Z'nnek cried with mock seriousness, holding the Book to his chest in feigned horror. "No foreplay in the library!"

Before he could manifest his massive double-ended scythe, we were interrupted. Again.

"Goddess," a soft-voiced shade called from behind me, "your mother awaits your pleasure at breakfast." The woman was a gentle unclaimed from Elysia a century past—I tried not to hold her ethnicity against her, but I'd never bothered to learn her name. I should do that.

Urth's nefarious nether bits, I thought. At that moment, the strangeness of swearing by the names of gods I knew in person, and nether bits I'd witnessed firsthand, struck me hard. *Will people swear by my genitals someday?* I struggled not to laugh at the absurdity.

"Very well," I said out loud, trying to recapture my daughterly irritation with my mother. "Thank you." I nodded to the shade, who hurried away.

Grievance always bitched in her nonverbal way to be sheathed unblooded. "Soon," I promised her in a whisper, "our enemies will come to us."

My hand outheld, I waited until Z'nnek put the Book in my palm after only a heartbeat's hesitation. "Thank you," I said with a serious smile.

With an exaggerated sigh, I followed my lovers from the library. In the primordial tongue, they chatted about some nonsense that they found funny from several thousand years ago. While I recognized their intentional temptation to exercise my linguistic muscles by eavesdropping, I couldn't bring myself to pay attention. Not even to learn more nuances of the ancient language of magic that had once been the mother tongue of mortals and immortals alike.

Absently, I spun myself a satchel to match my black-and-crimson burial shroud and placed Araeda'h's prison into the bag. More to keep it out of the way and keep my hands free than to hide it.

My mind was focused on imagining how to tell my mother *no*.

As it turned out, I needed to tell *everyone* no.

We arrived at a resplendent repast in the throne room where I'd first met Z'nnek. It had been a lonely place then, just a month ago. Now it was filled with warmth and light and food. Roast meats of all sorts littered trenchers atop the sideboard. Cornucopias of vegetables. Tureens of stews. Platters of boiled eggs and sliced cheeses. All the sun-kissed realms I knew were represented, and many that I didn't. Though I hadn't been consciously hungry before, I was now. I clapped and bowed my thanks to the serving shades.

"Warlord," Z'nnek said to my mother with a nod.

Tourak bowed halfway at the waist to her.

My husbands were nothing if not gentlemen.

She responded to them both with grim nods. I could feel her eyes track me.

Without acknowledging Madra, I attacked the feast. My mother had strategically placed herself at the center of the table facing the door we'd entered, so that regardless of where I sat at the long table, I couldn't be any further from her. At least I could arrange to have my mouth full when I did deign to speak to her. I knew I was being petulant, and I refused to stop.

My lovers and I took our plates to our customary end of the table. Z'nnek seated to my right. Tourak to my left on the same side of the table as Madra. A shade bent close to my mother, probably asking her if she'd like to be served. The warlord shook her head.

Although I'd not said I'd announce my decision first thing in the morning—or what passed for morning in Nethe, when the nighttime noises ceased and the daytime noises resumed—it was Alamar clan custom that any deferred judgment or decision would be declared at breakfast upon the day promised. And we both knew it. Profanity sufficient to describe my displeasure didn't yet exist.

She could at least have the courtesy to stew stoically until I'd eaten. And until my laggard allies arrived. It would be annoying to have to send for them to make an announcement I didn't relish giving voice to twice.

Fortunately, Goerranu and Mawzi saved me the trouble and arrived before I'd cleared half my first plate. The brown-garbed, birdlike goddess of secrets and lies picked at a plate of small fruits and nuts. The goddess of assassins and thieves, still wearing her heavy-lipped male face, guzzled a tankard of some steaming concoction that smelled bitter from across the room.

I wiped the last of the pork gravy from my plate with a flaky, curved pastry of some sort from a land I wished I'd visited during my life, if only for their baked goods. Licking my fingers like the hill folk barbarian I was, I grinned at my mother.

"Why should I go to the Conclave?" I asked without preamble.

Though I'd meant to put her on the defensive, she knew me well enough and had obviously prepared her arguments. She didn't blink or miss a beat.

Standing, she called in a clarion voice, "Goddess of Vengeance, Mother of Ravens, Founder of the Temple of Vengeance." She let my titles resound off the walls in the silence everyone else left to her. She turned to face me directly.

For my part, I resisted the urge to squirm as my mother pinned me to my throne with her maternal gaze. Childish embarrassment warred with aggravation at being challenged in my own palace. I hated what was coming. I hated that she was right. But I would not bow.

Madra continued, "Your faithful have been slain without cause. Your stronghold besieged without provocation. Will you answer the injustice?"

My anger threatened to boil over. I clamped down on the lid containing all the feelings she stirred within me. *I will not be provoked,* I swore to myself. *She's just angry and depressed.* But I had to say something. What could I say to her accusations? She was correct.

She glared at me, daring me to refute her. I couldn't do that.

Aiming for insouciance, I slowly put my boots on the corner of the table closest to Tourak. "I will be avenged," I pledged with a flippant wave of my hand that I did not feel, "but in my own due time."

"What of your promises?" Mawzi demanded in a growling voice. "Your oaths?"

If my priestess were present, she would wonder the same.

Tourak put his hand on my boot and gave my foot a gentle squeeze. I didn't need his reassurance, but I appreciated the touch.

"My promises keep themselves." I smiled at the assassin goddess. "I will not be rushed into an inopportune moment."

Goerranu sputtered. "This is the time they will least expect a direct challenge. They summoned you. They expect you to cower before them. Strike when they least expect!"

While she wasn't wrong, I wasn't going to take her bait. "Nor will I lend credence to a command from my purported equals. Attending the Conclave would cede power to them."

In the interests of self-distraction, I glanced at my fingernails—they'd been cracked and worn in life by training and work and war. No longer. My nails had the appearance now of a pampered love-woman. Yet, I could almost see the invisible blood soaking my hands.

When I looked up, I could see my mother calculating her next volley. She seemed a little deflated. Clearly, she'd expected anger alone to motivate me. Challenging me thus as a child, and if I were honest, even as a woman, she had always riled me enough to rise to whatever quest or task she set before me.

I've changed, mother mine. I'll not be manipulated into mass murder in my name.

"No." The shortest complete sentence I knew.

Her chainmail rattled as she banged a fist to her breastplate. "What, then, of your kith and kin?" Madra lifted her chin to look down her nose at me.

Memories of the slaughter of the Spring Festa just a month ago rose up from their graves in my mind. Fighting to the death. Rising from the corpse pit filled with my clansfolk. My boots dropped to the floor. I stood, shaking my head to keep the rest of me from doing the same.

Z'nnek tensed in his chair to my left. Tourak became still. Mawzi grunted. Goerranu meandered over to the sideboard, probably for more birdseed.

I blew out a breath I didn't know I'd been holding. I scowled at my mother.

"Your padra? Your bratra? Taken in demonic sacrifice!" Madra shook her head sadly. "Will you not avenge them?"

She was right about Padra. Though, I'd have to kill myself to avenge Nerren. No point in telling her that now. That one thought alone chilled the flames that had built up in my heart. I was just as guilty as anyone else. She expected me to war dance as she played my heart strings.

How could I riposte? I could *not* ask her if it would make her feel better —because I knew her answer, because my own heart beat the same. I just wanted a measure of peace for all.

"What will that accomplish, Madra?" I sighed. "Will one death bring Padra or Nerren back? Will a thousand?"

Her expression crumpled in a way I did not expect. Her lips quivered as if she were afraid to say anything but afraid not to speak.

Z'nnek saved her in the moment, to my surprise. "Bring them back? No." He rose to his feet on my right. "But to honor them by speaking their truth to power will preserve them in your heart." He raised a hand as if to put it on my shoulder, thought better of it, and dropped the offending hand to his side.

While I wanted to glare at him, my gaze was fixated upon Madra. Her eyes were full in a way I'd never seen. A single tear trickled down her cheek. She looked at Z'nnek with appreciation that she'd never shown me.

I whirled on Z'nnek then. "What would you have me do? Honor them with more death?"

He smiled weakly. "No. Keep the balance. But honor your kinfolk by demanding redress from those who've wronged you and yours. That's what Conclave is for! Preventing war."

Goerranu scoffed. Mawzi made a rude noise.

My body did shake then. With rage. And betrayal.

I glanced at Tourak for support. His traitorous face told me that he agreed with Z'nnek.

Walking away from them both, I stood across the table from my mother.

"I will not defile their memory with more blood, nor will I dishonor their sacrifice by—" I glared at my lovers. "—bending over for their murderers." I scoffed at the idea, at Madra.

The warlord took a deep breath and clasped her hands together in supplication. "Then—" Her voice broke as tears flooded down her face. "Then do it for me," she whispered.

In all my nineteen years, my mother had used many tactics to get me to do what she wanted. But none had ever been this blatant a manipulation. Crying was so out of character for her that I refused to accept that her tears might be real.

Bristling at the affront, I spoke through clenched teeth. "I. Will. Not."

For the first time ever in my experience, my mother fled.

CHAPTER 9

*B*reakfast gradually resumed its normal chatter around me. My traitorous lovers and my antagonistic allies alike left me to stand and ruminate. Their banal conversation ebbed and flowed around me like a gentle breeze. Whether they feared my explosion, if they prodded me again too soon, or simply had enough spectacle for the morning, I couldn't care less. Yet.

In my mind, through the powers of the crown I'd named Triumph, I searched for the presence in the palace that was Madra. She'd behaved unexpectedly, and that concerned me. My mother had always been a stalwart bulwark to shelter behind in my life. Sometimes, even from myself. Whenever I'd needed strength, she had been there to lend it to me. I was concerned for what or where she would go. And I was right to be.

If she'd gone to her rooms on the top floor of the palace to cool off or devise new schemes and stratagems to get her way, I'd be satisfied and then deal with the others.

If she'd burst out into one of the many gardens or training arenas to work off her anger against other shades or even angels, I would be reassured that my mother would recover her aplomb in time.

She did neither of those things.

Instead, she fled down the stairs. Through Triumph and my newly forged marriage to all of Nethe, I felt every hobnailed impact of her boots against the flagstones as if they beat upon my own skin. Beyond the moon-shaped gates of the eerie gardens, she began a rapid, almost linear trek over-land—away from the palace.

My heart thumped hard and slow, each beat a funeral drum.

I knew without knowing where she headed.

In desperation, I stormed out of the palace and took to the sky.

No one called after me.

I wouldn't have listened if they had.

In Nethe, the morning atmosphere was much like the night, only different in the quality of its sounds and the sensibility of its air. As if its denizens, and perhaps Nethe itself, echoed the memory of the lands beneath the changeable sun. Somehow, most mornings in Nethe felt brighter for all its preternatural darkness. Not this one. The normally gentle breeze carried a storm-pregnant weight upon it, mirroring my mood. Perhaps it was reflecting my own emotions back to me.

While I was angry with my mother, I could not allow her to do what she was surely intent upon now. The joy of flying eluded me yet again. The lovely, recent changes in the landscape did not draw my eye. Demon bones over eight thousand years old were still stacked in rude piles in all of the out of the way places. I loathed those remnants from before Z'nnek's supposed victory over the demon lords. I would avoid those desolate places. Until I discovered someday how to remake them.

Most of the unclaimed were content to while their eternities away in idle or indolent pursuits, far from the reminders of a time before Z'nnek's benevolence. Like most of Nethe's populace, I didn't usually even notice the ruins. Z'nnek had obviously arranged the landscape of Nethe to hide the blights from all but the most insistent or adventurous of shades who sought them out. Long-ignored sepulchers, tombs, mausoleums, and other aban-doned structures seemed to clamor for my attention today.

I headed straight for the worst of those.

The one that I'd only visited once. Yesterday.

Had I anointed Madra as one of my angels, and bestowed upon her the gift of flight, our race might have been different. Awing, she would have beaten me there.

As it was, she didn't run, but she moved quickly in her urgent grief.

I had to admit that to myself. She was grieving. But not just the loss of Padra, Nerren, our kinfolk, and her own life. She grieved what I'd taken from her moments ago: hope and dignity.

Shame rasped upon my soul for taking either from my mother in my anger and petty rebellion.

I could give her what she wanted: justice, war, vengeance. And become what I feared to be: a blood-soaked goddess no different from the high gods and the old in their utter lack of mercy and compassion for the mortal consequence.

I could lie to her, promise her the retribution she and—if I were honest —I craved. Just long enough to figure out how to placate her more permanently. And become what I hated: a manipulative tyrant willing to say or do anything to get my selfish way.

The scene was as I'd left it the day before. The sepulchers' stone doors were shut. Their grisly work secreted away in the noisome dark. Sluices trickled their black bile into the pool. The oblivion rippled and flowed out into its three tributaries that became the great rivers of Nethe.

I waited impatiently as the sense of my mother grew near.

Madra stopped at the edge of the slate-tiled expanse. Facing me, she lifted her chin and stared at me impassively.

As always, my patience failed before hers. "Please do not do what you came here to do."

Stepping onto the slate, she paced slowly toward me. Or perhaps the pool behind me. She said nothing.

"Madra, you have always been my guide," I said, modulating my voice carefully to keep it from cracking, "my refuge. Stay with me. Counsel me." I bowed my head, my hands clasped tightly at my waist. "Please."

Hobnailed boots stepped before my downcast gaze.

My mother lifted my chin until my eyes met hers.

"You've become a goddess for true, daughter. There's naught else I could teach you"—she smiled without warmth—"even if you'd the mind to learn it."

I felt the muscles in my chin quiver against her palm. But I refused to crack.

Not for the first time, I wondered who we gods could pray to for guidance and strength.

"There's so much of the clan history, the kinship ways," I said meekly. "You've taught me too little of our kith and kin."

She shook her head.

"Honor them!" I protested. "As you spoke true in my hall, they'll— I'll need someone to speak for them, to lead them..."

Her eyes were cold and distant now, considering me but not considering my words. "You've kin enough in this place," she replied. "Ask those countless dead. Or ask the living. You've no need o' me for all that."

Madra dropped her hand and waited. We both knew I wasn't finished.

I sucked in a great breath and balled my fists.

"What if—" I blew out most of my wind. "What if I told you that I would do as you ask?" I stood straighter, meeting her gaze and daring her to deny me. "Demand redress of the high gods and the old under threat of war?"

"What if?" The warlord narrowed her eyes. "Did I rear such a liar and a cheat and a tyrant? If you'll lie to me, daughter, pour it straight. Don't pose it as a question."

She'd laid it out just as I knew it in my heart. The finality of her decision swam there in her eyes. Could I deny her authority to choose for herself?

"You've no intent to war, child," Madra said with bitter sadness. "Why should you when you've been crowned with all this?" She surveyed my plush underworld domain. Even in this most horrible of its places, Nethe tried to be as welcoming as Z'nnek was.

I deflated. But I did not look away. She deserved the dignity I'd robbed her of at breakfast. I would return it to her with honors.

Numb, I nodded.

"What do I do?" she asked, her face an impassive mask.

I don't know if she was testing me, but it didn't matter. I'd give her what she'd earned, though it tore my soul to shreds. Strangling my heart, lest my self-pity leak out through my eyes, I steeled myself to do the unforgivable to my mother...again.

"Stand there," I said, pointing to the edge of the pool where there was no evidence I'd tried to murder Huund's emissary the day before. Curious.

Either Nethe healed itself or the wrathful shades had removed the marks of my indiscretion.

I didn't know if the ritual words were strictly necessary, but I told her what I knew. "Say: 'I am tired and I am ready.'" I took a deep breath. "If you are," I added hopefully.

Without hesitation, Madra strode to the edge of oblivion and announced in a clear voice, "I am tired, and I am ready."

As before, the screech of stone on stone announced the coming of the Thirteen. Their appearance was as shocking to me as ever. If she was affected, Madra showed no sign. Her expression changed not a whit when she quaffed the contents of Kragh's cup in one gulp.

Watching the ensuing rite of passage without flinching or intervening took all of the considerable will my mother had invested into me in my nineteen short years. I owed her that much and more.

When she'd thrashed her last, and the Thirteen horrors stepped back, a perfect midnight bubble burst forth from the oily blackness.

Of course, I'd expected her one defining memory to be the silver of Torr's moon. The color of justice and truth. The color of the paradise I'd denied her by claiming her soul as my own a few, long days past. The color of the god Madra and Nerren and Kausae and I had all worshipped in life. The same color as my sister's angel wings.

But.

Her most dear memory was the midnight hue of my heart.

I could not look away, scarcely able to bear the finality of her utter acceptance of me. My dark eternity blurred around me until nothing was distinct or certain anymore.

Bittersweet love for my mother leaked from my dying heart and urged me to peer into her dearest memory. I'd never forgive myself for not know-ing, regardless of how much it hurt. My awareness fell through the midnight membrane, into her moment. I became my mother.

"I know you," I said with awe in the formal highland way of greeting long unmet relatives. My daughter had risen from the dead. Alpine love, cold and strong as glacier melt, filled my chest. The object of my deepest love sat like a petulant child on a stone bier. Hard-won discipline alone kept my face from a silly smile at her chagrin. She always carried the weight of the world upon her heart.

"My beautiful, powerful daughter." I reached out a hand, hesitant, to stroke gently along Illyria's brow. I smoothed away the frown as I had when she was a child. My palm brushed her cheek.

She leaned into my touch as she always had. "Madra, I..."

"Hush, child," I said, "you've done much. And your priestess says you have much yet to do." My left hand cradled her other cheek. "There will be time enough for explanations and your self-recrimination later."

Tears spilled down her cheeks. I knew how much guilt and regret she carried. About everything. I knew to ignore her involuntary tears, too.

I pulled her to her feet, looking her up and down. Illyria was every inch the goddess I knew she would become. From the moment of her birth.

I smiled. And knelt at her feet, still holding her hands, still looking into her eyes. "I've always felt the divinity in you, my daughter. I understand why now. I will always be your mother." I bowed my head. "And your most devoted disciple."

The moment faded, but the icy shock did not, as I watched that one perfect bubble float up into the dark, sparkling sky to join all the other motes of light I'd failed.

Standing there, staring at the increasingly blurry stars, was all I wanted to do for the rest of eternity. But I also knew I couldn't tarry a moment longer.

I had somewhere else unavoidable to be.

CHAPTER 10

*T*yrr's golden moon rode the night sky high overhead as I soared in spirit toward my childhood home. Fragrant smoke dribbled from chimneys of the village homes below where extended clan families slept unaware of my presence. The gate to Alamar Forte was closed against the night, which had never happened in my lifetime.

I recalled my dying vision of the village, razed and smoking. Even if they could flee, there was no room for all of the village inside the walls. I shuddered.

Someone should do something about that lack. Right after I give Conseca her quest. And the Book.

Gilded light from Tyrr's moon bathed sleeping Alamar Forte and cast deep shadows. Vigilant, black-cloaked wardens stalked the top of the wall and the grounds. They couldn't challenge what they couldn't see.

From where I alighted on the hard-packed clan training ground, the windows of my shrine were as dark and cold as when I'd left it four nights ago and probably just as vacant. Still, I kept myself to the realm of spirit so none of my mortal kinfolk would notice me. In that moment, I gave no thought to *why*.

Rather than sneak into my own temple through the walls or ceiling, I'd decided to enter more conventionally. Perhaps I'd just not been dead long enough to be comfortable sailing through solid objects. My sister had been quite rude about it in her silver-winged role as Torr's messenger girl. All the other ascended that I'd become acquainted with seemed to have no qualms about ignoring the realm of flesh when it suited them.

This fine morning, it suited me to pull on flesh. I rather loved having wings, so I kept them in my angelic form. I paused at the door and listened to the moans from within. Not moans of pain, for sure.

"Oh, Memad," a woman groaned.

"For fuck's sake," I muttered, already annoyed with my priestess.

I adjusted Triumph on my head and shoved the lockless door open to stride in.

The hinges must've been well-oiled since my last visit. The heavy door gave only a slight scrape of wood on flagstone. Midnight curtains held the golden moonlight at bay. With my immortal sight, I had no trouble seeing through the dark. Z'nnek had melded many spells into the heart-shaped sigil of midnight scars carved between my breasts. By burning but a trickle of magic through the sigil, I could see the realms of flesh or spirit or both at will. So little time had passed in my eternity and yet I already took too many of my new powers for granted.

The shrine was different than I'd left it and far less empty. The blood candles in their niches were unlit. Heavy tapestries embroidered with ravens and feathers and crowns and swords hung along the walls, cordoning them off into private sanctuaries. Bronze braziers—currently unlit and cold —squatted at the four corners of the stone altar that dominated the open space. The altar upon which I'd lain like the dead for four days.

Now, the altar was covered with a simple crimson silk sheet trimmed with the black fur of a hill bear. A faint aura of midnight magic, much like my own, radiated from the altar. *Curious.* I did not recall making it so. Several inkwells, quills, and a scattering of parchments covered the silk. I wondered what they were for and who was writing with them.

I knew from Araeda'h—the goddess of magic trapped in the Book of the Forbidden I carried in a satchel at my hip—that my priestess couldn't read. The priestess who was still moaning in the far curtained corner being pleasured by a particularly annoying scion of the high god, Vayan.

After a significant misunderstanding with the thunderbird demigod in question, named Memad, I'd unintentionally made an enemy of Vayan, his father. One of my many errors that I'd yet to pay for. I'd sent Memad away to deliver a humble request to his father to restrain himself from interfering in my hostilities with the Chosen and the angels of the Holy Twins. Apparently, Memad had not understood the hint to keep away from Alamar. I couldn't very well have my priestess consorting with the son of an enemy.

My slippered feet whispered across the flagstones. In any event, no one would have heard boots and spurs stomping over the sexual crescendo building in the far corner. Though I was sore tempted to sweep the tapestry aside and expose the traitorous lovers, I didn't. That would be more rude than necessary. Amusing, perhaps, but rude. Instead, I peeked through the gap between tapestries. And was surprised. Again.

Where I'd expected to see my flame-haired, soon to be ex-priestess and her muscular demigod lover, a familiar young woman lay on a small cot. Eyes closed. Legs spread wide. Pleasuring herself. Which, on its own, was fine, even in my shrine. I was no prude, to be certain. It just seemed that—since my death—every time I'd tried to have sex anywhere but Nethe, I'd been interrupted. If there existed a god of fate, it seemed they often conspired to interfere in my love life. The Litanies spoke of no such god for me to be wroth against.

Nevertheless, the woman here and now was not who I'd been expecting. The lithe, brunette lass was barely half covered in a black cotton robe. As I watched, she squeezed one breast and twiddled a hard nipple. Her other hand stroked her core with increasing intensity as she moaned Memad's name again. Clearly warm and ready, she was a delicious temptation.

I struggled not to giggle at the absurdity of my cousin five or six times removed fantasizing about a very sexy—but very annoying—demigod. Though, I suppose every girl's a right to her fantasies. Being drawn to invite myself into her bedplay, I struggled to remember why I was here.

This young woman had been a child the last time I'd noticed her years ago, when I'd first begun my own womanly escapades at age fifteen. Beyond second cousins, nobody in the highlands cared much who tumbled whom. And she'd grown into a fine specimen, though a little skinny for my taste in female partners.

I sighed, regaining my composure with effort. Knowing it might take much to gain her attention, I called in my training ground voice, "Reenaa! Where is Conseca?"

Reenaa startled, eyes popping wide. She shrank back against the wall, clutching her robe around herself. The covering of her flesh was a little disappointing. Her pupils were fully dilated as she stared blindly.

"Who is it?" she demanded, startled but resolute.

Of course, she couldn't see me in the dark. But that didn't stop her from sliding a watered steel dagger from beneath her mattress. I couldn't recall if she were warden-trained, but I was proud of the reversed defensive grip she took. The blade between us did not waver.

Drawing magic from the worship that swirled in my little shrine, I manifested a fist-sized tourmaline in my palm and willed it to begin to glow. It was a trick I'd borrowed from Tourak. The small, curtained alcove filled with dark light. I smiled. I really tried to smile in a nonthreatening way.

My distant cousin must've seen something else in my face because she recoiled.

She hauled in a deep breath as if to scream.

"Reenaa," I said in a soothing tone, "you're safe." I raised both hands into the W of a warden's greeting with elbows on hips. Shadows danced in the tourmaline light as I moved my hands.

With a full body shake that reminded me of her delicious, now-hidden flesh, she visibly calmed. "I'd thought myself alone," she said self-consciously.

We stared at one another for many slowing breaths. She put the knife aside on her pillow and straightened her sleeping robe nervously. I waited while she gathered herself. Curiosity and kinship seemed to win her calm quickly enough.

"Those are beautiful, uh, wings," Reenaa said, with a shy smile.

A bevy of mildly inappropriate return compliments flooded my mind. Instead of giving them voice, I nodded to her and said, "Thank you."

I smiled again, more successfully, because Reenaa didn't flinch this time. Proof that I could be a gentler and more diplomatic goddess when I wished. "Why are you, ah—" I paused to look for a different word. "—sleeping in my shrine?"

She smiled with youthful radiance that took my breath away, her embarrassment and fear forgotten in a blink. "I'm apprenticed to Conseca. I'm to be your priestess," she said with hope. "If you'll have me." An eager blush colored her cheeks.

It was my turn to struggle with speechlessness. Conseca took an apprentice without consultation with her goddess? I scarcely knew what to do with one priestess, let alone two. Well, they were both sexy, and I knew what to do with— I yanked my mind back onto its not-sex-related track.

"I see," I said. "That's—" I didn't know what that was yet or how I felt about it. "That's an interesting choice." My brain flailed about, trying to recall what Reenaa had been interested in as a child. I couldn't. Who paid attention to annoying younger cousins?

"I'm sure you'll make a fine priestess," I said, in lieu of something wiser and more eloquent. Enigmatic and unpredictable completely eluded me that early morning.

Reenaa blushed as if— I stopped myself from thinking further along those lines.

Then she beamed at me. "I'll be your most vengeful priestess!"

It was impossible to imagine this enthusiastic creature taking revenge upon anything but my now-inflamed libido.

"Where's, uh, Conseca?"

My priestess-to-be cocked her head at me. "She's in the manor, a'course." With a wicked grin, she added, "She's taken to your old bedroom."

I should have asked what she was grinning about. I really should have. But I was distracted by the insistent vibrations of the Book nestled in a bag against my hip. Unfortunately, I ignored her as much as I ignored Reenaa's intimations.

The familiar walk, across the training ground past the clan hall to the family house, gave me just enough time to muse, but not enough time to actually figure anything out. I'd precious little time tonight to prepare Conseca for what was coming. What I wanted her to do. What I needed her to do.

In retrospect, I should have noticed that no warden of the night watch challenged my winged self in my predawn stroll across the training ground.

Rather than bang on the door and wake the entire fortress, I resigned myself to stepping into spirit once more. I was glad I'd practiced enough to move between realms without damage and pain, if I took it slowly. Weighing less than light itself, flying up and through my old fourth floor bedroom window was trivial, though it was uncustomarily shuttered.

My magical vision pierced the dark. I took in the room I'd called my own for most of my overshort life. Battleworn trophies still hung upon the walls: shattered shields, broken swords, cracked spear shafts. Spoils of war. Gifts, I'd naively thought, from the war god, Tyrr, and his justice-minded twin, Torr. Things I'd valued once. Perhaps I still did, but they seemed distant now, of concern in a life long past.

None of those symbols had changed.

But I had.

What was different in the room was the fresh-cut spring flowers that adorned the windowsill and the headboard. It no longer smelled like my room. Cleaner bedding, for sure. Perhaps brand new? And the tangled couple occupying the mattress. They were an attractive tableau. Conseca resplendent in her pale skin and freckles and flame-colored hair still inexplicably bobbed short. She'd never told me why she cut it—and I'd stupidly never asked. Memad was striking, his even paler skin cut with lightning-bright tattoos and a black mane of hair past his shoulders. The betrayal I'd felt earlier wormed its way back through my heart, chewing painfully. I must've unconsciously made a sound.

The thunderbird demigod cracked an eye. Blinked at me. "Illyria," he said in a soft rumble, "can it wait until the morrow?"

I shook my head, keeping my face completely still. I would betray nothing to the son of my enemy.

He sighed and whispered, "This is the first rest she's taken since you laid down next to your mother."

In my chest, I squeezed hard to keep my heart together. He couldn't know. I'd show him no weakness. After four careful breaths, I said at a normal volume, "I must be away long before the dawn."

Memad looked at me quizzically.

Stirring, Conseca nuzzled against him. She reached up to stroke his face. "Don't go," she murmured. "Don't go."

"Conseca," I said forcefully, forgetting she couldn't hear me when I was not flesh, "I must speak to you. Alone."

Eyes fluttering open, she rolled over and blinked into the dark. The little golden moonlight that sneaked into the room must have been enough. Her eyes found me easily and widened. "Illyria!"

Conseca rolled out of bed and rose easily to her feet, as naked as the day we'd met and just as heedless of her lack of clothing. Freckles and tempting red hair all the way down. Her ample but firm tits enticed me as she moved. I resolved to not be distracted. Killing her was not my intention, but how did one unmake a priestess otherwise? I hadn't known what I was doing when I anointed her. Problems with easy solutions never seemed to present themselves.

I realized with a start that I had not pulled on flesh. *She can see me in spirit! How? What other gifts have I unwittingly given?*

"My queen," she said, arms akimbo in the W of a warden's greeting. She'd quickly adopted that custom, at least. Concern lined her face. "I serve at your pleasure."

The one ring that flashed upon her finger reminded me: she knew my intentions. And she was right to worry. I took a deep breath and looked to Memad.

The scion of the storm lord stood next to my soon-to-be ex-priestess, naked in all his glory. I'd not realized, the few times we'd interacted, just how much his loincloth had concealed. After giving him a worthy appraisal, I raised my gaze to capture his.

"I must speak with Conseca." I had many questions, none of which I could ask in front of the storm king's son. And he would likely object to what happened next.

He nodded, expression wounded. But he glanced around for his discarded clothing, minimal though a loincloth and sandals might be.

"No, my queen," Conseca said. "You can trust him with anything you may tell me." Her volume was low, but her tone rang with strength like the poured sandstone walls of Alamar.

Her newfound confidence was fresh and full. And unexpected. So much for the obedient priestess I'd come to expect based on the Litanies and my life experience. Of course, I'd get the one obstinate priestess in all the sun-kissed lands.

"Is that so?" I kept my anger in a firm grip. *Was she telling me that she confided in him?* "Do you even know who he is?"

She relaxed her arms and stood with one foot canted, an open and unconcerned stance of negotiation with an equal. "He is an ally," she said softly. "An ally who risked his immortal life and the wrath of the high gods, including his father, to aid you."

In truth, I did not know why Memad had come to my aid at the bridge where I'd failed to slay Provax a second time. I'd assumed the thunderbird demigod wanted something of me. And he had. He'd asked me to retake centuries of memories from him that I'd only just returned to keep the peace with Vayan. I'd refused Memad's request, for many painfully obvious reasons.

With a glare at Conseca, I said, "Divided loyalties lose wars."

She blanched but did not retract her statement.

Memad, now modestly draped in his azure-trimmed white loincloth—if modesty could be attributed to such a tiny scrap of fabric—bent to lace his sandals. "It's fine, Conseca. I understand. She is wise not to trust overmuch."

Whirling so that her bobbed scarlet hair flashed in the trace of golden moonlight, she scoffed. "You'd *not* betray her. I know! You've done naught but help! You carried her broken corpse to me!"

I'd forgotten that. In my torpor, I'd thought Tourak had scooped me out of the freezing river beneath the broken bridge and borne me home to Alamar. But it had been Memad. The Book in the bag slung over my shoulder nudged at my hip. I ignored the meddlesome mad goddess. I would not be giving her to Conseca now, in any event.

It occurred to me that Memad might have valuable information, though. "Memad, what did your father say when you carried him my request?"

The thunderbird demigod inhaled deeply, expanding his massive chest. "He was not alone. The high gods had gathered in council at his court."

That wasn't exactly an answer. The high gods had not intervened in my flagrant disobedience of their command. I'd thought Memad had delivered my plea. But if he hadn't, why had the high gods not interfered? Because I was bound to a mortal form and they could not act against me? Was that why my conquest of the twin golden-winged war angels, Yunfak and Yanfak, had been so easy? Another forgotten memory tickled at my mind. Unbidden and unasked, Memad had fought one of them to a stalemate for me at the bridge. I remembered his clumsy attack and the two tumbling into the crevasse.

Memad continued, "In the presence of Tyrr, Torr, Huund, Raan, and the entire court of storms, I informed my lord father of your request for nonintervention and your promise to not escalate a godwar." He watched me carefully, perhaps expecting me to disbelieve him.

So, he had delivered the message? "And they agreed?" I found that hard to imagine.

The thunderbird laughed, a deep and rolling sound that invited others to join him in mirth. "No, not at all. They all disagreed about how to intervene and how to slay you, not whether to do so. All but Huund." He chuckled again. "By the time they finished arguing, your battle was long over. Urth and the other old gods convinced them that the point was moot."

I masterfully resisted the temptation to stamp my foot. Not an impressive gesture in slippers anyway. I closed my eyes and wished for someone to pray to for patience.

"And?"

"The only thing they could agree upon was to summon you to Conclave on the morrow." He smiled ruefully. "Huund gave Urth the task to deliver the summons."

Ignoring Conseca's gloating expression and now-divided loyalties, I mulled over the new information. The high gods and the old all wanted to kill me. That was obvious, expected. But they were divided about how to best accomplish it? That didn't make any sense. *What difference did it make how they killed me the next time?*

"Tell her what Huund said when Urth returned with Illyria's reply," Conseca prodded.

Perhaps priestesses had their uses after all, I thought.

With a shrug, Memad replied, "Huund proclaimed that she spoke with Amuun's voice and that all the gods, high and old and small, were to be summoned to Conclave"—he lowered his gaze—"after respecting your four days of mourning."

Interesting. But why respect my petty demand?

"Does that include you?" I inquired, curious to know how big the audience would be for my execution. I couldn't imagine any other reason than a trial and sentence of death for the high gods to summon the small gods to Conclave.

The big demigod shook his head, long black hair sweeping back and forth across his bare, lightning-tattooed shoulders. "My father's not trusted me since you and Z'nnek restored my memories." He sounded a bit wistful, but not upset by this fact. "Thank you, again."

I opened my mouth to dismiss him with my thanks, but said, "I need your help." *Stupid mouth. Why in all the fucks would I say that?*

Memad immediately knelt before me, just as he had in the training yard four days ago. And said the same damned thing. "It is I who have a debt to repay. Command me, my queen."

Fuck me with— I stopped myself. Cursing by the genitals and favorite sex toys of my fellow deities felt hollow now. Goddesshood sucked the joy out of so many things. But I was starting to feel more enigmatic and unpredictable in my divinity again. I thought about the memories I'd stolen from Memad and restored with Z'nnek's help. I recalled Memad's joy in speaking with Tourak about the thunderbird's long-dead mother.

"Swear your fealty to me and me alone—" I raised my eyebrows at Conseca.

My priestess nodded and lowered her gaze. *Good, we understand each other.*

"—upon that memory which you hold most dear. Upon your mother." I paused and waited. Knowing what I knew now of mortal souls, I could think of nothing more sacred than the memory of a worthy mother.

Without hesitation, Memad's electric eyes lifted to meet mine. "I swear on the memory of my mother, long taken but never forgotten, that I will serve no other god but you. Every thunderbird in my rumble is yours to command."

The ease with which he gave such a sweeping and unambiguous oath stole my breath.

In my immortal sight, his aura changed from Vayan's electric cerulean to my midnight. Shock ripped through me. I struggled to contain my amazement. I'd done nothing to effect that change. He'd changed his own aura, his own allegiance. I'd not known that was possible. I plastered a haughty smile on my face to cover my surprise. I had an enigmatic and unpredictable reputation to maintain, after all.

"That will do." I gave him a brusque nod. "Rise, Memad, avenger of the Raven Queen and lord of thunderbirds. Your first charge is to guard my priestesses with your immortal life."

I held out my hand, still keenly aware of my missing middle finger. He took it with a grin, and I lifted him to his feet. Giving my left to Conseca, I pulled them both into a close, conspiratorial huddle. We fell into an energizing hug instead.

It wasn't all bad to have a priestess after all. Or two.

I smiled and slipped the satchel strap over my head and extended it to Conseca. "I am entrusting her care unto you as much as I am entrusting your training unto her."

"To do...?" she asked, peering intently into my eyes.

"You discharged my last geas with aplomb," I assured her. "This one will be trivial by comparison." I wasn't lying, in the strictest sense of the word. I didn't intend her ill, but I wondered what the ring of insight showed her.

Because she seemed even more concerned now, I continued, "And I'll send Z'nnek along to aid you, too. I need him for the morning, at least. But he'll come to you soon."

Conseca took the satchel after a long hesitation. Memad watched with birdlike curiosity.

"Can't you train me yourself?" my priestess asked with trepidation.

I shook my head. "Before I forget... Araeda'h said to choose your next move carefully, whatever that means."

Conseca's lovely scarlet brows knitted together. "Why?"

I grinned wickedly, misunderstanding the question. "At dawn, I'm going ta' pick a fight."

When they didn't respond, I continued, "Listen carefully to what I need you to do, beginning with the protection of the villagers."

CHAPTER 11

The ragged lips of the mass grave were almost indistinguishable from the deep black of the veil of night. Only the dance of the gold and silver motes of guardian angels patrolling the void gave evidence of the liminal. Torr's silver moon had set and Amuun's sun had yet to break the dawn. All was just as it had been the fateful night of the Spring Festa a month past.

Once again, I lay upon the mound of the now-burned bones of my kin, roughly where I remembered "waking up" in my corpse not so many weeks past. So much had demanded my attention, but fresh guilt and rage at myself slithered through guts at having left them unmourned and uncelebrated for so long. When this sham of a Conclave was done, I would honor my beloved dead and move their remains to cavern tomb in Alamar where they belonged.

The voices of small gods arriving carried the short distance down the hill from the standing stones where the Conclave would be held. Where my father and brother and kin had been slaughtered. I wished for a way to eavesdrop. That would make it easier to recognize my cue to make my grand entrance into the sham trial I expected the high gods to hold for me.

"Remind me," Z'nnek chittered. The vocalizations of his vulture form were deeper and rougher than his naturally effeminate voice. "Why are the rest of us wearing our feathers?"

Tourak clacked his beak in raven laughter. I ignored them both. I'd already explained myself once. In the distance, I heard a three-pitch rumble that could only be Urth's greeting the Conclave. The old gods had begun to arrive.

Without access to Nethe's boundless source, I chose to reduce the magical burn of the spellwork of my sigil. Preserving my reserves removed the enhancements from my sight. I could make out only the shape of things in the predawn. As a big vulture, Z'nnek perched on the lip of the pit, his wine-colored plumage almost invisible in the dark. Tourak roosted on my armored left breast, regarding me with his one good eye. The rising of the sun began to reveal details as I watched. Fingers of pink and rose began to leech into the midnight of the sky. A few of my ravens circled overhead, angels in disguise. Far out of bowshot, a lone hawk circled high above on an early morning hunt. I wondered if the creature were mortal or angel.

"Tyrr and Torr have arrived," Tourak chirped in his cheerful avian speech. "Vayan is coming, carried by his freeti."

"How can you see that?" I demanded. There was no way he could see out of the pit we lay in together. Even in the growing light of dawn.

My archangel gacked. "Just look and listen," he clicked impatiently.

Z'nnek ruffled his wings and tilted his head almost sideways at me. "Do you not sense your unkindness?" He craned his long neck skyward toward the increasingly visible circling ravens overhead.

"Of course," I whispered. "They're always there, at the back of my mind."

"Then bring them to the front of your mind!" Tourak clacked his beak in amusement. "Not sense them. Sense through them." He made it sound like the most obvious thing in creation.

I did as he suggested. Reaching into the depths of my mind, I embraced all of my lovely ravens and pulled them to the forefront of my thoughts.

And fell into the bleeding dawn sky.

A confusing deluge of everywhere assaulted my senses.

Sights from thousands of eyes blinded me. Smells from thousands of beaks confused me. Sounds from thousands of ears crashed over me. It took all of my self-control not to screech in the overwhelming flood and give away my carefully arranged ambush.

A rush of magic drain dragged at me through the manifold connections. In panic, I fumbled in my mind to pour out several bottled souls from my stolen reserve lest I burn more of my remaining self than I was prepared to lose. I'd not even bothered to learn the names of those Grievance had taken from among the Temple Guard and the Legion in the last battle. Provax's and Yunfak's unique wineskins I left untouched among the now less than a dozen souls I kept imprisoned in my mind. Belatedly, it occurred to me that I could just as easily bottle the ambient worship in Nethe and expand my reserve without taking souls. Lack of foresight was expensive.

Panting, I shoved the vast flapping unkindness all to the back of my mind again. Blinking and blowing out a breath, I repossessed just my own senses. I glared at Tourak. He clacked his beak at me, clearly amused at my expression. He'd not wasted a lifetime of memories on magic before he'd understood its cost—he couldn't grasp my fear. He seemed unfazed by my glower.

"Perhaps," Z'nnek offered, "you should work with only one or two at a time to begin with." He made a chortling noise. "It can be a bit much to manage with so many so close."

I glared at him, too. This was something he should have taught me. Sooner. I sighed. If I'd given him the time to do so, as he'd asked me to do a month past.

"Can you sense me from among the unkindness?" Tourak offered in an appeasing tone. Maybe he'd made his point with the prank of luring me to overstep my ability? Maybe he felt a little guilty? He should. But probably not. That wasn't the way of ravens. Not Tourak's way.

Sifting through the flurry of feathered sensations at the back of my mind, I searched for one that felt like Tourak. He wasn't hard to find—he was the largest, most familiar presence in my mind, and the closest. Of course he was. Gingerly, I drew that sense of him to the fore of my mind. And found myself looking down at myself, which all kinds of disorienting.

We'd been deeply intimate in our short acquaintance and brief marriage, but riding behind his eyes was by far the deepest intimacy we'd ever shared. His warm, reddish essence embraced me without reservation.

Tourak spread his wings and launched himself into the sky. My joy of flying went with him. The irritation of the moment was wiped away by the splendor of the dawn. The thrill of flapping into a circular orbit. The love I felt in his mind for me. I forgave him—a little.

With a slide through the air, Tourak angled over the standing stones and the gods gathered there. Nearly a hundred immortal spirits stood. Waiting. To judge me.

The magic required to keep my connection to Tourak was far smaller than the heavy deluge required for the entire unkindness. It was a small thing, when I was not in a terror, to reach for Nethe from where I lay in this place of death and draw magic from my underworld realm through the shadow connection to avoid depleting my reserve.

He soared overhead, presumably out of sight or out of mind, since no one in the crowd gave him a glance. I listened as the small gods gossiped about the summons. There were twice as many guesses about the reason for the mass Conclave as there were small gods. I was amused that none of the wild theories I heard were correct. I listened more carefully as we neared the center of the circle of standing stones.

Tyrr grumbled, "She's late." His golden hair and burnished armor took on a bloody hue as the sun rose over the horizon.

"Perhaps she's not coming?" Torr offered. The silvery twin of the war god stood with his arms crossed, radiating boredom and skepticism.

The twin sons of Amuun could look more dissimilar, I supposed, but seeing them side-by-side was jarring. The Litanies did not describe them as fraternal twins, but in thinking about it critically for the first time, I supposed they had to be since they were sired by different fathers. Seeing them stand with their fathers caused me to wonder. I could see no similarities between Urth and Tyrr. Nor much the same between Vayan and Torr. Tyrr's broad, solid features were similar to no race I'd encountered yet, and nothing like the mercurial, animalistic traits that Urth adopted and shed continually. Torr's patrician features were much like the Elysians in their cast, and nothing like Vayan's aquiline nose and high cheekbones that clearly resembled Memad's.

Strange and curious, I thought.

Urth, mercifully dressed for once, in armor fashioned from tree bark and animal hides, said in his three-toned voice, "Huund is never early nor late."

Not talking about me then, I thought with a little disappointment. I expected to be the guest of honor at this soiree. *Perhaps she's waiting for me to appear. To put me at a disadvantage. Not today, bitch.*

"I mislike her plan even more now," Vayan grumbled. "She should be here."

The other high gods stood mute.

I expected the high gods and the old to refuse to mingle with the small gods. The high gods, of course, stood isolated at the center. But the old gods surprised me. They moved among the conversational knots of small gods and the cluster of high gods. Wherever the old gods went, a hush fell—until the old god asked a direct question or moved on. An interesting dynamic to see, for sure. I didn't bother trying to follow their conversations.

When I was long past bored and clinging hard to my wait-and-see plan, the messenger I'd danced with in Nethe arrived. She alighted with a precise flutter of her hawk wings. Garbed in the same manner that I'd last seen her, she seemed more imposing now. The nearest of the small gods bowed to her. A sinking feeling took hold in my gut.

"Is our guest of honor not yet arrived?" Siti asked.

The twins answered at once, "No, sister." Their voices clashing.

Sister? Her dark skin and her features, especially the upturned corners of her lovely eyes, were nothing like her brothers. Did she alone take after Amuun? Or not at all? While the Litanies gave no detailed descriptions of any of the gods, the many effigies I'd seen looked nothing like any of them in the flesh—yet I'd known them. But I'd not recognized the Lady of the Dread Hunt. A cold realization chilled me.

Huund lied to me! What else besides her identity was a lie? A moment of indecision crossed my mind. She had freely scouted Nethe in the emissary guise of Siti. No one had even challenged her but me. *What else am I ignorant of?* I used all of Tourak's senses to scan for signs of ambush. And found none.

Tourak circled more tightly, his mind awhirl with uncertainty—like my own.

Vayan interjected, "I told you we should raid Nethe and—"

"No," Huund said, cutting the air with her empty hand.

Torr took a step closer to her. "We will give her the courtesy of waiting a few moments before we render judgment in absentia."

That was more like what I expected from the Conclave. I refused to be judged in absentia or in any other way.

Huund scoffed but didn't say more. She looked directly up at Tourak. Our gazes met. She smiled with all the warmth of a predator. I released both my connection to my archangel and to Nethe's magic.

I'd best not keep her waiting. My war-grin clenched the muscles of my face.

The bones of my beloved dead rattled beneath me as I rose to my feet and leaped. The last time I'd tried to jump out of this very pit, I'd failed miserably. Today, even wearing the heavy plate armor I'd named Repose, I flew high and fast into the dawn, easily clearing the lip of the mass grave. I landed halfway up the grassy hill and began to march toward my enemies. And the place where I'd unwitting slain my brother and taken his soul. I drowned self-loathing beneath bubbling rage at being dragged back the place of my greatest sorrow and regret. They brought me here to make me feel weak, to make me afraid.

I will teach them terror.

Grievance scraped her way across the whetstone of my heart as I drew the thirsty blade. Light as a feather, Triumph clung to my brow and leant me her crowning authority.

A wordless ululation, the war cry of the highland wardens, burst forth from my throat of its own volition. My unkindness fell from the sky like black-feathered hail. I'd not needed to call them. My angels knew my heart and mind. They rose up from behind me by the scores from the tall grass of the steppes where they'd hidden, shedding their raven forms. They stepped from out of shadow where they'd lurked by the hundreds.

We surrounded the ancient circle of standing stones.

The gods waiting there quickly faced outward, forming a defensive ring. Shock, surprise, and fear marred the faces of the double line of small gods. Hells only knew what the expressions on the inhuman old gods' faces conveyed. Urth stood tall above the rest and scowled at me. Rage and defiance filled the faces of the high gods.

Except Huund. She looked calculating. And mildly amused.

"Tyrr and Torr," I shouted, projecting my battle voice to carry, "I heard your summons!" I rapidly closed the distance and halted within striking distance of the ring of small gods.

Goerranu and Mawzi stood in that line directly in front of me. The former gave me a put-upon look which conveyed her distaste for this plan. The latter grinned, as if anticipating the bloodshed she craved. Many of the other small gods had drawn weapons. Some just cowered against those in the second rank behind them. They were not my concern.

"But I came not to answer your summons!" I yelled, not lowering my volume in the slightest. "I came to demand justice and recompense from Amuun, mother of the gods, for wrongs done in your name!"

Despite the evident threat the unkindness of my angels presented, the small gods and the old could not help but turn to look at the high gods I defied. Tyrr was livid. Torr was growing angrier with every heaving breath he took. Well, I hadn't come to make friends.

Before anyone else could speak, Huund spoke in the same bored tone that she'd used when posing as Siti the messenger to my realm. "By what right do you challenge the mother of the high gods with naked blade and demand redress of wrongs?" she asked, her voice slicing through the stillness that filled the circle.

Though I'd not paid much attention to my tutors as a child, I had somehow captured the essence of the Litanies. In particular, all the details pertaining to my childhood infatuation with justice. The answer to Huund's question, I knew. What I didn't know is why the others deferred to her in her mother's absence. Where was Amuun? The game had subtly changed, but I still felt like I covered the board with more pieces.

Needing to say something, I improvised. "By right of victim, by right of kinship, and by right of liege," I called, still speaking as if I addressed the training yard, though I didn't need to yell for everyone to hear me. I could hear the wind rustle the grass when no one else spoke. I held my breath a moment, preparing to walk a fine line between truth and heresy.

Huund strode toward me, parting the small gods with her strong, thin-fingered hands. "Victim, perhaps, you may be, and kin perhaps as well," she said, stopping between Goerranu and Mawzi, just a sword stroke from me.

"But what liege do you own?" The goddess of the hunt and the hunted sounded curious.

There was no way she was ignorant of recent events. I didn't spy Amuun anywhere in the crowd. I wanted to hold out for my original demand. I couldn't very well ask my allies for counsel. Z'nnek stood silent behind me as we'd agreed. Goerranu and Mawzi stood beside Huund. This was all just legal foreplay to discount my rights.

All in or nothing, I thought.

"The clan of Alamar were many among the victims of the crimes I allege," I said. "I am their liege." Not technically true in the mortal sense, though many among them, like Reena, worshipped me now. I hedged, asserting leadership without professing goddesshood.

She didn't look surprised, which was disappointing. "They are sworn to you now?" She grinned, her wicked canine teeth gleaming. "Were they sworn to you when they were broken upon the wheel of woe by hammer and tongs?"

Suppressed woe erupted from deep beneath my heart at her blatant provocation. The amused wrinkle at the corners of her eyes told me she knew she'd scored. To her left, Mawzi shifted a hand to the hilt of her largest dagger. Goerranu didn't shift her position, but she put one hand to my bow that hung over her shoulder. My allies and my enemies all seemed to be ready for war. I did not want to even flirt with it. Yet. The heresy of declaring myself a goddess would ignite this volatile situation.

I refused to give Huund the satisfaction. With effort, I reined in my wild temper, but I could feel Grievance vibrating in my gauntleted fist.

"They were not sworn to me then," I said, as deadly calm as I could manage, "but their kith and kin and heirs are sworn to me now. I represent them as their advocate and champion. I demand justice from Amuun as set forth in the Litanies."

The hawk-winged goddess nodded to concede my point. I couldn't be sure, but I suspected that a smile had ghosted across her olive-skinned face. She held my gaze for countless heartbeats more.

Why am I talking to her? Why are they letting me? How did she sidestep my demand for Amuun's judgment? My thoughts swirled whilst I waited.

Huund raised her arms and her voice. "In the name of Amuun, I hear and accept the rights proclaimed to demand redress from those accused." She turned in a slow half circle to face the other high gods. "Do any present dispute my judgment?"

Shocking silence ruled the brightening morning. The gods of the world held their breath. She might be Amuun's daughter and eldest child, but... *How has she enthralled them all? Has she enthralled me?* Never in the Litanies had Huund spoken for her mother.

Completing her full turn to face me again, Huund said without expression, "Very well. By silent acclamation, on behalf of the Conclave, I accept all of your unstated grievances." She gave me the short quarter bow one gives to equals, and in the highlands, to those who've bested you in a bout. "I am prepared to negotiate recompense," she continued with an extended pause, "if you are prepared to accept?"

What the fuck just happened? I wondered silently, glaring at Huund's expectant expression.

The left eye of the goddess of the hunt twitched as if she stifled a wink.

Behind me, Z'nnek coughed. His hand found my shoulder and squeezed. I knew what he wanted without speaking—this was everything he'd advocated for, as had Tourak. Everything I'd resolved to fight for. And it had all been granted without challenge. I felt on unstable ground, my footing uncertain. Around me, the raven wings of my entire unkindness ruffled uneasily. Mawzi scowled, seeing the war she pined for bleeding away. Goerranu inspected Huund from behind, her eyes recalculating.

I had to say something. I needed time to think. The words came out gruffer and more surprised than I wanted. "What do you offer?"

Huund turned one foot out in a half open stance that reminded me of Conseca's recent, aggravating negotiation. "To commence negotiations, I am prepared," she said, "to offer an apology and blood compensation as decreed in the Litanies on behalf of the high gods to the clans of the highlands for wrongs done unto them by our Elysian worshippers."

I grunted at the understatement. The crimes against my kin went far beyond wrongful killing. I tried to gather the words to tell her where to stuff her apology and blood money. Similar sentiments were palpable from the anger I felt from my angels and the two allies I could see.

She smiled without warmth and continued before I could speak. "Additionally, I am prepared to restore those highland souls claimed by the high gods." She sighed dramatically. "Though we cannot restore their mortal lives without forbidden magic, we will commit them to other service—if Nethe will have them."

"Why would they—"

Huund held up a hand. "Please allow me to finish." She waited, presumably for my acknowledgment.

I glanced at the barely contained rage on the faces of the Holy Twins. They clearly hated this. A now-impassive Vayan and a curious Urth flanked the pair of golden and silvery gods.

Not trusting myself to speak, I gave her a curt nod to continue.

"We will grant amnesty to all who have violated the Litanies—"

Mawzi and Goerranu and I all scoffed.

Huund continued as if uninterrupted. "—and welcome you and Z'nnek and others"—She glanced left and right to Mawzi and Goerranu acknowledging our conspiracy—"into our Conclave as peers."

Amuun's holy glowing menses.

Behind Huund, small gods gasped and began to chatter in low voices. Mawzi and I blinked at each other in amazement. We both looked at Goerranu, who wore a mild frown, still gazing at Huund as if unable to solve a puzzle. The goddess of secrets and lies looked at me and gave a slight shrug. Mawzi bowed her head in defeat. It was my decision.

Stalling for time, I asked, "And we are expected to forgive and forget?"

"I expect no one to forget," Huund stated flatly, holding my gaze with a level stare. "In the interests of peace and justice, I must ask that all concerned forego vengeance."

Too late, I saw the trap. Rather than try to unmake me and risk the devastation of godwar, they would force me to unmake myself, to act against my nature—in the name of justice and peace. *Would my hold on the domain of vengeance diminish if I accepted her offer? Did I care? Why had I taken it up without a thought if it were not mine to bear?*

They couldn't've known that I'd bring overwhelming force to the Conclave. With reparations and the peace I thought I wanted on the table, did it matter? I knew I wouldn't slaughter the small gods to reach the others —there was no profit in slaughtering potential allies. Huund obviously gambled on it as well. Even if I gave the order to attack, the high gods and the old might escape in the confusion of the melee.

I hadn't wanted goddesshood. But I had it. And all its consequences.

The weight of thousands of eyes lay heavy on me. Heaviest of all were the haunting, dark eyes of the mixed-race goddess of the hunt and the hunted. She stood very still, preternaturally so. And watched me like her hawk totem might a hare hiding in the brush.

"I will negotiate in good faith," I said softly, "but I would see the details written before I relinquish my rights." *Or the threat of my unkindness and my avengers,* I promised myself.

My voice obviously carried in the bright morning stillness. The tension among the circle of gods eased. Huund appeared triumphant.

I stared up at the rising sun: the court of the sun goddess. The bastion of greatest power that none but the high gods had visited since the Little War. Perhaps I will meet Amuun herself after all.

"Of course," Huund said in a cheery tone pitched to carry to the ears of all present. "You will all come to Mother's court in Saetarra. Immediately! We will arrive at the best of terms in fewer days than you mourned your mother."

I bit my tongue to keep from lashing out at her temerity. Putting a time limit on our negotiations was fine, but her all but spitting on Madra's memory riled me something fierce. Why did she appease with one hand and taunt with the other?

I surveyed the crowd, still ringed by my unkindness of angels. Behind Huund, the Twins and Vayan scowled. The old gods, with their strange eyes, stared. Every small god considered me. Some with awe. Some with envy. Some with disdain. Some with curiosity. A few with...hope.

Urth's voice rang clear in its three-part harmony of male, female, and other. "Four days."

My renewed glare seemed to have no effect on the goddess of the hunt.

Huund cocked her head and gave me a lopsided smile. "The priests will need to learn to sing a new Litany." She nodded. "Soon."

That was the moment I realized I'd forgotten to pass along Araeda'h's nonsense final warning about gemstones to Conseca.

CHAPTER 12

*A*ll I wanted was to get through this farce with my dignity intact. The rosy dawn was past. Peach sky streaked with clouds hung above the Conclave filled with gods and goddesses, like me, who had not witnessed what they had come to expect. My confusion and uncertainty reflected in others' faces and postures. With my lovers—no, with my husbands at my back, I put on my bravest face and grinned.

Huund withdrew a long, thin horn that had been tucked unnoticed in her belt. The fluted ivory horn contrasted beautifully with her dark skin and wild hair. She drew it to her plump lips and pointed the curved instrument to the brightening sky. A plaintive wail bugled its long ululating call. The sound chilled my soul. Some primitive part of me quivered, in terror of pursuit or excitement of the chase—or both. I could only stare at her lips wrapped about the hunting trumpet. Behind her, the gods lingering between the standing stones stilled in fear.

The quavering clamor seemed to have the same effect on the small gods and the old. They all gawked unmoving at Huund, Lady of the Dread Hunt. The Twins and Vayan stood stock still, trying to evince a stoic mien, but I could tell the unexpected noise rattled them, too.

The goddess of the hunt and the hunted turned her sharp-toothed grin upon me. She seemed satisfied with whatever she saw in my expression.

"Please ask your host to make way." She waved the horn in her hand in a lazy circle to indicate my unkindness that still surrounded us. "It would not do to have any misunderstandings at this delicate juncture."

I boggled at her, mouth agape, not understanding. I was *not* smitten.

Over the distant horizon, hawk-winged hunters came. Not so numerous as my—what had Huund called them?—my host, who stood fast in the face of the onrushing threat, not reaching for weapons but looking to me for the command. The ring of approaching angels encircled mine. And they carried the terrible wounding boar-spears of legend: weapons that left their victims eternally bleeding.

Have I been doubly ambushed? My heart quickened. Huund was craftier than I had prepared to face.

Madra's voice urged me: *Never engage an unknown foe until you've taken their measure.*

Behind me, Tourak growled with readiness to fight. I felt his protectiveness, but I was loathe to risk him, or any of them.

Afraid for my lovelies, I raised my arms and shouted, "Let them pass!"

My host of raven-winged angels opened their ranks to permit access to the center.

Stalking without hesitation between my more numerous raven-winged host, the angels of the Dread Hunt arranged themselves into a silent double spear-line. Its point lay where Huund stood with me. As one, they whispered, "We come when you call."

Though softly spoken, they were heard by all. Had I not just been assaulted by a terrifying demon lord a day past, I might've flinched—but it was still a near thing. The small gods shivered. The old gods shifted their alien forms uneasily. The trio of high gods watched with feigned impassivity. The Twins crossed their arms, a mirror image of one another. Vayan waved toward the sky. I didn't look up to see to whom or what or why he waved.

Why surrender if they had us entrapped? I wondered. *Huund had the advantage...*

Like a mating hawk, Huund gave an adoring whistle. "Good, my pets. Please carry our...guests to Saetarra." She spread her hands to indicate the small gods. "It is many hours awing." Her demure smile was feigned.

I narrowed my eyes at her game. No one present was fooled.

Fearful eyes among the small gods gaped at the command. A burbling filled the standing stones. No part of this was what any of us expected at Conclave.

Yet, I had no intention to be carried anywhere. "We can fly ourselves wherever we must," I said, trying to keep the disdain from my voice.

Several close by among the small gods scowled at me.

With a quizzical look, Huund nodded. "You may, of course, but they"— she threw a thumb over her shoulder at the small gods—"cannot."

Neither small god nor old had wings to fly. Except for Z'nnek. And except for me. *Until Z'nnek gifted me the mantle of ravens, why was he unique among all the small gods in that one respect?* Upon that matter, the Litanies and Tales were silent. My already long list of unanswered questions for my husband continued to grow.

Clearly at a disadvantage, I waited and watched. Behind me, I could feel Z'nnek and Tourak sharing a knowing look about my wasteful haste to test the depth of every stream with both feet. My lot in life was to easily forget how little I knew.

"Why do we need them?" I asked, honestly confused about her intent. *Did she think they would be hostages to control me?*

Too late, Goerranu and Mawzi both gave me different hand signals to desist. I saw the narrowing of eyes among many nearby small gods as they frowned at me, perhaps taking offense that I thought they should not be included.

Huund laughed like heavy harness bells for chasing spring foxes or winter wolves. "Momentous times require momentous changes." She smirked and waved to her angels to hurry.

Behind me, his warm breath against my ear, Z'nnek whispered, "The small gods have not been invited to court at Nuuria nor Avaala since the Accord. And never to Saetarra." Out of sight of the Conclave, he rested his hand behind my hip. The lord of the underworld might keep his secrets, but he had my back.

If I objected more, perhaps I would alienate small gods who might become my kindred spirits. I needed allies. And I needed information to make sense of this strangeness. I'd play along with Huund's game until I understood it. I hoped I'd figure it out before it killed me. Again. Perhaps eternally this time.

The angels of the Dread Hunt obediently bowed to Huund and put their hands and knees onto the long grass of the steppes. Their transformation was subtle and gorgeous to behold. Where angels had knelt, huge, tawny hunting hounds rose, hawk-headed and hawk-winged.

I sought out Goerranu's attention. She did not look as surprised as I felt. While I'd known of the Dread Hunt, it was still terrifying to witness more than four dozen of the mythical canine creatures, as large as horses, materialize and subjugate themselves as mounts for the small gods.

At Huund's urging, the small gods stiffly sat forward of the hawk-hounds' wings, grasping white-knuckled fistfuls of feathers. Mawzi glared in my direction. Goerranu pointedly did not.

"Take them swiftly and safely to Saetarra, my pets!"

When the flights of hawk-hounds had mounted the skies, Huund slashed her open hand toward the rising sun. "Shall we?"

The Twins had taken the last two of the hawk-hounds for themselves. *Did they not have wings of their own like the angels of their hosts?* The enormous freeti I'd met in the court of storms lifted Vayan in his many arms. The trio took flight, trailing the Dread Hunt.

Huund stood alone at the ring of standing stones, with me and Z'nnek and my entire host, as if she had not a fear in the world. As if I could not even be a threat to her. She watched me with predatory stillness.

"Shall I bring my"—I hesitated on the odd word—"host?"

"If you do not trust me," she said, "you should." A sharp-toothed smile dared me not to. "But I am sure they have more pressing duties to attend."

Too many quick heartbeats passed while I wrestled with my distrust. Was Huund sincere in her offer of peace? Was the invitation to court a trap? There were too many unknowns at play now for me to calculate risks accurately. Z'nnek's comforting hand still rested at my back. *What was it Conseca said? All in or nothing?*

"Very well," I announced in a too-bright voice. "Return to your duty to the unclaimed, my pretties. And your usual roosts in Nethe!" I sent gratitude and love far and wide to all of the angels in my unkindness...and a sense of foreboding. *Prepare and watch,* I tried to tell them with my heart.

93

I turned, taking Z'nnek's hand in mine and grasping Tourak's. "I need no other escort than you, my lovers." I gave them a wicked grin that I hoped said, *Be ready!*

With no other warning, I launched myself sunward and forced them all to chase me into the sky.

CHAPTER 13

*W*e flew into the cloud-streaked, early morning sky. The rising sun washed the dawn colors into an increasingly brighter blue. I chased the Dread Hunt, and the exertion brought me joy. At last, my missing delight to fly rose up in my chest. Without looking, I sensed Z'nnek and Tourak on my wings, just below and behind. We were safe, together, for now. *Perhaps forever, if only I can discover the weakness of my new opponent. She must have some chink or blind spot I can leverage.*

The Elysian steppe fell away as we rapidly crossed over my beloved highlands, straining for altitude. The muscles in my shoulders stretched and warmed with my exhilaration. A dozen times higher than I'd ever flown, we cleared the barrier mountains that shone like tiny, sparkling white spearpoints. I felt grand to stay ahead of Huund. Until her hawk cry sounded loud and close behind.

The higher we flew, the more I struggled, and the more resolute I became to best her.

As I gained the rear of the long double line of the Dread Hunt's formation, Huund soared overhead in a dramatic roll resembling a dancer's pirouette. I imagined that she winked at me again as she took the vanguard. *Showoff!* Her sudden flourish reminded me to stop gawking over the awe of flying halfway to the sun and ponder the very real danger I was plunging toward. Far from my palace and my power, without my entire unkindness, my allies and I would be grossly outnumbered in the high gods' home arena.

The heart-shaped sigil on my chest tickled as it drew sips of magic from my reserves. So far from Nethe, I tried but could not draw from the ambient power around me. Perhaps I could not touch my home from so distant an orbit. Or I'd not learned the way of it in this other space, I supposed. So little time, so much to learn.

With the roar of the wind of passage, I couldn't very well speak with Z'nnek. Screaming, we might be overheard. Instead, I slowed just enough to fly parallel with my lovers to try a modification of avian speech in my angelic form. I pitched my wing feathers, my face, and my shoulders to ask, "What should I expect in Amuun's domain?"

Z'nnek laughed. Lucky for him, I couldn't hear it. His posture, widespread hand gesture, and headshake told me, "Be calm and patient." His annoying answer for most anything.

Fuming, I glanced to Tourak. What would he know? Had he ever been to the court of the sun? As an envoy or accompanying Z'nnek? It didn't matter. He shook his head, long black hair streaming out behind him as he flew. His face was an expressionless mask. He either knew nothing or would tell me nothing.

Aggravated, I pushed myself harder and flew higher. With no recourse to answer my myriad questions about our destination, I focused my attention on the Dread Hunt. And Huund. Instead of leaving her in my wake, I was chasing her tail. I growled and flapped harder.

The angels of the hunt possessed an additional powerful form beyond their angelic aspect. *How did I not know that?* I knew of the hawk-winged hounds, but I'd not associated them with Huund's flight of angels. My poor study or an intentional gap in the lore of the high gods? The Litanies that mentioned the hunting ways of the hawk-winged hounds painted them to be implacable predators. The angels of the Dread Hunt doubly so, with their broad-headed boar spears of wounding. Now I knew them to be one and the same. *Could I learn other forms than the raven and my angelic form? Could I teach my own angels once I knew?* Having options in war would be valuable indeed.

How could my angels prevail against foes who inflicted injuries that never ceased to bleed? What defense against them could I build, beg, borrow, or steal?

In neither the Litanies nor the Tales did any prey ever escape the Dread Hunt. *Could I brand my lovelies with healing and binding sigils like the one Z'nnek had gifted to me? Would it be enough for them to regenerate more quickly? Gain other powers to keep them safe?* I shook my head. *Better to prevent injury than heal it,* I thought. I needed to make time to consume Provax and discover the secret of Tyrr's invulnerable skin that he had worn when I defeated him. Soon. Until then, his bottle could languish on the wine rack in my mind.

The sun grew steadily closer. Its heat increased against my black-feathered wings and kissed my skin hotly. I struggled to breathe as the air got thinner. My sigil drew on my magic reserves more deeply now to heal me and keep my flesh functioning. If I burned much more, I'd begin to lose memories on the pyre of magic to heal and energize me.

Looking at the sun too long was painful from the ground. This far up, I had to intentionally stare elsewhere and avert my gaze to avoid the blinding glare. Eventually, I succumbed and began to fall behind. I accepted that I could not overtake her. I slid out of the realm of flesh and solely into spirit. The relief was immediate. Featherlight, I flew faster and with negligible effort and had no need to breathe. In moments, I was soaring above and just behind the double line of hawk-winged hounds. The small gods all seemed to cling to their mounts for dear life.

Had I been watching more closely, I might have seen Huund and her Hunt shift into spirit sooner. *Or had they ever taken flesh? I couldn't recall now.* I caught her looking back at me beneath her broad, brown-feathered wings. Shame at overexerting myself for no value rattled through my soul. *Had I learned nothing about conserving my power?* I'd lost much in the pointless war with the Chosen. There were still holes burned into my memories caused by spending myself beyond the point of reason.

Fortunately, the power of the sun had no effect on my spirit self. I could even stare into its full glare without being blinded. It was a wonder. *Why had the high gods created spirit, flesh, and shadow so differently? Would they tell me if I asked? Tyrr, Torr, and Vayan held no love for me. But perhaps Huund might? Her motivations were mysterious.*

Huund herself was a threat multiplier and an unknown. She'd

outthought, outplanned, and outmaneuvered me. *So far,* I reassured myself. *Nobody could win every battle.* I was certain I'd find a way to turn the war in my favor.

Still, I'd had a hundred times more angels than she now led toward Saetarra, and I'd felt severely disadvantaged. *What did she plan?* The Lady of the Hunt was not an enraged war god nor an overconfident god of justice and civilization like her twin brothers nor a blustery storm god like Vayan. Huund's Hunt tracked and killed the demons who snuck through the veil past the guardian hosts. *Her apology and reparations might become an anvil upon which to crush me.* She was cool, calculating, and implacable.

I see the anvil. Where's the hammer?

Amuun's host of angels guarded Saetarra and the veil. I wondered if they would be the hammer of my destruction. *How does hauling the small gods into the fray serve her trap? Are they hostages? Or fuel for the fire?*

My mind ticked over all the lore I could recall, despite the fact that those were all suddenly suspect in my mind. *Which—if any—were true?*

I was still churning over the strategic implications of my situation as the sky gradually darkened from blue into near black. Nothing in the Litanies or Tales prepared me for the midnight sky so far above the clouds. The brilliant motes of the veil guardians emerged, picked out like a scattering of jewels on a black velvet cloth. The hosts of Amuun, Tyrr, and Torr that patrolled the veil to keep demons at bay were hidden from below during daylight. Gold and silver motes of Tyrr's and Torr's hosts were evident. Torr's were sparkling silver, almost white against the midnight of the veil. I searched for Amuun's but couldn't distinguish the sun gold from Tyrr's war gold.

One sparkling white diamond stood out, growing steadily brighter. Soon, it became apparent that the gem hung at the edge of the sun's corona. Amuun's palace was only visible against the black sky. The sheer scale of the burning ball dwarfed any sense of grandeur the court of the sun might have held. Still, as we approached, the massive magnificence of Saetarra became clear.

Easily a hundred or a thousand times larger than storm-tossed Woazanayehn, the power of the high gods struck me squarely. Anxiety thundered through me. The court of storms that I'd visited against my will

—just once for the first time and only weeks ago—was Vayan's cloud-covered realm. I'd not taken the time since then to compare the power of that sky castle with the realms of other gods and my own. Nethe was flat and wide and undefended—nothing like the fortresses of the high gods.

Forced to confront the disparity in power, I studied the approach to Amuun's palace as I might if I were a besieging general or sneaking assassin. *Who knew? I'd rather neither, but either might become necessary.*

Gleaming quartz construction reflected the blinding sunlight. The domed palace hung upside down from the sun, pointing downward toward the realm of flesh. Transparent rosy crystal capped the entire palace, save for the large platform that ringed the gleaming cylinder. Tiny figures, in complementary shades of ivory and various metallic hues, stood guard in ranks along a parade ground the size of Alamar Forte. What kept them from plummeting toward the world below, I could not guess.

Closer still, I could see the turrets arrayed along the dome perimeter. Spaced every furlong or so, the tubes and crystal lenses poking out of the quartz turrets were eerily familiar. Larger versions of the siege engines the Chosen had brought to my gates only a few days ago. I'd never seen them in action, and I'd no idea how they worked—but I suspected their purpose to be one of massive, magical destruction. And I'd no desire to be on the receiving end in my first experience of their power.

I circled the platform, bewildered, as the hawk-winged hounds flipped over in some complicated aerobatics. They landed, paws and claws, upside down, not even sliding on the polished stone. Huund somersaulted and joined them, as if standing on the sky were a natural everyday occurrence. She chivvied the small gods from their mounts, which had landed between a double line of four ranks of stone warriors I doubted were statues. Though she had seemed to be ignoring my circling uncertainty, I saw Huund cast a smirk over her shoulder toward me. Her gleaming white teeth were as smooth and unforgiving as the marble she stood upon.

Armored in mirror-bright metal, the quartz golems stood twice as tall as the mortal gods who milled about between the golems' disciplined ranks. Each identical stone soldier stood with an ebony-hafted halberd, half again as tall as they were, in one hand. The watered steel blades of the halberds

99

shimmered gold and silver in the blinding sunlight. In the other hand, they each carried a short, wicked crystalline wand of unknown function.

The Litanies forbade such self-animated creations upon pain of exile to the Hells. The Tales often tempted their heroes with the power to create them. The mortals who gave in to the temptation always suffered at the hand of the high gods or the old. Often the Dread Hunt itself delivered the justice. Strange to find a legion of them here.

I imagined those stone soldiers would be far more formidable than the demon-bound terfs and other lesser golems that survived the veil and its guardians—or were created in defiance of the Litanies. Tourak and I had been assaulted by terfs the first time I left Nethe. All sorts of golems occasioned the sun-kissed lands from time to time, before the Dread Hunt tracked them and destroyed them. I'd seen many in Urth's service, patrolling the realm of shadow and his underworld domain, in clear defiance of the Litanies. I wondered if the high gods knew or cared. Perhaps not, for here were eight ranks of golems in Amuun's domain, arrayed on the upside-down parade ground as if on review.

Why should the Litanies only apply restrictions to mortals? In the highlands, any of our few laws applied to warlord, warden, and clan folk alike. I mastered my anger and focused on assessing my approach to the bizarre platform as I continued to circle.

From behind me, Z'nnek soared up toward the stone platform. He rolled over in his shallow climb, which I supposed became a shallow dive. Assuming his enormous vulture form, he used his massive wingspan to brake and stall. As he began to fall toward the waiting parade ground below, he resumed his angelic form and coasted to a gentle, if inelegant, landing on his feet. I got the unsubtle hint. But I wasn't sure I was prepared to take it.

My lord of the underworld had nothing to prove. As a mortal, he'd defeated the three demon lords who had ruled there before him. Prior to his inexplicable surrender to the Accord, he'd beaten the high gods in the godwar and laid siege to their paradises. He'd been their peer in all but name for eight millennia. Among the small gods, he was king. Fluttering down like a feather meant nothing to his image.

Conversely, all I had was a defiant attitude and a crown I'd been given as a bride gift. To my enemies—and myself—I'd earned nothing. The Twins and Vayan clearly had no respect nor fear of me. Huund's feigned apology and deferential mien must be false and hiding her disdain for me and mine. She'd only brought the small gods here to witness the negotiation of my case and to judge every move I made. *My political failure must be her endgame. Image was all in any game of politics.*

Clenching my jaw, I copied Huund's swoop toward the waiting ranks of golems. I could do no less than she. With a twist of my torso, I rolled and tucked into a somersault, just as she had midway through her descent. Then the pull toward the platform overcame the pull toward the ground far below the clouds.

I held in a frustrated screech as I fought to regain control of my tumble.

Too far! I flapped my wings, fighting the overcorrection.

The pink-veined quartz of the parade ground rushed up and smashed me across the face.

Through the haze of pain and nausea of the impact, all I could hear was laughter that rang like hunting bells.

CHAPTER 14

*M*y entire world was hard, smooth stone and pain. The cold, polished quartz of the parade ground crushed against my face. Murmurs and laughter leaked in around the edges. Squirming, I shifted to rise to my feet, expecting to leave both my pride and my blood on the ground.

Huund's voice rang rich with amused hunting bells. "Peace and hospitality, O Raven Queen! Welcome to Saetarra."

A warm female voice with feathery desert tones said, "Wait." Her accent reminded me of Goerranu. "Hold still."

Gentle hands stroked my hair back from my face and touched my cheek where I could feel the bleeding skin had split. Coolness invaded the stinging wound. The pain subsided. It was far from the worst I'd ever had, but I was grateful for its absence. For the absence of all my pains, actually. The healing coolness had swept over me so fast that I'd scarcely noticed.

Sliding my legs under me into a kneeling position, I considered the tan-skinned older woman who squatted beside me. Her wrinkles made her out to be Madra's age or a little older. A long, thick braid of shockingly white hair draped over her shoulder. She wore a simple, conservative sari made of pink cotton, embroidered with a long row of dainty white asters along the border.

The goddess wore no weapons or armor, only simple, pink-dyed leather sandals to complement her unassuming clothing. Her only adornment was a scarlet macramé sachet that hung about her neck on a knotted cord. Her scent was a pungent poultice of anise, mint, oregano, and too many other herbs, flowers, and spices to identify. An aura of soothing comfort embraced her, and me.

Mentioned seldom in the Litanies, Hayyek made frequent appearances in the Tales as the pacifist small goddess of healing, medicinal herbs, and midwives. My opposite in many ways, her light brown eyes held my gaze without deference and without challenge.

"Why are you missing a finger, Illyria?" she asked in a mild, motherly tone. Her glance at my permanently injured hand was a healer's inspection, not a judgment.

The question struck me as daft. I could ask why she seemed nigh elderly. *Some things just were. Were they not?* I thought. But she'd been gracious enough to heal me without being asked at the cost of her own magic. So, I humored her with the truth. "Because someone cut it off, I suppose." I caught my smirk as it escaped and twisted it into a sardonic smile. "He desperately wanted his brother's ring back."

She blinked at me, blank-faced. "I see." Though her tone said she clearly didn't.

Brushing off the strange conversational tangent, I stood as Z'nnek and Tourak reached my side. Hayyek rose from her crouch, straightening her sari.

I said, "Thank you for your aid and support, Hayyek." And I meant it.

"Oh, I don't support you, child," Hayyek replied with a grimace. "I oppose the vengeance you've come here to exact." There was no malice or reproach in her voice. Just fact.

Speechless, it was my turn to blink at my erstwhile benefactress.

"Are you well, Illyria?" Z'nnek asked, his mild tone belying the worried quaver of his voice. He would never scold me for allowing an enemy to touch me. But he would be well within his rights as one of my husbands to do so.

His concern was enough for me to get the message. I'd been careless in my embarrassment. I wondered for a moment how to clean my blood from the stone at my feet without drawing more attention. Leaving so powerful a conduit for my enemies was unwise.

Tourak's warm, solid hand on my shoulder told me he was both concerned and prepared.

My archangel knelt, glowing tourmaline in hand. He whispered, as Hayyek watched him intently. The dark light from the stone played across the pool of my spilt blood. The stain evaporated with a faint sizzle.

I found my voice at last. "If you don't support me, why help me at all then, goddess?"

"I help any I find powerless and in need," Hayyek said in a prim tone.

My breath left me in a whoosh. "Oh," I said sagely. *Powerless?* I ground my teeth. *Stupid, I might be, and clumsy, but powerless?* "I see," I replied aloud.

Tourak stood and squeezed my shoulder. I felt the reminder to keep my temper.

Laughter floated from over Hayyek's shoulder from among the small gods. Several were exchanging tokens of some kind. I recognized the transaction immediately: bets won and lost. The laughing god was collecting, obviously the oddsmaker from his posture and banter. I didn't recognize him from the Litanies. Many chagrin-faced gods were paying. Several glared my way or eyed me with disappointment. I was gratified that so many had bet on me—whatever the odds had been—despite my failure to satisfy their belief in me. I'd played the game often enough during festa bouts and other contests, even on the subject of one lover pursuing another. I'd even been the subject of bets before, won and lost.

But somehow this stung more than it had as a mortal—more was at stake. And my self-appointed ally Goerranu and my sworn sister Mawzi were among the bettors. One smiling, one not. Just as I wondered which had bet against me, Mawzi extended her hand to receive three glittering tokens from the gambling master reluctantly given. She was the only one being paid. I scowled as the betrayal of my bloodsworn struck me. My face burned now with more than embarrassment. Hayyek turned, following my gaze.

"Coyne," Hayyek said with disdain. "Ignore him and his games," she advised, turning back to me.

Z'nnek made a small noise of agreement.

My thoughts chased it down swiftly. From the Tales, then. Coyne was the trickster god of luck, surprise, gambling, and misfortune. Not important enough to be represented in the high gods' Litanies, but still a favorite among minstrels and bards and gamblers. I couldn't help but wonder what the odds had been that I'd fail. If Mawzi's winnings were any indication, at least three to one in favor. And she'd bet against.

"What do the gods possess of value to wager?" I wondered aloud. Giving myself something else to ponder than betrayal. It was harder than it should've been.

Z'nnek sighed and stepped closer. Tourak slid both hands onto my shoulders and kneaded at the muscles there. Hayyek stared at me in open surprise. She, at least, was frank with me. So, I focused on her.

"What value does money have," I began, "if every god can create—"

Z'nnek cut me off, sliding an arm around my waist. "We should discuss later, my queen," he whispered in my ear. "There is much for you still to learn of divine society."

I hated being patronized, and Z'nnek knew it.

"What do you mean, Illyria?" Hayyek asked.

The question seemed genuine, if baffling. And I thought about how to rephrase mine.

Tourak smoothly interjected. "We have not had cause to teach Illyria how to create a token of favor." He chuckled in his sexy way and nuzzled my neck suggestively. "We've been too busy making merry memories of note to have much need of the exchange of significant memories in Nethe."

Though she didn't look convinced, Hayyek nodded. Her gaze lingered on the three of us, taking in me sandwiched between my lovers in a way that made me think that she wasn't only curious about my lack of knowledge of divine society.

Z'nnek stood on tiptoes to whisper in my ear, "Not all gods may create the way you do."

Tourak caught my eye meaningfully.

Yet another secret? I wondered. *If the small gods couldn't create with magic, what made them divine? Immortality alone? Were the high gods so limited, too? If so, how had they defeated Z'nnek? Or enforced the Accord against him?*

"O-ho!" Vayan thundered. "Are you sure you have collected enough to pay me, Coyne?"

The god of thunder and lightning wasn't watching Coyne. He was watching me. Still, Coyne's face darkened as he faced the lord of storms.

Vayan's bluster was loud and grating. "You offered thrice better than even odds that the raven girl would take the coward's way down, did you not?" He stalked up to stand in front of Coyne, towering half a head over the god of misfortune.

I bristled at the implication. My lovers' various grips on me tightened. Hayyek sighed and turned to watch.

"I—" Coyne looked flustered. "She seemed—" His eyes met mine, but his mild embarrassment didn't cover the enmity I saw there.

The god of good fortune and ill hated me. And I couldn't imagine why.

Huund's bell-like laugh tinkled. "Surely you can't believe he took both of your bets of ten favors seriously, Uncle?" She maneuvered herself between the two. "I didn't take your bets seriously." Huund inclined her head toward me. "Who wagers ten favors on long odds that she would fail so spectacularly?" She winked at me.

My eyes narrowed at Coyne, but my growing anger wasn't directed at him. He was just an opportunist, nothing more. Vayan and Huund were trying to provoke me. And it was working.

Vayan guffawed, a forced and overly dramatic sound. "He owes me sixty." His eyes were still fixed on me. "I knew she'd fail."

Even though my lovers clearly wanted me to suffer the indignity, they would just have to forgive me if I recouped some of the pride I'd just lost. Eventually. I took a breath. Deep in my heart, Grievance quivered, ready and willing to try the storm god for this humiliation and the previous one in his court. Not to mention for the abuse Memad had suffered at his father's hands. Now that the thunderbird demigod was secretly sworn to me, his honor was mine to avenge.

But, if I directed my ire at Vayan, as he and Huund wished, or worse, my violence, I would kill this nascent second Conclave before it served its purpose. Though I couldn't see all of the trap yet, I had already taken the bait. And there was perhaps more to be gained with subterfuge. An audience at least to plead with Amuun for her mercy.

Between me and my antagonists stood Hayyek, a new acquaintance and an enigma. Someone who stated clear opposition to me and my goals yet was willing to give freely of herself to aid me, even if it was in a small way. If I picked the first fight I was offered, I would confirm her mistaken beliefs about me and perhaps never learn what motivated her. Though I couldn't explain—or wouldn't admit to myself—why I wanted to know her mind, I did.

Curiosity won, but I couldn't very well leave a blatant challenge unanswered. I would need to draw every eye to me by way of controlling the situation. Then release the tension in some unexpected way.

"Is that so?" I called louder than was strictly necessary.

I made a show of shrugging off both Z'nnek and Tourak, who tried to hold on tighter. But action always beats reaction.

Stalking past Hayyek, I scowled at Coyne as I approached him. I intentionally ignored Vayan and Huund. I struggled to keep my expression furious when the god of happenstance visibly paled beneath his tan. *Why would a god centuries older than I fear me? Especially here at the seat of power of those he seeks to curry favor with?*

Nose to nose with Coyne, I repeated my rhetorical question. "Is that so?" I sneered in his face, close enough that I could see my breath flutter his eyelashes.

He flinched.

I waited.

Behind him, Vayan and Huund sidled closer, presumably to pounce when I violated peace and hospitality offered to a guest. I'd figured that was their opening gambit. Without having to look, I was sure that Tyrr and Torr were also preparing to join the imminent fray. Out of the corner of my eye, I saw a flutter of brown on one side and a flash of black on the other. Goerranu and Mawzi. I hoped they moved to back my play, not stab me in the ass.

Reluctant, Coyne nodded.

I shouted, "Well, Am—" I censored myself as I'd been about to take Amuun's name in vain. In her own domain. "—radiant shit!"

Huund smirked at my near faux pas.

It occurred to me, not for the first time, that I really needed to find new things to swear by than the anatomy and excretions of the gods of the Litanies. Working to cover my stumble, I conjured as deep a belly laugh as I could muster, throwing my head back to laugh at the sky that wasn't the sky. All that lay above was the realm of flesh.

Disorientation rolled through me as I realized I was looking down upon the world.

With a tremendous effort of will, I kept the laugh rolling for several more heartbeats.

I wasn't sure I could get used to an upside view of everything.

Then I took a deep breath and feigned wiping tears from my eyes.

"If I'd known those odds, I'd've bet against myself!"

Looking over my shoulder, I winked at Hayyek. The goddess of pacifism gave me a thoughtful stare in return. The knots of the small gods all looked torn between anxious and relieved. My lovers were caught between amused and annoyed.

Turning back, I patted Coyne's cheek in fake affection. "Next time, be a dear and let me in on the action, eh?"

Coyne swallowed and, despite his fear, still looked angry with me. But he nodded.

Behind the god of long odds, Vayan, Tyrr, and Torr looked puzzled, but still ready to attack. The Dread Hunt all crouched motionless on their haunches, wings half furled, watching their Lady for a sign to attack.

But not Huund. She'd stepped back behind her uncle, Vayan. She eyed me with that calculating look again, which told me that I'd surprised her.

Good. Get used to it, bitch.

CHAPTER 15

*A*fter a nervous Coyne settled with a belligerent Vayan, a laughing Huund led us through the enormous gates into Saetarra. We left the ranks upon ranks of strange, still-unmoving golems and the haunting, predatory gazes of the Dread Hunt behind us. Clearly, the high gods held no fear of we small gods in this overbearingly white sanctum. Overhead, prisms and mirrors poured light into every space. So bright was the light, no shadows fell on the brilliant marble tile and walls. A strange sensation plagued me. I longed for a little less razor-edged perfection. Long moments passed before I realized I missed Nethe. I was homesick for the surreal, haphazard realm I'd once spurned. I owed Z'nnek an apology. An orgy of apologies.

I didn't know where we were going. I didn't know what we were doing.

But I understood the grandiosity Huund established by dragging us unwillingly through paradise. I vowed to not allow myself to be impressed. It was frustrating to not have the sense of connection and awareness of everything here that I owned in Nethe. So, I resisted the temptation to look over my shoulder to ensure Z'nnek and Tourak followed me. They'd won far more than my trust. We brought up the tail of the undisciplined column of small gods. For some reason, Hayyek lagged behind and walked beside me, though she seemed to pay me no mind, gazing at the splendor of Saetarra with a critical eye. Far ahead of the middle of the pack, Goerranu surreptitiously studied her surroundings, while beside her, Mawzi gawked.

While I had many things I should have been pondering, my thoughts of what to say to my fickle allies and how to make my case to Amuun for reparations were constantly interrupted by the sights. The vast halls we marched through were long, echoing chambers lined with more immobile golems guarding murals upon the walls and brightly colored statuary. Many of the pieces held captured banners and broken weapons and other battle trophies. I expected to recognize the statues from the Litanies, but they were all strangers to me. The images upon the walls depicted brutal fights, pompous parades, and baffling ceremonies. *Were these the histories of long-forgotten gods?* Some of the images were moving, playing through a scene as if the pictures were actors on a stage. They were so real I could almost hear and smell them. I resisted my urges to reach out and touch them.

Why was Huund showing these to us?

In the early scenes, beautiful mortals fought winged, scaled demons. The many races were well-armed and armored and outnumbered their foes, but they were vastly outclassed by the enormous flying demons who breathed fire and frost and worse. The powerful weapons of the warriors and massive magics worked by the mortal sorcerers were no match for their foes. As we walked, the mortals fought a retreating action toward a massive wrought iron gate blackened with age and fire. Beyond the obviously magical portal, constellations of stars wheeled in a multicolored void.

More scenes depicted the stages of construction of Saetarra and its defense. In her radiant and terrible beauty, Amuun stood amongst hooded figures robed in diverse colors, who directed the construction of the defenses. All of the people involved were angelic, winged folk, except for Amuun and the robed figures. The most striking of those was a woman with a riot of curly black hair, draped in glittering red-gold brocade with her hood pulled low, her face mostly obscured in shadow. She exuded an aura of command and was always central everywhere she was shown. The old gods were depicted rarely and were relegated to the background when they were infrequently portrayed. Several turns and hall segments later, Tyrr and Torr began to emerge among the seventeen, in place of or adjacent to Amuun.

My parents, my siblings, and I are different, but not so different as Amuun and her Twins. I walked on as that thought itched deep in my mind.

Sometimes the angels fought one another in the sky or on the ground. Other times, they fought various breeds of demon in a dizzying array of environments. Individual duels and the clash of hosts and hordes littered the walls and splashed gore everywhere for many minutes of walking until, at last, Saetarra hung beneath the sun before the blackness of the veil, its construction complete. The hallways had taken to gently sloping upward, but I didn't give it any thought at the time.

Though she'd started among the midst of the procession, Goerranu stopped to inspect a painting. Anxious, but resolved to confront them, I caught up with her and Mawzi as they stood still. The goddess of assassins stared at the goddess of secrets but uncharacteristically held her tongue. I didn't.

"What in the Hells?" I demanded of my allies.

I wanted to challenge them both for their bets and meant to wait for a response, but the object of Goerranu's attention caught my eye. The painting was an armored angel with wings and streaming curly black locks leading a host of raven-winged angels through the black, wrought iron gate and into battle against the winged and scaled demons from the earliest hall. I assumed she was the commanding, robed figure from earlier, or perhaps her daughter. Something about the woman's face was disturbing and familiar.

"What in the Hells?" I asked no one in particular, staring at the painting.

Mawzi nudged Goerranu. "She sees it, too."

Goerranu narrowed her eyes at me as if measuring my face.

"Fascinating," Hayyek said, engrossed in the painting as well.

Z'nnek said dryly, "Unless you wish to be late for your own parley..." He gestured ahead, past my shoulder, where the procession was turning a corner out of sight. He pointedly did not look at the painting on the wall.

Being lost in a hostile fortress held no appeal for me. The mystery of the raven-winged woman would have to wait. I strode after the disappearing column of small gods, leaving my retinue to follow or not, as they chose.

By the time I caught up with the main group, they had entered something like a throne room through massive brass-bound doors that gaped wide. I stopped in the doorway so abruptly that someone bumped into me from the rear. There was no other exit from the huge hall before me.

"Illyria?" Hayyek asked, not concerned, just confused.

Her cool hand rested against my bare lower back with unearned familiarity. It didn't displease me so much as it surprised me. Shoving aside the implications of anything but the tactical situation, I scanned the room. I confirmed there appeared to be no other way out.

Tyrr's golden-winged war angels lined the wall to my right. Torr's silver-winged angels of justice lined the other wall to my left. My unease was confirmed as I heard the other boot finally drop. *So much build up and misdirection for a simple ambush after all?*

My fingers ached to reach for Grievance. Every instinct screamed at me to fight and hold the door—the one exit. A glance over my shoulder confirmed only Hayyek, my lovers, and my allies filled the hall behind me. No contingent of the high gods' command to trap us.

I forced myself to wait and surveyed the battlefield. Three throne-like chairs carved from black granite dominated a dais raised four steps above the floor. Tapestries, battle trophies, and artwork depicting scenes from the Litanies accented the walls. Huund, Tyrr, Torr, and Vayan were already mounting the steps. The angels lining the walls might as well have been golems or statues. Not an ambush. Yet. Not until the door was closed and barred.

I clenched and unclenched my fists to relieve the tension in my fingers. *Where was Amuun? Surely, she would sit in judgment here in her own domain.*

A single long table made of polished, gold-veined quartz faced the thrones. Four lesser chairs, obviously for lesser gods, were arrayed at the table facing the dais. My fellow small gods clustered in small groups, eyeing the flanking angels, the now-seated Holy Twins on their thrones, and the knot of my little retinue in the doorway. Vayan stood behind the empty throne between Tyrr and Torr. Huund guarded the dais from one step down, regarding me with her remorseless eyes.

The goddess of the hunt invited me to the table and its seats with a wave of her hand.

Whispers burbled amongst the small gods. Coyne eyed me speculatively from a small group to my left, who were clearly making bets. My gaze slid over them all, not really seeing the rest. I ignored the ranks of golden and silvery angels along the walls.

Four chairs concerned me. One more than the thrones, obviously for weaker supplicants. While that annoyed me, it was fact. So, I put it aside. *Who should I seat? Was this an unspoken part of the challenge? What else could it be?* By choosing who to sit with me, I would show both strengths and weaknesses. The obvious advisors and the only ones present whom I could wholly trust were Z'nnek and Tourak. And I could trust myself. An enemy might give me crucial context and direction, if I do the opposite of what they recommend.

At that moment, I realized no one had brought angels but me. Notwithstanding the two ranks of the high gods' servitors waiting for us here in the inner sanctum. Huund had left her Dread Hunt outside. The small gods either lacked any, hadn't thought to bring them, or had been instructed not to. The Tales were silent about whether the small gods could raise angels. The summons to Conclave had not specified the protocol. I'd not even thought to ask Z'nnek the etiquette. Which is why I had brought one archangel—my husband—with me without thinking.

"Tourak," I said in an even tone without turning to look at him, "would you be so kind as to guard the door and ensure we are not disturbed?"

The warmth of his familiar grin on my back told me he understood. I strolled between the conversational knots of the small gods, my eyes only on Huund. Muffled footfalls behind me told me that at least Z'nnek followed me. And I hoped Hayyek did as well. The goddess of the hunt stood alone, one foot on the third step up to the dais, the other on the dais itself. *Would she take the empty throne behind her, between her younger brothers? Or was it reserved for her absent mother? Or did the empty throne send a message that no greater power was needed here?*

Behind me, the big brass-bound doors boomed to a close. Two strides and four heartbeats later, the crash of the heavy locking beam announced Tourak had read my intentions true. The high gods might need two ranks of angels to flank them in their most holy place. My single angel of death alone could bar the door against them all. I grinned to cover my anxiety.

The susurrus of conversation died as the small gods around me went still. Both of the Holy Twins scowled at me from their thrones. Vayan fidgeted as if he wished to pace, but mastered himself and remained still. Huund inclined her head in a sliver of a nod.

Leaving the leftmost chair, I pulled out the second and held it. "Z'nnek, my lord."

My king of the underworld gave me an evaluative smile. His lips twitched as if he wished to speak, smile, or kiss me. As much as I would love all three, I gazed into his wine-colored eyes and blew him a kiss. He sat without further ado as I assisted him with the chair. No harm in showing my clear allegiance and commitment any less than those on the dais.

With a half step to the right, I pulled the nextmost middle chair. The room overflowed with chilly calculation. I wanted everyone to wonder. My allies. The rest of the small gods. Most of all, the high gods. Who would I choose? And why? The entire room seemed to hold its breath.

"Hayyek?" I asked. I hoped she would be as forthright an advisor as she'd seemed so far.

Let the high gods know that I needed no war counselor here. My choice signified confidence and benevolence, though I felt neither. To my left, Z'nnek nodded approval, considering his folded hands upon the tabletop. Of course, he believed choosing Hayyek meant I would follow his strategy of conciliation. Her advice I would consider carefully.

A cool, soothing hand rested briefly on my bare shoulder and slid down my arm. Gooseflesh rippled across my skin. My nipples tightened. I told myself it was just the cold of her touch. Without other acknowledgement, Hayyek allowed me to assist her into her seat. Behind us, the conversation bloomed louder than it had been before. I ignored it, especially the under-current of disbelief I heard in Goerranu's whispers and Mawzi's grumbling.

Moving to the seat furthest from the empty chair of power, I withdrew the fourth and leaned upon the back with both hands. I schooled my face into an expression of ponderment. I wanted everyone to think I had not already decided for as long as possible. Everything in the arrangement of this room—Hells, this entire day—was too like the stupid gameboard in Araeda'h's garden. But play we all must. The key was to choose pieces of unexpected power.

Prolonging the wait, I considered each high god in turn. Vayan's glare met my blank stare. Torr's eyes narrowed, considering me as if for the first time. Tyrr feigned boredom, but beneath it was concern which caused me to wonder. Huund gifted me a slight smile when I turned to her last. We considered one another until silence fell across the throne room.

"Coyne," I called, still holding Huund's gaze.

Her eyes widened ever so slightly. *Good,* I thought. Echoes of my parents' voices across the training yard chorused in my mind: *Never do what your enemy expects.*

A huff of amazement preceded Coyne's question. "What?"

Goerranu scoffed. Mawzi growled. The other small gods quibbled about my strategy. Rather than extend my senses to parse their confusion, amazement, or acrimony, I took slow breaths and waited.

The shuffle of Coyne's goatskin boots made its way to my right. I turned my head to look at him and gave him a nod. Pale bone-white irises made his pupils look like black pips on dice. Angry dice. I'd not noticed that about him before. *Did his eyes change with his mood?* Speculation buzzed behind us. *Good. If he's angry, he'll be paying attention.*

"Why?" he demanded. "What do you want me to do?"

Z'nnek chuckled softly. Coyne's faced pinked with embarrassment. There was something there, some prior relational mystery that Z'nnek had not confided in me.

I resisted the powerful temptation to explain. *I'm preventing you from making book behind my back and tilting the odds in your favor,* I thought. *And I want your counsel so that I may do the opposite.*

But before I could speak, Hayyek said what I intended. "I believe she would like for you to sit, Coyne." But she said it with more gentility than I could ever muster, which saved him more of my sarcasm.

With another huff, he sat heavily in the chair. I slid his seat beneath the table without real effort. He wasn't as heavy as his attitude.

Brief laughter like hunting bells cut the conversation. Huund clapped her hands together once in the ensuing silence. "Thank you for not consuming all of what remains of the four of the days of our truce in choosing your advisors."

Truce it is now, eh? I wondered. *Not the genteel parley you invited me to?*

DAVE REED

She smiled like a wolf. "If you'll take your seat," she said, pointing to the empty power chair at my table, "I have a gesture of good faith that I would like to gift to you before we begin."

"No," I replied, heart beating faster with my intended challenge, giving her my crazy mountain cat grin. If she'd no intention to sit, then I would refuse on principle. "I'll stand."

CHAPTER 16

a hush gripped the hall. Huund stared at me, nonplussed. The Twins lost their scowls and settled back into their thrones, eyeing their sister with mild bemusement. Vayan finally began to pace. At my table, Z'nnek smiled at his hands—I could almost hear his amused inner monologue enjoying someone else being the object of my defiance. Hayyek sat with perfect posture and seemed to be in some sort of breathing trance, her long, thick white braid draped over her shoulder. Coyne leaned forward, elbows on the table, as if trying to distance himself from me. I wondered what odds he would be making if he had bettors to hand.

I resisted the temptation to smirk at the goddess of the hunt.

Huund glared at the empty chair to my left. "If you would—"

"Shall I summon the gift?" Torr's strong tenor voice interrupted his sister.

Closing her mouth into a prim line, Huund nodded without looking at me or at Torr.

Torr clapped his hands together with a deep sound, like a silver bell the size of the world. Overhead, the ornate ceiling began to dissolve into translucency then transparency before it was gone. Warmer air rushed into the hall, heating my face as I looked up.

More than one door after all, I thought, in awe of the magic. *Could I do that in Nethe?*

The great clear crystal dome arced overhead like an enormous lens, bringing the world far above—no, far below—into stark focus. Clouds and continents alike circled a morning's flight away. I'd always believed the sun and moons circled the world. From this vantage, the world itself seemed to turn. Nausea and vertigo battled with my will to remain unaffected as my eyes pulled me one way and my sense of weight pulled me another.

A silver-winged streak appeared at the corner of my eye. Turning my head to look aggravated my dizziness. I stumbled. My hand caught the back of Hayyek's chair. Without turning, her hand reached over her shoulder to cover mine. Cool energy flowed from her and settled me.

"Thank you," I breathed quietly to Hayyek, grateful for her unearned aid.

My benefactress said nothing, but sat quietly, her hand upon mine.

As I regained myself, I noticed Huund eyeing me speculatively with a raised eyebrow. When she looked up, I followed her gaze to the sky where Kausae descended toward us. My heart sank into the pit of my stomach for reasons that had nothing to do with my terror of the sky beyond her. Since our deaths, the arrival of my sister had been a harbinger of ill fortune.

Before Kausae had even winged her way to the floor, Huund spoke. "As a token of good faith, I—"

Torr cleared his throat loudly.

"—we," Huund continued smoothly, "give you the gift of kinship. We will return your sister from among the silver host to serve you." She smiled. "As you wish."

The knots of small gods at my back rippled with surprise like unto my own.

Hayyek's hand tightened on mine. She recognized the emotional trap at the same time, I'm sure, as I noticed the political one. Kausae was just as I'd last seen her when she'd delivered Torr's acceptance of Madra's sacrifice to his twin. Our mother had mistakenly thought to end the war with Elysia through her own humiliation and sacrifice. She had prayed to the self-proclaimed god of justice. Contrary to the tenets of his domains, Torr had agreed to her rape and demonic sacrifice upon the wheel of woe in tribute to his warmongering brother.

Z'nnek turned in his seat to regard me. "Illyria?" Concern wrinkled his face.

I stepped back and immediately regretted the loss of the comforting coolness of Hayyek's touch. My left hand fluttered at Z'nnek, out of sight of the high gods. "Leave me be," my fingers told him in the speech of birds. If he touched me, I might shatter. To his credit, he did as I bade him. I held my breath and watched.

My sister alighted, furling her silvery wings over the shoulders of her simple white robe. Her hand-and-a-half sword hung along her spine, just as it had when I last saw her. The amulet of encircled balance and scale lay in the hollow of her throat. A silver shield embossed with the same symbol adorned her left arm. She embodied the perfect servitor of justice, from her coiffed brunette braids to her simple leather sandals.

Every ounce of my will was required to maintain my outward façade of calm. Kausae did not know our mother was gone, dead eternal. She naively believed Padra served in Torr's host guarding the veil, though she had been unable to locate him—she believed Torr's lies. We'd never discussed Nerren nor how I'd mistakenly consumed his soul. Despite our unresolved issues and recent acrimony, my sister was all the family I had left in the world.

And she had been offered to me as a bargaining chip, as if she were of little value.

If I took the so-called gift, my sister would be under my protection and free to live out her eternity under the Accord in Nethe. Where she might become so distraught as to choose as Madra had. My heart clenched, but I refused to dignify that pain and submerged those memories deep beneath icy calm. I desperately wanted to keep Kausae close and shield her and enjoy her as my sister. We'd had too little time together under the sun. And she might be forever lost to me if I rejected Huund's indecent, implied proposal.

Kausae already had the eternity of her choice, serving justice She would hate me for selfishly taking it from her. She'd accused me of terrible things in our last fight in my shrine, when she'd delivered the high gods' ultimatum to me and to Z'nnek. There was no respect or love in her heart for service to the unclaimed. I was ashamed that I'd once felt as she did.

My sister bowed to Torr. "My lord." Her voice quavered just slightly with confusion.

Her god of the silver moon waved to me nonchalantly.

Kausae regarded me cautiously. She appeared uncertain as to how to address me in such a formal setting. She settled for neutral familiarity. "Illyria?"

While my sister might also hate me for not taking this one opportunity to reunite us, it felt unfair of me to even consider doing so for my own selfish reasons. I took a deep breath and tried to marshal as diplomatic a warning as I could give her. I felt the high gods watching me with intensity. My heart sank, but I steeled my resolve to play the unexpected game piece Huund had given me.

"Kausae, as a gesture of good faith in these negotiations," I began, "your lord of civilization"—I could not call him the god of justice any longer—"has offered to remand you into my service."

The abject horror on her face was confirmation enough for me. Her shoulders twitched as if she meant to whirl on Torr, but restrained herself.

"Indeed?" was all Kausae said to me, her lip curled ever so slightly in disdain. My elder sister was always more self-possessed than I.

Dreading the outcome, I walked past the empty chair at my table to stand between Huund and Kausae, giving the thrones my back. "The high gods," I said, waving a dismissive hand toward Huund and the rest, "believe it is my wish that you join me in Nethe." I stared into her eyes, desperate for her to hear my meaning: *It is my most earnest wish!*

Kausae adopted the hands folded before her stance of impatient waiting. Only a slight tremble in her fingers betrayed her nonchalance. I knew my sister. But she did not know me. And neither did the high gods.

"It is my wish that every soul determine its own fate," I intoned as forcefully as I could, channeling as much enigmatic and unpredictable goddess as I could muster. Perhaps I still did not feel like a goddess, but I knew I would never lord my power over those weaker than I against their will. "*I am not a tyrant.*"

The audience of small gods erupted in debate. I held in my smile. Huund had miscalculated her audience, thinking to use them to shame me into compliance with her agenda. Instead, I would suborn them into apostacy with the coin of personal sovereignty. In my heart, I knew that no one loved living beneath the boot of another. Kausae blinked at me. Understanding dawned in my sister's eyes. I did smile then. My sister knew me after all.

"As your fate has been given into my care," I announced, "I give *you* the choice. You may remain among the silver host if you wish." I tried not to sigh. "Or you may join my host."

Though I could not see the high gods behind me, I could imagine their chagrin and rage just from the shocked expression on Hayyek's face. And the lopsided grin that twisted Z'nnek's lips. Coyne stroked his chin, calculation creasing his brow. Though I heard Mawzi's deep, mocking laugh, I did not look beyond my table of advisors. I needed to hope a little longer that the small gods responded well to my heartfelt belief. I would need their support when my sister broke my heart. Returning my gaze to Kausae, I disciplined my face into impassivity and watched her hesitate for countless heartbeats.

Before my sister opened her mouth to make her eternal choice, Urth stepped forth from shadow at the foot of the dais to my left. A neat trick that I wanted to learn—and soon. It would beat flying here any day. Watching them slide out of shadow into spirit, bent my eyeballs a little bit. The sensation was akin to crossing my eyes for too long and trying to immediately focus on a target a furlong distant. Yet, I could see the twist of shadow and struggled to watch the magic in the making. I had observed Mawzi and Goerranu do the same. I could learn to do that.

Urth put one hoof upon the lowest step of the dais. They bowed low. The everchanging horned god addressed Tyrr in their tritonal voice of many-gendered disharmony. "The Final Beacon has been lit. She quests among the Mountains of Deylar for Preema's tomb."

The golden war god looked taken aback. "Her demons have breached the veil?"

Kausae gasped. Bemused, I glanced at her. A stoic expression covered whatever momentary shock she'd felt. She gritted her teeth in repressed anger, as she had since we were children. I wanted to ask what the beacon was and why it was final and who *she* was. But I decided it would all become clear if I just held my tongue and waited. I was content to become a bystander for the nonce. However, I couldn't resist needling my elder sister.

"Is that bad?" I whispered in mock concern.

Kausae scowled at me.

"No," Urth confessed. "They slipped almost unseen through the Levant. Many of my pickets were slain, but a few escaped to sound the alarm."

"Why did you let this happen?" Huund demanded of Urth.

Urth's hooves scraped on the marble tile as they half-turned to regard Huund with multifaceted insect eyes. "Leaving too few to guard the Levant Gate was another's choice," they said in a decidedly male voice.

Amuun's— I interrupted my lame blasphemy of the absent goddess's anatomy. *What in the ever-loving fuck are they on about?*

The spectacular rack of antlers crowning Urth's head began to morph into bull's horns. Their two massive, muscled arms spread and split into four then six shapely, feathered arms. They spread as if to encompass the entire hall.

Oh, eternal stinking excrement! They mean these thirty angels brought here to intimidate me? What could so many angels of justice and war be needed to guard?

Huund scowled at Urth before turning her baleful glare upon her brothers.

Torr intervened without a hint of chagrin. "Now is not the time for blame. We must act." The silver-haired god stood and gestured to his flank of silver-winged angels.

The angels of justice took a pace forward. Kausae made a small, jerky motion, as if she, too, meant to step forward and restrained herself at the last moment.

Torr assumed a formal posture and faced his contingent of fifteen angels. "Aid your brethren to secure the Levant Gate. Hold it against further incursion but beware of those who might seek to retreat through it as well."

"Good plan, brother!" Tyrr had risen to his feet while I watched my sister and her god. He waved dismissively to his own fifteen. "If we are fortunate, she'll be trapped, and we'll finish her endless campaign once and for all."

Tyrr and Torr spoke as one, "Go forth and secure the Levant Gate!"

Thirty gold and silver angels launched themselves out through the open ceiling through which my sister had descended moments earlier.

"I told you we should have ridden our own mounts," Tyrr muttered.

Torr scoffed. "She wouldn't hear of it."

The Twins turned to regard Huund. She hesitated and made a moue.

Whatever was afoot interrupted her game with me. And she was cross about it. Also, possibly annoyed with whatever her brothers had left insufficiently protected.

"Very well," the huntress said after several breaths. "The Hunt shall serve." With a sigh, she drew her fluted ivory horn again and blew long to summon the Dread Hunt.

When the horn ceased, Kausae asked, "My lord?"

With bemusement, Torr looked at her. "Ask your—" He waved a heavy hand at me.

CHAPTER 17

*H*ush had fallen over the high gods' throne hall. The horns of the Dread Hunt sounded in the distance. Mounted again upon hawk-winged hounds, the remaining high gods had fled with Huund leading the way. Only Urth stood on the steps of the dais now, motionless and everchanging. At the foot of the steps, I waited for the old god to walk into shadow. I wanted to see how they did it one more time. *Why did the ancient shapeshifter not grow wings and fly?*

Kausae stepped into my personal space, almost nose to nose. I mastered the urge to flinch. I'd show fear to no one, least of all my annoying kin.

"This is your fault, you know," Kausae hissed. "Always meddling. Always scheming. Always causing trouble." She didn't scowl, but I could see the tension between her shapely brows.

I looked back at her, confused. "What?" My hands spread wide of their own accord. "How is any of this my fault?"

My beautiful, spiteful sister scoffed. "If you hadn't called this Conclave, the Twins would not have withdrawn so many guards from the Levant."

"I didn't—"

"Save it," she interrupted me. "The damage is done. Just take me to the gate and make it right. The least you can do is help." She did frown then. "For once."

Stung, I tried to find the words to explain that I hadn't called the Conclave. The high gods had summoned *me*, not the other way around. Instead of explanation, what emerged from my mouth was, "I have no intention to waste time guarding some ridiculous gate to nowhere while they hunt demons without me!"

My elder sister scoffed. "Why do you always think you're the only one who can achieve anything? Do you honestly believe you can out-hunt the goddess of predators and prey?" She glared at me, daring me to say so.

As a matter of fact, I did, but saying so aloud wouldn't change my sister's mind.

Urth shuffled their hooved feet, huge hairy ungulate legs moving in a surprisingly delicate change of posture on the white marble steps of the dais. Their huge beetle eyes sparkled in the brilliant light of paradise. Instead of six arms, Urth now possessed two which they folded across their lean, androgynous, four-nippled chest as they watched me.

Urth's attention reminded me that the small gods still lingered, too. *Great, we have an audience for our sisterly dispute.* Kausae would just have to join me on the hunt, whether she liked it or not. I just needed to remain calm and remind her that, until she decided her own fate, she was under orders from Torr to obey me.

Kausae hummed with accusation at my long silence. "I didn't think so."

Irrationally, her impatience angered me. She'd always jumped to conclusions faster than I did. To me, it felt like she never actually thought about anything. My self-righteous sister always did what everyone expected: whatever she thought our parents wanted, whatever was popular with the clan, whatever the Litanies commanded. At least I considered alternatives!

I knew better than to retort. But… "I think too highly of myself?" I demanded. "Do you think your precious Torr is so weak that your aid alone could hold the Levant Gate?" *Whatever that is,* I murmured in my own mind. *Why is everything a secret?*

Kausae purpled, just as she always had when I scored—with words or swords. Her mouth gaped open and closed without making a sound, like a landed fish. I smiled with hauteur.

"You are both irrelevant children," Urth's tritoned voice rang in disharmony. The resonance of male, female, and other filled the hall. "Nothing you do will change the outcome."

I narrowed my eyes at Urth—they had backed down from me before. Kausae whirled, her wing feathers ruffling and puffing out in an avian dominance display. *Why does she feel she can defy the old gods, but not the high gods?*

Murmurs from everyone behind me were another reminder that my audience was much bigger than the judgmental old god. What Urth said might be true, but it was still rude for them to say it out loud. And I had every intention to make them eat those words.

Before Kausae or I could refute them, Urth continued, "Neither of you were conceived when last Huund drove the demon F'riida from the world. Bide here. Wait. I go to the Levant."

Kausae and I both bristled at the old god's command. *Perhaps we're not that different after all,* I mused.

I stepped closer to observe not only what I could see but also what I could feel of Urth's transition into the other realm. They reached through spirit and expertly sliced a portal with all four simian hands with an elliptical motion from top to bottom, both pairs of hands meeting in the middle. As Urth flowed back into shadow, a maelstrom of spirit and shadow swirled about them where both worlds now overlapped through the smooth doorway. To my divine sight, it seemed as if the air itself had come alive, bleeding whorls of ink drops and crystal tears. So close, I could feel the distinction. Spirit was crisp and bright. Shadow was smooth and weighty upon my skin. Tendrils of the two licked at me and then were gone with the horned old god as the portal collapsed into nothing behind them.

I could manipulate shadow to my benefit. Could I walk into shadow the same way?

I could see now that the separation between spirit and shadow was more vast here than in the realm of flesh below. Shadow was far harder to perceive here than in Nethe, where spirit and shadow blended freely deep beneath the world. I compared the eyes-crossing sensation of watching Urth descend into shadow with the feeling of drawing Grievance from within the magic of my own spirit and shadow. I knew I could change things from one into the other, and I thought I could sense how to walk between them now.

Before I could try to match these moments with the first time Mawzi had drawn me into shadow with her a week past, Z'nnek coughed behind me, a diffident noise.

It was hard to believe that I could identify the man by his effete mannerisms in only a month, most of which we'd been apart. The heart bond between us beat a slow, firm rhythm I'd felt since the wedding whenever we were in close proximity. Eternally grateful for his intercession, I smiled and turned to where he still sat at the table with Coyne and Hayyek. Kausae huffed her annoyance at my back.

The hall was still full of small gods. Why I felt responsible for them, I couldn't say—even though I knew that's why Huund had dragged them all into this. *How had she known I would when I hadn't known myself?*

Between Vayan's electrifying anal beads and Raan's waterfall of vaginal secretions, I couldn't pick a blasphemy strong enough to damn my predictability and Huund's abuse of it. Cursing used to be so simple before I began meeting all of the gods of the Litanies and the Tales. It occurred to me in that moment that there were many high gods and old from among Amuun's coterie missing from my Conclave. And countless small gods. *Where were the rest?*

I stowed away the thought to ponder when less of the world was aflame. I needed to get these gods, here in this moment, all busy first. Then I would deal with my sister. Again. Why the high gods felt we immortal nobodies could be left unchaperoned in their holiest sanctum, I would have to determine soon. *We could touch neither the magic of Saetarra nor the ambient worship of the high gods, so perhaps their other secrets could keep themselves, too?* In the meanwhile, I needed to set them all to tasks, especially Z'nnek and Tourak, while I took care of my next big problem myself. Especially Z'nnek and Tourak. The small gods could—

My brain flailed about for a moment as the utter dissimilarity between Saetarra and Nethe struck me full force. I had been thinking that I would set them to refreshments and ask my "chosen advisors" and my allies to organize a weighty discussion regarding my case before the Conclave, and the effect of the outcome upon the small gods and mortals alike. But there was nothing. In Nethe, we would have plentiful food and drink for our guests.

In Saetarra, there was only emptiness in the hall, scarcely decorated by the mostly colorless banners. There were no sideboards groaning with platters and trenchers. There were no shades to refill them or to serve those in attendance. There was no sign of life, no garden, nothing to relieve the stark white monotony. The throne room of the highest paradise was sterile and barren by comparison to my own. Neither would Saetarra let me conjure them. How had I not noticed that before?

"There's no food," I said to Z'nnek in a small voice.

He shrugged as if unconcerned by an irrelevant fact. Hayyek narrowed her eyes at me in speculation. Coyne boggled as if I were speaking a foreign tongue. Behind me, Kausae clucked her tongue to remind me to hurry up—just like Madra had to both of us when we were children. I knew very well that Huund and the Hunt gained a further head start with every passing heartbeat. My lips pressed into a firm line. Her disapproval only aggravated my frustrated helplessness.

Z'nnek asked in a wry tone, "Do you think Tourak still needs to guard the door?"

The irritating man was correct. I would have to put the truths together later when I had time to digest the differences between the paradise of the Litanies and my underworld.

I shook myself. The wrapping loops of my burial shroud dress resettled around me. My lover's understated mordancy got my brain moving. I would kiss his sarcastic ass. Later.

CHAPTER 18

*E*veryone in the glaringly white hall seemed as frozen as my mind had a moment earlier. Why the contrast between Saetarra and Nethe clenched me so I'd have to inspect some other time. For the nonce, I must dispatch my lovers and the rest so that I could drag my sister away undistracted. Regardless of whatever objections or tantrum she might throw.

"Tourak," I called, "please attend me." I smiled and held out my hand, wrist up, like a falconer might to a hunting bird.

He laughed. Pulling on his raven, he flew over the knots of small gods who stood between us. With his endearing, deep-throated buzz, he alighted upon my wrist.

"The Dread Hunt may require assistance," I said for the benefit of my audience. "As my mightiest archangel, please assemble half our unkindness to encircle the Final Beacon. If we provide a perimeter, perhaps it will make it easier for the Hunt to run down the demons that concern them so."

Kausae scoffed but didn't speak, which was fine by me.

Tourak cocked his head with a tiny shake, which was more than enough in the speech of birds to ask why we would help them at all. Then he gave me a deep, sexy squawk. Which I chose to interpret: "As you command, my queen."

Warmth thrilled through me. A month ago, being called his queen had irritated me greatly. Now, it lit my libido aflame, because I was his queen in truth. And he was my—

I smiled and decided in that moment that I would speak with Z'nnek again about making Tourak a king as well. Z'nnek had been right to offer Tourak the buzzard mantle. We three should rule Nethe as one. I should have pressed him to accept when we all married two days past. But I'd been distracted and not considered all the ramifications. And I'd taken him for granted, as I always did. Not acceptable. I would fix this. But not in this moment with so many not-yet-friendly eyes upon us.

I leaned close and kissed him. Then whispered against his feathers, "Keep the other half of the unkindness on alert in Nethe. Allow no interlopers to roam freely into our domain. Not all of our secrets keep themselves."

He looked puzzled, but we exchanged a nod, and he was gone, flying up through the open ceiling and down toward the world to gather our raven-winged host. I avoided watching him go.

"Z'nnek, my lord," I wheedled as I leaned forward across the table into his space.

He blew a mock, long-suffering sigh. His fruity breath was warm against my face. His lopsided smile made me happy. But I still needed him to be somewhere he wouldn't meddle. That was my job.

"I have a simple request." I nuzzled his stubby nose as if it was his beak. "Please convey urgency to my priestess in the matter I asked her to inveigle."

He raised both eyebrows, but not in surprise or question. I couldn't fathom what his expression meant. Perhaps in a thousand years, I'd learn his nuances. "Oh?" he asked.

"She will know the one I mean," I said. "The son of Vayan is with her."

Z'nnek scowled, a light expression of long-suffering disapproval. He'd only grudgingly helped me solve the first Memad problem I'd caused by mistake. And he was within his rights as husband and fellow monarch to worry that I'd caused another one.

"I know!" I straightened and raised both hands to forestall his objections about Memad. "But it's for the best, I promise." I winked at him, hoping he'd play along. "I'll explain everything when you return. Just please gather what she has learned and bring *it* to me." I hoped he'd understand that *it* was the Book of the Forbidden that contained Araeda'h. Or was Araeda'h. Or some other third thing that no one could explain.

"This is not how I imagined spending my honeymoon," he said.

"This is not the afterlife I'd imagined for myself, either, lover."

I laughed and kissed him across the table as he stood to show him that I'd no regrets. Then the vulture-winged lord of the unclaimed dead was gone, flying on an errand for me to retrieve a magic book. My afterlife never ceased to get stranger.

"Illyria," Kausae said in her most impatient tone.

Without turning to look at her, I held up a hand to forestall her. I knew denying her would have consequences for her choice to join my unkindness. The anticipatory heartbreak squeezing my chest would have to be soothed later. I had one more task to assign before I explained to my sister why we were not going to the Levant Gate. Whatever that was. My eyes sought out my erstwhile frenemies: Goerranu and Mawzi.

"Goerranu," I said, "my friend and ally." I held out my arms in an inviting mock embrace. And waited until she took the hint and approached close enough to whisper.

The knots of small gods began to converge as they hovered nearby, trying to appear not to eavesdrop. At least they were becoming a more cohesive group.

"We have a unique opportunity," I said, scarcely moving my lips, "to learn the secrets of the high gods and the old." There was no need to whisper, but I knew the goddess of secrets and lies couldn't resist the temptation if I pretended there was.

She nodded slightly, her doe-brown eyes never leaving mine.

I continued, "Let's use it to invite the other gods to our cause, as well as to learn as many truths beneath and behind the Litanies and the Tales as we can."

A wry smile twisted her lips. She knew something, or thought she knew something, that I did not.

"What?" I demanded.

"A tale for another time, my queen," she said in her mocking lilt. "Your instincts do you credit. You're growing into the sly goddess I knew you would be."

Trying not to feel insulted, I looked for the compliment in her statement. I chose to reciprocate. "You have been patient with me," I said more loudly, "during a trying time." I returned her wry smile. "I appreciate your loyalty." I truly hoped I could rely upon it. "And I reward loyalty."

I stepped to Goerranu's side and raised my voice for the benefit of the whole audience. "Mawzi, my sister in blood," I said, meeting the gaze of the goddess of crime, "will aid you in this. Please?"

There was a ripple of surprise among the small gods. Apparently, the blood oath I shared with her was not common knowledge. Well, it couldn't be helped now. Words were like arrows.

Mawzi gave me half a nod.

"I apologize to the rest of you gods," I said, intentionally not calling them *small gods*, "for the lack of hospitality here." I waved at the empty throne room with its sterile white decorations. "I am sure that the crisis and the unexpected urgency of matters that concern the high gods"—let them think that whatever the fuck was going on didn't concern me or them—"will pass soon. Then we shall feast." I gave a polite laugh.

Kausae groaned. I felt her step close behind me. It took effort not to bristle.

While I had their full attention, the small gods didn't respond with the mild felicity I expected of them. Didn't everyone love a feast?

"I go to assist them, to end this disturbance with due haste." I raised my right hand toward the open sky above.

Behind me, Kausae spluttered with irritation. I smiled, a bittersweet bend of my lips. One must enjoy the little victories. Even the ones that come at a dear price.

I pointed with an open hand toward the still locked and barred door. "There is much history of our world recorded here." It was a calculated leap of logic that the murals we'd passed, and perhaps hidden libraries, contained information, not propaganda. "We should take advantage of the high gods' hospitality and learn what we can of our predecessors."

Nothing. No response from my audience. *Why are they so hard to reach?* I wondered. *Did they not care that the Litanies were a lie?* Perhaps something more enigmatic and unpredictable was in order.

"Coyne," I said to the god of chance, still seated at the table behind me. "Will you give me three to one odds that I return with the trophy Huund seeks before she does?"

Kausae sniggered, acrid and bitter.

Surprise did ripple through the small gods then. Not smiles and acceptance, but it was progress. They conversed amongst themselves now in whispers. I looked over my shoulder to where my "advisor" still sat at the table. Coyne was not surprised. He was calculating. After a moment, he gave a reluctant nod. *Damn. I should've wagered four to one.* We exchanged smiles, his guarded, mine gleeful. A dull uproar began among the small gods, who were inexplicably fond of wagering, much like novice warriors attending their first summer Festa contest.

I used the opportunity to whisper to Goerranu again. "Find out why Z'nnek surrendered to these fools." I left unspoken an urging to learn all she could hanging in the air. We locked gazes until she nodded assent.

Taking many breaths and heartbeats to wrangle with my unease and looming vertigo, I prepared myself to face that irrational terror in the sky. I knew my sister. Kausae would follow, despite her annoyance and momentary disappointment with me. If I were successful, she would forgive me.

Something in Coyne's purposeful reckoning inspired me. Or perhaps I stood too close to the goddess of secrets and lies.

"Kausae," I exclaimed, "guide me to the Levant Gate!" Only the slightest guilt for my lie twinged my heart.

Without warning, I launched myself toward the upside-down world above me.

Not for the last time, I wished that there was someone I could pray to.

CHAPTER 19

Far above, the massive crystal dome of Saetarra focused the world below like a lens. Beneath my boots, the sterile paradise receded with every wing beat. As I flew up toward the dome and cloud-covered world beyond, my stomach threatened to crawl up my throat. I could not explain what squeezed my guts or why, only that it did. My eyes saw upside down and my body felt downside up. Something about being head down toward the cloud-dusted mountains above me but feeling pulled in the opposite direction threatened to scatter my wits. Clenching every muscle in my body, I willed myself onward and upward or downward or—

Whatever. I dismissed the dissonance between the downward pull of Saetarra on my body and the downward pull of the world on my eyes. Or tried to. I couldn't outrace Huund to her prey and gather the intelligence no one else would give me if I were paralyzed with vertigo. Perhaps a lifetime of forcing my body to act despite its feelings and pains served me well in that moment.

"Do you truly think to out-hunt Huund?" Kausae shouted from below and behind me.

"Again with the obvious?" I demanded.

Instead of telling her to shut up, I scanned the space before me. Off to my left, in the far distance already outside the dome, the gold and silver wings of Tyrr's and Torr's angels soared around the curve of the sun and higher toward the star-dusted veil. That would be the direction of the Levant Gate—whatever that was. A gate to one of the Hells, I supposed.

Briefly and disconnectedly, I hoped Goerranu, and her erstwhile mob of researchers, would uncover long-buried truths sufficient to overthrow the high gods. Inexplicable guilt tingled in my chest at the blasphemous thought, and I rejected the feeling. Unless Amuun and her fabled right-eousness restored what the other high gods had unbalanced, rebellion was the only path I could see. Yet I lacked so much information about how the divine world worked that the known unknowns were daunting, let alone the rest. If Z'nnek couldn't or wouldn't tell me why we must preserve the status quo, I would discover it for myself.

"Is that the direction to the Levant?" I hollered to Kausae, pointing toward the vanishing gold and silver wings and wishing she'd hurry up.

"Obviously!" she shot back.

Refusing to let her irritate me further, I watched the flight of angels of war and justice long enough to get a strong sense for where in the sky among the dancing constellations they were bound. To the place where Huund's prey—and mine—was presumably headed. That space in the sky, normally a spiraling constellation, was only a handful of glimmers now. The points of light which normally described the constellation were mostly absent. Committing the spot to memory, I directed my gaze closer at hand.

The Dread Hunt still rose toward the vast crystal lens, easily four minutes' flight in the lead. Curious about how they would exit, I kept my gaze on Huund and her angels of the Hunt. I would not follow them, not exactly. Kausae would catch up with me at her own pace, or not. As the Hunt approached the glistening, transparent material, I expected them to pause or perform some ritual to open a portal I could not see. Rather than slowing, the hawk-winged hounds accelerated. They passed through the dome as if it were immaterial. Good. I wouldn't have to aim for the same spot or figure out some new magical rite.

Flapping my own wings, my eyes tracked where their trajectory would take them in the realm of flesh while I banked in another direction on a divergent course. Not toward the Levant. Not following the Hunt. Some-where in between.

Kausae took station off my right wing. "I should've known you lied to me!" She scoffed so loudly it must've hurt her throat. "You'll never beat Huund!" she taunted. "You don't even know what prey she tracks. We can best serve at the gate with Torr."

Though I had no intention to catch Huund, I retorted, "Then tell me who she hunts."

Far beyond the Hunt and the dome, a bright red flare hung above the curve of the world. Its warning light just bled over the edge of night where Amuun's white sunlight gave way to the wan golden night lit by Tyrr's moon. I'd never seen what Huund called the Final Beacon before. The Litanies did not mention it. But the Litanies did wax eloquent about the dread hunting horns blown as they closed in upon their prey: demons from beyond the veil who'd snuck past the vigilant guard of the gold- and silver-winged hosts.

The sanguine light of the Beacon flickered across snowcapped peaks and fluffy clouds alike, which seemed to ooze crimson. I wondered if mortals could see the Beacon and guessed not. I never had, in my naïve years beneath the sun. At least now I knew for true the reason why the Dread Hunt blew its horns.

By the time we were halfway to the great lens of the dome, Kausae caught up with me and relented. "She hunts a demon, Illyria. An ancient and powerful one."

I didn't scoff or roll my eyes at her. Neither would have served any good purpose. "Of course, she hunts a demon, sister. That's what the Dread Hunt was created to do." That Litany, at least, was actually true. "Do you know anything that's not obvious?"

My dear sister bristled but didn't take my bait. "F'riida is a demoness and a sorceress who wields entropy and necrosis and poison like you wield a blade." Kausae's voice carried grudging respect that surprised me.

She paused, probably for me to acknowledge her compliment. I didn't.

After many wingbeats, she continued, "F'riida never goes anywhere alone. A score or more of powerful demons are always at her side."

"Well, that'll make the fight more fair," I boasted with a grin. I watched my sister long enough to enjoy her disbelief at my outrageous statement.

Then I focused all my attention on the rapidly approaching dome and beyond. The Hunt had spread their formation wide and looked to be approaching the Beacon in a full hunting semicircle. At the rate they flew, it might take them hours more to reach their goal. I wondered why they did not shortcut through shadow. When Mawzi and I walked through shadow, we crossed leagues in the realm of flesh in mere moments. If I could find the way myself, I could beat Huund at her own hunt.

It made sense that she didn't lead the Hunt from the Levant Gate down through shadow. Though Urth could have opened the way for them, it was a good tactic to trap a foe between two flanking forces. Perhaps the old gods alone were not powerful enough to chase the invader out of the realm of flesh? I'd not seen Urth nor the other old gods in battle. The one time I'd felt threatened by them, Urth had backed down from my bluff. Though, if I were honest with myself, I'd been backed by Mawzi, Goerranu, Tourak, and Z'nnek, all of whom Urth likely judged to be more dangerous than I.

I traced the line in my mind from where I suspected the Levant Gate hung along the veil to the place where the Beacon shone. Somewhere between, I hoped, was prey that even the high gods feared. Perhaps I, too, should've been afraid. I was too arrogant in those days to truly fear what I didn't know. A minor correction to my course aligned me ahead of the midpoint between the Levant and the Beacon, closer to the gate.

Kausae banked with me. Sighing dramatically, she continued, "F'riida works shadow as well as any of the old gods. She's of an age with Huund, at least. Maybe older than Amuun."

"That's interesting," I said with a grin. "Can Huund not walk in shadow?"

"Why would she?" Kausae sounded offended. "The high gods abide only in the purity of spirit. All of us do. Shadow is the realm of the old gods and…"

And the rulers of the underworld. Like me. I felt a twinge at my sister including herself among the pure. And not me nor my new family. I'd made my choice. It became all the more clear that Kausae would not choose me.

Her disgust should have been a warning. I left it unheeded as we approached the dome. As we closed the distance, I began to think about how little I'd paid attention to the distinction between spirit and shadow and the flesh they blended to create. Each realm was a different sort of weapon. One should always use the appropriate weapon for the fight. The small necromancies and other magics I'd been taught or learned the hard way were a blend of both. Creating with shadow and spirit felt more powerful than one or the other alone. Why would anyone eschew such an advantage? Surely the arbitrary 'purity' of one over the other was a stupid reason.

The spirit mass of the dome struck me like an anvil. Shards of intangible glass broke and grated along my innards. Triumph bonged deep and resonant, rocking my head with the impact. Grievance, sheathed in my soul, clashed with the crystal. Those shadow-worked items of power dragged on my spirit as my wings propelled the rest of me forward. So great was the shock of it that I felt no pain. Yet.

Realizing my failure and fearing the shame of a fall back to Saetarra, I mastered my panic. My wings beat to press my body against an immovable object. I quested with my senses through all of my being. Pain radiated everywhere. My wrap and the skirts of my burial shroud, too, were a blend of shadow and spirit. Z'nnek had warned me once, when he'd first watched me draw Grievance, not to work in shadow. Stupidly, I'd ignored him and not demanded an explanation of why.

Above me, Kausae had flown on unimpeded. She was just beginning to look back. Her face lit with concern and confusion. And a bit of gloating. "The high gods permit no shadow to pass their defenses, save through the well-guarded servants' gates," she called back. "Only those old gods with express leave, like Urth, can work in shadow here."

Fearing the loss of myself as much as a fall from this height, I reached for my purloined power. Before I'd understood, I'd burned so many of the memories that comprised myself in my ill-considered war with the Chosen, I'd forgotten my first meeting with Tourak and my proudest victory over Nerren. Only Tourak's generous sharing of his memories and Nerren's sacrifice of his own had restored me somewhat. I'd no wish to lose myself again.

Had I been half as smart as I believed I was, I would have slunk back to Saetarra and walked out the servants' entrance I'd first come through.

The magic of souls stolen from men and angels lay bottled upon the wine racks in my mind. Uncorking the imaginary reserves, I poured them all—all but the golden bottle containing Provax—through a magical sieve to destroy the cohesion of their memories lest they contaminate me. Now, I'd never know what Yanfak could teach me about his master, the god of war. The filtered power sluiced into the hungry, burning sigil carved in black scars between my breasts. I would thank Z'nnek, again, for the gift of that mark when next we collided. The heart-shaped mark of magical transmutation burned, glowing with heat the color of midnight. Its first purpose had been to hold my corpse together and regenerate my flesh. Now, having lain my corpse upon its burial shelf next to my mother's, I used the sigil to heal and regenerate myself from the concussion and contusions with the first draughts of other mortal's lives.

All the while, I frantically kept myself aloft by sheer force of my beating wings.

I could try the shadow trick I'd seen Urth perform, but I'd no chance to practice it. And I'd no leave from the high gods to work shadow in their realm. I'd fall back to Saetarra in embarrassment while trying to figure it out. The only option I could see was to change all of my shadow-worked items, and every part of myself that held shadow, into spirit. Transmuting all of that magic from one form to another would consume all of my reserves. Or more.

I loved Grievance and Repose and Triumph the way they were. I wasn't certain I could get them back into the same state again. In a month, I'd not much time to learn, let alone practice. I could fly back down and use the back door as I'd entered Saetarra. But that would shame me further in front of my sister and anyone else who might observe me. I'd be unable to beat the Hunt to the prey. Far above, I would wager that Huund was watching.

I screamed at myself in my heart, *Damn my ignorant arrogance!*

Using the rest of the deluge of power to transmute shadow into spirit, I pulled all of myself into the realm of spirit, leaving nothing behind—not my artifacts nor anything in the palace of my mind or body. I should have realized that if the high gods were so prejudiced against shadow, their defenses probably were as well. *That must be why Huund had walked me through the back door instead of flying through the dome. Traps within traps.*

Kausae had paused and hovered on the other side of the invisible barrier, self-righteous and haughty and something else. Perhaps sisterly concern? I doubted that.

139

I'd lost all of my momentum when I crashed into the dome. Only the continued buffeting of my wings against the wind of Saetarra kept me from stalling and plummeting back into the throne hall below. With every bit of shadow I possessed gone, my wings began to bite the air of the spirit realm again. I felt lighter, emptier, cleansed in a way I'd never felt.

I transcended through the great crystal lens without resistance.

And without my reserves of stolen magic.

CHAPTER 20

For hours, we flew toward a point I estimated lay between the mysterious Levant Gate and the Final Beacon that hung like a drop of glowing blood in the sky. The many questions I could ask Kausae tumbled over one another in my mind. *Where does the gate lead? Why do demons want to sneak through it? Why do the high gods care? Who in the Hells is Preema?*

Ultimately, none of those questions mattered in the moment. So, I reluctantly bent my thoughts toward more urgent ones. *How fast can F'riida travel through shadow?* I had to assume she was at least as fast as I'd experienced myself with Mawzi. If she'd left the world when the Beacon were first lit, I'd likely already have missed her. But if she was truly seeking something, that would take time. Of course, she would only flee the Hunt when she had no other choice but to give up her unknown goal. The Hunt must be some level of danger to her, or she'd just slaughter them or ignore them. Since she'd been driven from the world before, she must be less powerful than Huund and the Hunt feared, but perhaps craftier since she had escaped them more than once. And so was I.

"Where are you going?" Kausae demanded at long last. "The gate is that way!"

So much for accepting her place, I thought.

My nature bade me ignore her, but that seemed petty, given that she'd followed without too much complaint. So far. Leaving aside the true accusation of lying. I could've wished for less taunting, but she was my sister, after all. I relented. "Where do you go when you're playing a game of poach? Do you chase the ball?"

Kausae perked up, but looked confused. "I don't follow. What does that child's game have to do with this?"

A laugh bubbled past my control. She was precisely the type to stand next to one of the other players tossing the ball back and forth. Then try to pick off the ball as it arrived—she'd long been taller than me and the younger cousins. Until we grew into our paws. As a strategy, it never worked anyway unless the other players stood still.

"Weak players chase the ball," I said. "Mediocre players try to dominate one of their opponents." I smiled at her grimace. "I prefer to go where the ball will be in flight and uncontested." Against relative physical equals, I usually won at poach.

"That's a silly child's game." She scoffed. "That's not how anyone hunts."

"Would you like to wager something on that, sister mine?" I grinned.

As was family tradition, she huffed, but didn't take my bait.

Estimating the arrival of the Hunt upon the surface of the world and assuming F'riida would plan to be gone before they arrived, I adjusted my aim again, closer to the Levant. Now, I recognized the constellation of stars that danced around the location I presumed the high gods had gone. That must mean the flight of angels had arrived to fill in the Curl, which always pointed east. The lack of symmetricality of the pattern had never struck me as odd until now. *Who would build such a misshapen gate? Why did guarding it require such a specific moving formation of angels?*

I laughed away my absurd speculations. Kausae muttered unintelligibly, but loudly enough that I noticed she'd fallen silent long ago. *Had she resigned herself to her role? Or finally accepted that I might have a workable plan?* For the moment, I chose not to invite further scorn by asking.

Taking care not to burn my memories, I reached to pull in magic from the void around me and found only spirit here in the space between the worldly realm of flesh and the night black curtain of the veil. In Saetarra, I'd been completely unable to pull power to me. At some point, I needed to learn why. But here, I could freely gather what I needed. I fed that into my effort to search for the cross-eyed feeling and the sensibility of shadow that I'd felt when Urth appeared in the throne room.

I also searched for words in my limited primordial vocabulary to describe what I wanted as I tried to peer into the other realm. Araeda'h and Z'nnek had schooled me in the days since I'd retreated into Nethe. But little of it stuck to my mind—I was no scholar, for certain.

For another hour as we flew, the realm of shadow eluded me. Until I thought of the runes I'd once seen flicker across Mawzi's face when she'd looked out of shadow into the realm of flesh for me. A combination of nonsense syllables that felt like shadow. I formed them in my mind, in reverse, and gave them voice. Disorientation worse than the vertigo I'd felt in Amuun's realm punched me through the eyes. A splitting headache cracked from one temple to another.

With a gasp, I gazed into the dark, withered realm of shadow I'd visited once before.

"What is it?" Kausae demanded.

Seeing both realms at once, I resisted the reflex to release the magic with the pain. This portion of shadow was rolling svelte unlike the darkling forest that I'd walked through with Mawzi and Tourak. The grass looked desiccated and listless. No wind blew there. I could see for leagues. *Who had created the shadow realm this way? And why?*

A tall woman with sallow skin strode through the realm of shadow in the distance, a league and perhaps another half away. Her loose robe scintillated with many hues of sickly green, much like her flowing hair. She walked with a pair of long staves to support her, one in each hand. Several demons trailed behind her, the like of which I'd never seen or heard described in the Tales or the Litanies. They were each the size of a pony, with a squat torso sort of like a man, but with too many legs to count. Their bodies were armored with plates that shifted as they walked. Wicked pincers instead of arms and a stinger tail like a scorpion completed their visible armaments. Their flat, misshapen heads rose as high, perhaps, as the woman's shoulder.

So swift was their progress that I'd lose my opportunity to intercept them if I delayed. Having help would be better than charging into battle alone against an unknown enemy. But I was committed either way, though I couldn't've said why I was confident of gaining what I sought. I uncrossed my mind's eyes and shook my head, wishing the pain away. It didn't go.

Mawzi had needed me and Tourak to be in contact with her when she walked us into shadow. I presumed I would need the same.

"Kausae," I shouted, "take my hand!"

"Illyria, we don't have time—"

I halted my flight. The wonder of floating with no sense of falling might have distracted me any other time. I focused on blending the realms of spirit and shadow as I'd witnessed Urth do. The freely available magic ambient in the empty space around me made the miracle possible. My sense of the void around me began to thin and stretch taut as I funneled more and more of its inherent power through me. Concentrating on pulling and disrupting the smooth sensibility of shadow, I bent the bright feel of spirit toward it. It might've been easier with words in primordial I didn't know. I promised myself to pay closer attention to my lessons in the future. I demanded that spirit and shadow blend together with my will alone. But I wasn't able to peel open in a clean portal as Urth had done.

In frustration, I grunted and tore the shadow realm open with the claws of my mind.

A maelstrom of spirit and shadow boiled around me, swirling like a tornado, pulsing like a severed artery. I wanted to whoop, but maintaining my focus was more crucial. The cataract was already beginning to coagulate and seal. Both realms fought me to remain separate.

Kausae paused and reversed course, flying closer. "What are you doing?" she shrieked.

Speaking was hard while I concentrated to hold open the wound I'd inflicted upon reality, but I managed. "I see her. I'm going after her. Come with me!"

I reached out my hand for my sister. Tendrils of shadow and streamers of spirit dripped from my fingertips like midnight blood.

She recoiled from me, disgust and shock writ large on her face. Her wings flapped, lifting her back and away. "How could you?" she demanded.

My heart broke. I wanted Kausae to accept me for what I'd chosen. Shadow was part of my underworld, my afterlife. I needed her—wanted her

—to come with me. But if I waited and wasted time trying to convince her, I'd lose my chance. Before she could turn her back on me, I turned my back on her.

I gasped one last breath in the realm of spirit.

Then I plunged down into shadow. Alone.

CHAPTER 21

*M*y intrusion into the realm of shadow popped closed behind me, sending ripples through the desiccated grass. As I flew low over the subtly rolling steppe, I aimed myself for a point ahead of the group of buglike demons led by the tall woman in long, loose robes. She carried herself as if weary. My transition into this realm must have alerted some arcane sense she possessed. Her eyes tracked toward me. A mile distant, I felt our eyes lock for a moment. Then she surveyed the empty expanse around us.

With some terse, inaudible command, she halted her party and waited.

I alighted upon the sward about a quarter furlong from the group, between them and where I judged the Levant to be. My intuition told me that I had more to learn from her than the satisfaction I might gain from usurping Huund's victory. So, instead of pulling Repose on to armor myself, I kept my simple, nameless burial dress. The flowing wrap and long skirt were styled after some long-forgotten culture Goerranu had known. She'd given me one like it as a gift, and a trap. The echo of the betrayal buried within that original still rankled, but I brushed the irrelevant feelings to the back of my mind. The goddess of secrets had since re-earned a measure of my loyalty. And I adored the style.

I stood, emptyhanded. We studied one another, the demon sorceress and

I. Her long, flowing hair possessed unhealthy hues of emerald that seemed flat in the ambient sunless light of the shadow realm. Both of her staves were taller than she and carved with runes I could not discern from half a bowshot away. The hafts of the staves were crafted of something semi-translucent like amber, but not so wholesomely colored in their swampy hue.

Holding a resigned pose, the woman I presumed to be F'riida seemed content to watch me and await whatever I wished. She seemed inexplicably satisfied, as if she had at last found what she had long sought. For prey pursued by the Dread Hunt, she seemed remarkably unhurried and unconcerned. Her grotesque retinue arrayed themselves beside their mistress. Three to her left and three to her right, spaced a double arm's reach apart in a shallow arc. Crouched on their countless millipede legs, they looked ready to pounce. I wondered if they could throw the stingers that arched high above their long backs.

Did she know Huund hunted her? Had she found whatever she invaded the world to obtain? Those and a thousand other thoughts, like squirrels, chased each other around my mind.

Minutes later, I decided that if she would not speak first, I must, lest we stand here for all eternity like statues.

I raised my hands in the open W salute of highland wardens. "I am Illyria di Alamar Forte, lately become a ruler of Nethe. Some call me the Raven Queen." It occurred to me too late that we might not speak the same language. I'd not had trouble conversing with anyone from many tribes and countries since I'd lain down my mortal burdens, but F'riida—if that's who she was—hailed from some Hell beyond the veil.

A skeptical expression twisted her face. "Do you think a fake name would conceal you from me?" Her voice was a sibilant hiss, like a scaled monster sliding through the swamps of western Elysia. She tsked in mock disappointment.

Well, that's an odd response, I thought. *At least she understood me.* Aloud, what I managed to say was, "Pardon?"

"You've never been one to dissemble. Why start now?"

How could she know me? I wasn't trying to deceive her, but I recalled the other raven-haired woman from the murals in Saetarra with a face suspiciously like mine. *Perhaps she'd known that woman once?* Suspicions weren't enough for me to play this game with a sorceress older than I could guess. I was never good at lying anyway. Talking to her already felt a bit like conversing in non sequitur with Araeda'h. I hoped I would never behave that old.

I fished about for my enigmatic and unpredictable goddess persona.

"Humor me, F'riida," I said, gambling that knowing her name might nudge her to make more sense.

Her face remained an impassive mask. Her motionless warriors were unnerving.

Forcing a smile, I said, "We probably do not have long before Huund and her pack arrive to chase you from the world again. I would know what you seek." I chuckled, trying to emulate Huund's sly playfulness. "If your goal thwarts the will of the high gods, perhaps our interests align." I lowered my hands slowly to my sides.

"High gods?" She laughed then, sharp and caustic. "You've gotten careless in your ageless arrogance, Preema, if you think so transparent a ploy would stay my hand while we await your playthings. Or has perhaps senescence of the mind finally caught your frail mortality?"

She thinks Huund and the Hunt my *playthings? I wish.*

Her posture straightened, her apparent fatigue falling away along with some of her false humanity. Hiding within her borrowed form was a powerful divinity beyond the high gods' might. Her soul was suffused with the essences of scales and acid and fire. And something else I recognized all too well: the scent of bitter vengeance.

She drawled, "You seem to have healed from the gift I gave you during our last meeting. Allow me to replace it!"

"But we've never—"

The ill-colored staves whipped in circles as her wrists spun. But they were a distraction. F'riida reared back, snapped her head forward like a striking snake, and *breathed*. A cone of putrescence spewed from her unhinged jaws.

I leaped, already in motion before she spat her horrible magic. Powerful beats of my wings lifted me high above the wave of the attack. But its foul odor assaulted my nostrils. The liquid mass splashed down yards in front of her, extending to an arc well beyond where I'd stood heartbeats ago. The papery grass sizzled and burned in a wide swath where I'd been standing.

"Damn my curly cunt hairs," I muttered. A nasty trick that would be handy if I could learn it. I'd make magic my main strength someday. If it didn't kill me first.

The other demons gave me no time to study F'riida's spell, though. Their tails whipped like siege engines catapulting stingers up toward me. Furling my wings, I dropped half a dozen feet below the missiles' trajectory. My instincts and Grievance screamed at me to attack. But if I killed her, I'd never learn what no one else was willing to tell me. Instead of arrowing straight toward F'riida, I reigned in my nature and snapped my wings wide to bank away.

I dropped to the ground at the far end of the demons' arc. The closest bug was forty feet distant. From the flank, only one could attack me at a time without endangering F'riida and their fellows. Until they repositioned. For the moment, they could only come at me one at a time.

"If that's how you feel," I called with fake nonchalance, "I will not hinder your escape." *That alone will vex Huund,* I told myself, *but won't help me much.* My empty hands itched for a weapon. "I came only to parley, if you'll kindly desist."

The closest demon pounced. Its leap took it in a high arc. The monster probably expected me to launch myself in a skyward dodge again. But I'd been born to fight aground and trained that way long before I was given wings.

I stepped aside, avoiding the pair of pincers extended like spears. Its momentum carried the demon past me. The second, following low behind the first, was a surprise that nearly cost me a leg. Pincers snapped on air as I buffeted the creature across the shoulders with my wing. The demon lost its balance and plowed into the brittle grass, spitting up dirt from the furrowed ground. Knowing the third couldn't be far behind, I allowed the energy of my wing buffet to spin me. Grievance rasped from her sheathe in my heart into my left hand. Still entirely composed of spirit, her blade sliced through the scorpion tail of the second shadow creature as I whirled. With no effect. These demons were made of pure shadow.

With no time to formulate a proper oath, I roared with wordless frustration.

Then the third was upon me.

The sky would be no refuge from enemies with ranged attacks. I hugged my wings about myself. I dove toward F'riida to make it harder for her minions to attack me without harming their mistress. Rolling as low as I could, I tried to avoid the pincers and tail. But not low enough. A hard blow hammered the wing covering my left shoulder, tumbling me off course. I grunted with the painful impact but focused on drawing shadow from the withered land around me. There wasn't much, but I made it mine.

As I recovered my feet just out of sword reach, F'riida grinned at me and struck, whirling both staves in blurring circles that buzzed in the air.

The demonic sorceress gave me no time to reforge Grievance with the shadow-kissed edge I'd first created not so long ago. Reflex alone saved me. And perhaps chance. My blade slashed back and forth in the defensive arcs anyone would use with a sword against a wooden weapon. Miraculously, the spirit I'd transmuted Grievance into clashed with F'riida's staves. Her weapons were made of spirit and shadow, like mine usually were. Unfortunately, my blade didn't shear through them as if they were wood. My strokes knocked her spinning guard open as she struggled to recover the long weapons without being disarmed.

Instead of striking through that opening, I jammed the pitiful amount of shadow I'd drawn into myself through my blade. I'd no time for finesse or detail. I needed to be able fight both spirit and shadow, so I used what little I'd drawn to sharpen her to a blended edge. Wicked midnight gleamed along the length of Grievance once more.

"I'd rather not fight you," I said in as light a tone as I could manage as I stepped back out of reach of F'riida's longer weapons.

I casually swiped Grievance left-handed through the pincers of the third demon as it attacked. It had recovered quickest and moved to threaten my side. This time, Grievance did her grisly work. A pair of claws of the size of bear paws flopped to the grass in a spray of viridian ichor. An unnatural, keening wail pierced the air. With only my peripheral vision to guide my thrust, I buried Grievance in its armored torso. My sword hummed with satisfaction.

I whispered the necromantic incantation, "Your life is my life." The primordial words vibrated the shadow-kissed air about me.

The demon's pained shriek died as I stole its soul. The insect-like creature bore nearly as much power as the war angels Yanfak and Yunfak. I'd taken their souls in my war against the Chosen. I'd learned the hard way how to cage such a monster. My wineskin metaphor was better tutored and my magical imagination stronger now than before. With barely a struggle, I stored away the fresh soul in the wine cellar of my mind while holding F'riida's gaze. The corpse crumbled to ash around Grievance and littered the steppe at my slippered feet.

"When did you take to the sword?" F'riida inquired with mild interest, as if we sat at tea gossiping like two indolents. She made twin circling motions with her staves.

The misshapen scorpion beasts skulked into a new semicircle and began to close.

"Shall we parley?" I asked, pretending my heart wasn't in my throat and pounding harder than it had when I'd faced Baal. I whirled Grievance in a flourish, shifting her to my right hand. I slid into the stance of aggressive negotiation and raised my blade into high guard.

"Hold!" F'riida called in a sharp tone.

Her five remaining demons froze obediently. She eyed me with renewed curiosity.

"What do you propose, slayer of my matriarch?"

Well, fuck me with both fists, I thought. That made it easier to understand why she didn't hesitate to try to murder me. I'd've hated anyone who killed my mother. Even if it was me. I put that painful realization aside to examine later. Much later.

I forced a nonchalant smile. "Tell me what you seek here and, perhaps, why the high gods fear you so."

Suspicion clouded her face, but she must have reached a rapid conclusion. "Let us pretend, then, that I believe you have become so weak as to parley," she said with a devious smile. She leaned on her staves. "I seek you."

Electric surprise shot through me. I lowered Grievance to my side and stood straight.

With a snicker, she continued. "More correctly, I sought your corpse."

She shook her head in mock sadness. "Somehow, I knew you'd not had the decency to crawl into a hole and die."

Before I could inquire further, she asked, "Why did you hunt me?" Her alien, yellow-green eyes narrowed as she watched my face for something I couldn't fathom.

"As I said before, I wished to know what you seek and why." I tilted my head in thought. "Though I would remember if I'd slain your matriarch, I can appreciate your motive for seeking me if you believed that true."

"It is true!" she raged. "I watched her die in the torment, just as I watched my daughters wither and succumb to your spells! When we last met, I returned the favor." Her face twisted in a vindictive snarl. "A pity you recovered." She sighed, heavy with melodrama. "No matter. I'll remedy that shortly."

Somewhere out of my view, arrows buzzed through the air. The hateful whirring noise triggered my instinct to armor myself. I pulled Repose on, faster than thought, hunkering down. The heavy plate and chain clanked and rattled as I dropped into a comfortable, square fighting crouch. My left shoulder and wing ached where I could feel the contusion growing. I suffered the embarrassing realization that I lacked a helmet. *Diddle my tender sphincter,* I cursed silently. *Why in the fiend-humping Hells is it always archers?*

F'riida's demons sprouted feathers. The brown-fletched arrows were too numerous to count. No horns had announced them, but…the Dread Hunt had arrived.

CHAPTER 22

The demon sorceress and I stood alone on the withered grass of the shadow steppe. She stood without a care. I still hunched in a defensive crouch. Left and right, the big scorpion-tailed demons writhed on the ground. Their deaths were noisy, but no more grotesque than any others I'd witnessed. The energy their souls represented would be wasted, but I chose not to move to consume them and open myself to attack by either F'riida or the Dread Hunt. There wasn't even a listless wind in the shadow realm to blow away their ashes.

No arrows had struck F'riida, which seemed odd. I was grateful the Hunt's legendary aim was true. None of the hawk-fletched volley had hit me, either. Not trusting F'riida to refrain from attack but needing information, I snapped a look over my shoulder.

Huund stood unarmed almost a furlong away, one hip cocked to the side, watching us from the center of a broad hunting chevron a single rank deep. Arrayed beside her, the Dread Hunt stood impassive. They held the great ironwood bows described in the Litanies, arrows nocked at low ready. With a trivial command, Huund could have killed us both and solved two problems with one barrage.

Why didn't she? She clearly wants me eliminated. Would be easy to blame a simple mistake. What's her new game?

F'riida's laugh was like a cup of coffee from desert Cimmaron, small and dark and thick and bitter. Suppressing a shiver, I glanced back to be certain she hadn't moved. Leaning on her overlong staves, the sorceress feigned unconcerned weariness again.

Her rich voice filled the empty grassland. "Well met, again, little demi hound. I see that you have replaced the hunters you lost in our last meeting."

Demi? Demigod? Did that mean Amuun wasn't Huund's mother? Or a mere mortal her father? I would need a college of scholars to separate the lies from the truths in the Litanies.

Her belittling Huund amused me, but either the sorceress was bragging, which didn't seem like her style—at least not that I'd seen in our limited interaction so far—or she was more powerful than all of her dead demonic allies combined. *She'd killed a nontrivial number of the Dread Hunt during their last meeting?*

Huund's posture tightened, which confirmed the truth for me, but her training ground voice carried no hint of being provoked. "To your misfortune, your retinue is not so large nor powerful now as then. A pity."

There was no way I could shift my stance enough to see both my adversaries at once, but I tried. My gaze still had to whip back and forth to remain vigilant to attack. Neither F'riida nor Huund seemed to pay me any mind, which was mildly irritating. *What does a goddess have to do to be taken seriously around here?* If I hadn't wanted information from her so badly, I might have tried to take advantage of F'riida's distraction, since she refused to parley.

I did take advantage of the opportunity to reforge Grievance and Repose, using the soul of the demon I'd taken, into an alloy of spirit and shadow against the resumption of hostilities.

Feigning laziness, Huund drawled, "You may end this at your leisure, Illyria." She mocked a yawn. "I concede this trophy to you."

F'riida truly looked at me then. Her intensity gazed more deeply than anyone but my lovers had before. I'd felt inspected by many mortals and no few gods, but never with such intimate scrutiny. With an effort, I simply stood, without guile or attempts at self-protection. I'd not come to kill her, but to learn from her. The enemy of my enemy.

Huund had set me up to die easy if I behaved as I always had. This time, I meant to surprise us both. I intended to escape this trap through unexpected and peaceful means.

The old sorceress whispered, "You are in truth not Preema." Not a question. "Preema was never so weak." She scoffed at me. "You aren't even strong enough to be her shade."

"What are you waiting for?" Huund demanded.

Parallel strikes of both of F'riida's staves swept toward my injured left side. With Grievance low in my right hand, it was all I could do to dodge. Kicking myself up into a horizontal roll to tuck in between the long, sickly green weapons, I furled my wings and wrapped them tight about me. But not fast enough.

The lower staff clipped the tip of my already injured wing. I felt the furthest pinion joint dislocate. The impact spun me faster until I bit the dirt.

"Flaming cunt pust—" I grunted as crunched into the dry grass.

Knowing I'd need space and time to regain my feet, I swept Grievance low at her ankles without a glance. F'riida must've leaped over the blade or backed away with surprising speed. By the time I levered myself to a fighting crouch, her staves were already arcing back toward me from both sides in a pincer strike.

"I don't want to kill you," I huffed as I ducked beneath the staff to my right.

"Indeed." She chuckled.

Grievance leaped to add her weight and power to the staff's movement. Both ill-colored weapons careened into one another and rang with a sound like glass bells. The staves were jostled out of F'riida's hands, falling toward the unfriendly steppe. I watched them fall, amazed at how easily I'd disarmed her.

When I looked back, the sorceress had vanished. In her place was a rapidly expanding mist of verdant luminescence. *Well, un-fucking-lubricated Hells.* She'd taken a cowardly exit. *If she doesn't have a head, I can't cut it off.* I ignored the distraction of the cloud. *Where could she hide on the open steppe?*

Miles in the distance and through the dissipating mist, a squadron of winged figures appeared on the horizon. Their wings scattered hints of silver and gold from the flat, colorless light of the shadow realm. I knew better than to let them distract me from this duel. F'riida had to be somewhere nearby. Torn between whether to launch into the sky or hit the ground, I split the difference and spun Grievance two-handed in a waist-height arc.

Rotating all the way around, my blade connected with nothing.

The expanding mist enveloped me then in a pungent cloud that stank of bitter almonds. Where the moist embrace kissed my skin, it burned like a pyre. Crushing my urge to inhale deeply and scream, I tried to leap into the sky. Flapping my wings only spread out the surface area of the viridian fire searing my skin. The stench of scorched feathers blended with the biting odor of the cloud. The weight of the heavy mist dragged me down. The harder I strained against it, the faster the agony spread. I cut back and forth in all directions with Grievance in powerful double-handed strokes. To no effect. Panic rose up to choke me.

"Rest," F'riida's disembodied voice purred. "It will be over soon."

My only thought was absurd. *Now I won't be able to collect from Coyne.*

In despair and agony, I dropped to one knee and hugged myself. Releasing my wings to reduce the attack surface of my body was a terrible mistake. Drawing the magic of my wings back into myself brought the green bite of the mist inside my skin. The tiny pains of my damaged wing and shoulder didn't even register. I rattled my brain looking for a way to fight her. But I was dissolving from the inside and out.

I couldn't think. I couldn't plan. I couldn't fight.

All I could do was suffer. And remember.

I was as helpless as I'd been when I'd lain myself down upon the wheel of woe at Provax's mercy. The bright memory of pain flashed through the scars on my forearms and shins where the Elysian Foreign Legion had nailed me to the wheel. I'd expected the rape and humiliation Provax had intended for me. My only recourse had been to taunt him into killing me faster. Until he'd exposed himself and I'd remembered his one vulnerability when he'd rubbed it against my face.

This fresh pain intensified so much that I did try to scream then. Inhaling the foulness only brought the agony deeper into my chest. Gagging, I barely managed a hoarse cough which mangled my concentration. I felt myself coming apart.

F'riida didn't have Tyrr's invulnerable skin. But still, I couldn't bite the mist. That would only bring her power deeper into myself. She had already enveloped me, inside and out. Fighting her was like wrestling a larger, more powerful, and slipperier opponent. She covered more of me than I could ever cover of her.

But I didn't have to.

I could surrender. Oblivion in death eternal beyond this anguish would be a mercy. Give up everything I'd fought for and lost. My family was gone. Padra's soul broken on the wheel and eaten by Tyrr's golden eagle to feed the greedy god. Nerren accidentally consumed by my raging need for revenge and to restore many of my lost memories. Madra swallowed by despair deeper than the underworld. Kausae driven away by my choice to embrace an afterlife I hadn't wanted but one that repelled her. I could be free. My kinfolk had a steward now in Conseca and protectors in Memad, Tourak, and Z'nnek.

Z'nnek. He had surrendered to end the Little War. *Hadn't he?*

Even according to the Litanies, he'd lost nothing he valued. Exile from the sun-kissed lands was no hardship for the lord of the underworld. *Had he embraced that? To win by losing?*

F'riida was destroying me. Again. In the past month since my murder, I'd lost my memories—the essence of who I was—to carelessness and unrestrained vengeance. I'd consumed myself to power my war against the Chosen of Tyrr. I had been right to be enraged. I should be enraged now. There were still wrongs to be righted. The high gods had not been brought to justice. Tyrr and Torr and Huund must be made to answer for their flagrant disregard of their mortal worshippers. If I had nothing else left in the world, I would always have that.

In that moment, I understood the cold, remorseless wrath of the Thirteen keepers of Baal and Raam and Sett. I didn't know how they'd been wronged, but I didn't need to know the details. I felt them. A frigid gale blew through my soul, extinguishing the firestorm for just a moment. But it was enough.

That moment of clarity was all I needed. The demon sorceress had given herself to me. She was closer than Provax's cock had been against my face. I didn't even need to bite her to pierce her skin.

I knew less than a handful of necromantic spells. And I only needed one.

The simplest one I'd learned. The first and least that did nothing but leech life from whatever I touched.

I stretched out my hands to grasp the mist.

Unable to shout my defiance, I mumbled, "Your life is my life." The primordial words of the spell rumbled the mist around me.

Reaching out intuitively with my magic, as I'd done so many other times to steal a soul, I began to pull F'riida's essence into mine.

That's when the real fight began.

CHAPTER 23

*G*one were the desiccated steppes of the shadow realm. I retreated into my most treasured memory. Overhead, the sky of my mind shone with an azure so crisp and sharp it might cut diamonds. Brilliant white snowcaps speared up toward the midmorning sun. I stood on the cliff above Alamar once more in the place where I'd first beaten Nerren in a childhood climbing race. Where I'd consumed the entirety of Nerren's soul just days ago. Regret panged my heart. I'd never share confidences or be able to ask advice of my elder brother again. He would've known what to do now. I only had the memories he'd sacrificed to me, for me. I had to find a path forward for myself, alone.

Down below, my memory of kinfolk and clansmen long gone went about their customary early day business. Pleasant hickory smoke from chimneys wafted on a light breeze coming in off the plains of Elysia. The distant scents of breakfast greeted the brilliant morning sun. I didn't come to this place in my mind often. I wasn't sure why I was here now.

A huge, heavy shape cut the sun, casting a cold shadow over me. Fear beat down upon my self-confidence. Had I not recently endured terror inflicted by a demon lord, I might have broken and run. Still, it took an effort of will not to shiver and piss myself and instead to look up.

Massive bat-like wings seemed to cover the sky. A sinuous, scaly body with four clawed feet tucked close soared past. The demon banked and rose on the thermal that flowed up the cliff from Alamar below, leading with her long neck outstretched. Yellow ivory fangs as long as Grievance jutted from gaping jaws. She was so huge she could swallow me whole. Her spiked tail alone could lay waste to a phalanx or a building.

F'riida. I'd been afraid that she was more than mortal. *Why hide such power?*

The monstrosity screamed. My ears hurt from the concussion. I gritted my teeth against the pain. I'd dragged my doom into my soul. I could think of no way to fight such a demon. Not in that form. Not in the open. Not on the ground. Perhaps I could outmaneuver her in the air, assuming my weapons could even pierce her scaled hide. I couldn't fight her and win. My only path to victory was through the unfamiliar territory of peace.

Even as I was dying of her poison, I didn't want to kill her. Yet.

I'd meant to trap her in a metaphorical wineskin as I'd done with other powerful souls. But I'd no hope of doing that now. Her massive essence defied me. She was treating my mind, my imagination, as her own personal stomping ground. That meant I needed to control the battlefield. But how could I turn the tables?

Overhead, she inhaled with a huge sucking sound. Another scream, or worse, would ensue. I'd no desire to endure another. The safest place I could think of leaped to mind.

Imagining the entry to that familiar, comfortable memory, I manifested the archway in front of me. Shoving past the heavy purple curtains, I strode through as a gargantuan gurgle erupted behind me. A familiar foul stench stole my breath as burning agony splashed across my back and legs. The pain was so great that it only hurt in the abstract way that told me it would be unbearable soon. Fighting against shock, I stumbled deeper into the drawing room where I'd first fucked Z'nnek and Tourak. The gilded furniture of the salon was overstuffed and upholstered in rich shades of bronze and orchid, exactly as I'd first seen them. Plentiful candles bathed me in their warm glow.

I struggled to master the impending pain. I needed to keep it walled off and focus. I recognized its cause as a toxic blend of acid and poison. At least in my own imagination, I had enough awareness and control to understand it, but I'd no idea how to counteract it. My instincts raged at me to close the smoking curtains and shut out the mountaintop memory, to pull away from where my attacker dominated the sky, to hide. My deepest, primordial fears yammered at me to go anywhere else, be anywhere else. I resisted the completely natural urge to run and cower. I was dying. Distantly, I could feel my body crouching on the steppes of the shadow realm, succumbing to the noxious mist.

I desperately needed F'riida to stop her attacks and converse with me.

Here in my sanctum, she could not fit in her massive, winged demon body. I hoped she couldn't just destroy my carefully conjured illusion and claw me out. I needed her to listen, to dialog. Or I'd have to find a way to capture her or destroy her before she slew me.

"Truce!" I shouted through the archway past the sizzling hangings. "Talk to me, Hells damn you!"

Outside the smoldering curtains, a puddle of acid burned grass and stone. Over it, the chilling shadow loomed, blocking the sun. A great jaundiced eye with a pale green iris and a pitch-black, star-shaped pupil peered through the archway.

Her voice was as big as her nature and rumbled the ground. "Why should I bother with you, dying child?"

I wanted to sit on the overstuffed divan to show my nonexistent nonchalance, but that would aggravate the growing burn along my entire back and legs. I forced a smile past the rictus contorting my face. "There is no benefit to you to slay me, goddess."

She snorted. The pool of acid rippled in the wind of her breath. "Neither is there benefit to permitting you to live. You are inconsequential."

Lifting an open hand, with difficulty, to refute that statement. "On the contrary. I can aid you to gain what you seek."

When she didn't respond immediately, I plunged ahead. "I, too, want the truth. Preema is bound up in that truth that the high gods deny me. But—"

"They shan't deny me!" she roared.

The foundations of my mind shook. Somewhere at the edge of my awareness, my body was withering. I was almost out of time.

"Then why were you fleeing toward the Levant?" I challenged. "If you could have stormed Saetarra or Avaala or Nuuria, you'd not be skulking about in shadow!"

The monster growled, narrowing her great eye dangerously.

Rolling forward on bluster and desperation, I said, "You haven't found what you wanted in thousands of years." Angering her was a risk, but I was out of options. "You're tired, F'riida. Your quest for vengeance has gone on far beyond endurance. With my aid *and* the access an apparent defeat would grant you, we can learn the truth and find a way to end the lies."

Too many heartbeats passed as she considered. Better than being melted to death on the spot, but the raging pain outside and within threatened to consume me. All I could hope for was that oblivion would free me of it if F'riida did not see reason. I was gambling on my assessment of her bone-deep fatigue and her inability to single-handedly defeat the high gods and the Hunt. Getting rid of the monstrous demon lurking in my soul would have to be tomorrow's problem.

"What do you propose?" she rumbled at last.

I heaved a deep breath, hoping against hope to avert death and end my own pain. "Let us show them I defeated you. Relinquish your mortal form. Hide here inside me. Then I can demand a place among them as one who conquered that which they fear most. Let us use the secret trouble in paradise to our advantage."

F'riida scoffed, which blew smoke from the purple curtains. "Among the Seventeen?"

I didn't know who the Seventeen were, so I just kept going with my impromptu plan. "Amuun may not be in control any longer." Inspiration had been niggling at my hindbrain since I'd first met Huund. There was something there I'd ignored but provided an opportunity. "I will seduce Huund to gain access to the secrets they keep. She already fancies me," I lied. I hoped I'd read our conflicted chemistry correctly. She held some appeal. And she certainly was vain about her superiority. How hard could it be to tumble the huntress?

"You are a bold one, little raven." She sighed like a hurricane dying. "Very well. How do we convincingly fake my demise?"

Relief flooded through my ravaged soul. "First, you have to stop killing me."

CHAPTER 24

I became aware of screaming as the agony of the mist faded and I resumed awareness of the nameless shadow realm. *These shadowy steppes need a name*, I decided. I'd no idea what to call them. Yet. The Litanies held that they were some part of the veil separating the mortal realm from the Hells. I wasn't so sure that was true. Hells, I couldn't tell if anything was true.

My immortal body still crouched where I'd been hugging my pain and waiting doggedly to die. I surveyed my boring, grass-covered surroundings. Much had changed whilst I wrangled with the demoness.

Gingerly, I stood, enjoying the bright feeling of the absence of pain and not dying.

"Illyria!" Kausae hovered beyond the edge of the now-harmless-to-me mist.

Her yelling was the bulk of the noise my pain-fogged mind had failed to grasp until that moment. Other sounds I chose to ignore mingled together in an annoying burr. The sisterly concern that twisted her pretty face touched me. Perhaps I would have time to savor that memory later. Much later, because behind her, Tyrr and Torr loomed with a handful of their angels. Urth skulked behind them, which struck me as odd, obsequious behavior for an old god reputed in the Litanies to be of immense power. I wondered if Huund and the Hunt had closed the distance to my rear or still watched from afar. I resisted the urge to look.

I flexed muscles and rolled my shoulders. Repose rattled and clanked as she was wont to do when I moved. My armor comforted me in its midnight steel embrace. The agony was miraculously gone. Under F'riida's tutelage, I'd adapted my sense of myself to resist the necrotic combination of acid and poison that comprised her insidious attack. Her various forms were frightful and overwhelming. In time, I would steal them and master them for myself. But. For the nonce, I was grateful to count her a reluctant—if temporary—ally. Perhaps all a goddess could ever hope to have were lovers and frenemies. Sometimes they were the one and the same.

Together, we'd imagined for me something like the scales that covered her massive demonic form. Her refusal to teach me the massive demon form grated. She explained, in frustratingly simple terms, what I needed to do, but asserted that she could not change my self-image overmuch…without destroying my will in the process. I accepted the limitation and irritation. Painstakingly, scale by scale, I imagined covering myself with them.

Though I was on my feet and no longer being digested, I kept my concentration inward. Dealing with Kausae would have to wait a few more heartbeats.

I am ready, I told F'riida. Reaching out, I mimed the effort of gathering the mist around me into a tight embrace. I had to pretend to do what she was actually doing.

"I will consume every bit of you very slowly if you betray me, raven girl," the untrusting bitch rumbled deep in my soul.

But she shaped the sour green intangibility around me into a simu-lacrum of her mortal form as if she had coalesced from the green ether. The mist condensed into the new shape until the air between me and Kausae was once again clear. F'riida's false body thrashed like a living mannequin in my grasp about her throat. Her massive soul still reclined within my happiest childhood memory atop the cliffs of Alamar.

I shook the fake demoness, playing to the audience of the Hunt and the high gods. And my sister. The sickly viridian hair of the feebly struggling mannequin whipped back and forth.

Grievance lay at my feet like a forlorn, forgotten toy. I simply reached toward my blade and she leapt to my hand, hungry and ready. Holding her again—after so near-death an experience—brought joy to my heart and lit my face with a triumphant smile.

"Your life is my life!" I shouted the primordial curse as I drove Grievance through where I presumed the heart of the mannequin might be, if she were truly mortal, not a construct.

In my mind, F'riida huffed with a mixture of amusement and disdain. *"You are so dramatic, child. Just as your ancestor was. But I am curious. Where did you learn the most powerful spell in all of necromancy?"*

Pressing my lips together seemed the wisest course of action, since I'd no idea what to say in response. I'd understood from Z'nnek that he'd only taught me the simplest of all necromantic spells, though still as forbidden as any other magic. I concentrated on control of my spell, the vampiric drain of magic from the pretend sorceress in my death grip. The mist-induced pain radiating through me faded behind my deep focus.

F'riida's false body arced into a spasm and screamed a thin, inarticulate dying wail.

Yeah, I'm the dramatic one, I thought aloud in my shared memory haven.

From within, where she still crouched at the top of the cliffs of Alamar, I felt the great demonic soul give an amused, rumbling shrug.

The power I drained from the pitiful simulacrum by my spell was almost enough to overwhelm me. Lest I destroy the illusion entirely by consuming too much, I only took enough to refill my reserve and half again more. The excess magic lay next to Provax's untouched soul in elegant emerald wine bottles on the racks in my mind. I wondered idly if there would be memories in those bottles of F'riida's essence.

Before the frail shriek could fade, I released my grip on her throat and yanked Grievance from her body. With a quick spin, I slung my blade sidelong through F'riida's neck. Deep green ichor sprayed the dead grass in a glittering fan. Her severed head bounced and rolled several feet toward the dropped staves. The shocked expression on her mannequin face was a nice touch. Her death was somewhat as I'd imagined. What might have been my last resort to save myself had my attempt at diplomacy failed.

F'riida's false corpse collapsed to the steppe.

Sheathing Grievance in my heart, I strode over to the staves and bent to collect them. Intending to mark the weapons using the fluid from the open wounds of the burns I knew must cover my body, I was surprised to find myself actually covered in a sheen of light emerald scales instead of raw wounds and blisters where my skin had been. The imaginary protection had manifested in truth. Unasked, the demoness had loaned me her healing aid as well—I knew because the pain was gone. I would examine that suspiciously in the near future. Not knowing what to think about it, I stooped to stick my finger in the viridescent ichor oozing from the stump of her severed neck.

The raven rune had been the first I'd learned, almost by accident, when Z'nnek had offered me his first courting gift. I painted it across both staves in the sickly green blood before I pushed my will into possessing the magical artifacts. "You are mine."

"*That was unnecessary,*" F'riida complained. "*I spent a century making each.*"

Hush, I thought at her. *I'm selling the conquest.* The unnatural sheen of the weapons darkened to a shade of midnight that matched my aura and all the souls I claimed as my own. I was careful not to think upon any other intentions, lest she know my mind too soon. *Would you rather I leave them to be taken by the others?* I asked.

Her silence was enough acknowledgement.

We need to do something with your corpse, lest Huund—

A nova of silver brilliance exploded in my face. The tingle of unfamiliar magic washed over me. F'riida growled in unexpected pain. Flash blind, I blinked away purple afterimages and shook my head, barely able to see. Nothing hurt me, but F'riida writhed and huffed in the afterglow of the unfamiliar silvery power.

"*She thinks she can banish me so easily?*" F'riida roared.

Kausae screamed, "Release my sister!" and attacked.

Parrying frantically with two staves clutched in one hand, I batted her sword away. "Kausae, what are you doing?"

Grievance wailed at me to be drawn again and test herself against Kausae's long, hand-and-a-half claymore. I ignored the thirsty blade in favor of the staves I already held. Despite all her faults, I'd no wish to slay my sister.

For many wild heartbeats, my sister and I cut and thrust, parried and riposted. Her eyes were wild and enraged. I could imagine what drove her. She was beyond reason. I knew I had to change tactics.

Slay her and be done, hatchling, F'riida commanded. *We have an agreement to attend.*

I could kill my last remaining family in the name of expedience. That would satisfy my erstwhile ally and my own urgency. But I would be forced to live with yet more regret for eternity. That's not the sort of goddess I wished to be.

"No!" I yelled at my sister, slapping aside another vicious stab. "I am not possessed!"

Kausae grunted in disbelief and redoubled her attacks with ferocity. "I banish you!"

A massive silver wave burst from her words and blasted through me. Again, I felt nothing. But F'riida wailed and shook and thrashed inside me. That definitely seemed like a spell I should learn.

Giving ground, I continued to allow Kausae a chance to pause. But repeating my assurances had no effect. F'riida snorted and let me feel her aggravation and frustration as claws digging into the bedrock of the cliffs above Alamar.

Switching one staff into each hand, I began to use one for offense and the other for defense. Kausae's claymore, like Grievance, was heavier and faster than the long staves. But her blade lacked the reach of the staves and could only be in one place at a time. I focused my efforts on keeping her blade busy and away from me with one staff while I repeatedly pounded her sword arm and hand with the other. Disarming her seemed like the best option to get her to listen to me. Her attacks slowed and weakened. My hopes rose.

Until she intentionally dropped her own sword.

Kausae produced a dagger from her belt that I'd not noticed before. "Illyria! I know you're in there." She held the small blade to her own throat. "You have to fight her. I know you won't let me die."

The small blade was the personal knife Madra had carried my whole life.

My sister might be melodramatic, but she wasn't wrong. I just had no idea how to convince her that I wasn't possessed. The wounded demoness in my mind sat up with renewed interest in my ridiculous family drama.

167

"Kausae!" Torr thundered. "Don't! I command you to finish her!"

The ancient god of civilization cares for her, I realized. *We can use that.*

"Interesting," F'riida purred. *"Perhaps your ploy for emotional manipulation has merit after all, hatchling. Mortals always suffered such weakness. Their constructs seem to as well."*

Still pressing the family heirloom to her throat, Kausae turned abruptly to face the high god she had once—technically still—served. "What do you care?" she shouted. "You sold me like a prize goat to placate my sister!"

Disdain colored Torr's expression. The silver-haired god waved dismissively in my direction. His armor creaked with the motion. "That's not your sister anymore."

Inspired, I released Repose and swapped my armor for my burial wrap and skirts in less than a heartbeat. At least there was one advantage to being a dead goddess. I was certain during her life that my sister had wished she could change her wardrobe as often as she changed her mind. I waited for the span of four breaths before I interrupted the stare-down between my sister and her former master. That pause let me see that F'riida's false corpse was bubbling as if being consumed by acid. At least the demoness was thorough.

"Kausae," I pleaded. "Look at me." I spread my arms wide and dropped the staves.

She turned as the long weapons thumped onto the grass. Silver ichor bled from a shallow wound beneath Madra's knife. Tiny drops glistened like crystal tears as it dripped from her elegant fingers.

Slowly bringing my bare arms out in front, I said, "I am still your sister." I brushed my right hand along my left arm, scraping the scales away as if they were caked mud. Making certain she understood, I did the same for my other arm and scrubbed the scales from my face. "I stole her form," I declared, "to save myself from her venom."

"It was a poison," F'riida insisted with mild irritation, *"not a venom."*

Because the detail was irrelevant in the moment, I ignored the pedantic demon sorceress and willed my sister to believe me. The tiniest shake of her head denied me.

What else could convince her? I wracked my brain, but all I could focus on was the dagger pressed into my sister's immortal flesh.

168

Realization dawned. "That's Madra's dagger."

Kausae's eyes narrowed just a touch, but she was finally listening.

"I remember the first time you stole it." Genuine laughter bubbled up from my childhood. "You were so frightened when Madra discovered it gone that you helped everyone look for the stupid thing." I chuckled. "Did you ever figure out why she had the entire household turning the manor upside down to find it?"

Kausae lowered the blade but clutched it so tightly her knuckles were white. "Padra gave it to her on their wedding night."

We shared a nostalgic smile for simpler times we'd never have again.

"It's truly you?" she whispered.

I nodded. "Aye."

We collided halfway in the space between us, wrapping each other into a ferocious hug that spun us around. As we turned, I witnessed the other half of my audience. The Dread Hunt waited and watched a dozen paces away. Huund's face was a masque of bitter confusion and something else.

Is that envy? I wondered. *Or jealousy?*

Behind me now, Torr scoffed. I imagined the high god was disappointed that he no longer held sway over my sister. Which made what I must ask her to do all the more necessary.

Squeezing her tightly, I whispered into Kausae's ear, "I really don't want you to, but—"

She stiffened, but I clung to the embrace until she relaxed.

"You must choose Torr."

CHAPTER 25

I strode into the high gods' throne room for the second time with none of the trepidation I'd felt the first go round. My position here was reversed in ways I hadn't even considered yet. Making the high gods await my pleasure hadn't been my intention, but I didn't mind in the slightest. My mind pondered the problem of how to settle the complexity of a new Accord.

I'd chosen not to risk another fight with the big transparent dome over the shadow in my nature, particularly now that I hosted a demon in my soul. Instead, I'd opted to risk landing in the place I'd embarrassed myself. This time, with less to prove, I followed Z'nnek's example and floated gently on outstretched wings. But carrying the head of my vanquished enemy's false corpse was a salve for my ego. Though my only audience was my sister, who watched me warily as if I might turn on her of a moment. I didn't encourage her to speak, since I'd no desire to explain my reasons for pushing her to choose counter to both our desires. Sacrifices had to be traded for advantage in any conflict.

As we walked past the great, motionless golems, F'riida brooded silently, but I sensed she was on alert for betrayal and ambush. Perhaps it would've been kinder to try to put her at ease, but my concentration was elsewhere.

I'd traded more trust to her than I'd extended to anyone but my lovers. Perhaps more.

I was particularly proud of myself for remembering the route through the halls unescorted. F'riida only stirred in my mind when we passed images of the raven-haired woman I now knew to be Preema. The woman who wore my face. Well, perhaps I wore hers. The tip of the massive demon's tail twitched like a soundless snake rattle. I feigned disinterest, lest Kausae notice and ask questions I couldn't answer. My sister was preoccupied and mercifully oblivious.

Huund, Torr, and Tyrr waited impatiently, standing on the steps of the dais. The small gods had accreted together into a single group, with Goerranu, Mawzi, Hayyek, and Coyne lingering closest to the supplicants' table. The sense of the small gods was expectant now, though still with an undercurrent of trepidation. Of Tourak and Z'nnek, there was no sign.

A susurrus breezed through the crowd when I slammed my trophy down upon the table before my unused seat. The viridescent hair was matted with gore and was already beginning to stink. The best trophies always did. I scanned the room for an exaggerated time, noting the absence of gold-winged and silver-winged angels. Nor were any hawk-winged hunters present.

Interesting, I mused, wondering what that signaled from Huund and the high gods. *A new détente, perhaps?*

Since the high gods were watching with feigned unconcern, I played even deeper into my enigmatic and unpredictable goddess role.

Catching Coyne's eye, I raised a brow. With a rueful grin, he approached alone.

"What were the odds we agreed?" he asked coyly.

"I should've bet four." I scoffed and held up three fingers, which was easy since I was missing one on that hand.

While I'd no idea what I'd bet or even what I'd won, I was eager to learn more about this custom amongst the gods that was curiously absent in Nethe.

The god of gamblers sighed and made a queer five-pointed clasp of his fingers. After shaking his hand in this pose three times, he opened his palm. Three gemlike tokens scintillated there. He held them out to me.

"Let it not be said that I am miserly with a fairly won bet," he proclaimed. "Will you accept these?"

I examined them with what I hoped was nonchalance. One resembled a smooth, round, pink tourmaline. Another sparkled like a gold nugget that had been hammered into a gaming cube with different but indistinct markings beaten into each side. The last was a deep purple sapphire cut into the faceted shape of a lopsided cluster of grapes. I'd no idea what the significance of the different hues might signify until F'riida took notice.

"*Soul tokens,*" she purred. "*Interesting what small gods' favors he thinks you might accept.*" Her forked tongue lashed the air thoughtfully.

That prompted me to make all sorts of connections. Favors exchanged among the gods made sense when they could want for nothing. The sapphire was the same hue as Z'nnek's aura—I doubted the wine-colored stone of such a whimsical shape could be anyone else's soul token. *Whose were the others?* But now I'd have to tread carefully with no knowledge of what they could be redeemed for from the originator. *Why had Z'nnek gambled that token away?*

"*Perhaps bargain for some with more significance to our current endeavor?*" the old demoness suggested.

You know whose they are? I asked F'riida.

"*I know they are not of the Seventeen,*" she said dismissively.

Of course she won't tell me, I thought, *or she doesn't know. I'll have to find out who the Seventeen are, and soon.*

To play for time, I asked Coyne, "Why would you offer me those?" The sly god had to be testing me, so I might as well force him to lay his cards on the table.

"Another lost the favor belonging to Z'nnek." He shrugged noncommittally. "You played me well, and it seems fair to offer you the most rare and valuable I own."

Surprise whistled through me. Both because I'd guessed right and because of Coyne's estimation of its value, though it seemed perhaps he was overstating the case.

"Most rare and valuable, eh?" I jested with a smirk to make time to think.

That means they're tied, I thought, *to the god himself. But how? And of what value? Z'nnek had not warned me of debts he owed when we wed.*

"Z'nnek never plays," Coyne said with a slight pout. "It's the only one of its kind that I know of." His expression warned me that he expected to be suspected of cheating. "I won the favor in a fair bet."

If Z'nnek never plays, then someone else must've garnered a boon from him in some other way. Someone who was desperate to win. Or desperate to gamble. I stuffed the fresh jealousy down where the statue of Kragh lingered in my mind. I added this to the long list of unanswered questions about my king. The Tales often told of deals made with the trickster lord of the underworld. But neither the Litanies nor the Tales spoke of soul tokens.

Coyne winked. "I have at least one from most every other." He waved broadly around the room to encompass all the gods present in feigned magnanimity. "If you'd like another instead."

My gaze found Huund's by accident as my mind wandered. She blinked at me in surprise. We held the mutually unintended stare for too long.

F'riida chortled. *"Fascinating idea, hatchling."*

Coyne came to the same conclusion. With a snap of his fingers, he produced a glittering brown garnet talon in his right hand. I looked at him, at the new token, at the other three in his left palm. In the periphery of my vision, Huund shifted her weight from one foot to the other.

Unbidden, Araeda'h's words came back to me, *"Most gemstones can be trusted, but garnets cannot!"* Surely that was just a coincidence.

Without looking, I knew the idea of me holding her token was uncomfortable to the huntress. That favor could turn the tide of the Conclave, which was awaiting my decision, and save me difficult concessions. But, if I were to seduce her, I needed her trust above all else. Playing the long game was not my usual style. *What is more enigmatic and unpredictable than to do the opposite of the obvious?* I asked myself rhetorically.

I grinned at Huund. "I believe..." I paused to take four long, slow inhalations and exhalations, letting my wind rattle ever so slightly over my palette in the victorious breath.

The throne room seemed to collectively inhale and hold. Only my meditative breaths fluttered in the silence.

"Coyne, I shall accept the original three tokens you offered to settle our bet."

With relief and calculation in the squint of her eyes, Huund watched me stroke the sickly green hair of my grisly trophy.

CHAPTER 26

*I*n a rush to finish the Conclave business, I thrust out my empty left hand to Coyne. The throne room filled with anticipatory silence as I accepted three soul tokens from the god of gambling. Even F'riida sat up in my mind and watched. To my surprise, nothing exciting happened. The three gem-like stones rested in my palm without fanfare. Each felt different against my skin. Z'nnek's soul I recognized immediately. Genteel, smooth, and just a bit feminine. I felt that I could reach through the token and embrace him. That was something to be explored later, but somehow I knew I could commune with him. I hoped he'd join us soon and take his empty seat as my advisor. But the token gave me the sense that he was far away...and otherwise occupied.

The beaten gold gaming cube belonged to Coyne. I don't know how I knew the shiny, calculating sense of the token was his, but I felt certain it was. Yet another surprise from the god of chance. His gambler's eyes were watching. I wondered what bet he'd just made on me.

The pink tourmaline was cool and herbal, like Hayyek's healing touch. I sought her out in the crowd of small gods. She was easy to find. Her soul token seemed to draw my gaze toward her. We shared a long moment of eye contact and a nod. She began to walk towards me.

I smiled at Coyne and gestured to the seat I'd assigned him earlier. "Thank you."

The wisp of his smirk was all he gave me by way of acknowledgment. He nodded perfunctorily to Hayyek as she took her seat.

The purse at my belt already held Tourak's red-edged raven feather. I now knew what it was. The other three joined it with a soft clatter of polished stones.

Goerranu caught my eye. Urgency filled her expression. Perhaps she'd done as I asked? If she'd learned why Z'nnek surrendered, I could leverage his token to learn some other, more personal secret instead. Before I could take even one step toward where the goddess of secrets who stood with Mawzi, Huund whistled long and loud enough to impress highland wolf breeders.

"We have all been surprised, brothers," Huund said in a broad voice that filled the hall. With a smile, she inclined her head toward me and my table. "And sisters."

My heart began to beat faster, as if a predator had just spotted me hiding in the brush.

From her place upon the dais, Huund swayed down the steps toward me. "In my nineteen millennia, I have not seen her like." Emerald eyes, four shades darker than the enamel on her armor, pinned me in place. Amusement wrinkled her crow's feet just a touch.

My mind raced, seeking the danger in the ambush I knew to be there. My nineteen years seemed scant experience compared to hers. *What did she truly want?* I had her interest now, and that was the opportunity—and the thrill—I required. But I hesitated.

"She defied the children of the high gods in the name of justice," the goddess of the hunt proclaimed. "And she was right to do so."

Vayan's countenance crackled with disdain. Tyrr flushed red and scowled. His twin, the self-described god of justice, frowned and looked away. Their hawk-winged elder sister seemed oblivious to their chagrin.

A hush fell over the throne room as everyone waited for the next boot to drop.

"Winning the heart of the lord of the unclaimed was a mystery," Huund whispered loudly enough for everyone in the hall to hear, "but at last I think I see an inkling of why." She continued to stride purposely toward me.

"*I expected you to actually* do *something to woo her,*" F'riida complained. "*Your hesitance led me to believe this would be difficult.*"

For my part, I was as surprised as the demon sorceress when Huund winked at me.

The huntress stopped close enough that I could feel her breath on my cheeks. We were of a height, standing eye to eye. She was going to expect me to do something against my interests. In that moment, I became keenly aware that neither Z'nnek nor Tourak had returned yet. But I could hardly break eye contact to use their soul tokens to get their advice.

Huund spoke softly, like we were having dinner conversation. "But more than the four miracles her priestess proclaims in her new canticle, *The Book of the Damned...*"

Blinking in surprise was all I could do. *I have a canticle?*

"*You hardly seem competent enough to rate a priestess,*" F'riida commented dryly.

Huund gave me a lopsided, flirty smile. "I am impressed that the Raven Queen has ended a threat which skulked in the shadows with impunity for longer than I've been alive."

The claws of the green-scaled demoness clutched at the stones of my heart.

Huund took my hand and raised it over our heads in triumph. "A threat I myself was powerless to stop."

F'riida snorted, like a powerful demon sneeze. "*She's more dramatic than you are.*"

For once, the demoness and I agreed.

The goddess of the hunt and the hunted seemed oblivious that her siblings were on the brink of rage. Including Vayan, who'd sworn to end me only a few weeks gone for my unintended insult to his progeny, the three of them were now beyond enemies to me. Perhaps that was the result Huund sought, to seal my eternal fate by public acclaim. They might not end me now, today, but they would end me when they could.

"All hail the Raven Queen!" Huund shouted.

Deafening silence greeted her blasphemy. The small gods and high gods alike looked stricken. All Huund's possible intentions tornadoed through my mind. I had certainly wanted to conclude the Conclave swiftly, but this was too fast. I couldn't trust it.

From her perch atop the cliffs of Alamar in my imagination, the demoness narrowed her pale green eyes and clutched at the stone with her great claws. *"What is her game?"*

Fuck if I know, I thought.

The Lady of the Dread Hunt raised her other hand. This time, the shrill cry of a hawk soaring high above the mountains rang in her shout. "All hail the Raven Queen!"

Everyone but me echoed her words, "All hail the Raven Queen." Even the high gods mumbled the words. The throne room filled with my praise.

This is what it must feel like to go mad, I thought. Numbness hummed through my core.

She lowered our hands and took a demure half-step back. "Will you accept our reparations and the new Accord?"

"New Accord?" I asked dumbly.

"All that I offered before," Huund said diffidently.

In shock, I interjected, "Amnesty and reparations and…"

Huund gave me a predatory smirk. "And all the crown of Nethe must do in exchange is to release the shades from their internment."

There it is, I thought. *She expects me to commit Z'nnek as well. I just don't understand what she means or why.*

My fickle powers of erudition eluded me. "The shades?"

The hawk-winged predator smiled demurely. "After a suitable term of service, of course. We have no wish to hamper the lifestyle to which Z'nnek —and now you—are accustomed in your realm."

Why in the Hells would they matter to her? The shades were not prisoners in Nethe. They were honored guests, free to live as they chose. True, many accepted service, just as they had in life, but it was theirs to choose.

Confusion swirled in my guts and clouded my mind. I should wait for Z'nnek. The offer was too generous. I was clearly missing something obvious. But there was no downside that I could see. Pushing back would seem ungrateful and perhaps would lose all that was on offer for no reason. Peace throughout the world. Plenty and provision for my mortal kith and kin. An acknowledged place among the gods. It all seemed too good to be true.

What would be the harm in promising to release our guests from a condition they were never in?

Thinking of releasing the shades brought Madra to mind and her self-inflicted end at the hands of the wrathful keepers of Baal. *Is that what Huund wants for them all? If so, why?* I would not agree to that, but such was not the letter of Huund's words.

My gaze roved about the hall. When I looked over my shoulder, Kausae's eyes met mine. Perhaps sisterly intuition told her that I needed her aid. I needed something. I needed time to think. There was never enough time to think.

My sister nodded her concession, her assistance to me. "I have made my decision," she announced, to give me a reprieve.

The twitch of the pulse in Kausae's throat told me that she did not want this any more than I did. I loved her all the more for her trust. I vowed to myself to make our mutual sacrifice worth it. I was grateful for her aid.

Huund stifled a squawk of irritation. Torr sat up and faced her, his frown deepening.

Lifting her silvery wings to half spread, she said in a clarion tone, "I choose to remain in service to my lord, Torr."

The shock upon Torr's visage was almost worth my heartbreak. Almost.

The sympathy in the other eyes turned my way—Goerranu, Mawzi, Hayyek—all stung. I shoved those feelings beneath the glacier forming atop my heart.

Tyrr was glaring at Huund. Vayan looked back and forth between me and Kausae suspiciously. For his part, Torr looked unabashedly pleased. Coyne twitched as if he desperately needed to be among the other small gods, making odds and taking bets.

If I'd known then how to weave soul tokens, I too would have wagered against me.

Inspired by my sister's bravery, self-sacrifice, and unearned trust, I made my choice. Unconsciously, my hand found its way into my purse. My fingers brushed the carved bubbles of the grape cluster.

Forgive me for committing you without your leave, my love, I begged silently to Z'nnek. Wordless comfort and concern came back to me through the soul token I clutched in the fingers of my left hand.

I cleared my throat. Stretching out my empty right hand, I said, "On behalf of Nethe, we accept your terms, Huund." The royal we felt strange and false on my tongue.

The Lady of the Hunt grasped my three-fingered hand. Her palm was warm and firm.

Feigning surety, I said, "We shall release the shades of the unclaimed from any bondage in Nethe after a term of four years."

In my heart, I promised myself, *Which won't change a damn thing.*

CHAPTER 27

The throne room was silent. Uncomfortably so. The small gods, who'd never been invited to Conclave alone or en masse, seemed to have no idea how to react to the abrupt resolution. Hayyek and Coyne looked to me for a cue. As if I'd know! The others stood quiet, not even fidgeting, except Mawzi, who toyed with a long, wicked-looking knife. Goerranu raised an eyebrow at me, perhaps curiosity for my next move overriding whatever urgency she'd felt the need to discuss earlier.

In Alamar, we'd have celebrated a new understanding with an impromptu festa. Though I hadn't had the opportunity in Nethe—my recent wedding to Z'nnek and Tourak aside—I was certain that's what I would do after any big event.

But Huund, Tyrr, Torr, and Vayan busied themselves only with exchanging glares. I'd have to figure out what that tension was about soon. Since I'd presumably agreed to their chief demand, I would have thought they'd all be pleased. There was at least one important detail I hadn't figured out yet—why the rulers of the Twin Paradises obeyed the goddess of the hunt.

Still standing close to Huund, I placed a hand on her armored shoulder. The emerald steel of her pauldron was cool beneath my palm. She didn't flinch but twisted her head like a bird to regard my hand. I smiled and left the gentle pressure in place.

"How shall we celebrate our new Accord?" I asked.

Huund turned to face me, and my hand fell away. "What is there to celebrate in an unconsummated agreement?" The tiniest smile twisted her full lips.

Flirtatious teasing, I could deal with under most circumstances. But coming from a goddess who very recently seemed to want only my humiliating destruction took me aback. It occurred to me that perhaps she sought the immediate ejection of shades from Nethe, but I still couldn't figure out why. *What difference could all the shades in Nethe make? They'd been rejected by the high gods and left unclaimed!*

Still, Huund's verbal thrust was precisely the sort of opening my seduction would require. I treated Huund to a lascivious grin. "Perhaps only for lack of a bed." My eyes roamed the throne room as if in search of a suitable surface.

In my head, F'riida stretched and yawned like a great, scaled mountain cat. Her tail twitched. She made a show of indifference.

The goddess of the hunt and the hunted rewarded me with a birdlike twitter of laughter. "Is that sort of festivity commonly held in Nethe?"

Leaping onto the opportunity to suggest an orgy seemed far too premature, so I held myself back from describing my recent sexually charged nuptials. "We normally share a repast of some sort as foreplay," I hedged, feigning the ingenue, biting my lower lip just the tiniest bit. "What sort of food would you prefer?"

Inexplicably, Huund's face darkened. She looked back at her brothers, half turning away from me. "Perhaps bringing the Conclave here was a mistake," she muttered so softly I wasn't sure if she'd intended anyone to hear.

"Where are the Seventeen?" F'riida demanded again, like a querulous old woman who's forgotten she's asked and been answered repeatedly.

Could ancient demons be senile? Araeda'h seemed to be some days. Containing a sigh, I decided it was time to address the demon's insistence directly. *I've no idea who the Seventeen are,* I thought at her. *We're visiting Saetarra, Amuun's paradise. She rules here.*

"Did you not see them in the many halls you walked to get to this place?" F'riida grumbled, her claws digging into my mind, demanding attention. *"Amuun has always served Preema and the Seventeen."*

The aftershocks of that statement reverberated through me. The mother of the high gods, Amuun served no one. The demoness haunting me now had to be confused. But another demon, not so long ago, had confused me for Preema—whoever the Hells she was. That led me to wonder if Baal and F'riida might have more in common than I was prepared to deal with.

The demon huffed a grumpy noise. *"I don't know why you're wasting your time pandering to these servitors."*

I didn't know what to do with F'riida's absurdity, so I ignored it and focused on the here and now. Even if the high gods didn't understand the value of such a gesture to we who had been mortals once, I did. Winning over the small gods might not produce the army I might need, but the forbidden Tales always started with a small act of rebellion that led to a greater one, to the embarrassment of the high gods.

I tried again to reach for the magic of Saetarra. This time I felt repulsed, as if my occult senses had been lightly slapped away. The power was there, but it refused to respond to me. While I didn't know precisely how such things worked, Nethe had always been responsive and generous with her magic. To me. Perhaps the magic of this realm was denied to me? By whom?

"Would Amuun consent to creating a symbolic cornucopia?" I asked. "It wouldn't have to be..."

The goddess of the hunt narrowed her eyes at me. If I were prey, I'd be worried. Then her expression softened as rapidly as it had become stone. "I would not trouble my mother for such a trifle." A put-upon sigh almost convinced me that she and Amuun had as fraught a relationship as any mortal mother and daughter might. "She has much on her mind, as I'm sure you, of all rulers of a realm and a host, understand."

F'riida scoffed. The demoness didn't deign to clarify her disbelief.

With a smile for Huund, I said, "Much of what occupies my mind are such trifles. Little troubles me in Nethe but caring for my guests and my unkindness. I'm sure much as you do for your own Hunt."

I expected her to smile and concur. She did not. Her blank expression confused me. Her eyes watched me as if I were a curious cony alone under an open sky.

I didn't understand. But I didn't think Huund would explain, even if I pressed. She'd served me the solution on a platter. I was indeed the ruler of a realm. If Amuun and her coterie couldn't be bothered, I'd just take the party somewhere else. Somewhere that my word was law.

"Of course," I purred, trying to regain the playful banter. "I do understand." I lifted a hand, palm up, as if commiserating. "Then there's nothing for it…"

Huund nodded, beginning to turn away again. "That's for the best."

"Everyone!" I announced in my battleground voice. "You are invited to Nethe to celebrate our new Accord!"

"How is that going to force Preema to confront me?" F'riida asked. *"I'm willing to play your silly mortal games only so long."*

The shocked silence was broken by a quiet eruption of hushed conversation.

All four high gods looked nonplussed. Huund opened her mouth, said nothing, and closed it again. Vayan put hands on the Twins' shoulders and bent over to whisper urgently to them.

Coyne eyed me in a way that told me that I'd just raised my estimation in his mind. Mawzi rolled her eyes and turned away. Hayyek's face held a quizzical hope. The goddess of secrets and lies gazed at me with confusion knitting her brows.

"We could not—" Huund recovered from her surprise more quickly than her siblings. "We would not dream of intruding."

"It's no intrusion at all," I assured everyone, especially myself.

Z'nnek is going to be pissed at me. And rightfully so.

CHAPTER 28

Urth's haven was a dark, welcoming contrast to the sun-kissed realms we left behind. Escaping Nethe through these enormous tunnels not so long ago, with Tourak in tow, had been harrowing. I'd been nearly blind in the unfamiliar gloom and attacked by a demonic terf that had wandered through the veil. Today, the humid middle world above my comfortable underworld hugged me as if I were almost home. The tri-sexed god of creation and destruction had become an eclectic neighbor, not a terrifying gatekeeper.

My immortal sight revealed details of Urth's kingdom I'd been unable to see before. We flew through caverns too enormous for echoes. Stone daggers a mile high rose into darkness. Wicked crystals, like the teeth of world-eating monsters, lunged up out of the gloom. Behind me, Huund and the Hunt flew, carrying the high gods and the small. Before me, glimmers of fluorescent life littered the black, like writhing stars far below us. The urge to explore the vast variety of Urth's imagination tugged at me once again, but that would have to wait until I'd served the guests I led toward my home.

"We should invite Urth," I called to Huund, who flew just off my right wing. "And the other old gods."

She looked at me strangely, as if trying to determine if I were joking.

F'riida mocked me with snide laughter. *"Urth is no god."* She curled up inside my mind, radiating amusement, and rested her great, horned head upon her muscular tail. *"You are splendidly naïve, hatchling, or criminally uneducated."*

What do you mean? I demanded. I didn't understand. Urth ruled this realm. The high gods and the Litanies were— I crushed my sense of betrayal at that thought. Nevertheless, Urth and Z'nnek had a long, friendly relationship. Inviting one's neighbors to celebrations was just the polite thing to do.

F'riida scoffed but said no more.

"I'll send one of my ravens then," I muttered to myself, "once we've settled you." I wasn't sure if I meant Huund or F'riida—or both.

Nethe unfurled below me as I dropped out of the wide tunnel from Urth's realm. Tourak, bless him and keep him, had done as I asked. Half my unkindness soared through the gloaming sky in small formations. Dozens of my raven-winged beauties played complex, aerial tag in formations, armed with lance and sword and bow. In that moment, I realized that I had much to learn about war in three dimensions that I couldn't have learned as a mortal. Though, I was fortunate to have many in my unkindness who'd fought in the Little War and knew such things. Today was full of painful realizations.

Close by, my varicolored stars danced. Those simplest of shades hugged the stone sky of Nethe, seeking what? I could only guess. Perhaps release into the sun-kissed realms? Did any ever find their way to whatever they sought? It had not occurred to me to wonder where they were trying to go.

"Anamneses?" Huund's voice held awe. Her hungry gaze was fixed upon the dancing lights. "There are so many..."

Her reaction, as much as the strange word, struck me. I concealed my ignorance with a gentle riposte. "Did you not notice them before, Siti?" I teased.

A stoic mien clouded over her wonder. The predator reasserted herself. "Why do you cage them so?" she demanded, gesticulating at the stone sky, ignoring my reminder of her earlier, strange deception. "You must release them at once!"

My shoulders tensed at the unexpected command. Sudden protectiveness gripped my heart. Madra was out there among them. What would releasing them mean for her? What would releasing them even accomplish? I needed Z'nnek's guidance. And I'd let myself become too distracted and hurried to attempt to reach him through his soul token.

A laugh forced its way past my lips frozen in a rictus of a smile. "All in good time!" I swooped into a deeper dive, sneaking a peek over my shoulder.

After a brief hesitation, Huund followed me down, surveying my realm in judgment, I was sure. But she'd seen it before when she'd pretended to be her own emissary. I'd not figured out yet why she'd used that ruse. *What could she have hoped to learn?* Being manipulated into a new Accord with terms I didn't fully understand frustrated me, but I was in my own realm now, on familiar, defensible ground. I was queen here.

Worry that I'd brought doom in the front door shivered down my spine. The warmth of Nethe's welcome kept that chill from spreading through me. Its power swelled through my soul, and the feeling of magical starvation that had plagued me all day vanished. Though we never spoke with words— Nethe and I—since my wedding to Z'nnek and Tourak, I'd come to think of Nethe as aware and alive. It was as responsive and generous as my lovers. After the sterile whiteness of Saetarra, I was grateful to be home in my dark realm. It may not be the paradise I'd craved as a mortal, but now it was mine and I belonged to it.

Lest I forget later, I pictured the wine cellar of my mind. Torch-filled sconces lined the walls. Straw and sawdust upon the rough slate floor to absorb spills. Long rows of empty wooden racks cast deep shadows in the flickering light. I placed a clean corked bottle in each waiting holder. I filled each to the neck with the midnight nectar of Nethe's ambient worship. Never again would I find myself in need and lack the magic in my soul.

With simple thoughts and impressions, I asked Nethe to prepare for our arrival. It was fond of our shades and had a deep rapport with them. Those that preferred to serve responded well to its subliminal encouragement. Scant minutes later, food and drink waited for us in my midnight garden atop the palace.

Tourak waited for me there, anticipating my desires as always. As soon as I put boots on the flagstones, I hugged him fiercely and kissed him deeply.

He chuckled into my mouth. "I missed you, too, for the few moments we were apart."

I rolled my eyes. The time passed felt much longer than it had been. F'riida silently watched through my eyes, scanning my domain. I wondered how she judged it.

The Dread Hunt landed gracefully amongst the fruit trees and the ornamentals. Their passengers dismounted stiffly after such a long ride from Saetarra. And probably unfamiliarity with the mode of travel. The small gods gathered around Goerranu, Coyne, and Hayyek. Mawzi had moved behind me, swift and silent. But not unnoticed. In Nethe, I was aware of everything and everyone, if I cared to pay attention. If Mawzi wished to play the bodyguard for me, I would allow it.

The high gods approached, and my perception of them was more acute now than it had been ever before. Their power was greater than I'd realized. Nethe's estimation of their danger to me and to Nethe was concerning. It compared the risk they represented to hundreds of my own angels, all with images and sensory impressions and without words. Huund was just as large and dangerous as her brothers and Vayan. The small gods were negligible powers by comparison. Strange, to me, none of them seemed to reach for Nethe's magic as I'd tried in Saetarra—I hadn't decided whether to allow it or not, but I'd defer that decision until it was forced upon me.

Realization dawned. Amuun kept Saetarra from being permissive with its magic. Amuun kept the other high gods starving when they visited. Why? I touched Triumph where it rested upon my head.

"How did you wrest that bauble from Baal?" F'riida asked, mild curiosity not masking her keen interest in the slightest.

It was a gift, I said, leaning into my enigmatic and unpredictable goddess persona. Let the old biddy chew on that. I was grateful—again—that my unwanted guest could neither read my thoughts nor gain awareness of other parts of my soul.

"Perhaps I underestimated you," was her only response.

As the high gods approached and interrupted my epiphany, I felt a need to assert my authority here immediately. I was very conscious of the score and a half of my angels who feigned to lounge in the garden. My lovelies eyed the visitors with veiled suspicion.

"My guests," I called to everyone, "there is food and drink from many lands." I waved toward trestles groaning with the weight of many feasts. Platters of roasted meats and trays of grains and vegetables of all sorts accompanied pitchers and decanters and bottles. "Please refresh yourselves. Soon we shall divert you with other entertainments!"

Huund gestured over her shoulder toward where the Hunt waited. "You may go."

Even as surprised tickled me, my mouth got ahead of my mind. "They're welcome to stay!" I smiled as genteelly as I could manage. "There's plenty to share."

Again, Huund peered at me quizzically, as if I'd told a joke she didn't understand.

"As you wish," I said quickly, hoping my efforts here would soon turn for the better.

The Hunt took to the sky at a second imperious gesture from their Lady.

Everyone stood around, high gods and small, glancing at each other awkwardly as if they were virgins at their first adult festa, with no idea where or how to begin the orgy. It seemed as if they'd forgotten how to be mortal.

Vayan, towering a head taller than the Twins, grunted like thunder rumbling. "You will release—"

"A toast!" I shouted. "Please choose your favorite from among the wines and meads and other liquors. You won't offend Z'nnek if you do not prefer wine."

I chuckled at my own joke. No one else did. Vayan scowled at me but did not object.

Shades began to pour into goblets and glasses and circulate amongst the crowd, handing beverages to the small gods and the high. Mawzi gave me a tall golden goblet filled with a three quarters measure of a claret. Out of habit, I swirled it and inhaled the fruity notes of well-aged grape and pomegranate and a hint of thyme, stalling to think of what or how to toast. Stalling for Z'nnek to return. He did not.

Fingering the stem of her goblet filled with a sparkling white, Huund eyed me, patient and studious. The three other high gods grumbled to one another.

When everyone I could see had been served, I hoisted my own drink aloft.

"Our new Accord!" I clinked my goblet against Huund's and downed all my wine.

A clumsy chorus of "Aye" and "Accord" burbled through my garden.

Tourak whispered in my ear. "Illyria, what did you do?"

CHAPTER 29

*T*he urgency of Tourak's whispered question echoed in my ear. I surveyed the fragile beginnings of my new Accord celebration while my mind flailed about for an answer. *What am I doing? Why did I agree to something I didn't understand?* The small gods had tentatively joined my toast, and a few of them, led by Coyne, were sampling the varied fare provided. They were skittish as fawns in fresh alpine snow—as if they'd never been offered food before. Hayyek watched them, not yet joining in. I turned and lightly kissed Tourak and gave him what I hoped was a reassuring smile. I needed answers, and if I could get her alone, Huund was the most likely to provide them to me.

Surveying the high gods and the small, I realized their hesitation wasn't unfamiliarity—not entirely. In unguarded moments, when they thought themselves unobserved, I caught many of them gazing in awe about my humble home. Hayyek picked from a mango tree. She considered the fruit with inexplicable joy, turning it over and over in her hands before she took a bite. Her blissful expression warmed my heart as much as it surprised me. Not a highland fruit and by far not my favorite. It was just a mango. Others among my guests behaved much the same about the wine or the food. They gorged themselves as if my dark underworld eternity were paradise. Even Vayan gazed up with awe, his stormy gray eyes tracking the varicolored lights that danced across the stone sky of Nethe. They enjoyed what I had once spurned in a way I envied and craved to understand. *This was just Nethe!*

Tyrr and Torr were eyeing Vayan, who gave me a nonplussed smile—which was far better than the murderous glare he'd given me a few weeks past, along with a promise to execute me. But, he'd drunk to my toast from a hefty pewter stein. Huund triangulated among us. She held the pose of patient waiting with greater stillness than I could ever muster. Her mixed-race features were beautiful and wild, strong and refined. The Litanies did not tell of her sire, but I could see nothing of another god in her. I wondered if she ever wore anything but armor. I compared hers to my revealing attire. Emerald-enameled metal chased with gold filigree and boiled leather encased her dark skin from fingertips to toes.

Vayan hoisted his stein and drained the last of his ale. Wiping the foam from his beardless face, he said, "Now that you've had your fun, show us a gesture of good faith." He belched and a wicked grin flashed across his visage. "Release all the shades who've served more than four years, as you promised."

That wasn't what I promised, I thought and bristled, losing track of my curiosity about the reasons for his demand in my irritation.

He waved toward a trio of shades strolling through the far side of the garden, arm in arm like lovers. "And if they're not serving you at all…" He trailed off with a sneer.

"None are required to serve in Nethe," I said to the lord of sky and storm. "That has ever been Z'nnek's law. There are many who choose service, with our thanks."

Vayan scoffed. "Who but the unclaimed would serve by choice?" He eyed the shades who were doing precisely that.

The bittersweet memory of Z'nnek's overly generous offer to me when I'd first arrived in Nethe brought a wry smile to my lips. If I had taken him at his word, perhaps much of the blood and drama of the past month could have been avoided. Vayan narrowed his eyes at me.

I shrugged at the lord of lightning. "All must choose their own path in my kingdom."

"What sort of utter nonsense is that?" F'riida demanded. *"Who in the name of the Great Egg Layer is Z'nnek?"*

I didn't know how to respond to the demoness, but I was deeply grateful that, though she inhabited my soul, she wasn't privy to all my thoughts. I shoved a memory in her direction. The moment I first awoke in Nethe, carried thence by Z'nnek himself, and his very simple question: *"If you could be queen of the underworld, could you find a way to be happy here?"* He had earnestly meant every syllable—and I'd summarily rejected his offer as absurd in that moment. Yet, here I was now, my own and countless other deaths later.

And having recently seen the purported paradise of Saetarra with my own eyes, I was grateful now, for the first time, to Z'nnek for claiming me. And Tourak for inciting him to defy the Accord in doing so. If the twin paradises of Avaala and Nuuria were like unto Saetarra, anyone would choose Nethe over them, if the Litanies described them for true.

In my mind, the demoness blinked at me in bafflement. *"What in the Broken Shells happened to this world?"*

Before Vayan could open his mouth again, Huund gently said, "Can you leave it be for an hour, Uncle?" She glanced back and forth between us. "Illyria is being a gracious and generous host. The least you could do is mingle and entertain the newest members of our Conclave."

The storm lord's expression crackled with intensity and danger. The Twins exchanged a curious look. The moment hung in the humid air, waiting for lightning to strike.

I intervened before things got out of hand. "I apologize, Lord Vayan, if I have given offense. That was not my intention. I offer you peace and hospitality in all my realm." *Which I should've done the moment we entered Nethe,* I thought. "And a solemn promise to make good upon my commitment." *As soon as I figure out what it means,* which I did not say aloud.

Huund smiled demurely at me, which struck me as powerfully odd. "I'm sure there's some wager or another to be made with Coyne, is there not, Uncle?" She made a shooing motion toward her brothers and uncle.

Torr, of all people, clapped Vayan on the back and offered, "I have an idea for a game! Come along, Uncle. I'm sure you'll love it." He chuckled. "All these weighty matters we can save for a less public discussion later." The god of civilization gestured to his twin with a nod toward a crowd of small gods surrounding Coyne.

The trio of high gods wandered off toward the small gods clustered around a buffet, leaving me alone with Huund and Tourak. An eerie sense of foreboding squeezed my innards. Perhaps sensing my disquiet, Tourak laid a comforting hand upon my shoulder and stepped close. His touch didn't dispel my ill at ease, but it did soothe me somewhat.

"Huund," I asked, "what is the urgency? I don't understand." I wasn't sure I could even catalog all the things I didn't understand.

"Will you fly with me?" she asked, waving toward the eternal night sky of Nethe and presumably the—

What had she called them? Anamneses. Singular recollections. That they were. My mother among them. A bright sharpness squeezed my heart, and I blinked rapidly to keep my vision clear. I had eternity for self-recrimination and grief. In this moment, I had to focus.

It was not lost upon me that Huund wanted to take our conversation somewhere that the other high gods could not follow on their own. Their lack of wings was yet another unanswered mystery to me. Was it a simple choice for them to be served by others? I dismissed the plethora of unknowns as irrelevant for the nonce.

I squeezed Tourak's hand. "Please ask our unkindness to mingle with our guests and provide them with"—I paused to give him a meaningful wink— "diversion."

If the small gods and the high were unaccustomed to festa and food, the temptations of my lusty angels might baffle them amusingly. But, most importantly, keep them occupied.

Concern disappeared from his face, replaced with mischief. Then he moved away, waving to several of my raven-winged lovelies who had been surreptitiously observing our guests from the strategic points about the rooftop garden.

"Shall we?" I invited Huund and launched myself into the eternal night.

CHAPTER 30

fter Huund caught up with me, we soared without speaking for a long time. The thought of her scrutinizing my realm itched. But I kept putting it aside, since she seemed lost in thought, rather than surveying my lack of defenses. She circled lazily, in no particular direction but ever higher. Like me, perhaps, she was drawn to the glittering lights of the anamneses. F'riida's frigid silence kept my goal and my promise in mind: seduce Huund. Discover the reason for releasing the shades. Find Preema.

"A Czolidh wedding ceremony!" the Lady of the Hunt called in excitement as we neared a mass of them. Her giddiness was uncharacteristic of the stoic huntress I knew. "I haven't seen brood wives exchange crowns in…" Her expression became distant and…something else as she trailed off, but she turned her head so I couldn't see.

It was interesting that others could see into the anamneses. Not a gift I alone possessed.

F'riida made a noise too loud to be a cluck of disdain. *"Covens and coteries were common before we toppled Preema from her throne."* The massive demon chuckled, rattling my soul. *"Nonbreeding marriages fell out of favor in our new order."*

"I've never heard of it," I said to both of them. "Did they live far from Elysia?"

Huund held her tongue so long I thought she'd refused to answer. "Elysia would not rise," she said at last, "for ten thousand years after the Czolidh passed out of memory."

Lick my salty nipples, I thought. I'd known Huund was old. She was in the earliest Litanies, but she was much older even than Z'nnek. I didn't ask the rude question, though, to find out how much.

"You must've seen many wondrous things," I said with unfeigned awe as we sailed on.

With a huff, F'riida resumed her false nonchalance.

The goddess of the hunt eyed me with suspicion before she seemed to grudgingly accept that my statement wasn't mocking her. "I have," she said. A shy smile crept across her lips. "I'm flying with one."

I scoffed outwardly, but her faint praise thrilled me more than it should have. "Not hardly," I demurred. I wasn't being humble. None among the high gods had disputed with Z'nnek to claim me. I couldn't begin to imagine what I would do or see pass by during the rest of eternity. "I did scant little in my nineteen years."

Huund shook her head. "The first mortal claimed by the god of the unclaimed dead?" She laughed loud but didn't seem to be mocking. "I'm fascinated to know what is so unique about you that compelled the reclusive lord of Nethe to break the Accord."

I'd wondered that myself. A lot. Though Tourak had shared his memory of me as a child, once upon a time. That little incident seemed scarce enough reason to risk the ire of the high gods. *So what if I'd sheltered a wounded and dying angel trapped in his raven's body? What was the life of one angel to be weighed against all the denizens of Nethe? Against all of eternity? Surely there had to be more of a reason, didn't there?*

The goddess of the hunt watched my face as if trying to read my mind as we flew. If I had gods to pray to, I'd pray that she couldn't. Not for the first time, I lamented that lack of higher powers to appeal to.

Forcing a laugh, I tried to turn the focus back upon her. "Nothing nearly so fascinating as being the daughter of Amuun," I said, because I couldn't think of anything else.

My words felt lame, and Huund's face lost a bit of its merriment.

"I'll tell you a secret," she said in a tone that feigned playfulness, "if you tell me one, too." She made a show of examining anamneses.

F'riida twitched and sat up with interest.

My flirting game wasn't strong today, so I might as well play her child's game of trade-a-secret. "That's like betting against Coyne," I said, aiming for a disinterested tone.

"But you did!" She giggled, suddenly charming and girlish, which seemed very much out of character for her. "And you won!"

Not knowing how to giggle, I just laughed. "That was a sucker's bet," I declared, "for both of us. I should have demanded longer odds if I'd known how tough F'riida would be."

The ancient demoness snorted what felt like fire against the stone cliffs in my mind, but she did so in a manner that seemed mildly pleased.

We are all vain creatures, I supposed, in the privacy of my own thoughts.

The predatory gaze returned to Huund's face in a flash. "How *did* you defeat her?" she asked with deep curiosity.

Reflexively, I blushed, which would probably give away my sham. I used Huund's game to deflect her quickly. "Is that the secret you want to trade?"

"Someday," she replied with too much indifference. "Someday, maybe you'll tell me. When you want to. But, the secret I want to know is—"

She held a pause until I harrumphed at her. She laughed again like hunting bells. "Have you ever been with a woman?"

My turn to laugh. "That's hardly a secret! In the highlands, nobody cares who's throwing or who's catching." That seemed a very odd question from the ancient goddess of the hunt and the hunted.

I chuckled deeper at the thought. "I'm not rightly sure if I've been with more men or more women." Her request seemed so silly, it hardly seemed fair to ask her for a true secret. So, I returned her question. "Have you?"

"Yes," she said in a wistful voice, "but it's been a long time since anyone touched me that way." She sighed, looking lonelier than I'd seen anyone in my life. "My last lover was before the Accord."

Hells and damnation, I thought, *a cunt might wither away from disuse in thousands of years.* I knew I'd not let such an evil happen in my eternity.

"You're in danger, hatchling," F'riida grumbled.

In my mind, I waved a shushing motion at the demoness. I could read faces. I could tell when someone faked in the great game. Huund wasn't pretending.

To lighten the mood, I played her game like we were, perhaps, fourteen. Her favorite food seemed hard for her to choose between cony and venison. Mine was easy. We shared an embarrassed laugh at my cunnilingus joke. Our favorite colors might've seemed obvious, but neither of us revealed our auras to be our favorites, which I found interesting. Mine was scarlet, but midnight was a close second. She alleged hers was raven black like my hair, which I disbelieved, but secretly pleased me. We played in that vein for what seemed like hours. All the while, F'riida grumped at me until I shushed her enough that she stopped.

One simply cannot rush a seduction.

I'd been expecting Huund to pounce at any point. She wanted to know something that she didn't feel she could ask without the disarming game. I let her play. But she still surprised me.

"Why did you try to ambush me by the black pool?" she asked at last, her tone intentionally light, unoffended.

"Why were you skulking about my domain?" I reposted, irritated but feigning surprise. "Pretending to be your own servitor?"

While she could have been angry, like me, she smiled. "I didn't know how to approach you. Z'nnek has no love for the high gods. Why would you?" She frowned. "You'd just slain—" She drew in a long breath. "—defeated the Chosen of Tyrr."

There was something off in her hesitation, her choice of the word defeated. Did Huund have a connection to Saevera? The Chosen bitch I'd let live? At least until Conseca collected our due in full.

I considered what to say for many wing beats. One of the Chosen still lived. Another I carried in a bottle in my soul. Neither of which fact their aunt would find sexy. I needed a sympathetic but strong approach. And I needed to quell my irritation.

"I felt violated," I said at last. "You're right. I'd no reason to love the high gods." I laughed gruffly. "And here was one of their beautiful angels, spying upon my domain."

F'riida rolled her great yellow eyes. But Huund actually blushed beneath her dusky skin. A cute dimple peeked out for the first time.

"I don't think you truly sought to kill me," the Lady of the Hunt said. "I could feel your approach, but it seemed playful. So, I let you live." She gave me a wicked grin.

Unexpected laughter burst upward from my belly and spilled out of my mouth. I laughed longer than was strictly polite. Huund considered me as a hawk might watch a hare. But she didn't seem to be offended. To this day, I don't know what I found to be so funny.

After I collected myself, Huund asked, "What was that place? It had the feel of a shrine."

"The pool of oblivion?" I wasn't sure I should tell her. I felt sure that Z'nnek wouldn't want me to. I stalled. "Is that the secret you truly wish to trade?"

"What would you like to know in return?" she countered.

"Ask her where Preema is!" F'riida demanded. Clearly, the demoness had been biding her time until she could pounce on me with her reminder.

There were so many questions crowding my mind, I spent long moments sifting through them. I could ask what my unwanted tenant wanted and perhaps get rid of her sooner. But it seemed inopportune. What if F'riida was wrong and Huund didn't know? The old demoness was out of touch with the current divine situation and politics. What if I asked and Huund realized that I had interests that I shouldn't have? Preema was not mentioned in any Litany that I knew, nor the Tales. Would she suspect that I harbored her avowed enemy? No, better to ask the question related to the pool of oblivion. The question that I wanted—needed to know the answer to. F'riida could wait a little longer.

"I'll do better," I said at last. "I'll show you what the pool is for."

Huund looked skeptical. "And?"

"In exchange, you'll explain why the release of the shades is so damned urgent."

CHAPTER 31

*W*e stood on the charcoal tiles again, beside the pool of oblivion, Huund and I. This time side-by-side instead of at odds. The dark fluid rippled as the thin blood of demons spilled from the sluiceways in sickening waterfalls. Knowing that particular vintage of extinction flowed out into every river and stream in my domain chilled me. These three tributaries irrigated all of the vineyards and orchards of my kingdom. In my mind now, all the fruit of Nethe was suspect. My stomach churned with acid nausea. I poked at my memories, fearful that they were fading.

Ignorant of my discomfiture, Huund gazed at the beautiful raven-winged statue guarding the center of the pool. The Lady of the Hunt tilted her head as if trying to remember something. She sniffed, giving her nose an amusingly dainty wrinkle.

"Is that…" She inhaled more deeply. "Is that a pool of wine?"

"I married a vintner god." I shrugged. "It can't be much of a surprise."

Huund frowned. "It's just terribly—" She seemed at a loss for words. "Obvious?"

I forced a laugh. "Perhaps. Someone told me once that what we choose in life echoes in eternity." I regarded the statue, wondering if I would recognize Kragh's echo in Z'nnek's eternity when I heard it.

"Z'nnek was always too maudlin for my taste," Huund replied, guessing whom I quoted accurately enough. "All the dead seem to be." The huntress eyed me obliquely. "Except you."

"Thank you, I suppose," I said, unsure how to take the compliment. Suddenly too curious for my own good, I asked, "You've not died then?"

She laughed. "What is the nefarious, secret purpose of this pool?"

Miffed that she'd ignored my questions like every other god and goddess, I stuffed my annoyance down and smiled. "If we wait patiently, that shall become apparent."

I closed my eyes and lifted my face to the stone sky of my home.

Through Triumph, I reached out across Nethe. There were few shades nearby. But I only needed one. I allowed my awareness to expand and drift, seeking a shade who seemed faded and ready for oblivion. Past the fringes of the pool and its attendant sepulchers. Beyond the rivers that flowed from it. Furlongs. Then miles. I examined my subjects, rejecting those with apparent purpose and liveliness.

An aimless, faded spirit wandered alone through a wild, untended orchard downstream. He twitched and gesticulated, his lips moving as if speaking to himself, but either the distance muffled his words, or he made no sound. A pale-skinned, tattooed man, he must have been a fleshy boulder in life. I did not recognize the style or meaning of his blue and black ink. Though I didn't know if I could speak to him across such a distance, I felt that I could try.

"Are you tired?" I asked.

At my shoulder, I felt Huund stir. Her wing feathers ruffled a gentle noise, but she remained silent.

The shade lifted his gaze from the ground and turned. Across the miles, I knew he rotated to face me. "I—" His tenor was nasal in tone, a thin voice for such a thick man. "Is it finally my time?" Though his words were in a language I did not recognize, the magic of Nethe made me understand him clearly.

"If you wish it to be so."

"Will I suffer?" A pensive expression pinched his face.

The two ritual drownings I'd witnessed recently had not appeared to be enjoyable. But I recalled Z'nnek having said a confusing thing about souls choosing to be punished. Asking questions seemed better than making uncomfortable pronouncements.

"Do you deserve to suffer?"

F'riida's tail fidgeted, just a twitch. I had the sense that she studied Huund somehow, despite my eyes being closed. I ignored her obvious misunderstanding, grateful again that she seemingly couldn't perceive everything in my otherwise wide-open mind. I kept my focus on the tattooed man. His face and posture were wracked with long-held guilt and pain.

His whole body sagged, just a bit, and he sighed. "I have not suffered the eons here." He inhaled deeply. "I've not seen any of my kind in ages. Those I wronged in life have all gone." Long moments passed as his non sequitur hung in the air before he nodded.

Without knowing how, I shortened the distance for him. "Come then," I said.

I opened my eyes.

One step from the unkempt orchard where he'd been then he stood upon the lip of the pool before me and Huund. The goddess of the hunt gave a surprised tsk. My resident demoness startled, too, which made me smile. I was getting better at being enigmatic and unpredictable.

"I am tired and I am ready," the nameless shade said to me.

I wanted to soothe him. To stop the ceremony his words had triggered. Already, the horrid grinding of the stone sepulcher doors had begun. Surely the uncounted eternity of carrying the burden of his guilt had been punishment enough. But I also needed to keep my promise to Huund. I wanted to be a goddess who could forgive and forget. I wanted to be a goddess, too, who understood.

In the end, a few heartbeats late, I stepped back and drew Huund with me by the arm.

Huund studied the Thirteen as they drowned the guilty shade in the pool of oblivion.

I watched her as confused curiosity morphed into a predatory lack of empathy. Realization dawned on Huund like a bleak winter sunrise as an amorphous, brownish anamnesis floated from the churned up black waves. I was too distracted with watching her to take notice of the singular reminiscence that had defined him. By the time I thought to look, he was too far away. I should have asked his name. Regrets never do anything but pile upon one another.

"Their life magic flows through the rivers of Nethe," Huund breathed, apparently understanding something that I didn't.

"I suppose," I hedged, not wanting to ask a question that would lead the conversation away from the answer I wanted most urgently. "I have shown you the purpose of the pool." I chose my words with care. "Why is the release of my shades of such urgent concern?"

"But you are!" Huund declared. "Not enough and not often, to be sure, but"—she gestured toward the pool—"that must be why Preema included the demons." Her face pinched in deep consideration. "After Z'nnek slew their masters and slaughtered their hordes, this process is too slow to digest them all. No wonder each generation under the sun grows weaker!"

"My sisters and I would be more than willing to help with the remainder," F'riida purred in a low, dangerous tone.

Boggling at both of them, I demanded, "What are you talking about?"

F'riida maintained a prim silence.

"You're too young to have noticed," Huund rambled, staring off into the distance, "but the generations under the sun have been in decline." She pursed her lips in thought.

"Wandering priests have lamented such," I said, confused, "but what has that to do with demons? It always seemed like the usual complaint of every elder generation."

Huund looked at me, an earnestness in her eyes. "No, there are fewer and weaker in every generation to claim." She nodded, then shook her head. "Since Z'nnek slew the demon lords, each new generation of ascended has been smaller and more expensive to raise."

I didn't correct Huund's misbelief regarding the demise of Baal, Raam, and Sett, not because it wasn't my secret to share—though, in truth, it wasn't—but because my mind reeled at the time span. Decline for eight thousand years? The empty halls of Saetarra came to mind. Tyrr choosing to leave the Levant Gate unguarded, just to have a few war angels on parade to intimidate me. The entire Dread Hunt were less than three score. Why the hosts of the mighty high gods should be so few made no sense to me. Surely, omnipotent beings could claim whomever they wished and make whatever they willed. The Litanies said… My thoughts trailed off as more religious lies were revealed to me.

Shades were accumulating in Nethe.

Fewer and weaker generations were being born under the sun.

The high gods were frustrated with a status quo they couldn't change.

Z'nnek knew, and either didn't care or preferred it so.

F'riida seemed to believe she and her demon sisters fit into this somehow.

Why were the high gods taking such an obtuse tack to remedy this instead of simply commanding Z'nnek or me to do their will?

Of course, I'd been in a thoroughly defiant mood of late, but I was eight millennia late to the party. And Z'nnek had expressed nothing but amusement about their demands in the face of the longstanding Accord. Still, I felt like I was missing crucial pieces of the puzzle. Possibly more pieces than I actually possessed in the first place.

The Lady of the Dread Hunt turned to study me, which was disconcerting and brought me back from my frustrated woolgathering. I tried not to show my startlement.

To keep the conversational focus elsewhere than me and my yawning ignorance, I asked, "Why do your hosts—I mean all the high gods' hosts—need to grow at all?"

Huund scowled at me with suspicion, as if I'd inquired about a deeper secret.

F'riida chortled. The sides of her big demon body heaved. Her noxious breath choked my soul just a little. *"Hatchling, you ask the hard questions with such an air of innocence. I almost believe you."*

I was starting to get angry with everyone's obtuse assumption that I understood what in the fuck they're talking about. Yet, I was loath to seem ignorant.

Huund asked with injured pride, "Where are Nethe's hosts defending the veil?"

"A fair question," I retorted, feeling somewhat attacked, "but I'm unaware of any request for aid." I lifted an eyebrow at her. Thinking that surely

Z'nnek would not refuse such a reasonable request, I asked, "Has there been one?"

Her scowl deepening, Huund grumbled, "Your senior husband has always hidden behind his duty to the unclaimed."

Senior husband? I wondered. I supposed he was senior of position, but I'd always had the sense that Tourak was older. That seemed like something I should know. Still, I would defend his honor. "Tyrr and Torr ordered him out of the sun-kissed lands not so long ago, save for his duty to the unclaimed. They could have just as easily ordered he patrol some part of the veil."

F'riida scoffed, an enormous sound in my soul. *"They would seem weak to demand it."*

The Lady of the Dread Hunt smiled, her resentment and suspicion evaporating. "Just so."

She had answered my question obtusely. I felt I was owed a straight answer. As I sorted through how to directly rephrase without being offensive, Huund surveyed our surrounds.

"What lies inside these?" she asked, indicating the sepulchers. "Demons?"

The demoness hiding in my soul craned her sinuous neck. She asked, *"Indeed?"*

Bloody shits, I thought. *I don't want either of them poking their noses in there.*

CHAPTER 32

The Thirteen already marched back toward their various sepulchers. Huund had begun to drift toward the nearest, peering into its pitch-black mouth. Baal's prison. The huntress's leather boots whispered across the rough charcoal tiles. F'riida's talons clicked an insistent rhythm on my memory of the stone cliffs above Alamar.

Someone had taught me that it's far better to control the course of the inevitable than to try to sweep its tide. Maybe my father, but probably my mother. I'd no time for regrets over memories I'd sacrificed on the altar of vengeance. Striding quickly ahead of Huund, I blocked her path and sighed to express my misgivings. As much as I loathed lying, if I could find a way to keep Z'nnek's secret, I would. Though I was not a habitual liar, I owed my love and my king my soul. Deception was a tiny price to pay.

I would just stall her until the doors ground shut of their own accord.

"You have not given me a straight answer, love," I said with as much patience as I could muster. Though tempted to pull a seductive moue, I restrained myself for lack of recent practice. "I see no reason to permit you inside my unmentionables." I tried for a teasing smirk instead as I looked into her verdant eyes.

F'riida snorted, but it was a playful sort with little heat. *"Don't play with your food...for too long."*

Behind me, the tramp of the wrathful shades moved further away. Their footfalls took on a hollow aspect as they entered the chamber of horrors. Huund's eyes tracked them over my shoulder, her expression hungry.

"As you wish," she said, exasperated.

I smothered my smile, gratified at last to be recovering my ability to irk others.

"Since you must know," the Lady of the Dread Hunt explained with mock patience, "we are starving. While you"—she flapped both her hands around to encompass all of Nethe—"wallow in plenty!"

I snorted. I'd seen Saetarra, but I played dumb. "What do you mean?" I gazed up at the stone sky where no sun shone upon the twisted imitation orchards and groves and fields. "This—" I choked on my mixed feelings about my new home that I thought I'd resolved with my wedding. Then I decided abruptly to be vulnerable and let this play out like serious seduction.

"This poor excuse for a vineyard?" I demanded. I let all of my initial disappointment hang out at awakening in Nethe instead of Nuuria from the month past. Bitterness fountained up from wherever I'd repressed it. No faking was required. I was nearly shouting in her face by the time I finished. "This gloomy land where Amuun never shines?"

Something beneath Huund's armored expression cracked. "At least your mother can still speak with you," she whispered to herself, eyes downcast.

My breath whooshed out as if I'd been stabbed with my own sword. I knew she hadn't meant for me to hear. She couldn't've known Madra was gone, floating among the anamneses above us. The divine implications crashed down upon me, almost washing away my ungrieved feelings for my mother. And flooding me with empathy for the crestfallen Lady of the Hunt.

"Amuun can't speak?" I asked in a hushed tone.

F'riida growled with interest and stilled her incessant fidgeting.

Huund met my gaze. For the first time I'd ever seen, her hunter-green eyes filled with fear. Her breathing was rapid and shallow. Her dark skin was flushed. Her pulse beat fast and strong in her elegant neck. In that moment, she was prey.

"Well, well, well," F'riida said with a chortle, "the old construct's spring finally wound down. It took long enough."

I'd no idea what to do with that nonsense from either of them. If Amuun, the mother of the gods, the singer of the first Litany, and creator of the world could no longer speak, what chance did any of us have at happiness in eternity? What chance did Z'nnek and Tourak and I have for ourselves?

"That's not... What I meant was—" Huund heaved a breath and swallowed hard. Her shoulders settled. She blinked rapidly. She nodded, a seemingly self-comforting gesture.

She placed the tip of her index finger between her teeth, just the slightest pressure deforming her skin. Her face was a mask of anxiety. When Kausae used that manipulative gesture, it annoyed the shit out of me because so many other people found it endearingly vulnerable. When the Lady of the Hunt did it, I found it—hot. Attraction blossomed across the most sensitive parts of my skin.

She looked away. "At least not to me," she mumbled around her finger. "My *brothers*," she said bitterly, "would be wroth with me for telling you."

Too many questions crowded my mind. I shoved the sudden, unexpected crush of attraction down. My own miniscule problems were dwarfed by the queen of the high gods' refusal—or inability—to speak with her own daughter. Amuun's absence at Conclave and from my sham of a trial was explained. I wanted to ask how long and why and so much more. But the grinding of the stone doors of the sepulchers commenced.

Perhaps it was the shock of the revelation. Perhaps it was the utter vulnerability on display. Perhaps it was something else I didn't want to examine right now. I wanted—no, needed—to extend this shared moment. To gain more of her trust. Shared secrets opened as many doors—and legs— as expensive gifts. Z'nnek would just have to forgive me.

"Come quickly," I said. Worried, I added, "And you must speak of this to no one."

We raced the slowly closing sepulcher doors. And won.

I held Huund back by the elbow, just inside the deep entryway. The ambient gloom of Nethe was extinguished as the massive stone doors ground shut behind us. Darkness swallowed us whole. Huund stood stock still, without looking around. Hence, I assumed she could not see what I could see. Through Triumph, I made my will for light manifest within the tomb.

"Light," I murmured, for my guest's benefit.

A warm, orange-tinged light, like a handful of blood candles that cast no shadows, filled the chamber.

Little had changed since my last visit. Baal was still chained upon his blood-guttered altar. Four wrath-filled shades stood at the corners. In my rush, I hadn't noticed that the apparent leader of the Thirteen had chosen a different sepulcher this time. Their stitched-shut eyes were fixed upon the fallen demon lord. Watching for any growth of tissue to prune away, I supposed. I suppressed a shudder and watched Huund for a reaction.

Huund remained motionless. Her expression a blank slate. Her posture unreadable.

After an impossibly long time, Baal coughed, a moist, phlegmy sound— the first sign of life from his ravaged body besides the quiver of his heart and the drip of his blood. "You returned too—"

"When will you learn your place, demon?" I interjected, cutting him off before he could say anything damning. "If you ever wish to be free of this"— I gestured toward the altar upon which he was chained—"you'll learn to speak only when spoken to." I offered him the implication of what I would want in his place.

Eight unstitched eyes turned their baleful attention upon me. The weight of their gaze was palpable. The wrath-filled shades did not approve of something I'd said. *Very odd,* I thought. But I'd endured eight millennia of pent-up wrath from a demon lord. It would take more than mere disapproval to move me.

The demon apparently didn't believe me or didn't want the obvious. "I haven't had time to muster a proper greeting." His attempt at a chortle was consumed by a pained wheeze. "Come back in another four millennia. Or eight." His great vulture head, plucked of all its feathers, collapsed against the stone altar. His chains rattled.

Still gazing at the demon, Huund cocked her head to the right like a hunting hawk regarding a hare. Then she twisted her neck to regard me, a direct and unflinching stare. The movement was inhuman in its birdlike quality. There were no questions in her eyes, only calculations. I could easily guess at some of them.

"It seems we all have secrets," purred F'riida.

I could not guess any of the old demoness's calculations.

"If you've not come to end me," Baal pleaded in a pitiful, liquid voice, "leave me to my torment." He coughed, then spasmed with agony that rocked the sepulcher around us with a miniature quake.

"This is your big secret?" Huund scoffed. "This is Z'nnek's vaunted, gentle mercy?"

I flinched like she'd slapped me. More than I had when Baal tried to dominate me.

F'riida mused, *"Fascinating. You're not old enough for millennia to have passed. Your lover Z'nnek did all of this? For what purpose, I wonder."*

This eternal torment, even of a demon, was at odds with mercy. Yet, the genteel and forgiving—if awkward—lord of the unclaimed dead had made it so. True, he'd no sympathy for those who punished themselves. But the Z'nnek who loved me commanded this?

"I don't know," I mumbled, looking away. "I only found the source of ob —" I coughed, my chest suddenly tight, unable to say the word. "After you visited me. The first time."

"Everyone in Nethe drinks of oblivion," F'riida said, with admiration in her voice.

I scowled up at her huge form in my mind. *Of course, a demoness fond of poisons would approve!* I repressed a shudder. I couldn't show weakness to either of them.

"He didn't break Preema's mechanism after all," Huund said, her face working in concentration. "He just slowed it to a glacial crawl." She stared at Baal, her eyes following the trickle of ichor down its gutters to the floor to its drains.

My mouth hung open. My brain unable to put the pieces together.

F'riida answered the questions I couldn't ask. *"That's how I knew you were not Preema reborn,"* she said. *"The ruthless bitch imprisoned demons at the heart of her world to consume and digest the souls of the unworthy she had created then excrete the raw magic back into the world."* She grunted in grudging admiration. *"The whole mechanism was an ingenious way to raise hosts to fight us."* Her massive, scaled shoulders shrugged. *"Which is why Preema must die. You will find your ancestor for me to pay her bill!"*

The demoness' ravings were a distraction, but there was a nugget of something there.

All those anamneses seeking the sun. "They're all trying to be reborn," I whispered, "to try again to be worthy of being claimed." Awful realization roiled through me like boiling acid.

Madra had another chance. I might see her again if she found her way out of Nethe to whatever immortal spawning ground might be beyond the sun-kissed lands. My heart squeezed in agony at the enormity of what I'd stolen from Nerren and so many others by destroying their very essence. Even their anamneses were consumed in death eternal, burnt entire upon the pyre of my unholy vengeance.

Huund lifted one shoulder, as if my epiphany were obvious. She cocked her head to the other side as if I were a strange and unexpected thing to be considered from a different angle. The wrathful shades ignored us, their attention only devoted to Baal. The hapless demon lord chortled at my confusion, a wet and gurgling sound.

"You seem to have forgotten much," Baal taunted in a low, grinding voice.

In one agonizing moment, it all clicked. The high gods' starvation. The decline in new generations under the sun. The degradation of Preema's grand and terrible forge of souls.

I glared at the Lady of the Dread Hunt. "You want me to release all the anamneses trapped within my shades and the magic bound up in their souls." Nose to nose with Huund, I shouted, "You want me to *slaughter* the unclaimed!" The enormity of the crime she expected me to commit shook my very soul.

She only blinked as my enraged spittle dotted her cheeks. "Of course," she said in a matter-of-fact tone. "That's what they're for."

"According to who?" I demanded. "Amuun the Unspeaking?"

The goddess of the hunt flinched then. But in that moment, I was beyond caring.

"My mother was drowned in the vile vintage!" I spat with more feeling than phlegm, pointing at the foul font of blackness. "In a pool filled with the wine of oblivion!" I scoffed. "I've no idea why so many shades seek it out, but I'm going to put an end to it, once and for all."

211

Almost of her own volition, Grievance roared from the scabbard of my heart. The tomb rang with the sound of cutting steel. I drew the big, two-handed blade over my head, and turned toward Baal, ready for an executioner's strike. Midnight glowed from her blade, swamping the indirect light I'd conjured earlier.

"Yes," Baal croaked. "Yes…"

Four wrathful shades moved as one to block me from the altar where the demon lord lay. Their stitched-shut eyes tracked me. Their sewn lips stretched against ancient sutures in matching snarls. My own shades defied me. *Why? What cause could they have?*

"Preema must be dead for Godforge to have crumbled so far," F'riida said with grim satisfaction. *"Still, I must see her bones for myself to believe it."*

"Illyria," Huund soothed, sounding distant, "this isn't the way." Her hand was cool on my shoulder. "Please. Put down your sword."

"No." My voice shook with rage. And another emotion I had denied for too long.

As if she were talking to an animal caught in a trap, she continued in a low voice, "You don't understand the why of it."

"There can be no reason for such suffering!"

"Let me show you," she urged. "This world is so much bigger and more important than you know." She sighed. "Bigger even than the mother of the gods."

We'd both lost mothers in our own way. I breathed out, slow and careful, lest I shatter.

"Good. She'll show you the truth now," F'riida said smugly. *"Well done."*

By inches, I lowered Grievance and resheathed her, despite the sword's many disappointed wordless complaints.

I needed to know why.

"Take me to Amuun."

CHAPTER 33

*W*ith a mischievous grin, Huund launched herself toward the stone sky of Nethe. At least four heartbeats passed, probably many more, while my guilty thoughts sought out Tourak. And the party I'd argued for—then abandoned. Without inspecting too closely through my crown, I satisfied myself that Tourak had done as I asked. Though Z'nnek had not yet returned, all was well in my palace garden.

F'riida harrumphed. *"If you play too hard to get, you won't."*

I gave the old demoness a mental scowl and tossed myself skyward. Far in the distance, Huund had assumed her smaller, faster hawk form.

"Oh, it's to be a race?" I laughed and pulled on my raven.

F'riida scoffed and reclined on the memory of my favorite clifftop above Alamar.

I quickly learned that hawks fly more swiftly than ravens. By the time we escaped the open expanse of the stone-capped sky above Nethe, Huund had extended her lead considerably. There had to be some way for me to catch up. I found it when we reached Urth's middle realm between Nethe and the sun-kissed lands.

Her faster airspeed did her little good when she had to dodge around the massive stalactites and stalagmites and columns that held up the world above. As a raven, I could turn tighter, and I was more willing to skim closer to the unforgiving stone. I used that maneuverability—and my willingness to risk a high-speed collision—to make gains.

I took back half of her head start.

But it was not enough.

As soon as she emerged into the open air, I'd fall behind again. But I could use her own trick against her. On our first flight to Saetarra today—which seemed eons ago now—she'd shifted into spirit to conserve energy far sooner than I had. The expensive transition was easier for me now, still close enough to Nethe to draw on its bottomless magic. And, perhaps having had some earlier practice.

Eating up Huund's lead was trivial now that flying faster cost me almost no effort. Doubly so, because as a spirit, I just ignored obstacles and flew through the intervening stone. Of course, I missed enjoying the wonders of Urth's realm yet again in my haste to catch my prey.

A squawk of near triumph threatened to burst forth. I restrained myself from giving away how close the race had become.

I was beak to tailfeathers with Huund when we burst out of the cavernous underground and into the brilliant daylight.

"Fine," I cawed. "You win."

Huund returned a quizzical buzz. "Were we racing?" she asked with a sarcastic waggle of her wings.

I turned my beak to the sky, pretending diffidence. Hawkish laughter filled the sky.

Overhead, Amuun's bright white orb shone in the sky. More time had passed than I realized while we were below. A half a day or more.

For a time, I was content to soar with Huund, to follow her lead through the clouds and beyond. The earthtones of her plumage were resplendent in their predatory, hawkish way. She joined me in spirit, leaving the realm of flesh. We didn't race then, nor speak in the way of birds. It was enough that we existed and exulted in the glorious flight toward paradise.

When she did not turn toward Saetarra, though, I startled out of my reverie.

"*She will betray you,*" F'riida warned. "*She promised an audience with Amuun!*"

"Where are you taking me?" I demanded with a squawk and a waggle of my wings.

Though hawks have no way to grin, her amusement oozed from her posture and the tilt of her head as she eyed me. "Trust me," was all she replied with a flex of her talons and a toss of her crest.

Annoyed, I debated whether I should. She'd extended some trust in sharing. Belatedly, I wondered if her story about Amuun's incapacity were true. Not wanting to risk damage to our fledgling relationship, I didn't prod.

Instead, I debated with F'riida. *What if her story about Amuun isn't true?*

The demoness surprised me. *"What does she have to gain from a lie?"*

I shot a mental huff at her. *My trust. My vulnerability. She could be leading me to an ambush!*

Demonic laughter rumbled through my mind. *"Why would she do that now? She thinks you're more powerful than she is."* F'riida scoffed. *"She thinks you defeated me."*

Then where is she taking us? Why won't she tell me? I demanded, but didn't change course. I followed close on Huund's wingtip.

"This is your world, hatchling." She laughed and shifted her scaly bulk. *"Don't you recognize the shape of your own constellations?"*

This high above the world, the sky was black and decorated with gold and silver motes. The drawn bow of the Archer lay far off my right wing. The wheel of the Cart spun high and to its left. Others occupied their customary place along the utter black velvet of the veil: Wolf, Scythe, Raven, and the rest lay like jewels on a cloth.

Ahead of us, the dancing stars formed the familiar swirl of the Gate. In the Litanies, it was a symbol of transition, a milestone or a crossroads, often a place of refuge or to be guarded. Instead of feeling embarrassed, I was curious. As we flew closer, the stars became recognizable as individual angels flying in their formations. The Litanies never explained why the Twin's angels flew in those patterns to guard the veil. It occurred to me that I'd never wondered why the veil needed to be guarded at all. Demons snuck across the veil or broke through in some unspecified way, but the mortal world was protected from them all by Tyrr's host and Torr's host and the Dread Hunt.

Before I could formulate that question for F'riida, so that she could mock my ignorance, half of the flight of gold and silver angels vanished. Thirty or more heartbeats later, they reappeared. But they were in slightly different positions. And flying slightly differently. My raven intuition told me that they weren't the same angels. They moved like *others* in tiny ways that distinguish every creature from one another.

Huund was watching me carefully as we flew side-by-side.

"Do you see it now?" F'riida asked.

Beyond the dance of angels awing, I finally perceived the darker-than-black swirl in the veil. There was a hole in the nothingness.

As we flew closer, half of the guardians flew down through—no, into—that maelstrom. And vanished. I counted carefully then. Exactly thirty heartbeats later, they reappeared. But they were different. From the mortal point of view far below, the changes would be scarcely noticeable. Just a flickering of the stars. Easily missed. Or misunderstood.

Both F'riida and Huund watched me like, well, like hawks. It was unnerving.

Ignoring the awkward sensation, I started counting angels. Until the next half dropped into the blacker-than-black swirl. At least one hundred angels formed the constellation of this dance. Which meant that fifty more, at least, were on the other side of whatever that not-hole in the veil was.

"What in the Hells are they doing?" I asked.

"Not Hells," F'riida said with a chuckle. *"Heaven."*

I shuddered to think where a demon might consider Heaven.

"This is what I need you to understand," Huund told me with a trill and flutter of her flight feathers. "They constantly patrol for any sign of demon invasion."

My mind reeled. I clacked my beak and tossed my head. "That makes no sense," I told them both. "Why would there be demons in Heaven?"

A deep belly laugh rumbled through my unwanted guest.

Huund pulled up hard and flapped her wings to hover. Caught by surprise, I banked hard and twirled around, almost pivoting on a wingtip to return to her. Her nape feathers were up. She was angry. And I had no idea why.

"How do you know this is Heaven's Gate?" she demanded, snipping sharply with her beak and slashing the air with her talons. "You pretend to be so ignorant?"

Fuck me. Details of my two parallel conversations had become crossed.

F'riida chortled. In my mind, she gathered herself into a crouch, watching my interaction with Huund with greater interest than she'd shown toward anything else. Of course, a demoness would be amused by this disaster. I didn't even have time to curse her properly.

I released my raven form and assumed my winged goddess body in spirit. The transition gave me the space of a couple breaths to think, which did me no good. But my more mortal shape was somewhat more expressive —well, perhaps just more familiar. I wondered, not for the first time, if I even needed wings to fly. But I decided that experimenting under these precarious conditions was unwise.

F'riida still chortled at my discomfiture and watched the conflict with interest.

"Where else would *the* Gate go?" I shot back at Huund, deflecting. "It must be somewhere valuable or dangerous for one hundred and fifty angels to be guarding it!"

Those words made no sense, and I realized it as soon as they'd flown from my lips. There was no Heaven in the Litanies, beyond the Twin Paradises of Avaala and Nuuria, and the lofty realm of Amuun's Saetarra. Only a few of the apocryphal Tales mentioned the original home of the high gods: Heaven. A lofty realm which had given birth to the most powerful of our creators.

Huund assumed her own winged goddess form and looked utterly frustrated.

"I can't understand you," the goddess of the hunt and the hunted said at last. "Sometimes you're inexplicably naïve and—" She huffed and made fists. "Other times, you seem to know things no one should know."

Holding her body as rigid as a blade, Huund pointed at the utter emptiness around which Tyrr's and Torr's angels patrolled. "Through Heaven's Gate is the answer to your question."

Suddenly flaming hot and freezing cold at the same time, I held very still and stared into the shifting swirl of the void. My eyes ached from trying to capture its eerie motion and shapeless shape.

"Will you come with me?" Huund asked, a note of pleading in her voice.

The demoness in my mind rumbled a warning growl.

No one knew where I was, and no one would know where to look for me. I thought of Z'nnek, Tourak, Conseca, and Kausae—so many might be endangered if I vanished or died. Plus, I had no idea how the gate worked or where it went. Based on the defenses arrayed to patrol it in force, there was something on the other side too dangerous for one angel alone to investigate. A rolling cycle of fifty angels to a flight dove headfirst into that more than inky black. If I were to do this, more than at any time since I'd died a month ago, there would be no one coming to rescue me.

If I took time to figure out how to commune with Z'nnek through his soul token, he would probably tell me not to go—at least to wait. But I feared he knew the answer to Heaven's riddle and had simply not trusted me with the knowledge. There were many things he could have explained, and I don't know why he refused.

Should I fly into the unknown, there might be no path back for my anamnesis. Death would be death eternal.

Yet, I might never know, otherwise, why the high gods were so desperate to consume my shades. Here was a chance to learn a secret that neither the Litanies nor the Tales could reveal. And Huund would trust me more if I seemed to trust her.

As if sensing my uncertainty, F'riida whispered, *"She wishes your death. Why else would she take you to your doom?"*

I wanted to take F'riida's counsel, but I wasn't sure I could trust the demoness on this or any other matter. Perhaps she wanted me to go and judged me well enough that I would spite her if she warned me not to go. I could spiral myself in circles for days if I did not decide.

Huund was holding her breath. That, perhaps as much as anything, convinced me. This mattered to her. I could hope to discover why only on the other side. And would be in a better position to complete my seduction.

Tucking my hand into my purse, I clutched all four of the soul tokens I owned. *I am going through Heaven's Gate with Huund*, I told them all without waiting for a reply. *I will return as soon as I may. Bide until I return.*

I released the soul tokens and cinched the purse tight.

"Fine." I nodded and flew directly toward the center of Heaven's Gate. *"This will be interesting indeed,"* F'riida crooned.

CHAPTER 34

The shock of falling through nothing struck me like a forge hammer. The utter lack of sensation rang through me like I was a fragile bell. One pure note of no heartbeat, no anxiety, no pain, no demon, and no cares resonated through my soul. I had time only to wonder if I had died eternal.

Then the void was gone.

We fell into a gloaming sky not too dissimilar from Nethe. Stone-colored clouds hung overhead. Huund soared high and to my right. A strange amaranth sun kissed the distant horizon. Whether it rose or fell, I couldn't tell for sure. But some deep instinct told me that it was setting. Broad rays of pink and tangerine caressed the slate gray clouds above us. Their thunderous forms stretched across the world from edge to edge. The threat of a gentle rain permeated the air. And the magic...

Power roiled around me, through me, into me. I felt the tidal pull of it embrace me as if I'd finally come home. It was a welcome I'd not expected.

Below us, the flight of fifty angels of war and justice, resplendent in their golden and silvery plumage, whirled in their patrol pattern. They were spiraling back up from the black and white ruins below. Fear of being stranded in a foreign world—even a world awash in magical power—

gripped my heart with frigid talons. Fear of never seeing Z'nnek nor Tourak nor Kausae again pierced me.

A glance over my shoulder revealed Heaven's Gate.

The maelstrom of the portal was the same from this vantage as it had been from the other side, but inverted. Somehow, its presence comforted me. There was a way home. I relaxed and followed Huund down in lazy circles, luxuriating in the balmy, humid climate. The world beyond the granite and marble city ruins was greener than the highlands in spring and covered in a blanket of forest canopy.

Whatever this place had been, it sprawled ten times larger than Paerul and La Gran Catedral where I'd slain the Hierarch and taken his Book of the Forbidden. Or larger even than that. Easily a hundred times the size of Alamar Village in its span. Tall buildings were strewn across wide roads, both broken and ruined. Gold-veined marble and silver-streaked granite commingled in the jumble. There was no movement of people that I could see. No evidence of habitation. No smoke from chimneys. No lights among lengthening shadows.

"You must see this," Huund called over the wind of our passage. "Then you will understand everything."

F'riida chortled. I glared at her in my mind. But I could tell she was in no mood to spoil whatever surprise loomed for me.

The hawk-winged goddess led me straight to the center of the destroyed city where a massive domed structure had collapsed. The remnants of the architecture reminded me of Saetarra for some reason. The whole place, despite its current, lamentable state, bore the sensibility of a temple. I wondered what strange gods were worshipped here.

In the heart of the place was an enormous statue carved from something like black jade. As we approached from behind, I could see it was a curvaceous woman. She stood tall amidst the scattered debris in a commanding stance. Her shapely hands reached out, either to bless or to berate. Her hooded robe flared around her as if wind-blown. We circled to approach the tall, stately monument head on. Her features grew more distinct in the rosy, dying light until—

I felt as if I'd fallen through Heaven's Gate a second time.

Standing more than twenty times my height, the massive statue wore my face.

Though I have no memory of touching down, I must have landed of my own accord among the broken statues at the feet of my likeness. Power tingled up through my slippered feet as I stood in mute awe. I barely registered that they had been statues of people once. They had been broken off at the ankles. Perhaps the fall shattered them into myriad pieces, each larger than a horse. Those pieces were arrayed around the still standing statue who could only be me—or Preema. The sense of ripples of magic radiating outward through the ground from where I stood brushed against my shock, but didn't dislodge it.

Why this huge idol struck me so hard, compared with the many images I'd seen in Saetarra of the woman I knew in my heart to be Preema, I didn't want to consider. The magnificent scale? Perhaps the arrogance of her countenance frightened me. I knew that tyrannical feeling. I'd spent my life suppressing it, reining it in lest I do unto others what I feared most for myself. Perhaps it was the amulet that hung between her breasts, just as it hung between my own. An encircled raven awing. The same mark I'd impulsively given my first priestess.

I stared up at the berobed figure in awe and growing fear of the expectations of me others would have now. The expectations Huund would have of me now. An urgent welcome from the ripples beneath my feet agitated for my attention.

"My sisters' daughters will tear her down when I have confirmed Preema's fall with my own eyes," F'riida crooned. *"Alas, it would have been better if you had seduced the truth from the hawk-child."*

As if on cue, Huund stepped into my view, watching my expression with intensity.

I wanted to shout at her. But I restrained myself. Instead, I whispered, "Why didn't you warn me?"

"In truth, I didn't want to believe it." She lifted one shoulder in apology. "I still don't."

I glared at her until she lowered her gaze.

"She vanished before my mothers gave birth to me. Millennia before.

The Twins are—" She shuddered. "We all are starving. Now." She met my gaze and held it. "The hunger came slowly at first. After the Accord—"

"There is magic aplenty here," I interrupted. I could feel the rich power, deeper and vaster than what I was accustomed to in the sun-kissed lands or even in Nethe. "Take what you want!" I pulled in just the tiniest wisp of magic and conjured it into a blood candle. I blew upon the wick to light it.

In my mind, F'riida gave a fang-toothed grin at my dramatics.

The gentle glow of the amber light warmed Huund's crisp features. She met my gaze through the flickering candle flame. Her dark skin was flushed. Her eyes, haunted.

Spreading her arms to encompass the ruins of Heaven, she said, "As much magic as there is here, if we drink too deeply, the demons come. We can ill-afford to lose more angels."

"As I did, my sisters send their progeny to test them against your hosts," F'riida said. "Every generation must know the evil they stand guard against." Her long, forked tongue flickered between her fangs. "They must be reminded by blood lest, they forget."

I could protest my ignorance. I could demand that Huund explain it to me in detail. I could, but I wasn't going to give her the satisfaction. Nor the demon.

"The Tales aren't lies," I said with as much accusation as I could muster, "despite what *your* priests say." Speaking it aloud, I realized that the high gods' priests had never been—would never be—*my* priests. I blinked in rapid, cascading realizations as I waited for Huund to speak.

She only nodded.

"How could I be Preema reborn?" I demanded. "The Litanies say—"

Huund looked away, gazing into the distance. Was she wistful? Guilty? Worried?

"You must exorcise those lies, hatchling. They do not serve you. Not at all." F'riida huffed a sympathetic laugh. "But...it matters not for much longer."

"What am I supposed to do?" I asked them both. "I didn't ask for any of this."

Still staring toward the distant horizon, the goddess of the hunt and the hunted pulled her horn from her belt and blew it with all her might.

The fluted ivory blew a long, chilling blast.

Looking over her shoulder, I followed Huund's line of sight.

Three huge demonesses plummeted out of the slate-colored clouds. I knew their gender without knowing how I knew. In the sanguine light, their scales gleamed like polished metal. Each of the three was at least half of F'riida's size in her true, sinuous, scaly form. Probably larger than half. Red. Gold. White.

Gold- and silver-winged angels whirled into a practiced wedge formation and arrowed toward the threat of the incoming demonesses. Beside me, Huund hung the horn at her belt. She shrugged her legendary ironwood bow from across her back. She reached into the endless quiver of deadly broadhead arrows at her hip. Nocking a shaft, she drew the bow at the impossibly distant targets and took aim.

I wished I hadn't left Venatar's peerless bow that never missed with Goerranu. But wishes weren't horses. F'riida was right about one thing: I needed to exorcise the lies. Starting with the lies I told myself.

If, impossibly, I were Preema, if I were the primordial creator of the world I knew, then this Heaven was my home. Its stolen magic had once been mine. To survive, I would take it back. I would make it all mine.

Beneath me, volcanic magic surged through the lines beneath my toes. World-ending power beyond measure. Worship accumulated over centuries or longer. It hummed to the tune of my blood.

Without moving a muscle, I reached out with my senses and grasped more ambient magic than I had ever tried to channel at once. It felt strange. I tried to filter just the familiar shadow magic, but I couldn't separate it from the realms of spirit or flesh. In a hurry, I decided not to care and just *pulled*. Far more than Araeda'h had promised would destroy me if I ever attempted such a thing. If I were going to die, I would do it on my terms. And I would take all my enemies with me.

Huund loosed her shaft.

As I gathered magic, I fearfully watched the red demoness. Her wings flared wide. She inhaled deeply. Then breathed a ragged cone of fire across the flying wedge of angels. Gold- and silver-winged guardians screamed in agony and defiance as they plowed through the attack. Many fell smoking from the sky.

The golden-scaled demoness morphed into a bat-winged mortal form, similar in size to the angels. Huund's arrow sailed through the space where the golden demoness's previous bulk had been. The golden demoness hovered below the host of angels that soared through flames and began to weave a massive net of lightning.

The white-scaled demoness dove below the tops of the ruins and I lost sight of her.

Full past bursting with power, I hesitated. If I were who Huund and F'riida thought me to be, this fight would only perpetuate the cycle I had begun in a previous incarnation.

"My sisters' progeny come at your call," F'riida said with delight. *"You may not have asked for death."*

The green demoness's gaping grin mocked me. *"But it will take you at last!"*

CHAPTER 35

'riida's betrayal should have come as no surprise. Should have. But I'd let my guard down after I'd invited her in. Because I'd learned a tiny bit of the truth from her and with her, I'd felt we had come to a mutual understanding that was more than détente. Stupid of me. Now I had two problems. Once I opened myself to Heaven's magic, its deluge threatened to flood me beyond my capacity to hold it. I tried to turn it off as I would channeling spirit or shadow or flesh magic at home. But that effort failed, and I could not resist its flow. And this enormous monster, who inhabited the safest place in my mind, was bent upon my doom. In my natural form, I stood atop my memory of the cliffs above Alamar and glared up at her in defiance. And fear.

Somehow, I had to solve both my problems at once. Existence was never content just to fuck me. It felt compelled to bugger me at the same time.

"Illyria!" Huund's shout dragged my attention back outside my body. "Do something!"

Several arrows whizzed skyward from the huntress's bow in rapid succession. The surviving angels of the host had reformed a defensive hedge around us, bristling with silver spears and golden pikes. I wondered how many heartbeats would have to pass before the next fifty reinforced the flight of angels being destroyed in the sky.

Bloody prolapsed fuck holes, I thought. *Right. Three problems.*

The massive red monster which had roasted the gold and silver angels seemed oblivious to the hawk-fletched arrows puncturing its glittering scales. Banking lazily, it soared past the massive statue of... I sighed in denial. But that gave me inspiration.

"I'm thinking," I huffed at Huund, which I regretted when I inhaled the burned stench of the screaming and the dead.

Her jaw dropped in astonishment. "Why? Just do whatever you did to defeat F'riida three more times!"

"Give me a minute!" I resisted the urge to squawk at her in outrage. I wasn't about to do what I'd done with the demoness three more times. I should never have done it once.

F'riida was holding back. I was certain she would pounce on me as soon as I engaged with the other demonesses. A two-front battle was never optimal. I needed to reduce my problem set to something more manageable. Preferably to zero. None was actually my preferred number of problems. I itched on the inside and the outside with frustration.

Closing my eyes, I focused on my internal battlefield. The pure flood of magic channeled into my own self-image. The power was too great to contain in any wine vessel I could imagine. So, inspired by the absurd, egotistical monument, I built myself, growing me into statuesque proportions in my mind. Before the demoness could blink, we were on the same eye level. And I was still steadily growing.

"Pick on someone you own size," I challenged.

Within heartbeats, I was looking down at F'riida.

She reared back to buffet me with her massive wings. I stepped in so close that all she could do was pound on the back of my armor. *When had I donned Repose? Was I losing track of time or memories again?* I shook away the distracting thoughts and grabbed her around the neck with both hands. This demon had seemed so powerful before she gave away her power in a ruse to get Huund to believe she was dead. A ruse intended to gain my trust. Now that I was awash with Heaven's grace, she seemed a threat that I could manage. I didn't know why she didn't draw in more power to challenge me the same way I did, but I grabbed the advantage and squeezed it for all it was worth. And her neck.

F'riida tried to roar. She belched her noxious acid, but I held her jaws up and away from me. Still, I gagged on the smell. The burning bile splashed across the rocks where it smoked and bubbled. Pieces of my soul sizzled and burned, but I refused to think about the loss of those memories now. Fear of losing more memories I'd only recently recovered drove me to fight harder, to end this faster. Battling the Chosen, I'd sacrificed and forgotten my first meeting with Tourak and my first childhood victory over my brother Nerren. Gods knew how much else. I'd nearly forgotten myself.

Today, I burned the bottomless fountain that was the magic of Heaven.

As I grew even larger, I heaved her up and over onto her back. Her wings and tail thrashed the dry grasses and rocks. All four of her claws scratched at my armor enough to be irritating, like a house cat angry about being bathed. Straddling her scaly chest that no longer seemed so massive, I knelt over the monster I'd invited in. With both gauntleted hands, I crushed her horned head against the rocks of my favorite childhood refuge. At the foot of the cliff below, the memory of Alamar Forte seemed tinier to my much-enlarged eyes.

"Hold still," I demanded. "I don't want to kill you, but I will if you try to distract me while I deal with your sisters' daughters." I glared into the one slitted eye that I could see.

When she didn't respond, I shook her for good measure. "Yield," I ordered with a tightening grip. I could feel cartilage and bone creak in protest beneath my fingers. Her throbbing pulse beat at my palms. Her attempts to scrape me off with claw and wing grew increasingly feeble. At that moment, I could have possessed her soul and poured it into yet another bottle containing my enemies, or simply crushed her spirit into formless magic for use in some other purpose in the future. For some reason, I didn't.

I refused to examine why I didn't want to. But I would, if she forced my hand.

Too many heartbeats later, I'd resigned myself to just kill her and be done with it when she jerked her once-massive-seeming head in a brusque nod. I released the pressure enough that a wheezing breath expanded her laboring chest between my thighs.

"Good," I said. "Bide in silence while I convince the others to negotiate."

"Why?" F'riida croaked.

Good fucking question, I thought as I turned my attention back to the fight for Heaven. *Why didn't I destroy the traitorous demoness and be done?*

The lie I told myself? I had no time.

Turning my attention outward, I scanned the sky for enemies. Mere moments seemed to have passed. The red demon circled around to my left at about waist height. That was annoying. I never wanted enemies behind me. Absently, I backhanded the monster out of the sky. I looked down and watched as it crashed through the statue of Preema and skidded through the rubble of the ruined temple. The statue of my past self began to collapse.

I blinked. My actual body had grown to match what I imagined in my mind. Hells, that would require some thought to figure out. Not for the last time, I wished my magical tutelage with Z'nnek and Araeda'h were more thorough.

Lightning cascaded around me in a massive, shocking web. It *hurt* in a way I couldn't describe. Muscles twitched. Sphincters clenched. The porkish stench of cooked flesh filled the air. I screamed and felt the ground tremble beneath my hobnailed boots as I stumbled toward the golden-winged demoness the size of a large dragonfly. I absently noticed her very female nature while I fought against the lightning web that constricted my arms to my body. F'riida had called them all her sisters' daughters, so I guessed that made sense. Not nieces, so not really blood relations. Kinship of choice, of the heart, I understood. I staggered closer to her as I realized my balance was off. Godsdamned lightning. Someday, I'd master the elements.

My scream seemed to have tumbled her a bit. Given that she seemed tiny now, about the same size as the angels in the host who had grounded to form a defensive ring around Huund and me. Belatedly, I realized I should be careful and not step on anyone accidentally. I dropped my eyes to look at the ankle-high winged figures below. Then spotted the white-scaled demon who was sneaking out of the rubble to our rear.

"Behind you!" I thundered at Huund.

A fresh charge blasted through the net around me. Gritting my teeth on another scream, I left the huntress and the host to deal with the third. I needed this net gone. I tried to slip into spirit so that I could ignore the constriction. And found that didn't work. I couldn't separate the realms of spirit, shadow, and flesh. They were all one here. Not good. I had barely begun to understand the three realms of magic when I could deal with them separately. *Maybe that's why I couldn't shut off the deluge of power once I invited it in?*

The magical flood had apparently caught up with my new size and I began to feel close to bursting again. I needed to discharge it somehow. I couldn't continue to grow forever!

The golden-winged demoness fluttered close. "I never thought to see you myself," she crowed. "I will be the most honored among all my sisters!"

Discharge? My thoughts were fuzzy. Worse, F'riida was beginning to struggle against my hold around her throat. I should beat her to death with her own staves. The two disparate threads intertwined in my mind. I manifested the midnight fighting poles I'd possessed after our faux duel into my left hand. They were convenient for my new size. I jammed the ends against the stone at my feet and crushed the hafts of both against the lightning web constricting me.

With a clear path to follow, the web discharged through the staves, scorching my fist in the process. I held in a scream of agony but refused to release my weapons. The discharge blasted a crater into the ruined tile of the floor. Shrapnel showered Huund and the remaining angels. My tormentor gaped in surprise. Taking advantage of the concussive distraction, I snatched the demoness out of the air with my undamaged hand, trying not to crush her fragile, golden bat wings. But not caring much if I did.

"Hold still," I ordered my tiny captive, "or I'll end you in a most ignominious way." I gave her a shake in my fist, just to reinforce the point.

Her head lolled, blonde hair flopping about loose.

A glance told me the red demoness had regained her feet. She was battered but preparing to launch herself back into the fight. I winced as I twirled both staves in my damaged left hand and struck the ground between us. Because I wasn't used to accounting for being so much larger, it had a much greater impact than the warning I expected to give. The ground rippled away from the point of impact like a quake that knocked my target off her feet. And rattled my hand with bone-jarring pain.

"Stop fighting," I shouted through gritted teeth, "or I will end you all!"

"Illyria! Just kill them!" Huund's shout was small and far away. "But be careful of us!"

I looked down sheepishly. Huund, the entire surviving host, and the white demoness were regaining their feet. I didn't stop to count how many had been crushed or injured by debris or grounded lightning. Frost covered a cone between the demoness and the host. Two of the host had apparently frozen solid in some sort of ice attack and shattered in the quake. I'd apparently knocked them all down with my last warning strike. Or my shout. Or stumbling around.

I needed to get back to normal size to negotiate. F'riida's question still rang in my head. *Why not just kill the enemies who had attacked me and mine?* With a shock, I realized that I'd adopted Huund and the host of Tyrr's and Torr's angels as my own. *That complicates things.*

One problem at a time, I told myself. I watched the two demonesses that I wasn't currently squeezing while I focused on the magical problem first. Outgrowing my ability to manage it was bad. Araeda'h had described the explosive result of channeling too much in graphic detail. More than once. I had work to do and no time to die. Now that I realized that it was not spirit or shadow or flesh, but some strange fourth thing, I gained a sense of its origin and closed myself to its inflow. It seemed so simple, in retrospect.

Refraining from a sigh of relief for having one less problem, I glared down at the tiny woman-shaped demon in my fist. "Will you and your sisters parley?"

"No!" Huund shouted.

The host clashed their silver spears and golden pikes against matching shields in a challenge toward the red-scaled and white-scaled foes they could see. The smaller, differently colored versions of F'riida crouched and readied themselves to resume battle. Maybe the host thought reinforcements would arrive soon. Maybe Huund was just ready to die eternal. In very few moments, three lesser demonesses had reduced the host of fifty by more than half.

At last, I began to understand the high gods' dilemma. With fewer and fewer angels to defend Heaven's Gate, and however many other gates there were, attrition like that became unrecoverable at some point. Perhaps they were already starved beyond that.

Their shields gave me an idea. Looking around what had once have been a massive, domed temple like Saetarra, I made a snap decision. I couldn't trust Huund to keep the peace. There had to be another way. Padra had long ago drilled into me: *You win every fight you avoid, son.* I knew that was Nerren's memory, not my own, but I was sure our father had trained us both the same. I would honor their deaths eternal by blazing a peaceful trail. I released my staves, stowing them away next to Grievance in my heart to face my foes unarmed.

Envisioning a dome like the one above Saetarra, I poured the stolen power of Heaven to enclose the defensive circle of angels around Huund in a translucent midnight bubble. I needed mine to block spirit and shadow and flesh, to contain whatever Huund might try. Pouring all of the strange magic of Heaven that engorged me into a shield that I trusted to contain my warlike... *Um, what we were to each other? If this was Heaven, where was I born? One of the Hells? F'riida hadn't rejected the label of demoness, but weren't we the demons to the denizens of Heaven?*

I was sure my thoughts were making no sense, but somehow rang clear and right.

The clashing of weapons on the shields of the host became muted. I could see Huund glaring at me through the shadowy dome. I turned away, as much to hide my smile as to regard my accidental hostage. As I ruminated upon my disturbing thoughts, I set the slightly crushed, golden-winged demoness on her dainty feet at the edge of the translucent raven-black shield as an act of good faith.

"I will not destroy you," I rumbled in the biggest, most goddess-like voice I could muster, "if you respect the rules of parley."

CHAPTER 36

I'd shrunk a bit in manifesting the cage for Huund and the Twins' angels, but I still stood as tall as the statue I'd toppled by accident had long moments past. The scaly, white demoness clawed her way atop the smoky dome that trapped Huund and the host within it. Her claws clacked on my unforgiving magic. While she was enormous compared with Huund —or me, mere heartbeats ago—the monster was now a quarter of my size. Still a danger, but... Then she inhaled and reared back as I'd seen F'riida do before deploying her most devastating attack.

No, fuck that, I thought.

I didn't know if her breath would harm me much at this size—or her little, mortal-sized sister at my feet. I wasn't inclined to find out. Her mistake had been to trample upon my shield and my offer of peaceful parley. I lifted my hand toward her.

"Bhaerrah!" the tiny gold-winged demoness shouted. "Wait!"

Frost sparkled in the air around the rearing demoness's fangs. She showed no sign of stopping herself. Whatever she was preparing to do, it wasn't small. F'riida chuckled weakly through the chokehold in my mind.

I made a fist. The shadowy dome of my magic bubbled up around her before she could exhale. Encapsulated nose to tail, she expelled a blizzard against the inside of the smoky barrier. The ice shattered against my magic

—and it *hurt*. I stifled a grunt of pain. While I couldn't identify *where* exactly it hurt me, the burning cold stabbed through me. I hoped it hurt her, too.

With a squeeze of my fingers, I crushed the magic shell smaller and smaller, until the white-scaled monster was curled up like a baby chicken inside an egg. The tiny enclosure separated from the dome like a soap bubble rising from a bath.

"No!" F'riida cried, shaking the earth beneath us in my mind.

"Don't hurt her!" the little golden-winged demon below me wailed.

Still pained, I growled. "Too late."

With a crooked finger, I beckoned the ball wrapped around the white demoness. It rolled down the dome toward me and bounced until I stomped it to a stop with my oversized boot. Rubbing my armored sternum to ease the freezing indigestion that seemed to be settling into my core, I scanned the rest of the battlefield.

The red-winged demon pulled herself toward me on all fours, dragging a broken wing behind her. There was a dangerous gleam in her eye. Her tiny golden sister made pleading noises and beat at my shins with her small hands. I wondered why she didn't deliver a more effective magical attack. To prevent further silliness, I scooped her up again in one hand. With the other, I drew a dagger-sized version of Grievance and laid it against my new hostage's throat. Splitting my attention between two conflicts was dangerous. Four was suicide.

Faintly, Huund yelled through her own prison, "Kill them, Illyria!"

Five conflicts, if I counted Huund and the angels. If she and the Holy Twins' host attacked my dome somehow.

"Why can nothing ever be simple?" I complained to everyone and no one.

The surviving angels continued to beat their weapons on their shields. The sound was like children at play clacking sticks together. F'riida mewled impotently in my mental chokehold. My golden-winged hostage flailed and made helpless noises in her midnight eggshell. The white-scaled demon trapped inside my magic scrabbled ineffectually at the barrier with her claws. I scanned semi-consciously for new dangers and wished I could ignore them all.

Except the red demon dragging her broken body toward me on her belly. She had most of my attention.

"Maal!" my tiny hostage screamed. "Parley!"

I met Maal's demonic gaze and held it. I felt a certain kinship and sympathy with her. Not too many days ago, I'd been similarly humiliated by Provax. I'd had nothing to lose, and I'd never have surrendered but to save Conseca and my kin. If this monster refused to surrender to overwhelming defeat, I could admire her for it. Even as I destroyed her and her sisters.

How I could read the expressionless, scaly demon face, I could never say for sure. But I beheld her defiance at war with her love for both my hostages, white and gold. *Which will win?* I wondered and waited. In my heart, I knew that, were our positions reversed, spite would win.

At last, her horned head sank to the broken rubble. The scales blurred and rippled as her body reformed into a tiny mortal woman with close-cropped, fiery hair and leathery, red bat wings. She rose slowly from where she lay prostrate. One wing was mangled and misshapen. She spread her empty hands wide and limped toward me with her head lowered in submission.

"What is your name?" I asked as I placed my gilded hostage upon the ground again. Reluctantly, I sheathed Grievance, unblooded in my heart.

"Oorgaana," the gilded demoness croaked, working her jaw and neck.

I shrugged in apology. I'd been as gentle as circumstances permitted.

She pointed at the approaching winged woman. "Maal." With a look of concern, she gestured to the demon curled beneath my boot. "Bhaerrah."

Booting the ball toward her sisters, I opened my fingers wide to release Bhaerrah. She tumbled snout over tail. Before she shimmered and assumed the form of a pale-skinned woman with long bluish-white hair, I could see that her own ice magic had taken its toll on her as well.

Good, I thought. *Serves you right.* Yet, I pitied them in their humiliation.

"Why?" Huund hollered, her voice attenuated by the magic still imprisoning her.

I wondered about that myself.

The three demonesses held hands, faced me in a line, and bowed their heads. If they'd been highlanders or Elysians, that pose would mean acknowledgement but not submission. I wondered what it meant to them.

235

"Why?" F'riida asked in a strangled whisper in my mind.

"Something my father and mother always told me," I said to everyone, and myself. "You win every fight you avoid."

The three demonesses, the noisome host, and Huund fell silent. They all watched me with some mix of confusion and concern and hope. The green-scaled demoness in my mind ceased her struggle, her great body relaxing into submission.

"I did not come here to fight," I insisted. "I came here to learn."

My eyes roamed the destroyed, arrogant beauty of a temple that had once been. My gaze lingered on the newly broken statue of…Preema. I rejected that identity. Even if I were truly her, I did not wish to be as she had been.

"I do not like what I have learned." I glared at Huund.

Huund glared back. The Lady of the Hunt might be powerful at home. Here, though, she was not even powerful enough to challenge me. I was as baffled as she…and more relieved. How I knew enough to survive this confrontation, let alone snatch victory from the jaws of my enemies, I did not yet understand. Nor would I for some time.

Suppressing a shrug, I turned to watch the colorful demonesses, but they stood unmoving and regarding me with confusion.

Whatever part of me recognized this world and was embraced by it in turn, I refused to be the tyrant my past self had evidently been. We might share a face and a form, but we shared little else. Whichever deepest of my memories—my anamnesis—held the key to my essence, it was still subject to my choices. Later, I would have some serious soul-searching to do in order to discover those secrets. I doubted anyone here could tell me. For now, I would be as I chose.

You are home now, I said to F'riida in my mind. *Show me how to release you and I will.*

In my mind, I took my hands from around her throat and stood. Something had changed for both of us. She was beaten, and I knew she would present no further threat. No longer needing to be huge to dominate her, I released the massive magic of Heaven to shrink back to my customary size. The power sluiced away less eagerly than it had come, as if unwilling to abandon me. F'riida twisted to her feet, rocking her shoulders and hips as she stood. I didn't mind looking up at the scaly green snout. My fear of her had sublimated.

"What would you have us do?" Oorgaana asked, in a voice that no longer seemed tiny.

Opening my eyes, I found myself eye to eye now with my recent foes. They stood almost too far away to have a conversation. I would have to ask Araeda'h or Z'nnek or Tourak why my internal perception of size was tied to my external self-image. The scales F'riida taught me had been much the same.

With a thought, I released Repose to swap the armor for my more customary burial wraps. The crimson and black silk seemed more appropriate to the negotiation I wanted to have.

I smiled at the demonesses. "Why did you attack them without provocation?" I gestured toward the remaining angels of the host, still trapped beneath my smoky midnight magic.

Outrage blossomed on all three faces. "They— You— We—" None of the three could seem to find the words to explain.

"You would attack any invader in your home," F'riida's mortal-sized voice grated as if it had been crushed. *"To them, you are the tyrant their mothers deposed less than a brief century ago. The monsters you've caged are, to them, merely the instruments of your will."*

The very idea of Huund and the Twins' angels being my tools was ludicrous. I glanced at the subjects of my thoughts. They watched me warily, now quiet and skittish as unbroken yearlings. They had no idea what would happen next.

But I did.

CHAPTER 37

*H*uund pounded on the transparent midnight magic of my dome that entrapped her and the surviving angels of the Twins' hosts. "Illyria! Release me!" Her expression was difficult to read: part scowl, part wonder, part something else.

I chose to let her wait, since I wasn't sure I could trust any of those things. Huund would not want what I wanted from these three docile, vanquished demonesses that stood demurely before me. The Lady of the Hunt would meddle. I was certain of it. But I was tired. Exhaustion skulked at the edge of my awareness. I'd learned something new about channeling the magic of Heaven—almost too late. The lesson had taken much of my energy.

The fourth docile, vanquished demoness inside me waited more patiently than I'd ever seen her. I was afraid to know why, but I was grateful for the respite, however brief it might be. In her mortal form, she stood tall and motionless in my mind and studied me.

Taking a few moments to recover as I surveyed the aftermath around me wasn't to punish Huund. Or so I told myself. I lost count of the corpses of gold- and silver-winged angels strewn about the ruin of the temple. More than the original fifty must have joined the battle at some point while I was distracted. All the more reason to send these demonesses to their mothers with my request for Conclave.

"What do you hope to accomplish?" Huund demanded, her voice sounding far away through the magical shield.

After a deep breath, I stopped being petty and released the dome. The massive quantity of magic I'd channeled into it popped out of existence like a soap bubble burst. I could feel it rush back into the latent, ambient power of Heaven. Huund hurried to my side, watching the still immobile demoness trio.

"How did you manage?" F'riida asked, her tone curious, feigning boredom.

I could tell she desperately wanted to know. Not telling her because I didn't know sounded exactly the same as arrogantly refusing on principle. Neither was my style.

"A woman must be permitted some secrets," I snarked aloud to both Huund and F'riida.

The huntress and the demoness in my soul both regarded me with a fusion of vexation and admiration. Their chagrin warmed my ego. I chuckled, which drew the attention of my soon-to-be messengers. The expressions of the young demonesses tightened with expectation.

"That's right!" Huund hollered at them. "You should be afraid!"

Resisting the urge to shush her, I took four steps toward my intended emissaries.

The surviving angels encircled us all, spread about in a circle fifty paces across. They menaced the docile demonesses with their polearms and inarticulate taunts. By my count, Tyrr's and Torr's host had little to brag about. Twice or thrice their number lay on the battlefield. Many broken in a fall from the sky. Many burned to charcoal or shattered into still-frozen pieces.

All three ignored the jeers of the tormenting angels. Their eyes rested on me.

"They surrendered to me," I said in my battle ground voice. I'd never been elected warlord of a clan as a mortal woman. But I'd learned from—was descended from—some of the most respected in Alamar's history. "They have my protection."

The taunts ceased. Huund cast a shrewd gaze at me, not the surprise I expected. Everyone stood waiting for me to find a subtle way to ask them to carry a message of peace. Without giving away my intentions to Huund.

"What do you want of them?" F'riida asked. "Why did you spare my sisters' daughters?"

I want you to leave, I thought at the emerald-haired demon sorceress.

The Lady of the Hunt inquired with seeming obsequiousness, "What shall I do?"

"If I do that, my hatchling," she said, "your game with Huund will be up."

"Runny shits," I thought aloud.

With a surprised huff of laughter, Huund turned to me, head cocked to one side. "You seem to get ahead of yourself often, Illyria." She smiled wryly. "Did you not have a plan for what to do with them…" She chuckled. "If you won?"

Although I was not a child anymore, I couldn't resist the temptation to stick my tongue out at her. Her throaty, bell-like laugh drew everyone's eyes. There was a different woman underneath all that lovely, frightening armor.

"I am considering," I said, loud enough for everyone to hear. In truth, I was out of ideas.

"Do not presume to speak for the high gods," Huund warned gently.

I chuckled, then stopped myself abruptly. Beneath my dark amusement lay a hysteria that would undo everything if it were released.

"Tell me what you want to tell them," F'riida suggested. "I will give them your message in our speech." She gave me a genuine-seeming smile. "And Huund will not be any the wiser."

How will that work? I asked the traitress. *You just warned me that letting you step out of my soul will give away my game. How would speaking a demon tongue be any different?*

The wicked grin that lit F'riida's face made me shiver. "Explain it away just as you did the scales you 'stole' from me."

I scowled at her, but it made a sort of sense. *What's the catch?* I demanded.

F'riida shrugged. "You must allow me to speak through you."

"No, that won't work," I mused aloud, as much to refuse the demoness as to keep everyone waiting apprised that I hadn't forgotten them.

Huund blinked rapidly. "What won't work?"

240

I stepped closer to the goddess of the hunt and the hunted, cultivating an air of intrigue. "You brought me here to show me this." I gestured around the ancient, destroyed beauty strewn with fresh carnage. "Why do we fight them?" I asked.

Surprise or confusion or disbelief or something flooded over Huund's face, only to be washed away by disdain. "To keep them from coming through the Gate! You saw what F'riida could do." she whispered with forceful emotion. "And to reclaim *your* rightful dominion!"

"She lies," F'riida drawled. *"She's not old enough to know that."*

"Then why didn't you destroy the Gate?" I asked them both. "That would solve all kinds of problems."

F'riida nodded. *"My sisters are content to use the incursions of your little hosts to train their daughters. To remind us all why we must remain vigilant."*

Huund deflated. "We can't. We've tried."

I shook my head. "Why not just guard the other side? Why all this elaborate patrolling?"

"They"—Huund stabbed an accusing finger at the quiescent demonesses —"sneak through and kill more than if we meet them in battle here!" Then she grew wistful. "We remind ourselves of what paradise the demons took from us. And we watch for an opportunity."

Her vitriol sounded personal, and unconvincing, given what I'd witnessed of the four demon sorceresses of my acquaintance so far. But I supposed if I'd been fighting and watching my own die for thousands of years, I'd be bitter and uncompromising, too. For the first time, I wondered at how Z'nnek had kept his aplomb beneath the high gods' thumbs.

"That may be my fault entire." F'riida chortled. *"My sisters are in the main content to ignore your—Preema's—failed experiment. I alone refused to accept the détente."*

There was a fact to examine. Failed experiment? I needed time to explore F'riida's knowledge of history, which was more ancient even than Huund's. As much as I wanted to get her out of my head, I finally realized I needed to seduce her, too. At least metaphorically. I'd been focused on a goddess of the false Litanies when I'd been carrying around an older entity feared by the same high gods who professed the lies.

Could I trust the demoness who had just blatantly betrayed me? Should I?

My intuition not to trust Huund with my intention to negotiate with the demon-mothers was sound. She was too mired in her own reasons to fight forever. I could empathize, but I also could not condone eternal war. Countless generations of mortals and immortals had been slaughtered on the altar of this conflict. Everything had to end sometime. Peace was worth a risk.

Tell them, I thought at F'riida, *I will meet their leaders in four days to negotiate a peace.*

I gave the demoness control of my body to speak through me.

CHAPTER 38

$\mathcal{W}$e fell out of the numbing void that was Heaven's Gate. The familiar blue and white and green world below us was a cool bath for my soul. Mountains. Steppes. Clouds. Oceans. Even the dusty sands of the deserts. The brilliant white of Amuun's paradise warmed the left side of my face. I basked in the sun as well as relief that F'riida had returned control of myself to me.

I had gambled that she would. And inexplicably won.

Too bad Coyne hadn't been around to make odds and take my bet.

In the aftermath of F'riida's brief exchange—in a language I did not understand—with the younger three demonesses, I had rushed Huund and the rest to return. Huund had demanded to know what I'd said, so in the end I just flew off without her and hoped she'd follow. After two near brushes with extinction, I was as anxious to return to Nethe and consult with my lovers about my plan for peace as I was to meet Amuun for the first time. So, first to Saetarra, to meet the mother of the gods, and then home.

What did you actually say to your sisters' daughters? I asked F'riida as we soared away from Heaven's Gate. I had not understood the growling, roaring language the demons spoke amongst themselves. With little alternative, I had trusted F'riida to arrange a meeting with the demon matriarchs.

"Oh?" F'riida asked with false coyness. *"I just promised that—if they would meet with you a fortnight hence—you would surrender your right to Heaven."*

Irritation coursed through me. Everyone thought they knew better. *I told you four days!*

"You will need the time, hatchling," F'riida said mildly. *"Trust me."*

I suppose fourteen is about the same, I grumped. In my mind, I frowned at the blithe demoness. *And I don't like the word surrender,* I thought at her, *but it's near enough the truth. Nethe is my home. I've no need of a war for Heaven.*

The demoness watched me in a calm, disturbing manner.

Huund flew behind me with the bedraggled, battered flight of silver- and gold-winged angels. They weren't my problem, and I hadn't really given them much thought. I knew that the hosts of the high gods would likely be a threat to what I wanted in some way, and I resolved to ponder the problem of the Twins and the Dread Hunt and the old gods in the future. After my audience with Amuun and my reunion with my lovers.

But the hovering ranks upon ranks of gold and silver angels awaiting us was unexpected.

Kausae in their vanguard. I nodded to her in surprise. Something had changed. She regarded me without expression. I would have to defer our reckoning.

Tyrr and Torr broke from where they had been conferring with a knot of their angels and the double score of the Dread Hunt. They flew astride winged mounts I'd only heard of in the Litanies. A golden, eagle-winged griffon. A silvery hippogriff with the head and wings of a snowy owl. Knowing the Dread Hunt, I imagined these mounts were a second form of the Twins' own archangels. What would mine be? Was that a secret Tourak had kept from me? Why? Or had I simply forgotten...again?

Tyrr scanned the ragged lines of angels behind me. "I see that you did not require rescue after all, *sister.*" His tone was dismissive and not quite disappointed.

I blinked at the abrupt greeting.

Huund scoffed. "I know it seemed overlong to you, but I was gone but an hour."

While siblings squabbled, I surveyed the hosts drawn up around Heaven's Gate. Beyond them, the constellations of unchanging stars had vanished. The velvet black night of the veil that cradled the sun-kissed lands of my home was devoid of the sparkling diamonds I'd taken for granted all my life.

The Twins had gathered the last of their hosts to lay siege to Heaven's Gate.

The massed hosts of the high gods were fewer than half the number Nethe could boast.

How had they beaten Z'nnek? How had they forced his surrender to the Accord?

F'riida nudged me. *"Pay attention, hatchling."*

The Twins had been arguing, and I had missed something vital in my distraction.

"… a month was more than we agreed!" Tyrr grumbled, jutting his square chin at his brother. "He made us wait."

Huund frowned at the angry god of war. Tyrr had the petulant expression of a child denied a promised toy.

Torr petted the glossy feathers on his mount's head. "A few extra days changed nothing. A minor adjustment to our longstanding protocol. As it turns out, our beloved *sister* was able to rescue herself after all." He gave her a wan smile. "What, pray tell, was the delay, *sister*?"

It was clear to me that the Twins resented Huund. But they also feared her. Why?

"What protocol?" I asked, thinking it an innocent enough question.

All three siblings aimed their glares at me.

With a nod, Huund announced, "I am at last convinced." She locked gazes, first with Torr and then with Tyrr. When they stifled their objections, she continued, looking me in the eye. "Beyond Heaven's Gate, time passes more slowly."

"She is not so deficient of intellect as I gave her credit for," F'riida whispered with mild amusement. *"I wonder if she has learned the magnitude."*

The non sequitur confused me. "How much more slowly?" I asked the huntress.

F'riida chuckled and took a seated position upon the damaged stones. With her ankles crossed and her hands upon her knees, she looked ready to meditate. I supposed it was better than her massive, scaly bulk occupying my thoughts. I looked down upon my memory of Alamar at the foot of the cliff. The nostalgia for the crisp alpine air of my refuge failed to soothe me as it usually did.

"For them"—Huund waved a hand that might have encompassed the army of angels or the whole world—"it has been a month or more."

Shame and surprise warred within me. I'd left guests unattended! I resisted the urge to snatch Z'nnek's soul token and reach through the little pebble to touch him. The words that escaped were little more than a breath. "A month?"

With a dismissive shrug, Huund said, "We don't know why. It just is."

Torr threw up his hands. "Are you *not* going to tell—"

"You must tell Mother," Huund interrupted him, giving me a meaningful stare, "what you told the demons. And why." She raised one suspicious eyebrow.

"She talked to them?" Shock was not an emotion I expected to see on Tyrr's face.

"Yes, yes, dear *brother*," Huund said in a mocking lilt. "Talking is something other people do rather than hack things with a sword."

Apparently, there was no love lost for the Twins from Huund, either. The golden twin scowled at his sister. Torr chuckled at his brother's expense.

Huund smirked at Tyrr. "She bested three of their sorceresses like swatting flies and then proceeded to *talk* to them. After they surrendered."

"Indeed?" asked Torr with renewed surprise. "Surrendered?"

His brother scoffed. "She let them kill enough of mine first." He pointed at Torr. "And yours." The god of war shook his head. "They've never shown us mercy." He glared at me.

I felt challenged to explain myself, which I was loath to do under the friendliest of circumstances—which this was not. My mind was still reeling from the fact that a month had passed in Nethe while I'd spent an hour or less in Heaven. So many responsibilities shirked, albeit unintentionally. So many things could have gone wrong in my absence!

Conseca could have been slain by Saevera.

The highlands could have been lost.

They could have invaded Nethe.

Nethe. With so much time passed, I felt I should go home first. Saetarra.

I glanced at the citadel of the sun goddess where it orbited her shining white namesake. Or perhaps the sun was named for her? I shook my head to stop the woolgathering. Explaining myself to the siblings seemed pointless. My need for the comfort of home was strong, but despite my worries, Z'nnek and Tourak and my loving unkindness would always be there for me. This close to Saetarra, it would be wasteful not to make a brief visit. And, perhaps, warn the mother of the gods of what I intended to do. With or without her blessing.

Why I was tempted to ask F'riida for input, I don't know. But I refused to do so. The demoness sat with supreme stillness, like a monk from the east islands, and watched me intently. Feeling like an involuntary pupil again made me irrationally angry.

Channeling that anger into my impression of an enigmatic and unpredictable goddess, I smiled as coldly as I could manage at Tyrr. "I will speak with Amuun first."

With a nod to Huund, I flew lazily toward paradise. Past the angry gods. Past the waiting army of angels. Daring them all to defy me.

CHAPTER 39

*D*uring our march through the sterile white corridors of Amuun's idea of what paradise should be, Huund tried to engage me in conversation. She was the only spot of effervescent emerald and earthtones amidst the starkness, but I wanted none of that. So, I ignored her until she stopped trying. She'd manipulated me enough. To be fair, though, I'd done the same.

While my own deception was far from harmless, hers seemed so. Her surreptitious visit to Nethe in disguise. The all-for-show trial of the Conclave and her complete submission. The diversion through Heaven's Gate. All of those had been to illuminate my ignorance. I still wasn't certain what her ultimate goal was, but I was now sure she was no threat to me and mine. She knew who I was, or had been, and now accepted it as fact. Time would tell if she would be an ally, or more. Whatever her distractions had been about, whatever my attraction had been, they had delayed me from getting what I'd wanted all along: justice and mercy from the mother of the gods herself.

However, the Chosen of Tyrr and his warpriests in Elysia *had* violated the sanctity of Spring Festa. They had poisoned and murdered my kith and kin and clan folk from across the highlands. And did so in violation of Amuun's own Litanies and the teachings of the high gods' priests and priestesses. Tyrr's twin, Torr, had stood by and profaned his domains of civilization and justice by doing nothing to prevent or correct those evils. Surely, at my earnest appeal, the mother of the gods would set all that to rights.

I ignored the naked, armed statuary of ivory and iron that lined the halls. I ignored the ever-shifting portrayals of mysterious glories long past—none of which derived from the Litanies. I ignored the armories and libraries and all the empty spaces devoid of life. Instead, I ruminated upon my version of paradise in Nethe and how best to secure it against all comers. The realization that Saetarra wasn't refusing to supply magic when I tried to channel it saddened me. The magic was simply not there. What seemed inexhaustible in Nethe was absent here.

An irritable unease gripped me. I could not shake it free.

At long last, the goddess of the hunt and the hunted hesitated before an unassuming, curtained archway much like all the others we'd passed. "Illyria, I—"

"Whatever it is," I said, "we can discuss it." I huffed. "After."

She looked at me, concern etched into her face. "You just need to be prep—"

"Later," I dismissed with a raised hand. I took a breath. And pushed my way through the heavy, ivory-colored panels of silk brocade that guarded the entrance.

The garden which spilled out before me on the other side was not what I expected.

A riot of jungle flowers filled the hothouse. Brilliant sunlight in rays of pure white and stained gold speared through the colored skylights to pierce the greenery. The damp air kissed the exposed skin of my arms. Trilling of colorful tropical birds perched in the oddly shaped swamp trees covered the susurrus of insect mating calls. I'd never been to visit the eastern isles from where at least one of Huund's parents hailed. But I'd heard them described. I'd met the olive-skinned traveling monks and shrewd traders. And I might as well have just walked off a white sand beach into their jungle homeland. Vine-wrapped statues of duel-fighters, ascetic monks, and other stranger sorts from the eastern isles peeked out from among the overgrowth.

Off to one side was a small pagoda surrounded by artfully arranged orchids and lilies and other weird flowers I couldn't name. Bent over, tending the blossoms, was a frail east islander. She was dressed in a simple style that belied the richness of the silk and cloth-of-gold of its make.

"Mother?" Huund called from my side. She was uncharacteristically hesitant.

The woman tending the flowers stood erect to see Huund over the intervening undergrowth. "Oh? Did you bring me the seeds?" she said with a tonal accent I was unfamiliar with. "I so do need new varieties to plant."

Huund gave a dejected sigh. "She doesn't recognize me most days." The hurt in her voice was genuine, and I'd no reason to disbelieve my eyes.

The elderly woman's face was unmistakable. I'd seen it on a hundred idols, countless tapestries, mosaics, friezes, and illuminated in holy books. Amuun. Creator of the world. Bringer of light. Mother of the gods. According to the mendacious Litanies. The brilliant blood orange topaz diadem that hung against her forehead like the setting sun confirmed the truth.

But there was none of the majesty or power I'd come to expect. Here was just a confused older woman from the eastern isles tending her flower garden. She was not the youthful beauty portrayed in the Litanies. Nor was she the fearsome warrior-goddess who'd burned entire cities to ash with the power of the sun for the mere crime of defying her will. Only her radiant, sun-embroidered clothing met my expectations. And the crown of paradise upon her wrinkled brow.

"Well?" she demanded in a querulous voice. "I need my seeds."

Huund caught my elbow and guided me through the cultivated tumult of greenery. "Mother, I've brought someone who wants to meet you."

Still processing my surprise, I allowed myself to be guided. In the highlands, a woman in her dotage would be cared for by her family much the same way. A long life lived well did earn one the right to one's eccentric pastimes, after all. Glancing about the intentional disarray of the false jungle, I was glad for the first time to have died young. I was certain that Madra, too, warrior-mother that she had always been, was glad of her oblivion to avoid such a banal fate.

When we approached closer, Amuun's eyes widened as she stared at me.

Huund removed her gauntlets and stuffed them through her belt. She laid gentle hands upon the goddess of the sun to soothe her. Just a daughter concerned for her senile mother. The hawk-winged goddess stood protectively next to the mother of the gods.

After a long pause, Amuun said, "I wondered when you might return."

I didn't respond, since I didn't know what to say. Should I play the part of Preema? Or try to convince the old woman of my true identity? Neither would earn me what I came to get. I would want to say that, in that moment, I was not shocked by yet another confirmation of my origin—this one from the goddess I'd revered all my life. But I was.

Amuun stared at me, concern building in her eyes. "I've done as you asked since you gave me the crown," she said with trepidation. Her hand strayed to touch the diadem she wore. "I need to keep it," she said with reluctance, "if you still want more hosts for your war."

Your war. My war? With no memory of what could have possessed anyone to make war with Heaven, I could only speculate based on my limited nineteen years of experience. Anyone who came to dislodge me from my home—Alamar in my mortal life or Nethe in my eternity—would be in for the most bitter war I could make. Though my briefest visit to Heaven had felt welcoming, to be sure, it had not felt like home. I'd no desire to fight for reasons not my own.

Amuun made an odd sound, endearing humor and fearfulness burbling together. "It helps my flowers grow."

Huund patted her mother's shoulder and made reassuring noises. "The new flowers are even more lovely."

"Take the crown," F'riida purred. *"That's the only way you can ensure the peace you have promised."*

The demoness haunting my soul watched my hesitation from her meditative stillness. It was a stillness that vibrated with an intensity that would have frightened me only hours ago. While I could admire her newfound ability to actively wait, that wasn't my strong suit or my style. I was all in or all out, and that was how I would always be.

Why would I need that? I demanded of the demoness in my head. *I already promised my surrender to the demon matriarchs. This pitiful goddess couldn't defend Heaven's Gate much longer, let alone retake Heaven. I don't need more power to make peace. I only need resolve.*

"Am I the only promise of peace you've made?" F'riida murmured. Her vast,

scaly bulk reminded me of a languid mountain cat sunning itself on a highland cliff. *"Have your high gods used the power of this place to its best effect?"*

While the demoness made a strong point, I was disinclined to take queenship of all the gods for myself. I'd not wanted what I had already been given. And I'd only taken what I'd been forced to by circumstance to enact my vengeance. If I were done with that, if I were to lay down my grievances, I did not need nor want Amuun's pretty bauble.

"She can keep it, right?" Huund asked into my prolonged silence. Her concern for her mother touched me. There was a woman beneath the predator after all.

"All her knowledge," F'riida crooned. *"All her power. Think of yourself and yours."*

The demoness had finally learned my weaknesses. But I didn't need to armor them anymore. I only needed to embrace them. *I am thinking only of me and mine,* I told the temptress. *This empty shell knows nothing I need any longer.*

Amuun's expression had grown increasingly concerned with my lack of answer. Her face was a mask of pitiful trepidation, like one a child might wear in fear of punishment or disappointment at losing a treasured toy.

Me and mine must be my focus, I mused as much to myself as to F'riida. *I will return to Nethe to protect my unkindness and my guests. After I make peace with Heaven, I will make the most of what remains of my eternity.*

"Why would I have need of it?" I asked dismissively. If it made the old woman happy, I hadn't the least care for control of this sterile, empty paradise. She could keep it for all I cared. We had no need for the sun in the underworld.

Both Amuun and Huund looked relieved.

Hesitant, Huund inquired, "Was there anything you wanted to ask of Mother?"

Her timidity surprised me. Her vulnerable expression resonated with my own recent memories of Madra. I would have been—truly had been—afraid of anyone taking anything from my mother. I'd killed her to protect her from Provax.

The ancient goddess needed my pity. Taking anything from her would be cruelty I was unwilling to mete out. "No," I said solemnly. "You have a lovely garden. You have done well."

The demoness in my soul said nothing.

The mother of the gods beamed like a child who'd been praised for completing the simplest of chores.

Acceptance was hard. Mercy was a mild balm for the burn of disappointment. But I was confident that it would heal…in time.

Gratitude shined in Huund's eyes. That soothed some of my sadness.

The Lady of the Dread Hunt gave me a watery smile. "Come. Let us speak of our future together," she said, offering me her bare, outstretched hand.

CHAPTER 40

*H*uund led me by the arm out of Amuun's unruly garden. Our transit through the barren halls of paradise was a blur to me. My only thoughts were of the satisfaction the senile mother of the gods could never give me. After all I had fought and bled and died for. All the others who had fought and bled and died in my name. For justice. Their names and faces marched through my mind. My own mother. I refused to accept that it had all been for nothing.

Huund made soothing sounds and stroked my arm as we strolled aimless through the sterile expanse of Saetarra. "We will find a way," she whispered, "together."

My mind rejected the possibility that this was the end of my quest. Atop the cliffs of Alamar in my memory, I stood staring blindly across the highlands. Wearing her mortal form, F'riida stood at my back. She wrapped her arms about me and rested her chin on my shoulder.

"We will find another path, hatchling," the demoness murmured in my ear. *"Take your leave of the huntress. There's no point to further her seduction."*

Tyrr and the other culpable high gods must still be held to account, I whispered to the sorceress who shared my mind. *The world is broken and there must be a way to fix it.*

Mindless, almost of its own accord, my body let Huund guide my slow walk down the endless white corridors. The goddess of the hunt and the hunted murmured unintelligible words of comfort all along the way.

F'riida hugged me quietly and permitted me to dither. She reminded me more than a bit of Madra in her own pale-green-skinned way. I didn't know why she still haunted me after I'd presumably done what she asked. At least, what I had promised to, in the very near future. I didn't know how to release her, but she must know how to leave on her own. That hardly seemed a pressing matter. Later would come a time when I would have to figure her out.

Before I could truly begin ruminating on the options left to get what I needed, Huund led me into a boudoir filled with mahogany furnishings and alabaster upholstery. The accents, of course, were emerald and gold like her armor. She wore a ruffled gown the color of frost with brown hawk feathers embroidered along its trim. I hadn't noticed her change in clothing. But the lovely attire suited her at least as well as her armor had. It did reveal many more enticements.

I turned toward Huund and she released my arm. We awkwardly regarded one another. Her expression was concerned and curious. A touch of the winged predator lurked behind her eyes, just enough to be intriguing and unsettling.

"I'm sorry," I said. "You've been a gracious hostess and I'm being a poor guest." I examined the new gown she wore well. I brushed a feather-light touch across the foamy white lace decorating her brown velvet sleeve. "This is lovely."

The queen of the hawks smiled. "I've had nearly ten thousand years to adjust to her..." She sighed. "Her condition." Her smile took on a brittle quality. "You've had but ten minutes. It must be overmuch to accept."

"All I've known is the Litanies," I admitted. "And the Tales." I shrugged. "The reality of the divine is all foreign to me." I took a deep breath. "You've shown me more of the truth of the divine—and myself—today than I'd learned in a month in Nethe." Though that lack was in no small part my own fault. My lovers were not to blame. Not much.

I waited for her to respond, wanted her to respond. To defend the Holy Litanies. To refute the blasphemous Tales. To tell me what I'd seen with my own eyes was false. She simply watched me until the moment passed.

Then the eternal white light of the sun beckoned me toward a balcony, a bit like the one in my own boudoir in Nethe. I wondered if the view was better.

I took a step beyond the massive, canopied bed that was decorated to look like an ivy-vined trellis hung above it. Gilded stags and hounds chased one another across the duvet spread over the mattress. The decor of Huund's private chambers was as predictable as I might have guessed. Ivory. Emerald. Gold. The hunting motif wasn't subtle, but neither was Huund. She and I were alike in that way. No artifice. We showed the outside world who we were on the inside without reservation. Well, I did, mostly. I'd been pretending to seduce Huund and found that I wasn't pretending anymore.

The balcony overlooked the sterile stillness of Saetarra. An army of statues guarded every empty street. Unused buildings lined those same streets. The sun shone its unforgiving white light through the crystal dome overhead. Its similarity to Preema's temple in Heaven was unmistakable. I'd built— No. Preema had built this.

"We've both lost our mothers in a way," Huund said, joining me on the balcony. Her lace ruffles tickled my bare arm.

Unable to speak for a moment, I glanced sideways at her.

In that moment, she was close. Too close. And not close enough.

Her lips captured mine. Not in a predatory pounce. An invitation to be hunted.

F'riida hummed a pointless warning.

It might be—certainly was—unwise, but I needed Huund in that moment.

Suddenly sick of her maternal meddling, I closed the demoness off in a part of my soul where I couldn't see or hear her. Having already dominated F'riida, I tossed her into the deepest part of my mind. And locked her away in the darkness where even I never looked. Seducing Huund had been her idea after all.

I stumbled into a clinch with Huund. She gracefully matched me like a dancer. Our bodies squeezed into a desperate embrace. Her mouth hungrily devoured mine.

Huund pressed me back against the balustrade. Her lips trailed kisses down my neck. Her teeth nipped delicious little bites of my skin. Her clever fingers unwound the red and black brocade strips of my burial shroud to expose my breasts. I combed my fingers through her wild black curls, enthralled by what she was doing with her tongue.

Her leg thrust between my thighs as she leaned down. My bare skin hung over open air as Huund bent me back to suckle at my nipples. Euphoria as high as we were above the empty city below filled me from soles to crown. A sigh escaped me when she stopped.

With a teasing step toward the bed, she beckoned me with her emerald eyes and a wicked, wet grin. I laughed and pounced on her this time. Our demanding kiss warmed me all the way through.

Struggling to remain pressed together, we staggered through the boudoir, shedding clothing. Her ornate gown was ridiculously complicated to untie. She was amused by my unfamiliarity with overly formal attire. She seemed to enjoy my struggles. Exposing and exploring her intricacies was all part of the fun, I supposed.

Hours and uncounted orgasms later, we lay tangled atop the duvet that we'd never bothered to peel back. I toyed with one of her small, athletic breasts. She drew lazy circles around the edges of my swollen labia with a teasing finger. I laughed, sated and expectant at the same time.

"Yes?" she asked with a coy quirk of her brow. The pressure from her fingers became more insistent.

"This is better than what I imagined," I said as I pressed myself more firmly against her hand, "when I set out to seduce you."

Huund smiled, all victorious predator. "Oh, and why would you do that?"

Embarrassed, I ducked my head against her collarbone. Admiring her breasts was easier than meeting her gaze as I confessed.

"I had a grievance," I said with a sigh, "that I unfairly blamed you for."

She chuckled, which did pleasing things to her anatomy. "Everyone blames the gods for anything they don't like. Even other gods."

It seemed like she inhaled to ask a question, but then didn't speak.

"Don't hesitate," I said without looking up. "Say what you feel. I deserve it."

"I was just wondering," Huund replied with a smile in her voice. "Grievance is the name of your sword, I'm told. Is that so?"

It was my turn to laugh. I was surprised and curious. Not many who'd seen Grievance had lived long enough to spread its name. "Yes, it is. How do you know that?"

"Will you show her to me?"

Somewhere in the depths of my soul, F'riida howled and beat at the walls of the cage I'd put her in. I was beyond being paranoid like her. There was no reason for fear in this place.

Lying naked next to Huund, I supposed we were past being shy about anything. In answer, I drew Grievance from my heart as gently as I ever had. The black steel blade still rasped against my soul as she came into existence. I held the big, heavy sword above us. Light from the eternal sun winked silver highlights from the runes etched into the metal forged of spirit and shadow. *Perhaps*, I thought, *it is time to lay down my Grievance.*

Huund's face lit with appreciation. "May I?"

F'riida's wordless howl from the depths of my soul might have been a warning. I was tired of being on guard, on alert, being forewarned. I hesitated. But that was the old me. The Illyria conditioned to be ever vigilant, ever ready. I couldn't be that way forever.

After a heartbeat's pause, I handed my sword to the Lady of the Dread Hunt.

Taking the hilt in both hands, she sat up and straddled my hips. The long blade reached almost to the false ivy canopy over her head. I suddenly felt more naked than I ever had. With that sword, I had fought and slain mortals, gods, angels, and demons. My Grievance had killed my own mother. Shocking clarity shot through me like ice water in my veins. I did not like the goddess I had become. *Who could I be without Grievance?* I wondered to myself.

Running admiring fingers over the runes in the blade of spirit and shadow, Huund asked in a nonchalant tone, "What do you remember?"

"Remember?" I asked in bafflement. "About seducing you?"

Huund chortled and wiggled to grind her crotch against mine.

"No," she said, still focused on her examination of Grievance. "From before. When you were Preema. Your anamnesis."

"I, uh, don't," I said in surprise. "I've never thought about it." I hadn't known what an anamnesis was until just recently. "Do you?"

She laughed then, like the little hunting bells I remembered from our first meeting. "I've never died," she said in an emphatic tone. She shrugged. "I'm not sure I can. My mothers gave birth to me eleven thousand years ago, before they—"

Her face darkened as if she were remembering Amuun before her dementia. I could scarcely imagine how hard it had been to live with that secret for so long. How many other secrets were there? For example, the Litanies were silent on the matter of Huund's father.

"I do suppose Z'nnek would have told me if he was your father."

Huund made a sour face. "He's half my age."

I laughed at her reaction. She had mentioned nineteen thousand years several times, but I'd chalked it up to an exaggeration based on my own nineteen years. Perhaps she meant it literally? My mind reeled to consider that timescale. Z'nnek's eight thousand years had been inconceivable, though I knew Tourak was older still. But she'd said *mothers* plural.

Even more curious now, I asked, "Your mothers?" I supposed there was no reason divine parentage had to follow mortal rules. It had simply never occurred to me.

"Amuun loved the goddess who freed her." Huund's voice took on a distant quality. Her lean, muscled arms wielded the big hand-and-a-half blade with ease. She rested the hilt of Grievance on one bare hip as she reminisced.

In surprise, I held my silence, afraid to interrupt the blasphemous confession. The idea of Amuun being trapped was as absurd as the idea of her becoming senile had seemed yesterday.

"I suppose I understand the attraction," Huund mused. "If I were caught in a trap for uncounted millennia, I might mistake my relief at being released for love of the person who unshackled me."

The goddess of the hunt and the hunted looked down at me. And smiled her predator's smile. It aroused me and I pushed my hips up against her.

Wanting to prolong the foreplay, I asked, "Who is your second mother?"

She grinned playfully. "Oh, I think you've met her. Can't you guess?"

The clamor from F'riida's cell grew in ferocity, rattling deep in my soul. I couldn't imagine why the demoness would not want me to know these truths. I'm sure she had her reasons, but I refused to consider them valid.

She had betrayed me before and now would warn me not to do what my heart yearned to do most? I regreted only trusting unwisely.

Carefully, I examined Huund's face again. She shared some of Amuun's east islander features. The slanted, heavy-lidded shape of her eyes. The sharp cheekbones. The unusual, light coloration of her eyes. Her build was lithe and lean, like Amuun. But the darkness of her skin, the fullness of her lips, and the kinky curls of her hair were unlike any of the other high gods. The old gods were all too alien and inhuman to consider.

"She is one of the small gods?" I couldn't imagine why that would be hidden from the Litanies. There were many from dark-skinned peoples among the ascended mortals. Like Z'nnek, some even were mentioned in the Litanies. A few more, like Mawzi, in the Tales. If it were Mawzi, that would explain much.

Huund tilted her head in a familiar way that I'd seen someone else do. Recently. A metallic glint in the emerald of her iris sent a shiver down my spine. My libido was washed away in the tide of the second shocking realization in so short a time.

"Araeda'h?" I gasped.

"Indeed," she replied with an insouciant grin. "You've shown me yours," she said, hefting Grievance in her left hand. "Allow me to show you mine."

Bending low, she kissed me gently as she reached beneath the pillows.

My third shock in so many minutes came without warning.

When she sat up, she held a wicked, familiar athame in her right hand. The wavy bend of its blade and its inner veins of fire mesmerized me. It was no longer imbued with my aura. Huund had repossessed it with her own hawk brown. When I'd taken that athame from Saevera, I'd not recognized its similarity to the heads of the boar-spears of wounding carried by the Dread Hunt. Spears that delivered bleeding wounds that never healed.

I gaped in surprise at my secret seducer.

Saevera was not the daughter of Tyrr.

I had to warn Conseca and Z'nnek.

With a ferocious scowl, Huund plunged her blade into my heart.

CHAPTER 41

I don't know how it had come to this. Around me, the ruins of my greatest temple burned. Above me, the dome of perfect diamond erected to commemorate the hundredth millennia of my too-brief reign was shattered. I had ordered it raised as part of the celebration of my ascension to divinity. Great sheets of immortal crystal fell as the fighting in the sky raged on. The granite floor sparkled with glittering shards that reflected broken pieces of me. Overhead, the remains of my hosts of angels, still following my final command, fought the many-colored demons for possession of Heaven.

But the war was already lost.

I removed my simple, raven-black slippers and stood barefoot upon the bloody stone.

At my feet lay the Seventeen. Some dead. Most dying. My chosen mantle-bearers, each the war leader of an angelic host. Eagle. Owl. Hawk. Thunderbird. Phoenix. Proud, winged predators all. Sorcerers and sorceresses who'd served me faithfully for lifetime after lifetime. They had done everything I'd asked.

But that had not been enough. Again.

Countless corpses of my ancient enemies littered the granite flagstones of my broken temple, their iridescent scales glittering. They had been powerful demonesses and sorceresses in their own right. Worthy adversaries. Red. White. Blue. Green. More colors than there were in the rainbow. These enemies were first invited into my Heaven by my own subjects to depose me, lifetimes ago. The same subjects whose corpses were strewn about, ten or twenty or a hundred for every demoness who died. Seventy years by their reckoning, and seven hundred and seventy-seven times that many years had I lived to prepare for this moment.

And I failed.

Again.

Only two choices remained.

On one hand, I could take my fallen and retreat back into Godforge once more for endless millennia. I could rebuild even more hosts against the day of my triumphal return to retake Heaven, which was mine by right of birth and millennia of rule. Since I was the first of my bloodline to attain immortality, the children of Heaven—my rightful subjects—had become ungrateful and chafed under my dominion. History had taught me I could trust none but my Seventeen. The rest were just children who lived small lives for mere decades. They could not understand. But they could betray. And they could be reconquered, I was certain of it.

On the other, I could deny my birthright to my enemies. Here, in this place, at this time, my blood and my blood alone could set fire to Heaven. The civilization that my ancestors and I had built was infused with our might and our will. Beneath the soles of my bare feet, the magic lay ready. All I had to do was surrender. Simply slit my wrists and bleed upon the lines of power that twisted through every rock and tree and village and soul. To ensure that what was mine would always be mine, I had bound Heaven entire to me. When my heart stopped, the world would end. An unimaginable conflagration with the power of ten thousand suns stored in the heart of Heaven would burn it all to ash.

They knew it, of course. My enemies had never engaged me to slay me. They sought to entomb me for all eternity and thereby secure their stolen domain from my immortal wrath. So, they fought with a restraint that me and mine did not share. That weakness alone had given me the opportunity to flee Heaven the first time with the Pillars of Creation. And the second with my life. And the third. If my enemies ever realized the key to my immortality, they would invade Godforge to steal the Pillars. But that secret I alone would bear into eternity.

With my Seventeen, I had created Godforge to amass an army to retake my birthright. The demons had easily crushed my first army of constructs. And my second horde of demons. But I had learned from the defeats of my armies of metal and magic and blood and stone. After millennia upon millennia of refinement and evolution, the finest and most powerful of my new children—eighteen hosts of angels gifted with flight and the full power of sorcery at their disposal—had poured through Heaven's Gate with my raven-winged avengers at the fore.

And they had all died in my name.

I had no idea what made my eternal enemies more powerful than I. Whatever they fought for was greater than my will, it seemed. I had been unable to divine neither its nature nor its power. Everything was in my favor here, in this place, at this moment. And yet, for some unfathomable reason, I did not prevail.

Could I do it all again a fourth time?

The only untouched portion of my temple was the towering statue of me surrounded by statues, almost as impressive, depicting my Seventeen. Why the demons and my rebellious subjects left them intact, I do not know. But I did know that I was weary. For myself, I did not relish yet another grinding eternity. But for my sacred Seventeen? Only for them, to honor their loyalty and service, I would try once more.

With my sword, I swept their heads from their corpses to collect their anamneses and their mantles. I gathered the remnants of my Seventeen into the pockets of my ceremonial robes. Instead of a triumphal return garbed in black and scarlet silk, I prepared to flee Heaven once more in bloody, bedraggled rags.

I manifested my raven wings and prepared to take flight. I set my eyes upon the Gate which led back to Godforge. Unexpected, remembered pain pierced through the middle of my back, betwixt my wings. I did not recognize the toxin upon the blade, but I knew the slow, unerring press of that point toward my heart would be fatal.

"You slew my daughters. All of them," F'riida whispered in my ear. "You slew my matriarch. I am revenged!"

I refused to flinch or gasp in agony.

The sorceress's toxic breath burned my neck. "That's what I said to Preema there at the end. Do you understand now, Illyria?"

Still as a statue, the demoness stood behind me. On all sides was the frozen tableau of that final, fatal moment. My soul ached with remembered loss and disappointment. And resolve. I stood immobile, in those same blood-soaked robes, pockets full of the Seventeen's power, a heart filled with regret and resolve, poised with wings spread to launch myself into the sky.

Time seemed to stand still.

I was sure I didn't want the answer, but I asked anyway. "Where are we?"

F'riida walked around to face me. Her green-scaled skin and long, veridian hair were the same as when I'd first fought her in shadow. Except she was haggard and tired. She had been exhausted before but was more so now. The sorceress seemed at death's door.

She stopped an intimate distance from my face. Eye to eye, we breathed the same air.

"Have you not guessed, hatchling?"

I shook my head. I refused to speculate and admit what I did not want to know. I let my arms fall and my wings fold.

"This is your anamnesis, child," F'riida said in a gentle voice.

That couldn't be so. I asked a different question. "How did you stop time?"

"Unlike a heart, time cannot be stopped, Illyria." F'riida clucked. "You can gain mastery over the perception of time. With skill, you might control its speeding faster or slowing down. But its inexorable march cannot be stopped."

"This is an illusion you're using to trick me," I lied. It felt too real to be true, like the memories I'd shared with Z'nnek and Tourak through the wine of remembrance. I refused to acknowledge how like Madra's anamnesis it was.

"This is no trick. This is the deepest memory in your soul." F'riida gave me a disappointed little smile. "You know it to be so."

I stood immobile and refused to acknowledge her words.

She sighed and continued, "Had you not tried to lock me away, I might never have found the truth I was seeking all along."

"No," I said, denying the import of her words with all my being. "I am not a tyrant!"

The demoness smiled with a wan fondness that reminded me of Madra. She placed her smooth, cool hands upon my cheeks to force me to meet her gaze.

"You are not," F'riida agreed. "Perhaps that tyrant died upon my blade or by my toxin after she escaped my vengeance." She shrugged and dropped her hands. "It doesn't matter. I suspect that you have done more to kill Preema in your short lifetime than I ever could."

I shook my head with as much violence as those words shook my soul.

"We are out of time, youngling," she said in a rasp that was probably meant to be soothing—might have been, were I a demon child. "Will you keep your promised surrender?"

My eyes sought hers in surprise. "Why does that matter now?"

I gazed around the frozen ruin of a temple built in my image. "What could make up for...this?" I spread my hands to encompass all the death and destruction. Compared to my little war with the Chosen to keep the highlands free, the devastation of Heaven was infinitely worse. And for no better reason than entitlement.

I scowled and shook my head. "I would surrender a thousand times before I caused—"

"Huund is going to kill someone," F'riida interrupted me, "in the space of a few heartbeats." Her smile held a fondness I had not earned.

Moving at last, I nodded and straightened, accepting that judgment. "I deserve no less."

F'riida shook her head. "I only regret that I will not grow to know better the honorable woman who slew Preema."

CHAPTER 42

*H*uund's athame plunged into my chest. The wicked blade slid between my ribs, just below my breast. Yet I felt nothing pierce my heart. Nothing but shock. I lay atop the embroidered duvet with Huund astride my hips. Her heels locked beneath my thighs. Her cunt hairs tickled mine.

With a grin, I said, "What sort of new foreplay is this?"

"So innocent," she cooed. "So precious." Hunting bells giggled without mercy or remorse. "So surprised. You don't even know you're going to die."

Our gazes locked. I couldn't look away from her cold, emerald eyes.

Araeda'h had warned me, and I'd let ambition, arrogance, and lust blind me to the obvious truth. The surprise of her betrayal, after our long, intimate interlude, beat upon my already numb heart. Huund's face bent with cruelty as she watched me die. It hardly seemed real.

"You are so naïve," Huund drawled. "You'd give away any hope of Heaven in exchange for what?"

I knew my answer, yet I could only stare at the cruel lips that had so generously kissed every part of me. Surely I was misunderstanding our new game.

Huund laughed. "You were too easy to seduce." She clucked. "I'm so disappointed."

She twisted the athame between my ribs.

I expected to feel my life draining away.

Yet I felt nothing.

If our roles had been reversed, if I'd jammed Grievance into Huund, I would already have begun to draw her magic out by the bucket. She would be shriveling inside, losing her power as I sucked the soul from her flesh. Just as I'd done with Deffaen, Venatar, Provax, the twin archangels of war, Yanfak and Yunfak, and every single one of my victims.

A glance down showed me—and Huund—that I bled green. Sickly ichor oozed out around the hilt of the dagger and drizzled down my naked belly.

Together, we gasped, "F'riida."

I clamped my hands around Huund's on the hilt of her blade.

Huund tried to yank the dagger out of my chest—her second mistake.

We each raced to take advantage of the reversal.

Being quicker, she might have had a chance. But I already held her hands fast. Being heavier and stronger, I bucked my hips against her crotch. We rolled over and she lost her grip on the dagger. I heard Grievance clatter to the floor behind me. Holding the athame in the wound with one hand made me clumsy. If I yanked it out unprepared, a catastrophic fountain of blood would be the best case that could happen.

In hindsight, I should have pressed my advantage and pinned her then. Perhaps to strangle the life from her. Or I could've yanked the dagger free, risked exsanguination, and used that against her. My next mistake—I'd lost count of how many I'd made by that point—was to lunge for Grievance.

Lifelong habits die hard.

By the time I tumbled to my feet on the other side of the bed toward the door, Huund had flung herself off the balcony. She was far out of reach, even if I'd held my sword. Her hawk wings spread wide to catch the air. Her naked, sweating body glorious in the brilliance of Amuun's sun. Too bad all such beauty must come to an end.

The haunting horns of the Dread Hunt welcomed her into the sky.

She craned her neck back and forced her jaws impossibly wide. A screech of frustration and rage tore the air—a terrible hunting hawk sound. She turned, flapping her wings to hover half a bowshot away. And pointed at me.

With a laugh, I beckoned her to come back and play.

That's when I saw the vanguard of the Dread Hunt swoop onto the balcony.

"Monthly bloody drizzles," I swore.

All thoughts of toying with my prey evaporated. Muscles clenched from throat to sphincter. Cool realization of the ambush washed away the sex and adrenaline.

I could have stayed and fought. I should have. But I could feel F'riida dying inside me.

If I could get F'riida to Hayyek, the goddess of healing might save her.

I snatched up Grievance and fled.

Leaving my nameless burial shroud spread across Huund's boudoir, I ran naked and afraid down the sterile, unforgiving halls of paradise. I must have pulled the athame from my chest at some point. Grievance swung heavy and hungry in my right hand. In my left, I held the dripping dagger. I ran. Until I was so thoroughly lost, I felt it would take them time to find me. Finding an unguarded exit should have been easy.

Then I noticed the trail of green ichor droplets I'd left for them to follow.

No wound marred my chest. A quick self-inspection of my nakedness showed me that I was unhurt. There wasn't even a scar where the blade had pierced me. I dropped the dripping dagger. And shook all of the sickly-colored blood from my hands that I could. It should have been melting my flesh, but it wasn't. Because F'riida had granted me her own immunity. I gave no thought, then, to the depth of the relationship I'd shared with the demoness in so short a time.

Wounds eternally bleeding. That was the legend of the Dread Hunt's weapons. The pool of ichor around the dagger swelled as I watched.

F'riida! I shouted at the demoness who thrashed upon the clifftop in my mind. I must have carried her up from the depths of my anamnesis without realizing it. *Talk to me!*

As my flesh huffed and puffed to regain its breath, I watched the demoness's body in my mind. She seemed to be breathing. Her eyes were closed. Her hands were clasped tight over her heart. Her face was wracked with agony.

Tell me how to save you, I demanded as I knelt and scooped her now-frail form into my lap. My fingers searched her chest for wounds, but there were none. Around us, the cool alpine air of remembered Alamar grew more chill.

Slits of her eyes peeled open. *"You already have, hatchling,"* she said in a delirious, agonized voice. *"Atone for my daughters and all is..."* Her eyes flickered shut. *"...forgiven."*

I wanted to hide in my mind, to reason with her, to demand she help me, to tell me how to heal her. I opened my eyes instead.

Rather than stand, still naked and afraid, in the hallways of an enemy paradise, I pulled on Repose. The heavy plate settled across my shoulders and embraced me like a lover. The rattle of chainmail was a comfort. The hobnails of my riding boots scraped across the sterile marble floor. Now, I stood armored and afraid. And furious.

Healing. Hayyek. That had been my forgotten plan. I produced the pink soul token from the purse at my belt. All my concentration focused upon the sense of the goddess at its heart. *Goddess,* I prayed, *I have need of your healing.*

To her credit, the matronly goddess of healing didn't ask where I was or why I'd been gone for so long. "How are you hurt, child?" was all that she asked when she appeared in my soul. Her gaze left my face and fell upon F'riida. "Not you?"

Not me, I agreed, nodding at the demoness who lay dying in my arms.

Hayyek didn't quibble. She didn't ask me to explain the demoness in my mind. Instead, the lovely matron knelt beside us and laid her hands upon F'riida's head and heart. The goddess of healing closed her eyes.

"I feel that she is dying, but I sense no wound." Hayyek asked, "What happened, Illyria?"

Huund stabbed her. I couldn't manage to say more. An inexplicable lump clogged my throat. As my thoughts had been when Madra announced her intent to oblivion, they were still.

Huund's voice echoed down the hall, "You're making this too easy, Illyria."

I got a tighter grip on my emotions and ignored the Lady of the Hunt.

"The wounds inflicted by the Dread Hunt are no poison," Hayyek said softly. "They are no wounds of the flesh at all." She laid her cool, soothing hand against my cheek. "Those wounds bleed the soul." The goddess sighed. "The Litanies say not even the blazing might of Amuun could cauterize them."

Closer still, perhaps just around a corner or two behind me, Huund's mocking voice called. "A blind and crippled hound could follow your trail."

I snarled but didn't waste my breath in reply. I was out of time.

Amuun, I thought to Hayyek, *is the key, but I need more time to get to her.* First, I needed to keep F'riida alive long enough to get to the mother of the gods. A bad idea came to mind. *Thank you, Hayyek, you are a blessing!* I kissed her and released my hold on her soul token, dropping it back into my purse. She vanished from my mind.

The dagger lay at my feet in an ever-growing pool of F'riida's blood. The first trophy I'd taken from the damned Chosen. The athame that I'd slain my own brother with. The evidence that Huund was connected to Saevera, perhaps even her mother. All of these things, and also a connection to Huund, maybe sympathetic power over her if I could learn the right magic!

Would the wound continue to bleed if the weapon that inflicted it were destroyed? That course might not heal F'riida, but—

As fast as my thought, Grievance struck through the smaller blade.

The athame shattered. Sparks flew from the white marble. Green blood showered me and the moving mosaics on the walls.

In the distance, Huund screamed in pain.

My face contorted in death's grin.

My hobnailed boots rang on the tile as I ran in search of the mother of the gods.

CHAPTER 43

*T*he baying of the hounds of the Dread Hunt echoed from the stone walls and the omnipresent statuary. I ran, seeking a defensible corner or a place to hide and think and remember. The specter of lost memories licked my spine with chills. I had been cautious with all the magic I used! I shoved irrational the terror down deep.

There had to be a way to find Amuun, save F'riida, and escape this hellish paradise. The soundless moving friezes celebrating the millennia of Preema and the Seventeen mocked my every stride. Rows upon rows of statues of every imaginable mortal shape and hue seemed to watch me with a calculating gaze. The galloping clatter of the Hunt's nails on the tile chased me around each corner. I wracked my brain, trying to remember the way back to Amuun's sanctum.

Reaching into my belt purse, I sought a pebbled surface among the soul tokens. As my fingers grasped the lopsided cluster of grapes, a sweet smell of vintage wine filled my nose. The effeminate presence of the vulture god filled and warmed my heart. I had missed him more than I allowed myself to acknowledge until that moment. *Z'nnek, my love. It's time.* My body ran on instinct alone while I hugged him when he appeared in my mind. Half my attention looked for the curtained archway that led to the mother of the gods' mad garden. The other half enjoyed our reunion. Perhaps our last.

His deep affection reflected in his acceptance and lack of questions about the green-skinned demoness in my soul—or my unplanned, month-long absence. "I knew you would return," he said. "What do you need?"

I am in Saetarra. I skipped over my abortive trip through Heaven's Gate, my ill-fated seduction attempt, and all my other failures. *Huund and the Hunt are bent on killing me.*

"We could traverse through shadow more quickly, but the way was closed soon after you vanished." Z'nnek looked distracted for a moment. "I thought Urth and the old gods were just being petty for your poor hospitality."

Containing my irritation was hard, but possible, which I considered a victory.

"Not the time for humor, love," I said through gritted teeth. "Huund stabbed me with—"

The lord of the unclaimed dead lost his teasing manner. "Illyria, there's no—"

I'm fine. I'm not bleeding, I interjected. *I should have reached out to you sooner.* Although I already knew the answer, because none of my unkindness were near, I asked anyway. *How long, my love?*

Z'nnek looked incredulous, but he sighed. "Hours at least." He pressed his lips into a thin line. "We will rush."

I hadn't known the old gods could deny Z'nnek access to the shadow realm. How was that even possible? I didn't have time to make sense of it.

I love you, I said and released his soul token. We would have to save ourselves.

F'riida, wake up! I demanded. *I need you to guide me back to Amuun.*

The demoness mumbled, either unintelligible or in a language I did not know, delirious but not dead.

As I ran past, the motionless statues inspired me in a way they hadn't before. From Preema's anamnesis—my anamnesis—I knew those statues to be constructs. Those golems of stone and steel were built to fight in the first invasion of Heaven. Relegated to be mere decorations for thirty millennia, they might still serve me if I only knew how to command them. Alas, Preema had not left me a memory of how to use that power, only its tanta-lizing existence. I did wonder why Amuun had not yet activated them in my pursuit. Did the diadem not give her that control? Had Preema decommissioned the constructs into nothing but decorations?

Plunging through a curtained doorway that looked familiar, I hoped to find Amuun's wild garden. I did not. The rows of empty cages were disappointing. They filled the cavernous room up to a ceiling three or four times my height. A thick layer of dust covering everything put me in mind of the state in which I'd found Nethe's armories a month past. None of the barred cells held anything now. Most were too large to imprison a mortal man, but many were smaller. I didn't have time to examine them or ponder what creatures they might have held once. And I'd no interest in kicking up a sneeze-inducing cloud by traipsing through the ankle-high drifts.

I backed out of the room into the hallway.

Two winged hounds growled behind me.

My breath caught in my throat. My head whipped around to peer over my shoulder.

There was no time for escape. The first charged low toward me. The second spread its wings and pounced high. I dodged to the side, ducking low. I couldn't take the chance that their claws or fangs caused wounds like their weapons. My pauldron scraped against the wall. I punched the first hound's muzzle away. The second hound sailed over us, jaws snapping on empty air where I'd been a moment ago.

Grievance sang her hunger, joyful to be unshackled once more. The blade barely bit through the back of the first hound's neck. But that was enough for the first forbidden magic Z'nnek had ever taught me.

I growled the spell, "Your life is my life."

A soul as vast as any archangel I'd swallowed with my necromancy poured through my sword like blood through an embalmer's funnel. The memories, the magic of that construct's soul, sloshed into a fresh wineskin that I created for it. My brief visit to Heaven had left me full to bursting. I'd need to find something to do with my overfull metaphors of magic soon. The wineskin became a fermentation vat in the cellar of my soul.

Somewhere far away, a hawk screeched her rage and loss. Just as I would, Huund knew when her angels died.

The hound flopped to the floor, boneless. Its wings twitched and thrashed as he died and began to wither. I didn't linger to consume the remainder of the flesh.

I was glad to be done with running.

The second hound spun on her heel to face me. She assumed her angelic form. The hawk-winged beauty held a boar-spear in both hands. The weapon the Dread Hunt was most feared for—the weapon that would be a more powerful version of Huund's little dagger. She prepared to charge.

I set my boots and readied Grievance in a high guard.

"Mother!" Huund's words were faint—I felt them caress my soul as much as I heard them with my ears.

An unbecoming, snide comment about crying to mommy died on my lips.

Huund wailed. "She has killed one of my pets!" Her tone was aggrieved as much as it was petulant. "Help me!"

The feel of her voice gave me the sense that Huund knew where I was. We'd been too intimate too recently. She had my scent. I despaired to realize the playful chase had been for her enjoyment. Until I'd killed one of hers. Now the hunt would begin in earnest.

Amuun's querulous voice boomed through the hall. "What is the meaning of this?"

"Illyria," F'riida gasped. *"You must escape. You must ensure peace for my sisters' daughters. My life is worth that!"*

I growled again, frustration vibrating through me.

All along the hall, the friezes of the Seventeen and Preema were replaced with enormous depictions of Amuun. The visage of the confused goddess of the sun scowled at me from every panel of mosaic. She looked befuddled. And afraid.

"Mother!" Huund screamed from somewhere out of sight, but closer. "She means to take your crown!"

She wasn't far wrong, if her mother did not do as I demanded. If the false creator of the world did as I asked, I had no care for her bauble. In perfect hindsight, I was woman enough to admit I should've taken it when I had the chance earlier.

The many enormous images of Amuun touched a hand to the diadem that hung upon her brow. "You can't have it." Her feeble voice resonated through my boots as much as it rattled my eardrums. "I need it!"

I didn't know if Amuun could see me, but I presumed so when the statuary began to come alive. The hawk-winged angel blocked one end of the hall that was now full of armed constructs in motion. There were too many of the glittering marble and steel statues. If I stood still, I'd be trapped at both ends of the hall in a blender of marble and steel. I was sure that more angels of the Hunt were coming to avenge their fallen.

"Damn my moist bits," I swore under my breath.

"Take her," the elderly goddess murmured. "She must answer for her temerity." Her larger-than-life wrinkled visage nodded. "Yes, yes, she must answer to me."

I turned to run back the way I'd come.

The formerly sterile paradise came alive with constructs of all shapes and sizes. Many of the stone warriors were heavily armed. Spears. Pikes. Glaives. Swords. Others carried strange devices that resembled smaller versions of the siege weapons the Elysian Foreign Legion had carried to Alamar and abandoned unused after their defeat. Some statues were my size. Most were larger. None as enormous as the behemoths that guarded the exterior gates to Saetarra, though. Those would not fit into the halls through which they chased me. For that I was thankful.

I searched as fast as I could for anything that would lead me to Amuun.

Trapped in a blind corner, Grievance chopped through a stone soldier that surprised me.

"Your life is my life," I murmured by reflex.

Its halberd clattered to the floor in two pieces. Its surprised expression matched mine. The soul in the machine sluiced down the funnel that my sword provided. It was alive! The soul was strange to be sure, but it had been trapped in the construct for tens of thousands of years of servitude. Had it been mortal once?

Amuun had no angelic host. Were all the souls she claimed imprisoned in constructs? If not, had they been trapped in those vessels for tens of millennia?

The magnitude of my—of Preema's—evil struck my heart like a physical blow. Countless souls. Unnumbered lives had been created and snuffed out

275

to serve one woman's vain ambition. The reality of it took my breath away. In some nebulous way, I felt responsible. I carefully poured that soul into a crystal decanter to question later. I left the shattered statue on the floor and continued seeking an exit. But trying to avoid another fight.

I will end the cycle, F'riida, I swore as I ran. *One way or another. But you have to live to help me find Amuun!*

The demoness nodded once, a curt gesture in my mind, as she struggled to sit up. She didn't speak, but she pointed and I followed her directions. Surely her memory had to be better than my guesses. I wished I'd paid attention as Huund led me away to her boudoir. Had I the breath or time, I'd kick my own mental ass for days.

Many minutes and turns passed, but we didn't seem to be getting anywhere that seemed familiar. My frustration built to a bursting point.

In the distance, I saw three hawk-winged hunters at a junction of the hallway. Grievance and I both longed to charge them. Behind them, ranks of armed constructs filled the corridor.

"Illyria—" F'riida gasped.

"Fine!" I ground my teeth. "There must be a fucking door or window here somewhere!"

She pointed down a side passage. By that time, it seemed like F'riida was choosing turns at random. I ducked down narrow alleys, rushing through rooms without looking for more than an exit or an enemy to avoid.

I found an enormous room big enough for a legion to parade through. Along one wall were floor to ceiling panes of clear crystal two stories high. Grievance would likely make short work of the windows.

But on the other side, gold and silver hosts of angels descended through the cursed dome that hung over Saetarra. The sky was empty of constellations. All of those guardian angels had come to hunt me. Had we been in Heaven, I probably could have gathered enough power to crush them all. I could make everything right with enough power.

In that heartbeat, I understood Preema better than I ever wanted to.

The chase became more desperate thereafter.

I don't know how many hours passed, if even just one.

I would have fled Saetarra at F'riida's urging then, if I could. The constructs, the Twins' gold and silver hosts, and the angels of the Dread

Hunt all seemed to be herding me. Wherever that was, I refused to go. Tantalizing glimpses of Huund, Torr, and Tyrr behind the ranks upon ranks of implacable warriors taunted me with thoughts of killing them. But they were never truly within reach.

I did everything I could to break their ever-closing pattern, but Huund was the goddess of the hunt and the hunted. I had been arrogant to think I could out-hunt her. And now I couldn't escape her.

At last, I took a chance to duck through another curtained doorway.

And found myself in Amuun's wild garden.

The frail mother of the gods stood in her odd little pagoda with her back to me.

CHAPTER 44

$\mathcal{M}$y boots crunched through the overgrowth of Amuun's garden. There was no point to any pretense of stealth. The senile old woman wasn't even on her guard. I ignored the dozen or more motionless constructs that littered the space. All I wanted was for Amuun to heal F'riida—or order Huund to do so. I had no idea how to do it myself. Then we would leave Saetarra, probably forever. There was nothing I wanted here.

"You walk boldly where you should fear to tread," the faux mother of the gods declared. Her back was still to me, but her voice was firm and clear. She clucked as one might do with impudent but stupid chickens. "Huund promised you would be easy to herd into my trap."

I boggled at her. "Trap? I was *trying* to come here, and she was preventing me!"

The old goddess cackled. "I will not suffer you to amble into my garden and take back what *you* gave me in trust with your own hand."

I stopped in surprise, not knowing how to process what Preema had done to enslave Amuun, or how Araeda'h might have undone it. I believed Huund's parentage, but it was hard to imagine enslaving a woman I'd believed to be the mother of the gods.

Knowing I needed to say something, I guessed. "Have you been diligent in your trust?"

She stroked her carefully coifed hair, as if she were simply daydreaming. "I am no longer the obedient slave you made me. Araeda'h saw to that. It is not yours to reclaim any longer."

Lack of context gave me pause. I glanced around the garden in search of something to anchor my understanding. A grassy clearing several paces wide separated me from the strange little pagoda. I studied her posture, her stance. This couldn't be the same woman who was on about seeds earlier. *Had that all been an act?*

"I'm here to take nothing," I assured her, hoping at least some part of the Litanies were true about her vaunted mercy. "I come to b—" I choked on the word. I started again. "I came to request your mercy for my ally. Beyond that, I will leave with only what I came with into *your* paradise." I didn't say aloud, *Besides some illusions and misbeliefs about you that I lost along the way.*

She whirled. Her wizened features contorted in anger. "You would take everything from me!" she raged. The garden shook with the violence of her emotion. Out of sight, songbirds squawked in terror. "You would throw it all away!"

I held up my empty hands, spread wide in the warden's salute. "I want nothing from you except your aid," I promised. *F'riida first, and then reparations for the highlands,* I thought. "The mercy of the mother of the gods is much lauded in the Litanies."

"You want to replace me." Amuun looked off in the distance over my shoulder. "She told me so…" Her voice trailed off as if whatever memory she'd grasped was slipping away.

Scoffing, I said, "I've no desire to rule the gods nor the sun-kissed lands. Those are too many demands, too much politics. I am content with Nethe and my husbands."

She began to say, "I do not—"

"Let me show you!" I interrupted, impatient and grumpy.

I closed my eyes and focused on my internal world. Shaking with the effort, I gathered all that remained of the demoness in my arms. The green-scaled body was a shadow of the powerful sorceress she had been not so long ago. But she lived. I could feel the fading power still pulsing inside her.

Somehow, we had become entangled more than I thought. Separating our souls as gently as I could, I reversed the invitation I had extended to F'riida. I didn't want to cut or tear or do more damage to her than she already suffered in saving my life. Even dying, she was a massive soul. Pushing her toward the surface of my own existence hurt in an exquisite way. I could only imagine that must be what childbirth might be like.

Sweating with the strain, at last I manifested the demoness into the real world. I clutched her to my breasts, suddenly loathe to be separated from her. But Amuun scowled at me, understanding slowly dawning on her aged face.

With reverence, I laid F'riida upon the grass and stood to address Amuun.

F'riida croaked, barely a whisper, "No, daughter! Run!"

The mother of the gods looked confused. "I'd not believed that *you—*" She tilted her head to one side to regard F'riida from a different angle. Disbelief colored her words. "Is it true then? After all we sacrificed in your name, you would surrender Heaven?"

It was my turn to be confused. I opted to move forward anyway. "I wish for you to heal her. That is true."

Amuun drew herself up to her full height, seeming larger than she had been. The air around her crackled with power. "You would abdicate to the demons!" she roared. With a thunderous clap of her hands toward me, she shouted, "Slay her!"

Frustrated, I spat. "Lick my—"

I didn't have time to finish whatever lame curse I'd been about to spew when every construct in the garden came to life. And attacked me all at once.

Javelins crisscrossed the air where I'd been a moment before. With two powerful flaps of my wings, I'd thrown myself up and back, away from F'riida's prone body. Grievance sang her steel bloodlust as she leaped from my heart into my hands.

"I don't want to kill you!" I shouted at Amuun.

She raised a hand to point toward me. The Litanies attributed unimaginable magical power to the goddess of the sun. I'd no wish to discover their truth for myself. Fear pushed me to dodge down out of the sky.

In a shallow swoop, I slashed through three constructs without bothering to reap their souls. I wished them whatever peace they could find. If I lived long enough, Z'nnek and my angels might arrive to take them to Nethe. That was a problem for later.

The door was my problem now. I could handle the constructs currently in the garden. But I needed to prevent more from joining our little party. I could see no other exits than the one the Hunt had herded me into. The massive skylight overhead did not look to have openings.

When the silver-winged and gold-winged hosts of the Holy Twins began to settle around the edge of the great crystal panes forty feet above me, I realized I had been very, very stupid. Probably stupid for the past month since I'd died. Certainly for the recent hours.

Perhaps it was the presence of my sister among them that brought me to my senses. Kausae had witnessed almost every flagrant embarrassment I'd ever suffered. She'd always gloated over my failures and escapades when we'd been mortals. I expected that she would be, but she wasn't gloating now. She looked scared and disappointed. So was I.

While I might not have the best memory for faces of past lovers, I never forget anyone I've seen across from me on the battlefield. There were none among Kausae's compatriots that I had not seen on different sides of Saetarra during my zigzag evasion. The same few score angels had crossed back and forth, like the angels of the Hunt, to be seen wherever I needed "encouragement" to take a different path. They had indeed herded me here…without needing the entirety of the Twins' hosts. I'd been stupid.

I had been still thinking like a mortal girl of a mere nineteen summers.

I had let my nether bits and my arrogance swamp my better judgment.

Had carrying F'riida changed my thinking? Worrying for someone else?

I had let my fear induce panic and cloud my thinking.

I had not been thinking at all like an immortal, a necromancer, a goddess.

Still, I had been outmatched, outthought, and outplanned in every way at every turn.

I had let my enemy arrange the battlefield and array against me as she willed.

In all my urgent flailing around like a teenage novice having sex for the first time, I had failed to consider that the divine could step into spirit and ignore walls. Or skylights. And so could I. Unless Saetarra had been warded with magic to stop me, like the dome had been built to block shadow, anyone among the divine could walk in or out at will. I'd done it myself more than once. Urth had stepped through shadow into the throne room.

I expected the small contingent of the Twins' glittering hosts to fall through the ceiling and attack.

But they didn't.

Now that I realized I could have left Saetarra at any time, simply by taking an unexpected direction, I wasn't going to. I'd put F'riida at the mercy of my avowed enemy and she still lay there on the grass before Amuun. I wasn't going to leave her here.

I wasn't going to leave at all.

Not now.

I was angry.

My rage was entirely at myself. But I intended to take it out on everyone else.

I expended some of my anger on the immediately available prey. Grievance made short work of four more constructs as we danced among the twisted jungle trees and swamp grass. Although I never felt in danger, I used the terrain to my advantage so that they could only attack me by ones and twos. I left their souls where they fell. I had no appetite to consume more of those who'd suffered as they had. They would not suffer more at my hands.

All the while we fought, the Twins' hosts looked on, immobile and uninterested. In the moment, I was too busy to wonder at the blessing of that. The slight distraction let a javelin catch me unawares. The light spear punched through my abdomen, puncturing leather and shredding chainmail as it flew entirely through my body.

I screamed in surprise as much as pain. Crashing into a tree I should've dodged, I fell to the loamy garden floor. Statuesque warriors of marble and granite mobbed me then, stabbing and kicking and slashing.

That's when I realized all the constructs I'd slashed apart had risen to threaten me again.

Surrounded and prone, I carelessly spun the wick of my heart sigil to burn hotter than I ever had. The abundance of Heaven's power poured out of my reserves to regenerate my body and armor as fast as the constructs could wound me.

One at a time, I fought to regain my feet, Grievance reaped souls. "Your life is my life."

Only when no spirit remained to animate them did the statue warriors crumble into sand.

Destroying the hapless constructs didn't make me feel much better. But killing one at a time allowed me to focus on Amuun. My war dance carried me ever closer to the odd little pagoda, but incidentally, not as if I were intentionally fighting toward the mother of the gods. It was the only way I could think to sneak across the battlefield and take her unawares. I would just find myself returned to where I'd stood before in a few moments.

When the last construct fell, head and shoulder and arm severed by a cut through the chest, its soul stored away in the cellar beneath my heart, I stood over F'riida. I turned to face the ancient goddess. I expected her to look afraid. Instead, her expression was a mask of hate. The topaz diadem of the sun hung upon her brow like a blood orange beacon.

I shrugged and Repose's pauldrons clanged. "I do not want your silly little crown." I sighed. "I do not want the temptation that comes with that kind of power. For I know that I might use it." The weight of my anamnesis, the weight of Preema herself, was heavy in my chest.

Amuun scowled at me, disbelief vibrating through her.

I said, "If you will not help me in my very simple request. If you will not heal my ally"—I hoisted F'riida's impossibly light form into my arms, careful not to cut her with Grievance—"then I will take her and go in peace."

The demoness mumbled, "No, no. You don't understand. She will..." Her voice was pitiful. She struggled in my arms, her eyes wide and staring over my shoulder, directly into the blinding sun.

"You will not!" Amuun spread her arms as if to embrace the scores of angels high above us and screamed, "Kill her!"

The angels descended then, stepping into spirit and falling gently into the garden. They formed a near-perfect circle around us. There were at least four score of them, if I had to guess. Whether I could defeat so many alone was anyone's guess. Had I the power here that I had briefly held in Heaven, they would be no threat to me. Could I truly surrender that as promised?

"We have been commanded," Kausae called in her highland warden's training ground voice, "by our lords and masters, to ensure that Illyria does not escape Saetarra."

At the periphery of my vision, I could see the golden-winged angels of war and the silver-winged angels of justice twitch. They wanted to intervene. They wanted to obey the mother of the gods. But somehow, my sister held them in thrall. Perhaps with her words alone? Was reminding her peers of a strict interpretation of what Tyrr and Torr had ordered enough? Perhaps I had much still to learn about command from my elder sister.

Then with a clatter, Huund and the Dread Hunt arrived. They stacked up in the tiny doorway where I had entered. The Lady of the Hunt was at the fore.

"Hold the line!" Kausae shouted. "Do not let anyone pass lest Illyria escape!"

The angels of the Dread Hunt tried to press through the gold and silver circle. And were summarily denied by the Twins' angels.

For a moment, it seemed as if Huund and her mother would explode in apoplexy.

My older sister had her moments. Nobody could make people enraged like Kausae.

F'riida tried to climb out of my arms. "Illyria, you must—"

Amuun pointed both her hands at me like spears. "Then die!"

The diadem flared brilliant orange like a thousand pyres.

The world went white.

The grass at my feet burned to ash in a blink. The oppressive humidity I'd been ignoring boiled out of the air. Heat more terrible than anything I could have imagined scorched my skin. The smell of burning hair and flesh —my hair and flesh—filled my nostrils. My sigil sucked power out of my stores and burned it so hot the sigil felt like a branding iron.

As she'd done in the Litanies, Amuun had called down the power of the sun to smite me.

F'riida roared as she had once, not so long ago in my mind, when the great winged beast had sought to slay me in retribution for the slaughter of her daughters. Her hands clawed at my shoulders, launching her over my head, and the weight of her was gone from my arms.

Huund screamed, an inarticulate hawkish cry of pain and fear and defiance.

Above me, the enormous scaly bulk of the demon, in all her glory, beat her wings mightily against the blinding light of the sun pouring down through the shattered skylight.

Time slowed.

In the shadow of the demoness, I was safe for a heartbeat.

Before the first massive shards of crystal crashed into the flaming garden, I stepped into the odd little pagoda. My boots thumped on the roughcut wood.

I spun with all the power and regret I could muster.

Grievance slashed.

"Your life is my life," I whispered my vengeance and my heartbreak.

Though I didn't want it, I took the head and soul of the mother of the gods.

CHAPTER 45

*A*muun's memories disappointed. The deluge I expected to be the most powerful I'd ever consumed was naught but a dribble. By comparison, the archangels and demigods, which had threatened to overwhelm me with the volume of their souls, had held more vitality. At the end, she had truly been a sad, bereft, and senile old woman. Well, far less than half of one, perhaps.

I was no expert necromancer, but there seemed to be vast gaps where tens of millennia of memories should be. If Huund were Amuun's and Araeda'h's daughter for true—and I'd no reason to doubt it—she'd lived far more than nineteen millennia. But I didn't have time to examine even the pitiful remnants of the goddess who once was. That would come later.

First, I must end this charade of a standoff.

Amuun's trifling soul sluiced like a sigh into an amphora in the wine cellar of my mind.

Her daughter was still screaming incoherently as I stooped to pluck the diadem of the sun from the surprised brow of the dead mother of the gods. White ichor of little power spilled upon the roughcut floor of the pagoda. Amuun's milky blood haloed around her in a slowly spreading pool. The diadem she'd coveted more than her own life weighed heavy in my palm.

Triumph gave me dominion over Nethe. This bauble would grant me control over the sterile paradise of Saetarra.

In my other hand, I considered Grievance for a moment. My body was battered, scorched, and probably damaged in ways I didn't have words for yet. Though I was in no condition to fight, I wanted to. I owed Huund wounds a thousandfold. I knew without looking that F'riida's massive corpse laying smoking on the ground behind me. The sense of her I'd carried for only a short while was gone. I'd avenged her upon Amuun. Even if I'd been capable of dealing more vengeance upon Huund, it would be for naught in this moment if I died before I could fulfill my final promise to the demoness who'd called me daughter.

So, bluff it would be.

With reluctance, I sheathed Grievance in my heart.

Even Huund fell into an expectant silence as I turned toward the circle of waiting angels.

As I strode uncaring through Amuun's milky blood, I kept my eyes averted from where I knew F'riida lay. I didn't want to see the ruin that Amuun's godray had made of her, nor did I want to draw attention to her remains. I would claim her anamnesis in a moment.

In my right hand, I hefted the blood orange diadem. With my left, I took Triumph from atop my brow. I held them as if approximating their weight. Compared to the gaudy diadem, the crown of Nethe was elegant in its cool darkness. At last, I realized what Triumph signified: Z'nnek had abdicated his throne. To me. There would be time enough to question his wisdom and intentions. Later.

"Not since the third invasion of Heaven," I said, projecting my voice to fill the garden, "has the same person worn both the crowns of Saetarra and Nethe—"

"You can't!" Huund screamed. "You've no right!"

I grinned at her, hiding my weariness and pain. The goddess of the hunt and the hunted had fallen into my trap more readily than I expected. I was making shit up as I went along, but apparently it sounded formal enough that she felt the need to challenge me.

"By the Litany of Battle," I crowed, "This diadem is spoils of war." I hoisted the blood orange topaz high over my head. "Do any others have an entitlement to it?"

The Lady of the Hunt wanted the crown of the sun. I had seen how see she coveted it when she'd first introduced me to Amuun. I knew her heart without the need of magic. I could still taste her on my tongue. Had I been sufficiently tutored in magic, I might have done something with that fact. I hoped my scheme wouldn't depend upon training I didn't have.

Huund met my taunting gaze with a predatory glare. I read her intent in her eyes.

She was calculating whether she could take me in single combat. Or whether her Dread Hunt could overpower their gold and silver peers to get to me. I needed to take the latter off the table as an option. A pitched battle would be harder to bluff my way out of.

"Are you heir to Amuun, mother of the gods?" I challenged. "Are you the true daughter of the sun?"

All eyes were on Huund. Had her so-called brothers been present, she might not have hesitated. But the Twins had no wings of their own. That fact niggled at the back of my mind, but I put it aside for later. I needed to press Huund to assert her right by inheritance and fight me, or back down in a public way in front of four score immortal witnesses.

"Before I slew her, Amuun was enfeebled, a shadow of her former glory," I declared. "Anyone with access to her garden could have slain her and taken the crown of Saetarra at any time!" I held out the diadem toward Huund. "Yet you did not!"

The goddess of the hunt had been angry with me before. Now she was positively enraged. "I would never kill my mother!" she shouted. "I'm not like you!"

I hardened my heart and let the insult, which by rights should have slain me, strike my emotional armor. It was true, after all. "You are not like me," I agreed. "I obey the Litanies!"

Huund's outraged expression tightened into menace.

Given how she had tried to tangle me up in the Litanies at Conclave, not so long ago, it amused me to trip her up with them now. She looked dangerously far from amused. A beatific scowl graced her features. Were we not openly mortal enemies, I might have become aroused.

My slow, careful strides carried me out from under the pagoda. It wouldn't do to fall over and shatter the illusion of my bluff. With a flourish I barely had the energy for, I hung the diadem of the sun upon my brow. Awareness of Saetarra, its resources, and its defenses flooded my mind. As I could with Nethe when wearing Triumph, I could inspect or command any part of my new realm. And more. Saetarra was not built to be a paradise. It was built to be a fortress. Yet it was starved of power by comparison to the plenty of Nethe. Paradise had withered in the millennia of Amuun's rule, but perhaps through no fault of her own. It wasn't that I'd been prohibited from drawing power—there just wasn't enough blood left in the stone.

"By right of inheritance"—I placed Triumph's cool circlet atop my head with a click against the chain of the diadem—"will you challenge me?"

The two crowns did not collide so much as acknowledge one another, as if they were two long separated parts of a greater whole. Through me, the vast reservoir of worship and power in Nethe merged with Saetarra's empty well. The sterile white paradise breathed a relieved sigh in my heart. The Twins must each wear a crown like them to control Avaala and Nuuria. I couldn't recall if Vayan did. No matter. More jewelry for me to collect at length.

Kausae nodded to her gold-winged and silver-winged peers, who stepped apart to leave Huund a clear path to me. The huntress's fists were balled. Her face was flushed. She vibrated with obvious rage. Yet she hesitated for reasons I couldn't guess.

This had to end here, one way or another.

I raised my hands wide, not accidentally reminding Huund of the blazing ball of the sun above us. I'd no idea yet how to command its godrays, but my onetime lover couldn't know that. Could she?

Holding my arms high was going to get tiring if I didn't force the issue. All I wanted was to go home. And I was afraid that I might not get to.

My voice boomed through every hall and chamber in Saetarra, "You will challenge me, or you will kneel!"

Huund flinched.

Her viridescent eyes locked upon mine in defiance.

She took a stuttering half a step forward.

And launched herself.

CHAPTER 46

*W*atching Huund soar away with her Dread Hunt through the shattered skylight did nothing to ease my growing anxiety. Amuun's garden—no, *my* garden—was still full of broken statuary and scores of twitchy gold and silver angels of the Twins' hosts. Delicious Huund would continue to be a problem, I felt sure of it. But she would have to be tomorrow's issue.

These angels who obeyed my sister's whimsy—for which I was grateful —were an immediate danger. They had just watched me slay the mother of the gods and take her crown from her severed head. They might have a notion or two of what to do about that. Especially since Z'nnek and our hosts had not yet arrived. I felt Tourak and my unkindness were close. Z'nnek's larger hosts of vultures and buzzards would be with them. I thought I only had to stall for time.

Bluffing the Lady of the Dread Hunt seemed trivial by comparison to staring down four score angels of war and justice. Perhaps my sigil had been damaged by Amuun's solar godray. Despite pouring kegs and vats of stolen magic from Heaven into its midnight fire, my body and soul felt as if I'd been hammered flat by all the gods. But I refused to show weakness. I reared my head so that my double crown might flash in the still-blinding sun, glaring about the mess with as much regal disdain as I could manage in my abused state.

How my sister—who'd been immortal about a half an hour longer than I—had parlayed her ascension into such influence that both the angels of war and the angels of justice followed her lead mystified me. But she was a gift horse I could look in the mouth some other time. For the nonce, I would leverage that familial blessing for all it was worth.

"Kausae," I called without looking toward her, "did your master and his brother have any other orders for you?" I waved imperiously toward the increasingly hostile angels. "Or only that you were to prevent me from to leaving Saetarra?"

With all the defenses of paradise at my beck and call, I couldn't imagine anywhere safer to be than Nethe itself. Reaching out with a small part of my attention, I began to summon more of the brutal fighting constructs toward the garden. Unless the Twins' hosts of angels were necromancers, they might find the unkillable constructs a bigger challenge than I had. Also, I began to awaken the enormous guardian constructs which had first greeted me during my embarrassing arrival. Perhaps I should construct similar guardians for my own realm.

Infused with the surfeit of power Nethe had accumulated in eight millennia, Saetarra began to recover itself.

Looking outward, I found my sister had approached with her customary swagger. "Certainly. To keep you from escaping Huund," she said in a loud voice for every angel filling my garden. She smirked at me and waved a dismissive hand at the retreating Dread Hunt, far off in the sky. Then her face grew deadly serious. "Yet there is more, *little sister*," she said with mock disdain, "if you've *time* to hear it."

Her compatriot angels watched us with predatory interest.

I knew Kausae well enough to know when she was pretending. What her game was, I couldn't guess. But I could play along. "I've got all the time in the world," I said with as much arrogance as I could muster, "until my host arrives. But to be a proper hostess, I have summoned a few of the guardian constructs to keep us company."

I gave her a playful hurry-up gesture.

Her genuine scowl informed me what I already knew: I didn't understand what she was trying to tell me. She was always bad at giving subtle clues.

I resisted the urge to shrug. My body and soul hurt. An ungrieved hole ached where I'd grown used to hearing F'riida's snarky voice. Whatever game Kausae wanted to play, she would just have to be more clear about it. My sense of Tourak as archangel of my host was so near that I looked up, expecting to see him. Not quite yet. Still, the rhythmic march of hundreds of fighting statues filled the halls of Saetarra beyond the garden. Many of Kausae's angels glanced at the one doorway. Not anxious, perhaps, but with mild concern. They'd watched me fight the deadly constructs and perhaps understood their capabilities better than I.

Kausae spread her arms wide in an uncharacteristic hugging gesture. We'd always been competitively close in age. She'd never been physically affectionate with me. Still, I humored her and reciprocated. I had time. Through my double crown, I ordered the two companies of constructs to form up in the hall.

As we hugged, my hands brushed the scabbard of Kausae's huge hand-and-a-half sword that was slung across her back. I could feel the electric power of its lightning, even sheathed. A tingle of envy still trickled through me that she'd won the eternity I'd coveted as a mortal. After an obligatory single breath, I tried to pull back from the awkward embrace.

Kausae clung to me and whispered fiercely, "Tell me you did not summon your hosts."

I blinked in surprise. "You want me to lie to you?" I whispered back.

"Hells damn it, Illyria," she grumbled. "You fell into her trap."

I pushed her back hard then, gripping her by the shoulders so I could stare into her eyes. "What trap?" I demanded. I was pretty sure I'd already fallen into several of Huund's traps. But I'd escaped or defeated them all.

"They only sent a small flight with me," Kausae murmured, keeping her voice low for just us to hear. Her face pinched with worry. "A distraction!"

"So? They were enough to keep me here." I didn't understand her concern. "Because I was being stupid," I admitted.

"You're still being stupid!" she snapped.

"True," I muttered, "but rude."

"Madra is still in Nethe," Kausae stated with a frustrated grunt, as if I were just not understanding the blatantly obvious. She'd made that same sound the first time she'd tried to explain why all the young highlands boys and girls wouldn't leave me alone when I was thirteen.

While Madra might, in fact, still be in Nethe, my sister did not know she was our mother no longer in truth. Only the most naked, most vulnerable part of her remained. Though I didn't need to breathe, I suddenly felt an acute lack of air.

Unable to speak, I just boggled at her. *Maybe I'd damaged myself again in all the recent excitement?* My thoughts quested through my mind, seeking holes or gaps. I didn't feel like I'd lost any more memories or capacities. *I should tell her about Madra.*

With another frustrated huff, Kausae whispered fiercely, "If you left Nethe undefended, the bulk of the Twins' hosts and the old gods will have *liberated* all the shades."

My heart froze. Madra was a defenseless anamnesis. Worse even than slaughtering the hapless shades to release the magic in their souls, they might liberate Baal and the other demon lords to perform their original function. Everything in our mad world had been created or placed for a specific purpose. After failing as my—no, as Preema's—second army of reconquest, the demons had become the digestive system of Godforge. Perhaps they had been even before. *What of Urth and the others? What had been the purpose of the high gods and the old?*

I shook out the pointless thoughts.

"No," I said. "Urth has always been an ally to Z'nnek. They wouldn't—"

"Don't be naïve," Kausae interrupted. "The old gods serve the high. If Amuun"—she glanced at Amuun's corpse with a mild grimace—"or the Twins command them, they'll obey." My sister always took things in stride better than I did.

"Wait," I said, still refusing to accept her premise. "How do you know this?"

She hissed, "Because my orders are to join them in the pacification of Nethe after Huund finished with you." Kausae looked up in the direction the Hunt had vanished, and my unkindness was approaching. "I should go." She sighed. "Before he gets here."

DAVE REED

As soon as I found F'riida's anamnesis, I would tear a hole in the veil and rush to Nethe, the blockade of the old gods be damned.

I looked up to see a distant black wing getting larger by the moment. In a few heartbeats, a great, wide V of angels filled the sky. My unkindness had arrived at last. There were so many, though, it was obvious that all three hosts had come. I felt Tourak approach even though I couldn't see him clearly yet.

My eyes sought out the viridescent soul I expected in the ruin of the garden. The shock of the incinerated demoness rattled me. Kausae put a hand on my shoulder. I just blinked at the corpse that was all but ash and charcoal.

"She protected you?" my sister asked.

With a head shake, I pushed my threatening emotions down into the dark with Preema's anamnesis. I would never claim it as my own. I had to focus on the here and now. As I searched the devastated swath of garden with my immortal sight, I warned all the guardian constructs to expect my lovers and our combined hosts—to treat them as honored guests. It was well that I remembered, as the sense I gathered from the denizens of the fortress was that they had been given other, more hostile orders with regard to any save me, the Hunt, and the hosts of the Twins. I momentarily considered reversing those orders, but I had just summoned the Twins to Conclave, so I left my new order to Saetarra and its army of artificial guardians to welcome them. So long as they behaved.

Kausae turned back toward her fellows.

Urgency fell upon me like rain. "Wait," I whispered and closed my eyes. Z'nnek and Tourak had taught me, without really teaching me, that soul tokens were formed of significant memories. The first shape that came to me was the stupid wine bottle metaphor Z'nnek had first inspired in me. I was a vintner's wife after all. No use in denying it. I could be the bottle to his grapes. I smiled.

After all, nearly every significant memory I had in the afterlife had involved wine.

Perhaps my new anamnesis at the end of my eternity would be the moment I shared the wine of remembrance with Z'nnek. Not the tormented memory I'd shared, but the grace and kindness he'd shown me in the sharing. A wine bottle would make a fine token, I was sure. I just needed to find a singular memory to link with the symbol for Kausae.

I reached into my heart and found the dearest memory I shared with my sister. I'd hated her in that moment when she escorted our mother to her self-sacrificial execution to end the war with the Chosen. But I understood now. I would do the same for her. Just as she had done for me in agreeing to remain Torr's pet in Avaala. We were more than family.

I began to squeeze that singular memory into two equal portions through the winepress of my mind. When I tried to pour half of its essence into a tiny, smoky midnight bottle, I realized it was the wrong shape. The most significant memories of my afterlife all held another familiar, singular shape that was closer to my heart.

Manifesting my first soul token into my palm, I pressed it into Kausae's sword hand.

"Thank you," I whispered with a heartfelt nod. "When you've need of me, sister mine, call my name and I will come."

She looked confused but clutched the tiny midnight sword so that it was hidden in her fist. Shock widened her eyes. I felt the electric presence of my sister's soul through the effigy of Grievance I had gifted to her. Soothing strength and assurance were all I sent back.

Loudly, I announced for the loitering gold and silver angels, "Tell the Twins that I summon them to Conclave here immediately!" I slashed my empty sword hand for effect. "Bring them to me now!" I didn't have to fake being angry.

If I'd had anything left in my heart but terror and rage, I'd have laughed at the absurdity of my demand. Me? Summon the high gods to Conclave?

Kausae did laugh. A cold, mocking laugh loud enough to echo throughout the garden. "Our mission is complete!" she shouted to her fellows. "With me!" My sister took flight, still calling, "To Nethe!"

Her compatriots echoed her summons to war with wordless shouts as they followed the long-vanished Hunt into the brilliant, eternal sunlight. The wind of their powerful wings stirred the mountain of blackened ash into a choking cloud that filled the garden.

A glint of sickly green at the heart of that storm caught my eye. I stared at it, barely daring to hope against hope.

The immediate threat abated for the nonce, my heart pounded with fresh fear. Desperate, I clawed Z'nnek's soul token from its place in my purse atop. I had to warn him.

The facets of the tiny, lopsided cluster of grapes jewel glittered in the unforgiving sun.

Then crumbled into nothing.

LEAVE A REVIEW

If you enjoyed reading *Raven Queen, Ascend*, please consider leaving a review on your platform of choice. It's a much appreciated thank-you I give to all the authors I adore, too.

https://davereed.me/raven-queen-ascend-leave-a-review/

THE TEMPLE OF VENGEANCE

Read every volume of the series in print:

Death Descends
Raven Queen, Arise
Righteous Disobedience
Raven Queen, Ascend ← **You are here.**

Coming Soon:

Righteous Indignation
Raven Queen, Avenge
Righteous Determination
Raven Queen, Atone
Righteous Redemption

Free for my newsletter subscribers.

https://davereed.me/temple-of-vengeance/

ACKNOWLEDGMENTS

The number of people required to imagine, create, draft, and publish a book is staggering. Sitting and writing alone in the dark, I'm certain I've forgotten many who have inspired me and aided me in my quest to put this book in your hands. I am sorry if I forgot you.

In all the Universes, the one person after my Creator whom I credit as my Muse, my soulmate, and my biggest fan is my wife of many decades, Samia. Thank you, my love.

My lovely and talented editrix, Susan Bischoff, has been an indispensable midwife to this book—she came lately to the series and has immersed herself in its madness at great risk to herself and her sanity. Jaye Rochon, my marketing witch, is the critical core of my brand and marketing team. My cover artist, Katrina Curry, produced masterful work in a very short time. I am grateful to all of you.

Special thanks to the members of my various weekly writers' workshops: Estee Whitaker, Madeline Slovenz, Chris Madsen, Malin Fjellstroem, Tonja Davis, Lance Tracy, Krystal Garrett, and Chris Griffith. You suffered through all the terrible, horrible, no good, very bad versions of this book over the past eighteen months. I am in your debt.

Most of all, thank you, dear reader. This book is for you.

ABOUT DAVE REED

If you want to read the sexy bio written by my marketing team, you can find it on my website: davereed.me/about

This is not that. This is deeper. This is why I write.

In our confused modern, global culture, we have some deep-seated puritanical (and other traditions) roots of our evil. Don't get me wrong, it's not just politically warped monotheistic mythologies to blame. Even our purportedly secular global culture likes to pretend the essence of humanity is good and kind and bright.

It's not.

My purpose is to remind us of what marketing and politics prefer we forget: we are two-souled creatures. We are light. We are shadow. We are both—which makes us more. To be our best selves, we must embrace our duality. We are both wave and particle.

In my opinion, not only is utopia not possible in our Universe of scarcity, but it would also be stagnant and terminally boring. There's no story without conflict and stakes and risk and pain—and growth. That's all monster territory, all shadow.

The way humans make sense of the Universe is through story. It's so fundamental to our nature, we don't even notice it. I believe it's in our DNA.

Since the Toba Event, we have evolved to be *Homo narrans*. We can't even think without using story.

In my philosophy, better stories make better people.

To that end, I don't write the heroes you want.

I make the monsters you need.

THE WORLD OF THE RAVEN QUEEN

Only those characters who appear in this book or have some bearing on its events are included. Although many other characters came and went during *Death Descends* and *Raven Queen, Arise* and *Righteous Disobedience*, if they don't figure significantly in the telling of *Raven Queen, Ascend*, they're ignored. (Sorry, Antarro. Not sorry. Maybe you'll get a footnote in *Righteous Indignation*. Maybe.)

Spoiler Alert: Descriptions captured here are at the beginning of the events of *Raven Queen, Ascend* without spoilers for this book. These descriptions do include significant spoilers for the three chronologically previous books.

THE LOVERS

Illyria di Alamar Forte

The youngest child of the warlord of Clan Alamar. Born to a warden family in the rebel Elysian highlands, she spent her first nineteen years in devotion to Torr, the god of civilization and justice, training for her warlike duties with the singular desire to become a Temple Judge in Torr's service. During the events of *Raven Queen, Arise*, she was betrayed and killed on the night of Spring Festa by warpriests known as the Chosen of Tyrr.

After making a courtship deal with Z'nnek, the trickster lord of the underworld, Illyria is reborn as the Raven Queen who is seemingly destined to ignite the next godwar which may destroy the world. Along the way, Illyria gathered a menagerie of misfit lovers, allies, and powerful enemies who followed in her wake to aid her or blocked her path to thwart her quest for vengeance against the Chosen of Tyrr who killed her and her family and her kin.

Z'nnek

Lord of the underworld Nethe and god of the unclaimed dead. Z'nnek makes a deal to return Illyria to the sun-kissed lands in exchange for permission to court her. In violation of the Accord, Z'nnek claimed Illyria's soul during her mortal lifetime, without her knowledge, at the request of his oldest friend and archangel of death, Tourak. This claim, unbeknownst to her and unintended by Z'nnek, ultimately thwarted her lifelong dream and dragged her onto the road to war for justice and vengeance. Illyria is almost entirely unaware of Z'nnek's origin story, related in the prequel *Death Descends,* and his ancient relationships to Araeda'h, Goerranu, and Kragh. She is only aware of Z'nnek's first wife, Ru'mael, as the story is related in the Litanies.

Tourak

An ancient, one-eyed archangel of death who is devoted to Illyria for deeply personal reasons she forgot, due to burning her own memories to power her magic in her monomaniacal quest for vengeance. Tourak shared his memory with Illyria, using the wine of remembrance when he believed that Illyria would have to choose between him and Z'nnek. In the childhood memory that Illyria had inadvertently sacrificed for its magical power, she had saved Tourak from humiliation and death at the most vulnerable point in his afterlife.

FAMILY AND FRENEMIES

Araeda'h

The self-styled goddess of magic whom Illyria believes to be mad. Illyria finds Araeda'h trapped within the pages of the Book of the Forbidden after stealing it from the Hierarch. Araeda'h remains a difficult ally and frenemy to Illyria and Conseca. There is ancient history between Araeda'h and Z'nnek (from the prequel *Death Descends*) which Illyria jealously suspects but does not know. There is recent history between Conseca and Araeda'h from *Righteous Disobedience* that Illyria suspects but does not know.

Conseca maern Azzar

An escaped Azzarrean bedslave who became the first priestess of the Raven Queen, despite Illyria's best efforts to dissuade her. She remains in service to Clan Alamar and is the keeper of the only shrine to the Raven Queen in the sun-kissed lands. Despite the divine drama which Illyria dragged them into, Conseca and Memad became lovers in *Righteous Disobedience* and remain devoted to Illyria and to one another (which Illyria does not yet know).

Goerranu

Goddess of secrets and lies, who assists Illyria in her quest for her own nefarious reasons. She remains a devoted frenemy to Illyria. There is history between Goerranu and Z'nnek (from the prequel *Death Descends*) which Illyria suspects but does not know.

Hestaer di Alamar Forte

Mother to Illyria and called Madra throughout, she was a warden and wife of the warlord of Clan Alamar. She was eventually duly elected warlord of Alamar in her own right after the Spring Festa massacre that killed her husband, her son, both her daughters, and many of her kin of Clan Alamar, Clan Pluutar, as well as other unrelated rebel highland clans. When Hestaer attempted to make herself a sacrifice to Tyrr, in exchange for amnesty for Illyria and an end to the genocide of the highland clans, Illyria killed her and claimed her soul to save her from the looming demonic sacrifice and death eternal. Madra is now an aimless shade wandering Nethe for eternity, having lost her entire family save Illyria.

Kausae di Alamar Forte

Eldest daughter of Madra and older sister to Illyria, who was also killed during the Spring Festa massacre. Because her soul was claimed by Torr, she was taken to the paradise of Nuuria, where she serves as an angel of justice. Kausae's claim by Torr and subsequent ascendance are a source of jealousy for Illyria and friction between the sisters. She is sent to Illyria thrice as an emissary in an effort avert godwar during *Raven Queen, Arise*.

Mawzi

Goddess of thieves, pirates, and assassins, who assists Illyria in her quest for the promise of war against the high gods, whom she views as unjust oppressors. She remains a bloodsworn ally to Illyria and occasional frenemy. Mawzi is frustrated by Illyria's reticence to resume hostilities to end the tyranny of the high gods and the old.

Memad

The demigod scion of the storm lord Vayan was accidentally transformed from enemy to ally in a dramatic aerial misunderstanding, during which Illyria took four centuries of his memories. When the stolen magic of the memories were restored to Memad, he was forced to reevaluate the person he had become against the person his mortal mother had reared him to be. Grateful and rueful at the reawakening, Memad risks himself and his position as an immortal child of a high god to aid Illyria for reasons Illyria doesn't truly understand. Memad and Conseca became lovers during *Righteous Disobedience* (which Illyria does not yet know).

Nerren di Alamar Forte

Only son of the warlord of Alamar and elder brother to Illyria. When Illyria found him broken upon the wheel of woe, Nerren asked her for the warrior's mercy. Thinking she'd granted his request and sent him on to the afterlife using Saevera's athame, Illyria accidentally took his soul. She carried it and growing guilt until her fall on the bridge. After speaking with Nerren's spirit and with his blessing, Illyria consumed the magic of his soul to restore herself and rise again to ultimately defeat Provax to end the siege of Alamar.

BOOKS, RITES, RITUALS, AND CEREMONIES

The Litanies

Primary religious texts throughout the world in the era of the Raven Queen which describe a purported creation myth centered around the high gods. The principals of the pantheon are the mother of the gods, Amuun, and her twin sons, Tyrr and Torr. The Litanies deal almost exclusively with the high gods to focus worship upon them through ritual and prayer.

The world itself is never named in the Litanies, but they do describe various Hells beyond the veil to which mortals might be banished for various sins. The Forbidden include the worship of demons or small gods, belief in prophecy, or the use of magic of any sort.

According to the Litanies, the purpose of mortal life is to earn the privilege of being claimed by one of the high gods for an eternity as an ascended angel in one of the various paradises maintained by each high god.

A few old gods are mentioned and only one small god (Z'nnek) is referenced by name. Z'nnek is included in the Litanies primarily to describe his function as god of the unclaimed dead and his surrender at the Accord which marked the end of the Little War (the last godwar). A few old gods are mentioned in passing in the Litanies, including Urth. Several small gods are referenced by appellation to forbid their worship specifically, including Nameless (Goerranu) and Faceless (Mawzi).

The Tales

Allegedly apocryphal stories promulgated by one or more unknown small gods and their secret human worshippers. The Litanies are silent on the nature of the Tales. The Tales themselves laud many of the small gods by name and celebrate their exploits and their domains. The high gods and the old are often the butt of subtle sarcasm and overt jokes throughout blasphemous Tales. Despite prohibition and persecution by the priests of the high gods and the old, many bards and other entertainers regale their audiences with the lurid amusement of the Tales, when there are no priests about.

The Tales routinely refer to the use of magic and hint at every mortal's birthright to use it. As lord of necromancers, Z'nnek is often reputed in the Tales to make deals with mortals in exchange for forbidden knowledge. The Tales also relate stories of fallen demons who were slain during many an ancient godwar by Amuun and her coterie.

The Accord

Ancient pact of surrender between Z'nnek and the high gods, which ended the Little War eight thousand years prior to the era of the Raven Queen. The Litanies describe its terms loosely, focusing on the limits to Z'nnek's purview and power. The Tales are nearly silent on the subject of the Accord, though the Tales do contain a few references which question its validity. Z'nnek and Tourak have refused to explain to Illyria the reason for Z'nnek's surrender.

Conclave

Formal gathering called by the high gods for some purpose, usually the judgment of small gods' infractions or to communicate a new Litany or other edict among the divinity. Attendance is not optional.

Two Conclaves are mentioned specifically in *Raven Queen, Arise*. Z'nnek attends the first during the events of the book, but Illyria is never privy to what happens there. The second is the formal summons of Illyria herself that is pending at the beginning of *Raven Queen, Ascend*.

Magic and Memories

Sometimes used as synonyms. All memories are composed of magic. Not all magic, as Illyria understands it, are memories. The Litanies are silent upon the subject of both, other than to prohibit the use of magic. The Tales obliquely state: "We mortals are but only what we remember." Many of the Tales describe the use of magical spells in detail. Illyria discovered the hard way, during *Raven Queen, Arise*, that the world and its denizens are composed of two types of magic: spirit and shadow. Combined, spirit and shadow comprise the realm of flesh where mortals live and die in the sun-kissed lands.

The two types of magic are also names given to parallel realms which can be visited separately. The veil is a realm synonymous with the realm of shadow which is a buffer between the realms of spirit and flesh and the Hells beyond. Both realms are invisible to mortals, who exclusively inhabit the realm of flesh where spirit and shadow commingle.

Within the realms, conscious beings—mortal and divine—are entirely composed of magic in the form of memories, which are the most potent concentration of magic in the world. All of life, including the use of magic, requires energy to perform and consumes either freeform, free-floating magic or magic concentrated into flesh or memories. By using the spells Z'nnek carved into a heart-shaped sigil between her breasts, Illyria learns the hard way that the price of using magic beyond her reserves is the loss of her her own memories, consumed by the sigil in order to power its spells.

Illyria learned in *Raven Queen, Arise* the rudiments of how to manipulate spirit, shadow, and flesh, as well as how to transmute one into another in order to cast magical spells and to create objects. Z'nnek warned Illyria, for unspecified reasons, never to draw upon shadow nor to walk in it. Despite the warning, Illyria asked Mawzi to lead her and Tourak through the veil (the realm of shadow) when Illyria deduced that travel through the realm of shadow was faster or more of a shortcut (Illyria is uncertain which) than to travel through the realms of spirit or flesh. Illyria also ignored the warning to create her sword named Grievance and her armor named Repose from both spirit and shadow.

The High Gods

A pantheon of deities who, according to the Litanies, created and govern the world for the benefit of mortals. Such benefits include affording mortals the opportunity to earn the privilege of being claimed, and thereby earn an afterlife of immortal service to one of the high gods in the various named paradises. These include Saetarra (the sun), Avaala (the golden moon), Nuuria (the silver moon), and Woazanayehn (the court of storms).

Each of the high gods is given dominion over an area of mortal life, called a domain by the Litanies. Amuun is the goddess of the sun, creatrix of the world and of mortals in her own image, and the mother of the high gods. Tyrr is the god of war and conquest. Torr is the god of justice and civilization. Vayan is the lord of sky and storms. Each of the high gods maintains an angelic host of servitors to guide mortals and enforce the will of the high gods.

The Old Gods

Strange, alien gods of uncertain or unknown purpose, who do not typically resemble mortals. Mentioned in passing in the Litanies, the old gods seem to serve some sort of secondary function in the world and always appear to defer to the high gods. Urth is the only old god named in the series so far. Despite Amuun's position as the creatrix of the world and of mortals, Urth is known as the god of life and creation.

The Small Gods

Mortals who ascend to a state of divinity but are not claimed by a high god. Small gods are largely ignored by the Litanies and are the primary focus of the Tales. Each small god seems to have a specific, narrow domain of some aspect of mortal life. The Tales hint that it is possible for any mortal to ascend unto divinity through extraordinary effort worthy of worship within a new domain, or by challenging a small god for their existing domain.

The Demon Lords

Fallen lords of the underworld. All three demon lords (Baal, Raam, and Sett) were alleged to have been destroyed by Z'nnek during the events of *Death Descends*. By overthrowing the demon lords and purging Nethe of its demonic hordes, Z'nnek took all three of their mantles upon himself, and their associated angelic hosts, as the god of the unclaimed dead.

ALLIES AND ENEMIES

Amuun

Mother of the gods and creatrix of the world. Ruler of Saetarra, the solar paradise. Illyria has not met Amuun but frequently swears by Amuun's various physical attributes and genitalia. Amuun is reputed to be the most merciful of the high gods. Amuun is the mother of the Holy Twins, Tyrr and Torr.

The Chosen of Tyrr

Four warpriests born to the last Hierarch of Elysia (in order of birth): Provax, Venatar, Saevera, and Deffaen. Each are alleged to have been selected by Tyrr himself to lead the faithful among the Temple guard. Each was given a gift of magical power. Illyria comes to believe during the events of *Raven Queen, Arise* that they are, in fact, the bastard demigod scions of Tyrr himself. The Chosen, led by Provax, are the architects of the Spring Festa Massacre which resulted in the slaughter of Illyria and her highland kith and kin. In *Raven Queen, Arise*, Illyria is successful at killing three of the four Chosen she swore an oath to Conseca to murder.

Deffaen

Son of the Hierarch and a Chosen of Tyrr, gifted with a ring of insight that provided him knowledge of others' intentions. He was raping Conseca when Illyria first encountered him. Without forethought or warning, Illyria cut him from groin to navel before she later killed him to spur his siblings to pursue her. Illyria took the ring from Deffaen's corpse, but lost it to Provax in their second battle on the bridge when he cut it off, along with her right middle finger. Illyria later stole it back when she killed Provax and gave it to Conseca when she was consecrated before Clan Alamar as Illyria's first anointed priestess.

The Hierarch

One-time high priest of the Elysian Temple at Paerul, and purported father to the four Chosen of Tyrr. Illyria killed him when she stole the Book of the Forbidden from the Grand Temple at Goerranu's behest, in exchange for promised answers about the high gods and their mysteries. Illyria has reason to believe, from his memories, that the Chosen are truly unascended demigod bastards of Tyrr.

Provax

Eldest son of the Hierarch and a Chosen of Tyrr, gifted with Tyrr's own invulnerable skin. Illyria first hurt him by biting him in the Spring Festa battle when he cut her throat. She subsequently burned that memory by accident, among many others, in her headlong pursuit of vengeance. After surrendering to Provax and his inevitable attempt to rape her, Illyria realized Provax was only invulnerable to weapons. She bit him a second time during his attempt to force fellatio and was able to use her necromancy to steal his soul, which is still imprisoned in an imaginary wine bottle in Illyria's mind alongside several others.

Saevera

Daughter of the Hierarch and one of the four Chosen of Tyrr. She is gifted with the rituals of demonic sacrifice to glorify Tyrr through a magical athame of channeling. By her own admission, Saevera is as ruthless as she is depraved. She alone among the Chosen survived the events of *Raven Queen, Arise*. Although Illyria stole the athame after her return from the dead and marked it as her own, Provax retook it during their second battle and returned it to Saevera before his final battle with Illyria.

Torr

God of civilization and justice. Younger of Amuun's Holy Twins. Ruler of Nuuria, the silver moon paradise. Illyria has not yet met Torr but spent her nineteen years as a mortal devoted to and worshipping Torr in hopes of spending her life as a Temple Judge and an eternity as an angel of justice.

Tyrr

God of conquest and war. Eldest of Amuun's Holy Twins. Ruler of Avaala, the golden moon paradise. Illyria has not yet met Tyrr but has slain for revenge three of the four Chosen of Tyrr, whom she believes to be demigod scions of Tyrr. Illyria has also slain two war angels of Tyrr's host, Yunfak and Yanfak, in *Raven Queen, Arise*.

Urth

Old god of life and creation, who controls and patrols the shadowy middle realm between Nethe and the sun-kissed realm of flesh. Urth has long kept friendly relations with Z'nnek but desires the Book of the Forbidden for their own purposes, which puts them at odds with the rulers of the underworld.

Venatar

Son of the Hierarch and a Chosen of Tyrr, gifted with a magical bow and arrows that never miss their target. Illyria captured him when he ambushed her. He was later traded to Provax by Illyria's mother, in an attempt to sue for peace. Illyria took the bow when she captured him and later killed him with his own bow at the battle of the bridge where she left the bow on the field when she fell. Goerranu recovered the bow and used it to aid Illyria in the final battle for Alamar.

CONNECT WITH DAVE

The best way to connect with me is to join my newsletter, Dark Tidings: davereed.me/newsletter. I read every reply and I respond best to polite inquiries. Through the newsletter, I occasionally, but not too often, share book news, my thoughts about dark fantasy, and frequent recommendations for other great books.

Although I don't spend enormous amounts of time on social media (other than spreading memes that amuse me), you're always welcome to connect with me on your favorite platform:

https://davereed.me/

https://twitter.com/davereedme

https://www.facebook.com/DaveReedMe/

https://www.pinterest.com/davereedme/

https://www.linkedin.com/in/davidreed/

CONNECT WITH DAVE

https://www.instagram.com/davereedme/

https://www.amazon.com/author/davereedme

WORK WITH DAVE

Writing a novel can be hard and lonely. But it doesn't have to be. If you're inspired to create your own story, I'd love to join you on your adventure. You can find me at BookShaman.com.

I'm a Story Grid Certified Editor, and founding member of the Story Grid Guild. I've been helping my clients with developmental editing of their novels and screenplays as well as chapter-by-chapter scene coaching for their works-in-progress since 2020. I joined the staff of the Story Grid Scene Writing Workshop as a coach in June 2024 and the Story Grid Writer Mentorship cadre as a mentor in January 2025.

I'm available for hire as your writing adventure guide. Book a free campfire chat and let's see if we might be compatible narrative quest companions.

BookShaman.com